BAD KiTTY
SCHOOL DAZE

NICK BRUEL

ROARING BROOK PRESS
NEW YORK

For all teachers everywhere

Published by Roaring Brook Press
Roaring Brook Press is a division of Holtzbrinck Publishing Holdings
Limited Partnership
120 Broadway, New York, NY 10271 • mackids.com

Our books may be purchased in bulk for promotional, educational,
or business use. Please contact your local bookseller or the Macmillan
Corporate and Premium Sales Department at (800) 221-7945 ext. 5442
or by email at MacmillanSpecialMarkets@macmillan.com.

Library of Congress Cataloging-in-Publication Data is available.

First edition, 2013
Full-color edition, 2022
Book design by Jay Colvin and Veronica Mang
Color by Crystal Kan
Printed in China by RR Donnelley Asia Printing Solutions Ltd.,
Dongguan City, Guangdong Province

ISBN 978-1-250-78238-0 (hardcover)
1   3   5   7   9   10   8   6   4   2

• CONTENTS •

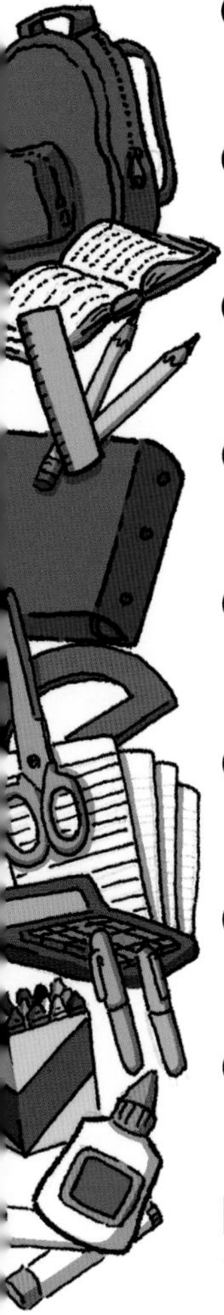

•CHAPTER ONE•

ONE FINE DAY

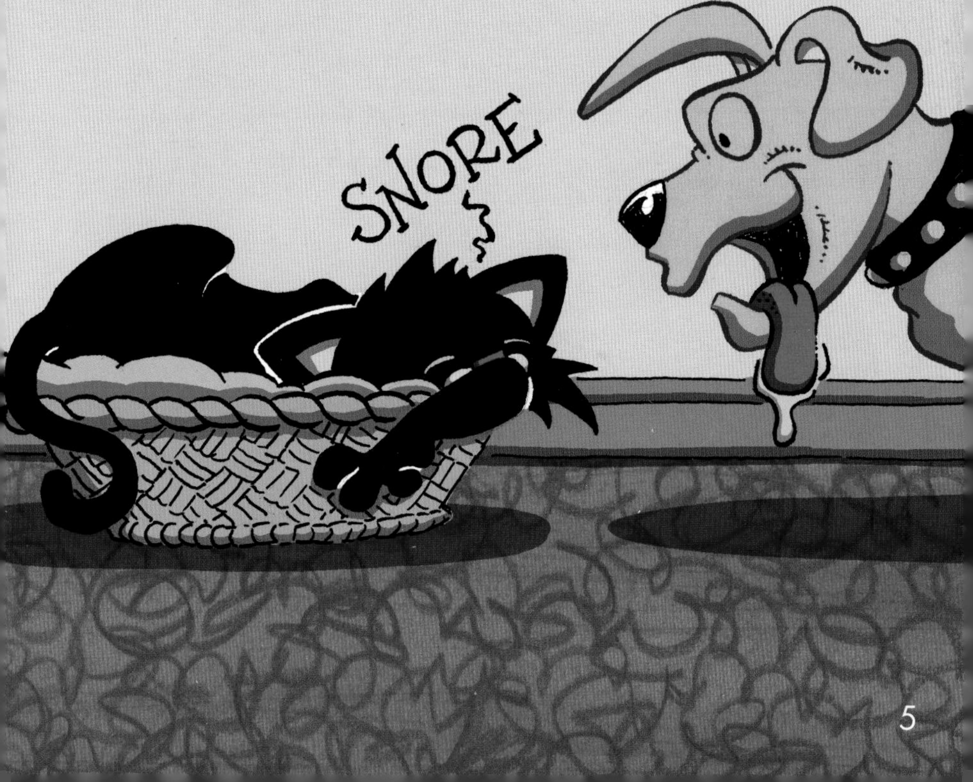
SNORE

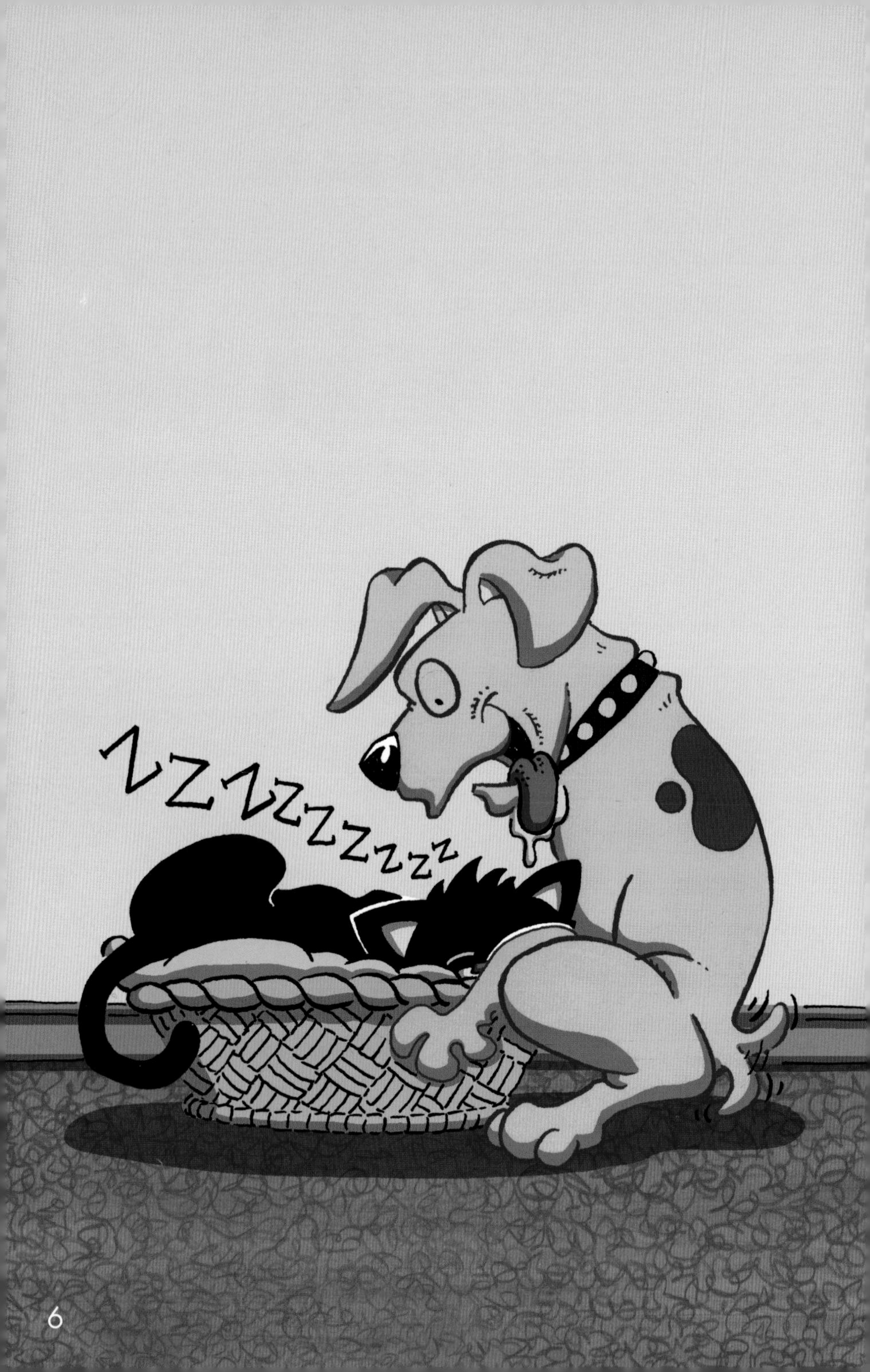
ZZZZZZZZZZ

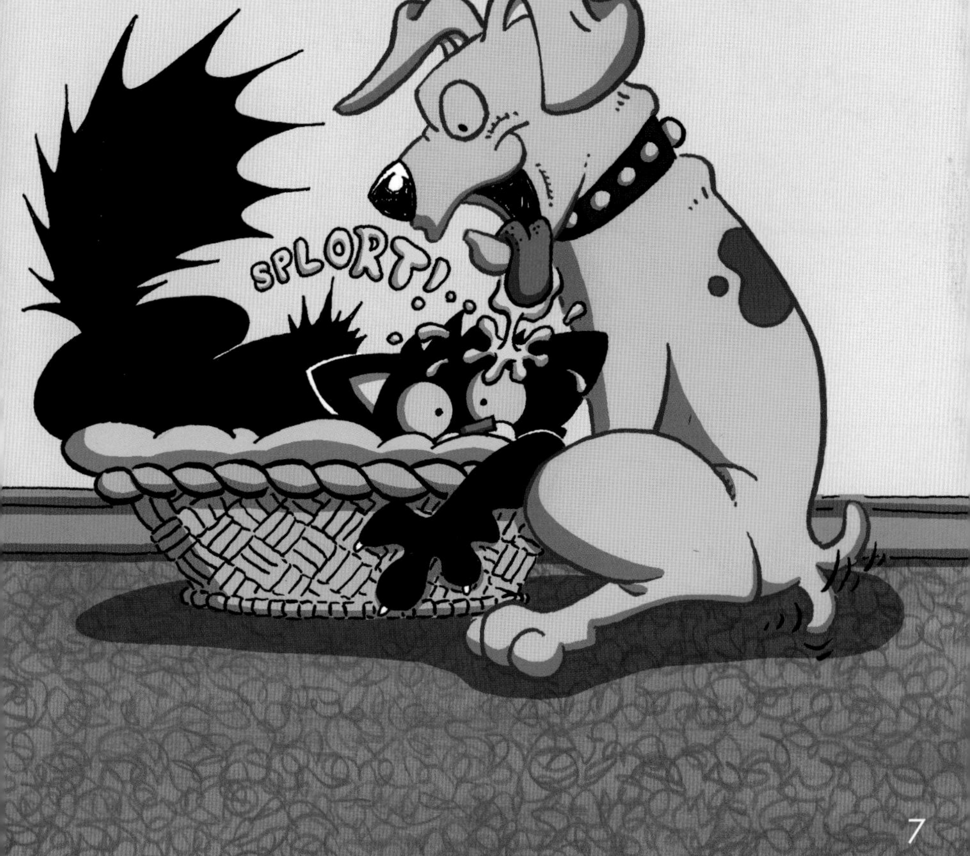
SPLORT!

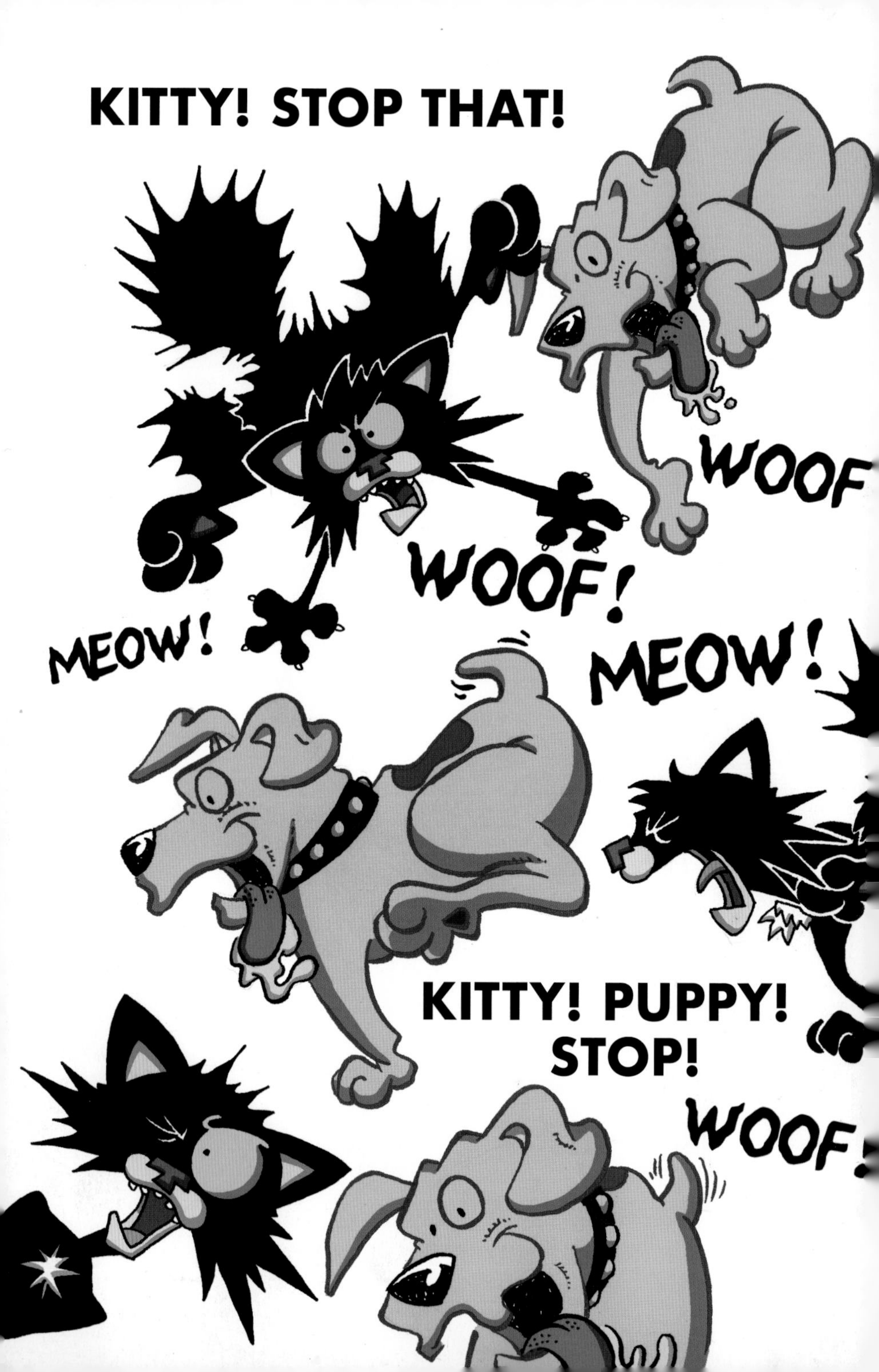
KITTY! STOP THAT!
WOOF
WOOF!
MEOW!
MEOW!
KITTY! PUPPY! STOP!
WOOF!

BOTH OF YOU, CUT IT OUT!

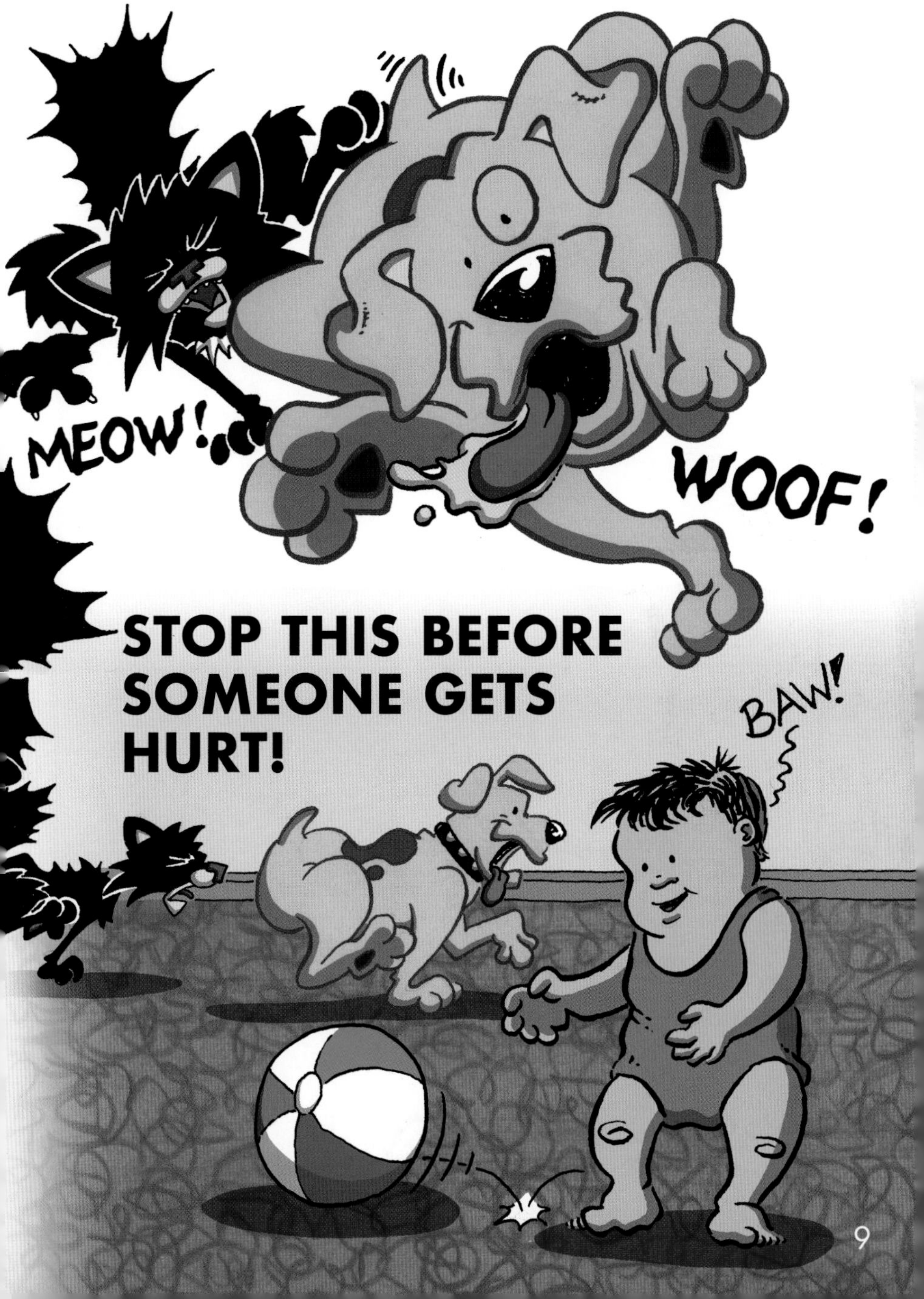
MEOW!
WOOF!
STOP THIS BEFORE SOMEONE GETS HURT!
BAW!

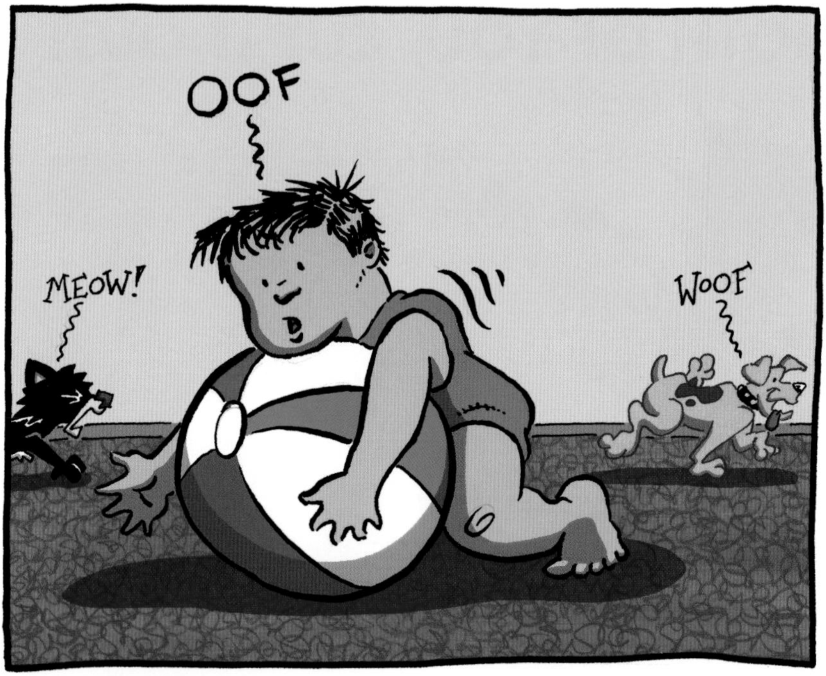
OOF
MEOW!
WOOF

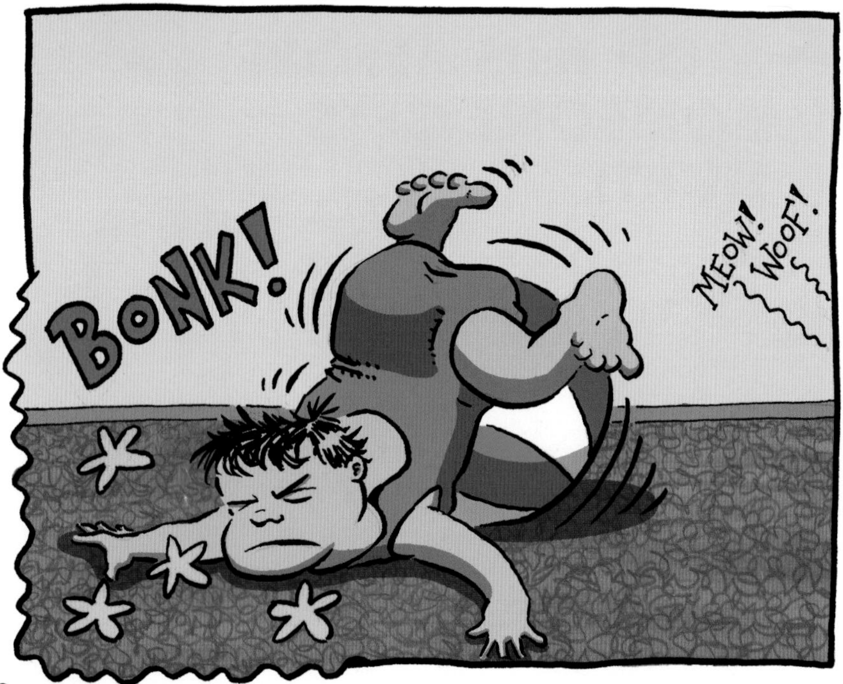
BONK!
MEOW!
WOOF!

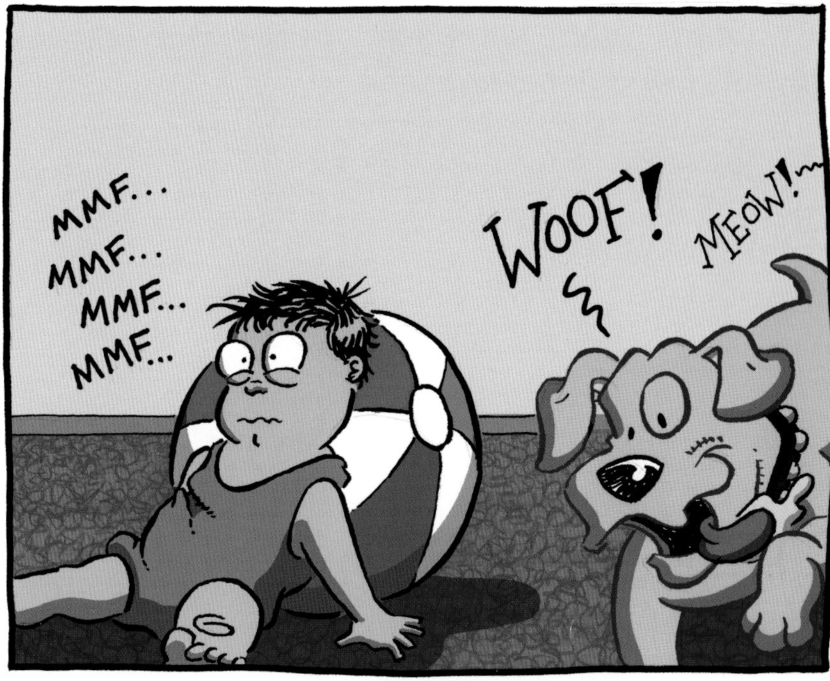
MMF...
MMF...
MMF...
MMF...
WOOF!
MEOW!
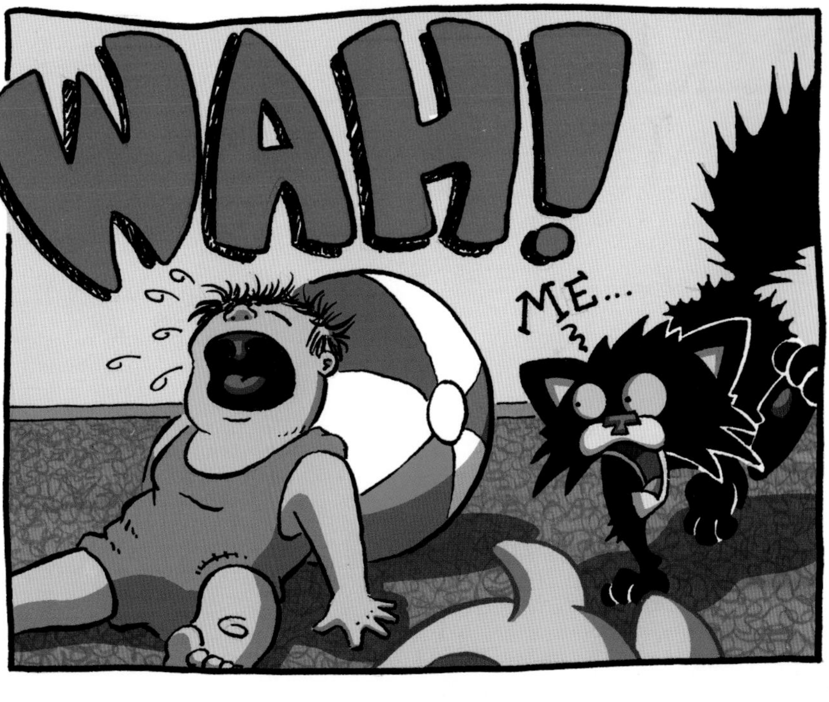
WAH!
ME...

Oh, dear! What happened, Baby? Did you fall down? How did that happen?

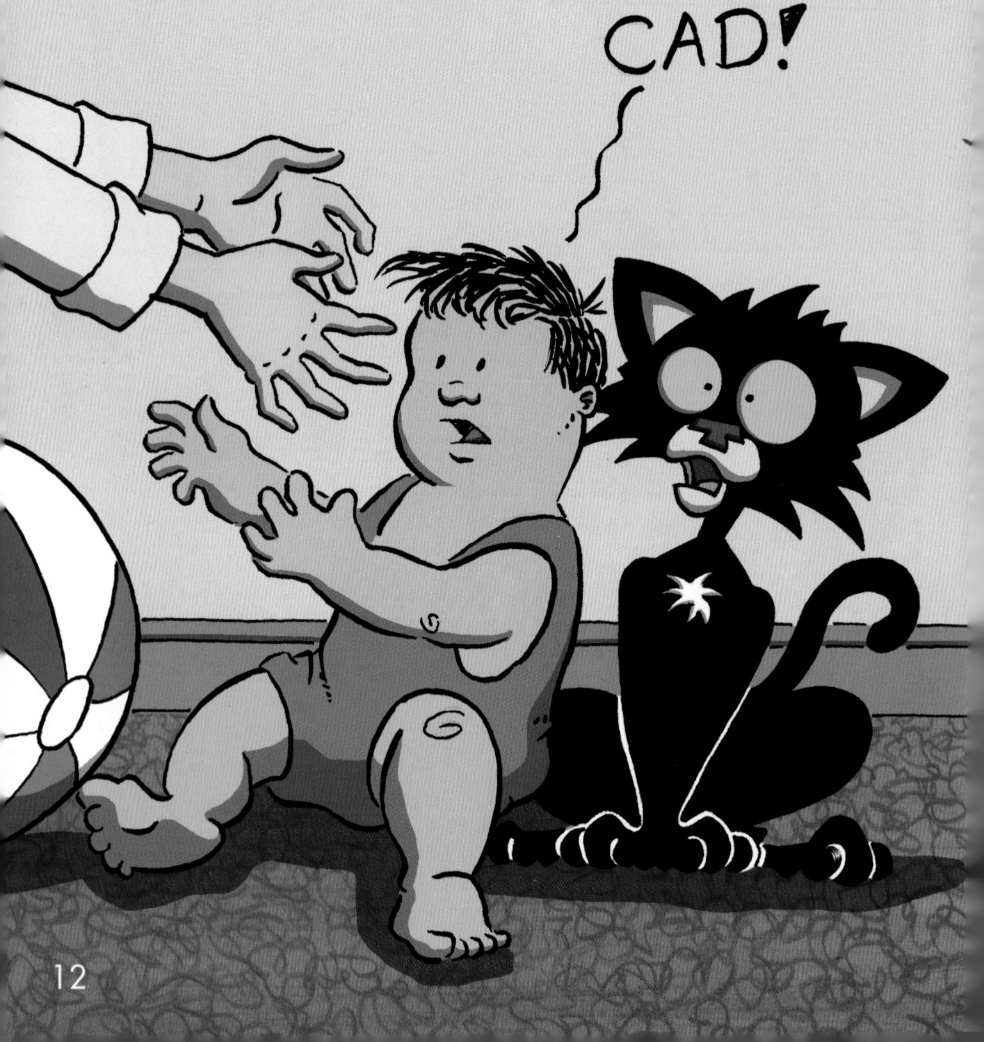
CAD!

The cat did this? Well, I'm not surprised. Tsk, tsk, tsk. The way those two were running and horsing around. But I'm sure it was an accident.

Kitty, it's time for us to have a little talk.

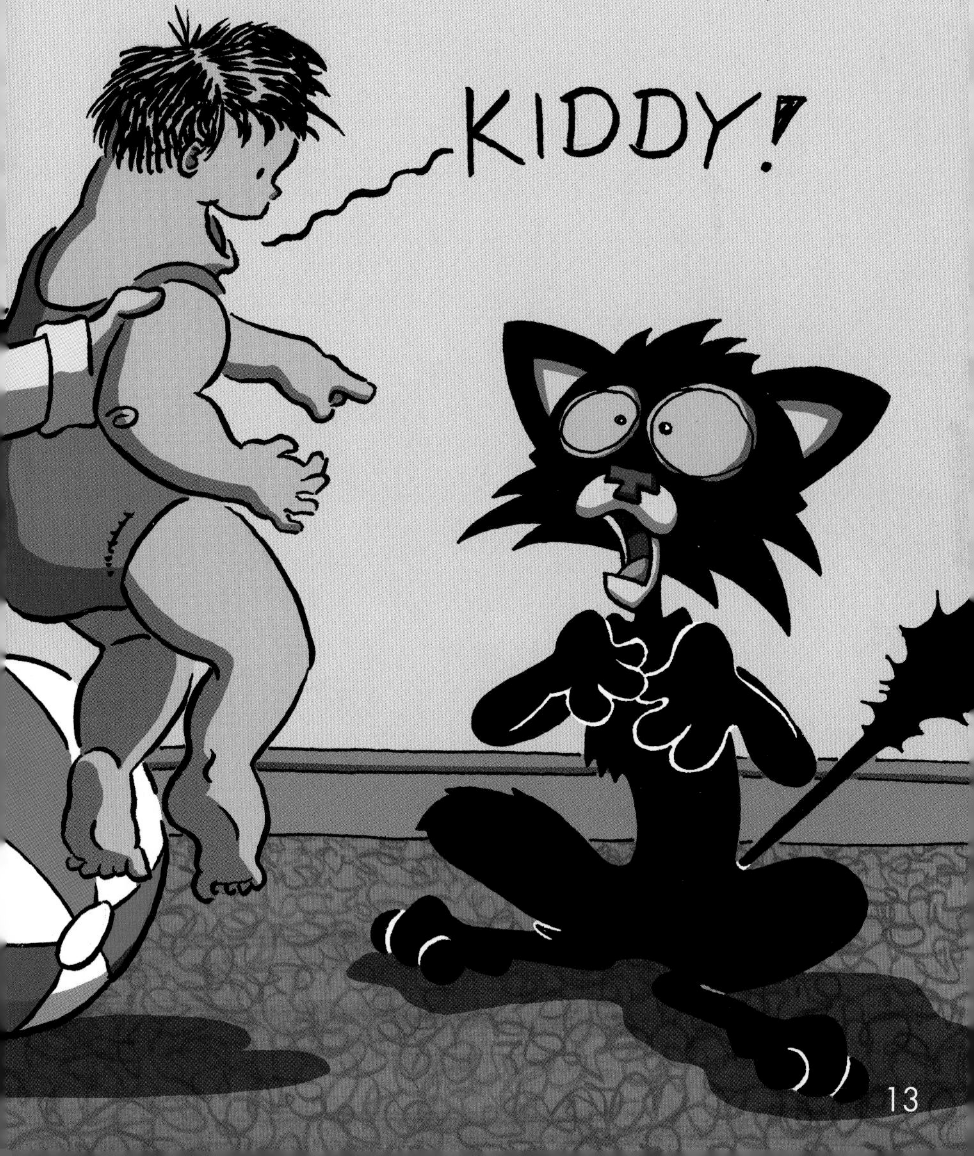
KIDDY!

Kitty, I've had enough of your SCREAMING and HISSING and FIGHTING. It's time we did something about your behavior, your nasty temper, and the fact that you never seem to listen.

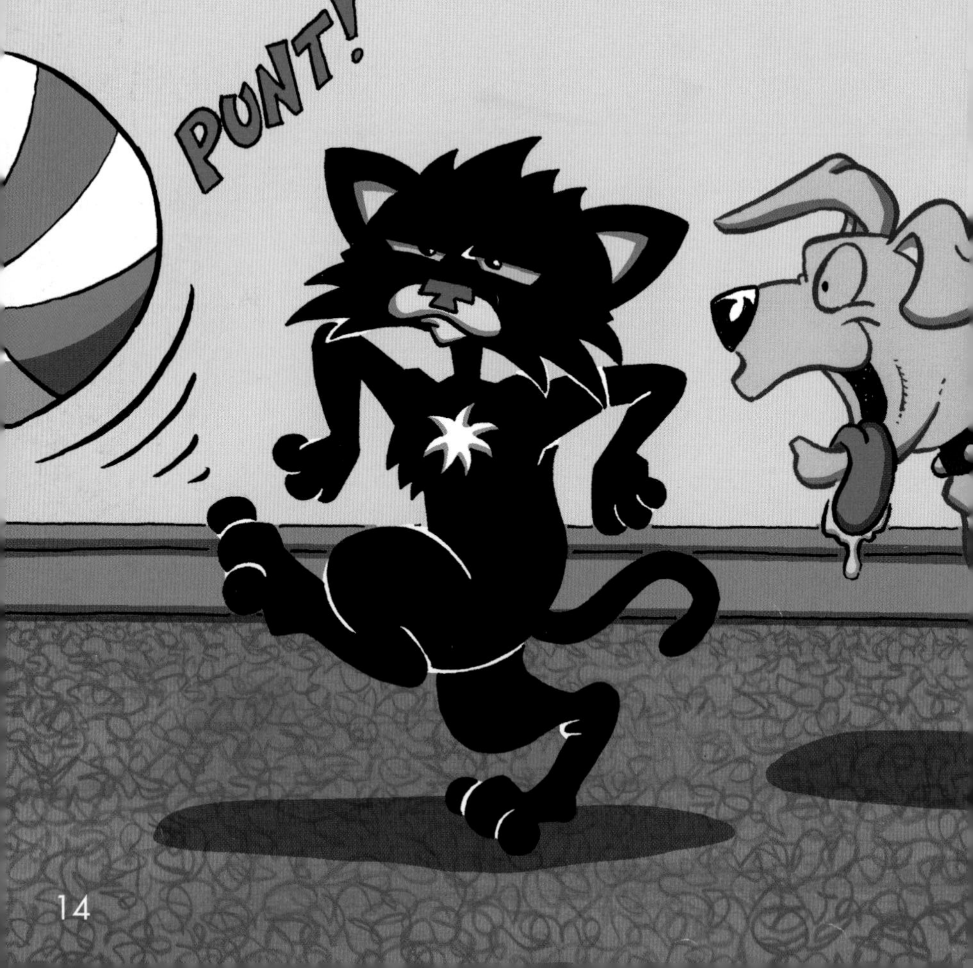
PUNT!

And that goes for you, too, Puppy. That drooling problem of yours started all of this.

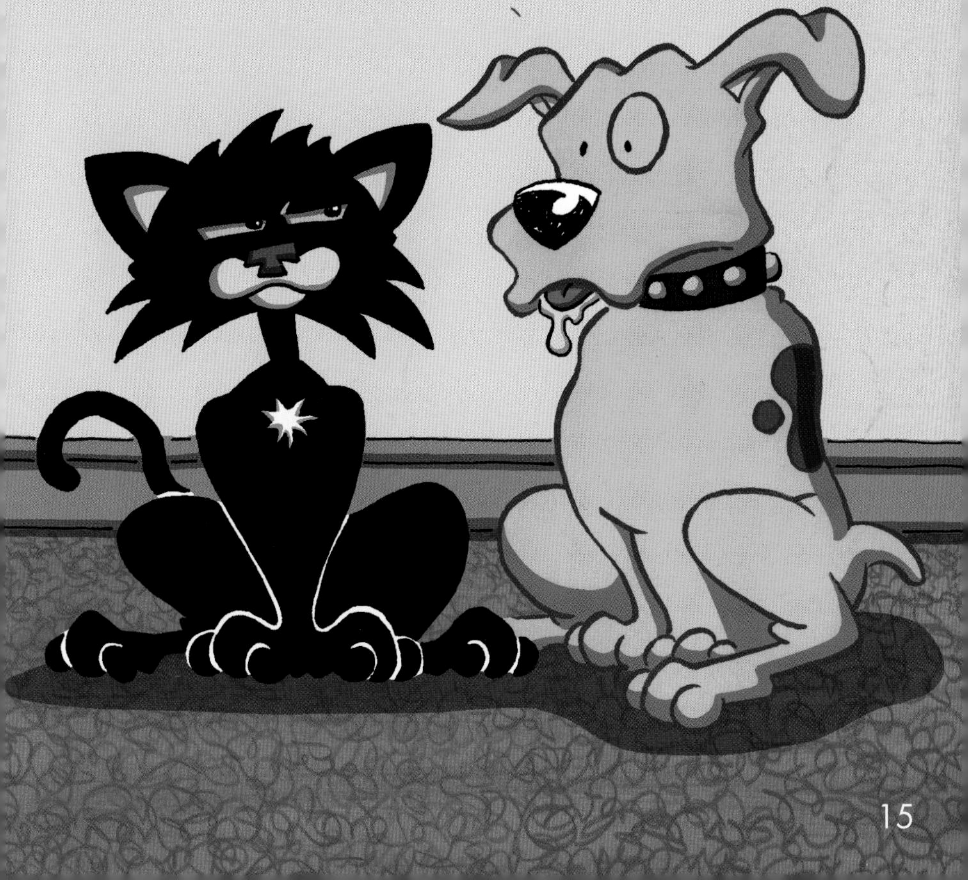

That's why I've decided it's time for both of you to go to . . .

SCHOOL.

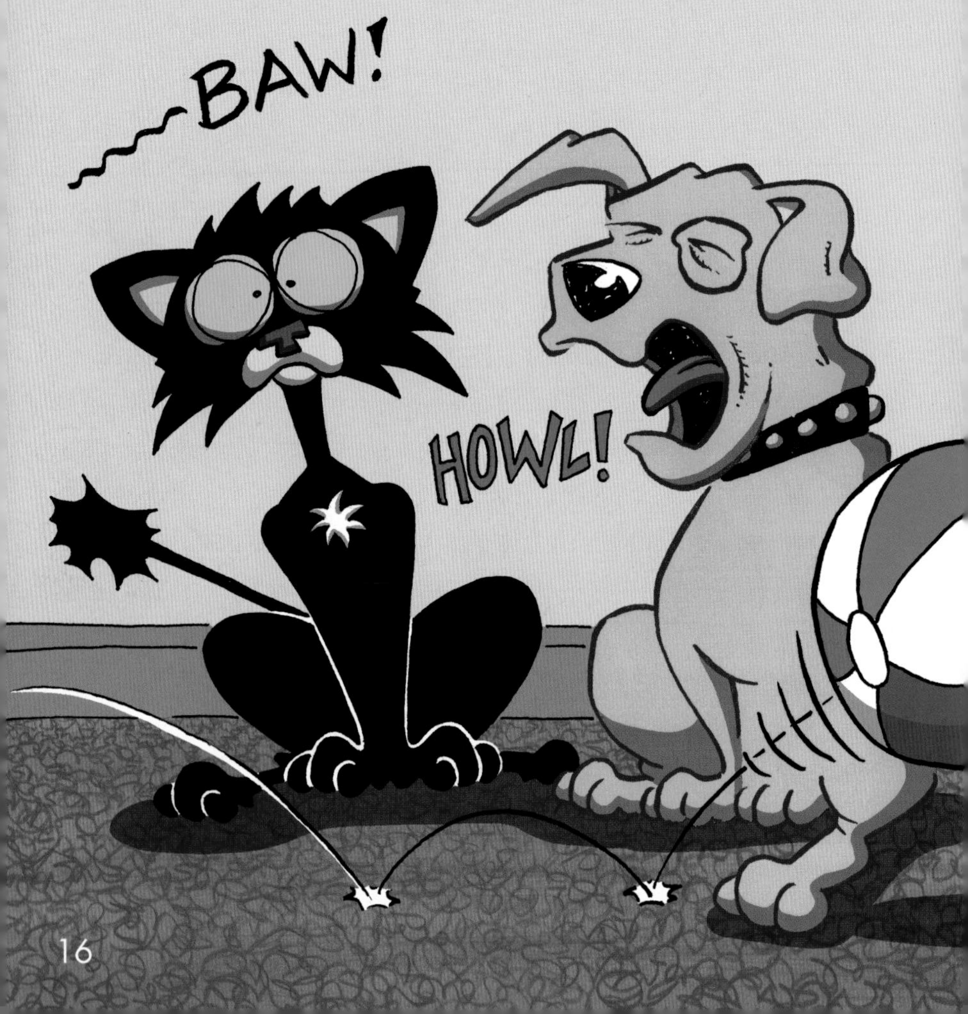
BAW!
HOWL!

• CHAPTER TWO •

THE NEXT FINE DAY

HEY, KITTY! I just got back from the store, and look at all of the super-cool school supplies I bought for you! They all feature your absolute FAVORITE . . .

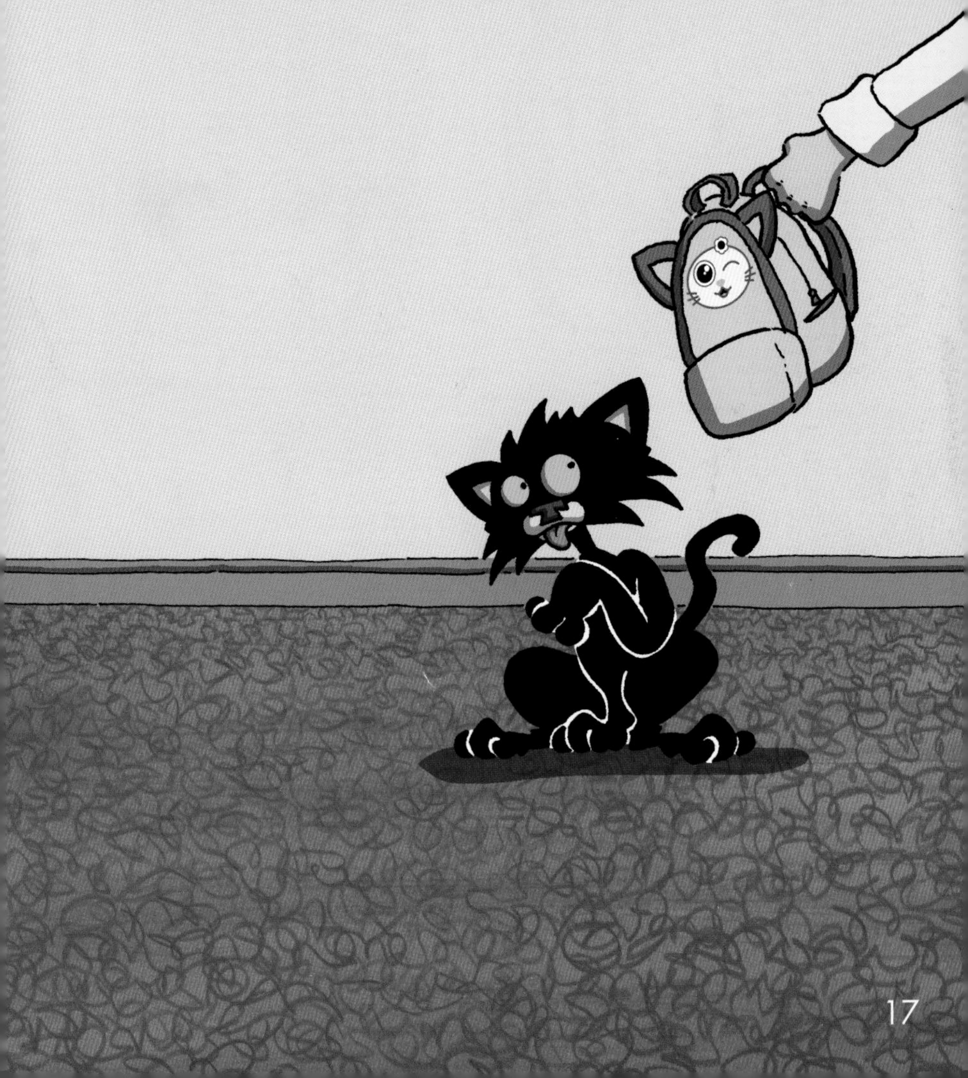

Love Love Angel Kitten

Love Love Angel Kitten
Backpack

Love
Love
Angel
Kitten
Notebook

Love Love Angel Kitten
Eraser

Love Love
Angel Kitten
Pencils

Love Love
Angel Kitten
Bowling Ball

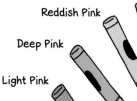

Pinkish Pink

Reddish Pink

Deep Pink

Light Pink

Pink

Love Love
Angel Kitten
Crayons

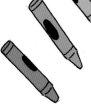

18

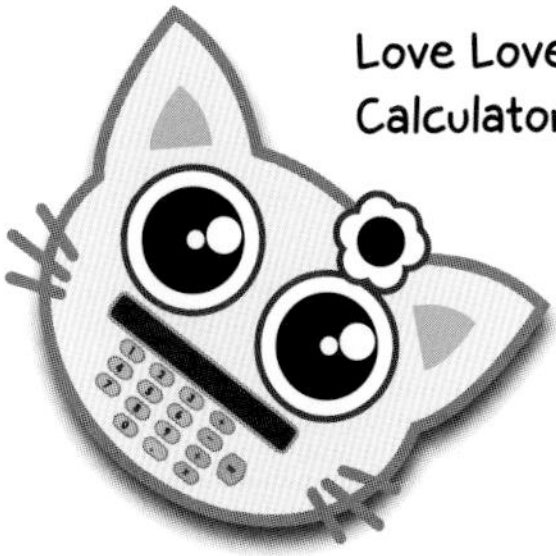

Love Love Angel Kitten
Calculator

Love Love
Angel Kitten
Gym Shorts

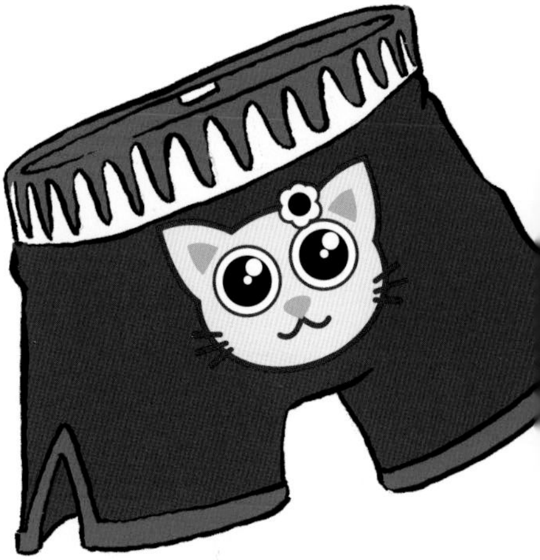

Love Love
Angel Kitten
Tractor
Tire

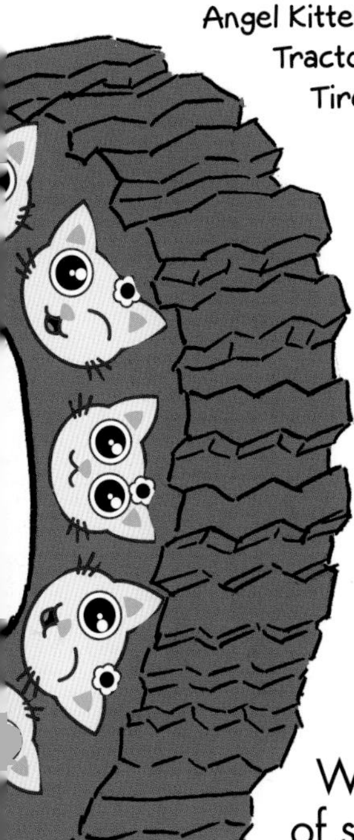

Love Love
Angel Kitten
Cinder Block

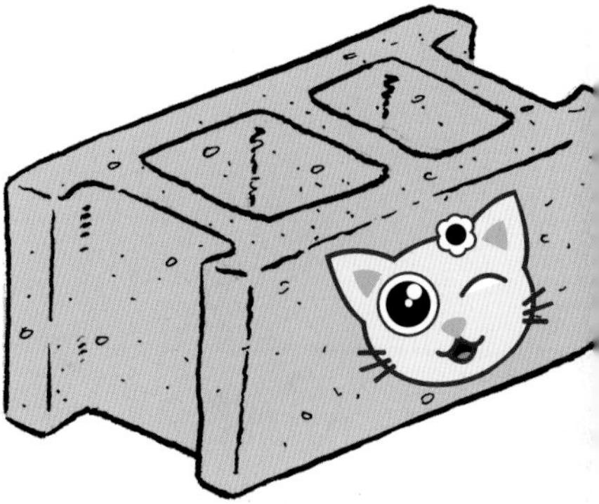

Love Love
Angel Kitten
Ruler

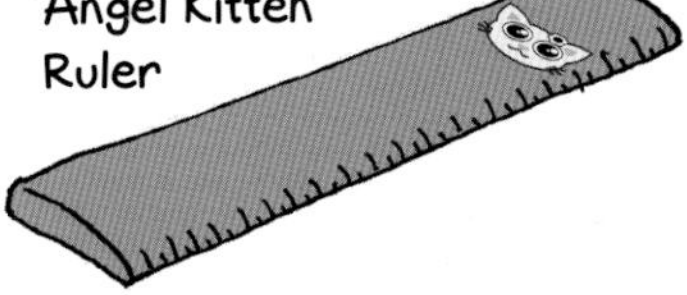

Whew! That's a lot of stuff! Oh well . . . Let's put it all into your backpack.

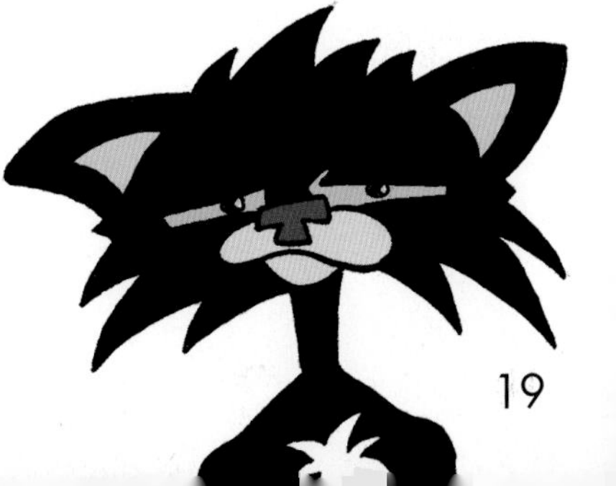

Awww, look at you! All ready for school.

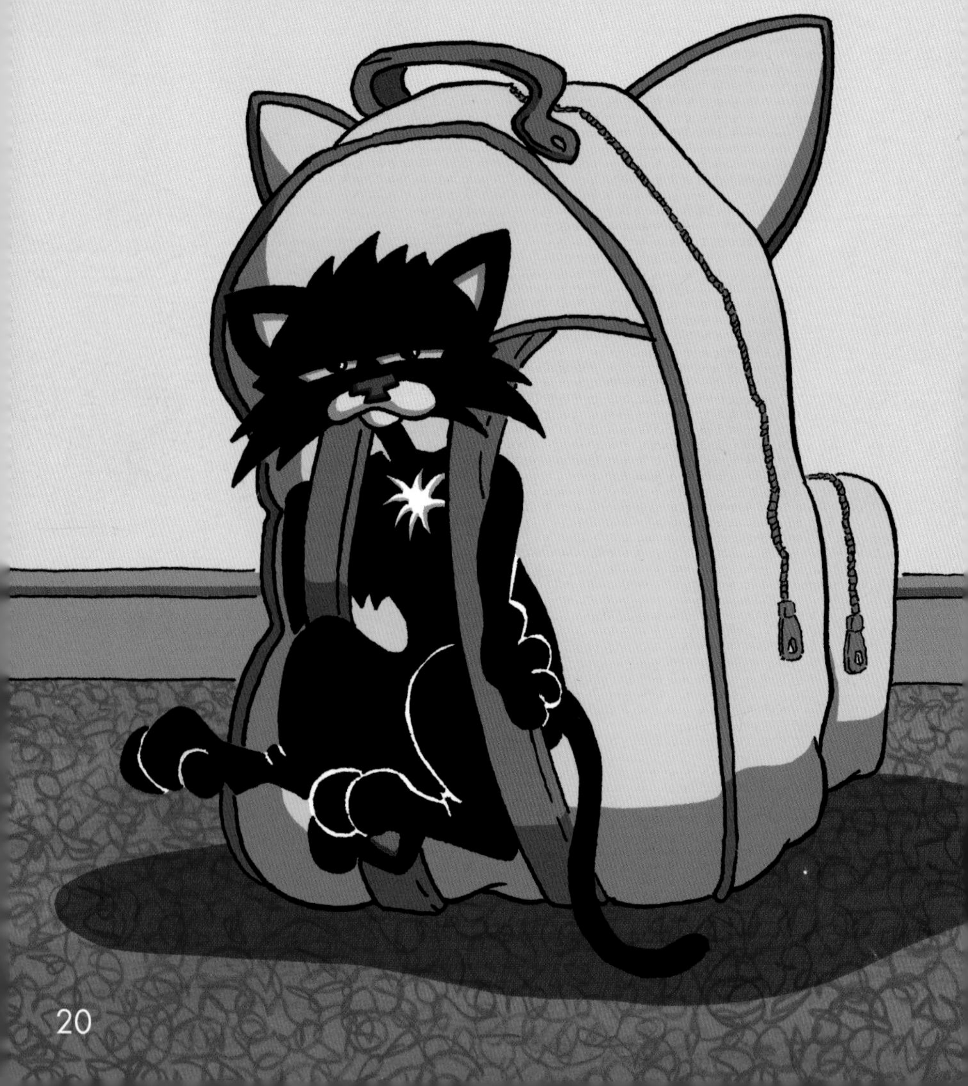

And so is Puppy! Did you pack your bandanna, Puppy? I hope so, because you'll need it if you start drooling again.

We better hurry. You guys don't want to be late for the school bus!

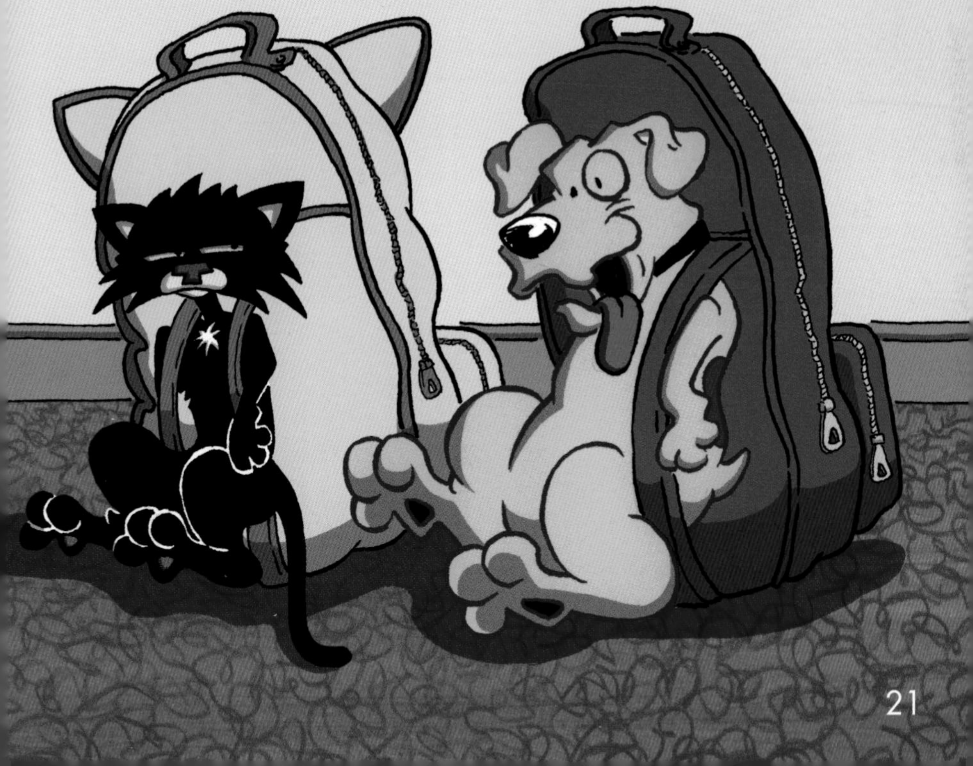

HERE IT COMES!

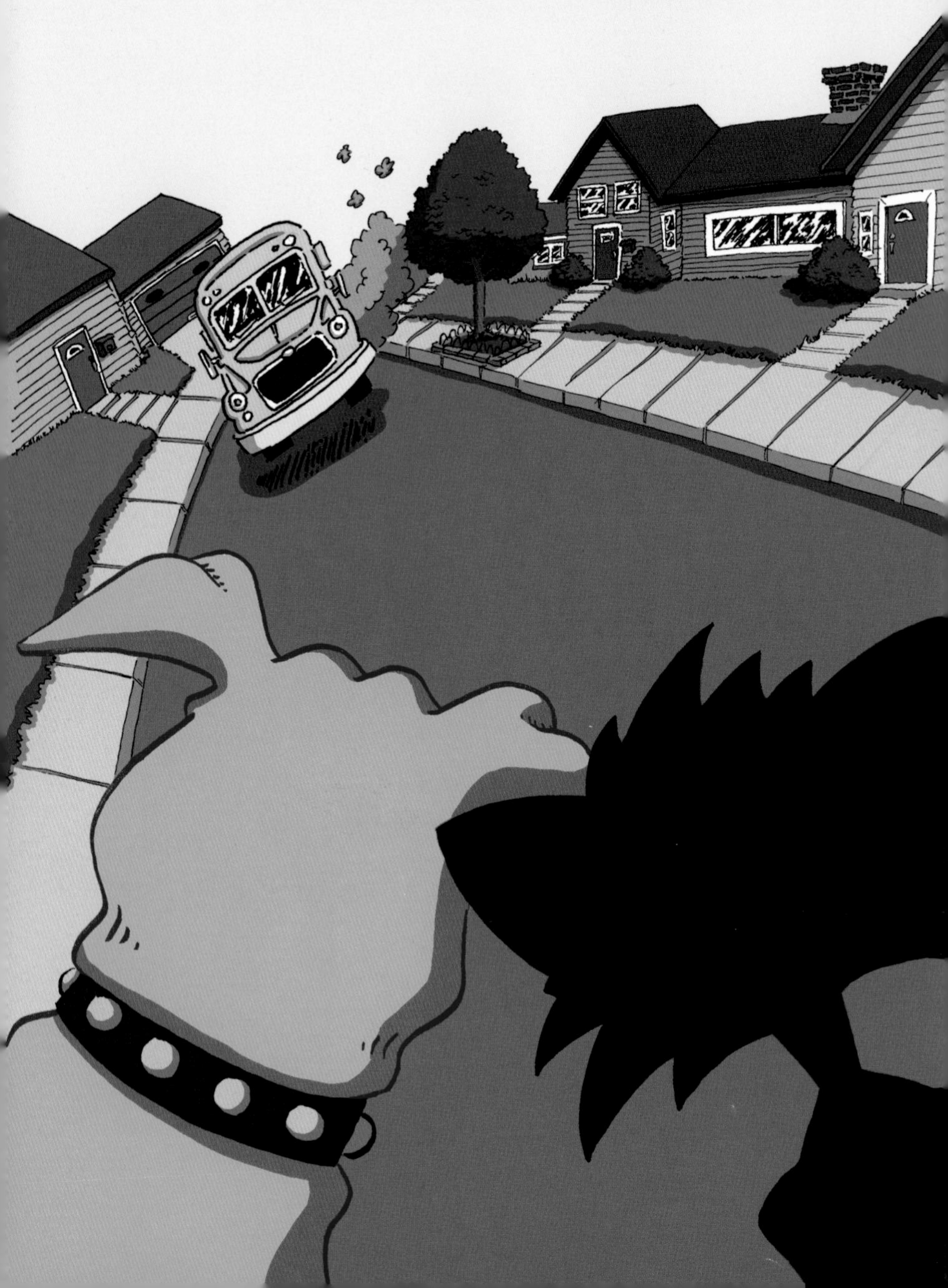

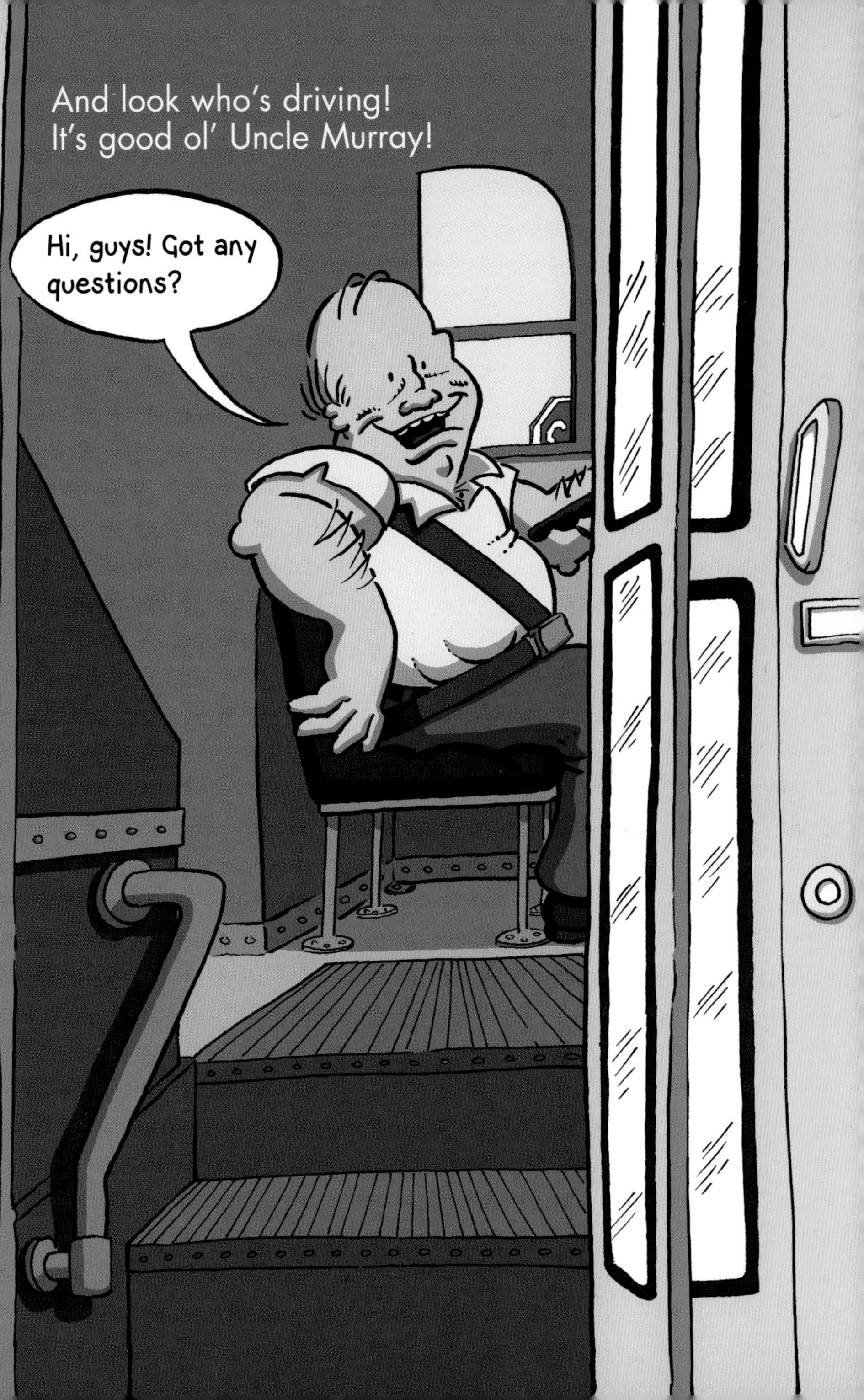
And look who's driving!
It's good ol' Uncle Murray!
Hi, guys! Got any questions?

WHY DO DOGS CHASE CATS?

Hey, do[n't] blame th[e] dog for t[...]

Dogs don't just chase cats. They chase lots of things, because that's what dogs like to do most.

Herder dogs like border collies are bred to chase sheep and keep the flock together. Hunting dogs like hounds and dachshunds are bred to chase foxes and rats. Police dogs like German shepherds are trained to chase criminals. And dogs chase all of these things not just because they like to do it, but also because they're so very, very good at it.

When a dog chases a cat, he's not chasing because he's being mean. He's chasing the cat because of instinct. Instinct is that part of an animal's brain that controls how an animal is going to act. Birds can fly because their instinct

MEOW*

*Albert Einstein once said, "Peace cannot be kept by force; it can only be achieved by understanding."

24

tells them how. Fish can swim because their instinct tells them how. And dogs chase other animals because their instinct tells them it's an important thing to do.

So when a dog sees a strange cat for the first time, his brain tells him that he MUST begin chasing the cat. It doesn't help that dogs are also very territorial, which means that if the cat is anywhere near something the dog thinks he owns, like his bone or his backyard or his house or even YOU, then he will feel compelled to chase that poor cat away.

Cats, by the way, have the same instinct as dogs. Cats are extremely good at chasing other animals, only they chase animals much smaller than they are, like mice and rats. Most dogs are bigger, sometimes MUCH bigger, than cats. So cats do not generally chase dogs.

I like dogs, but they better not chase my school bus!

Dogs, however, do not have the same sense of caution as cats and will often chase things much, much bigger than them. That's why they'll sometimes chase cars.

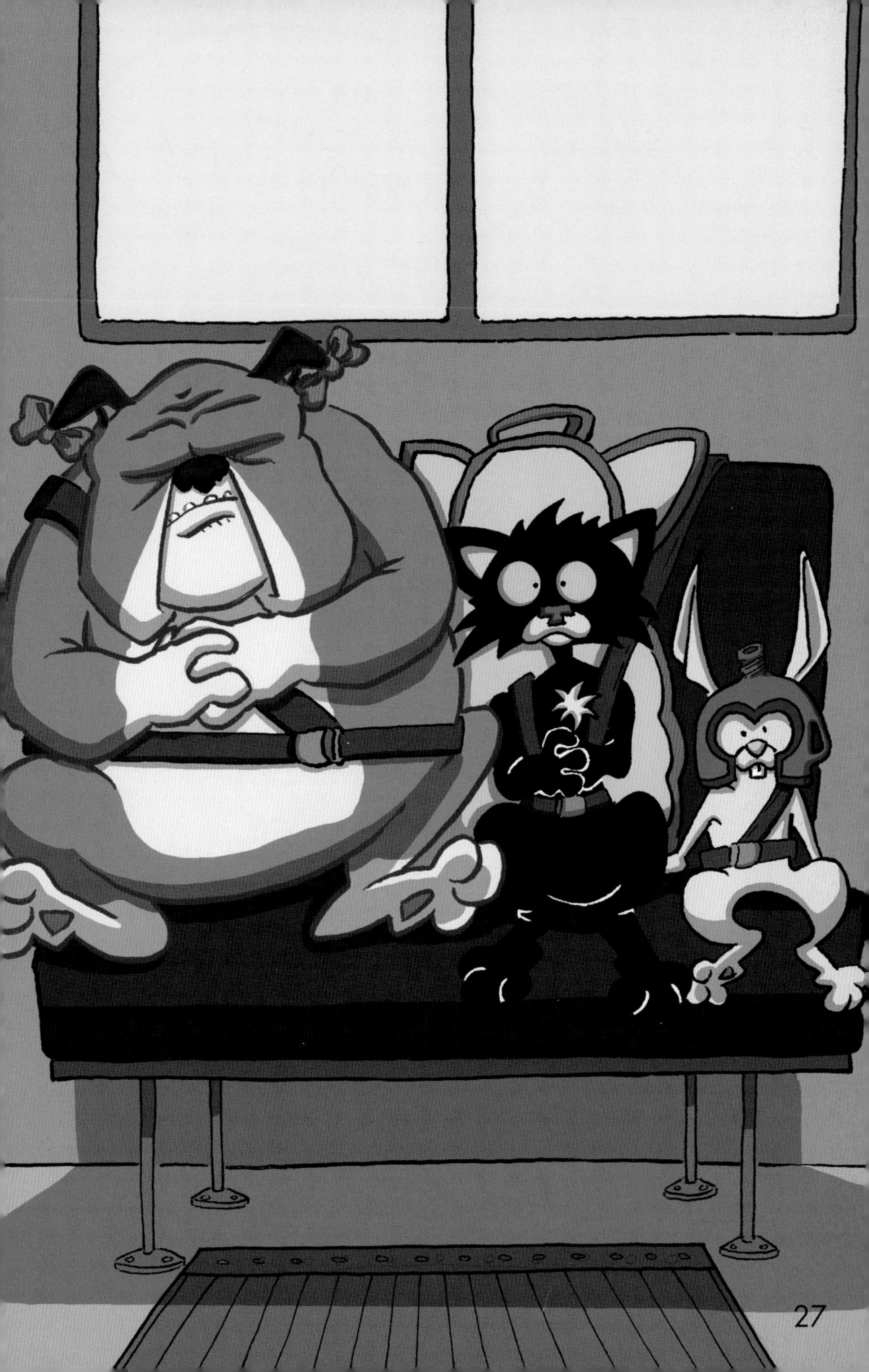

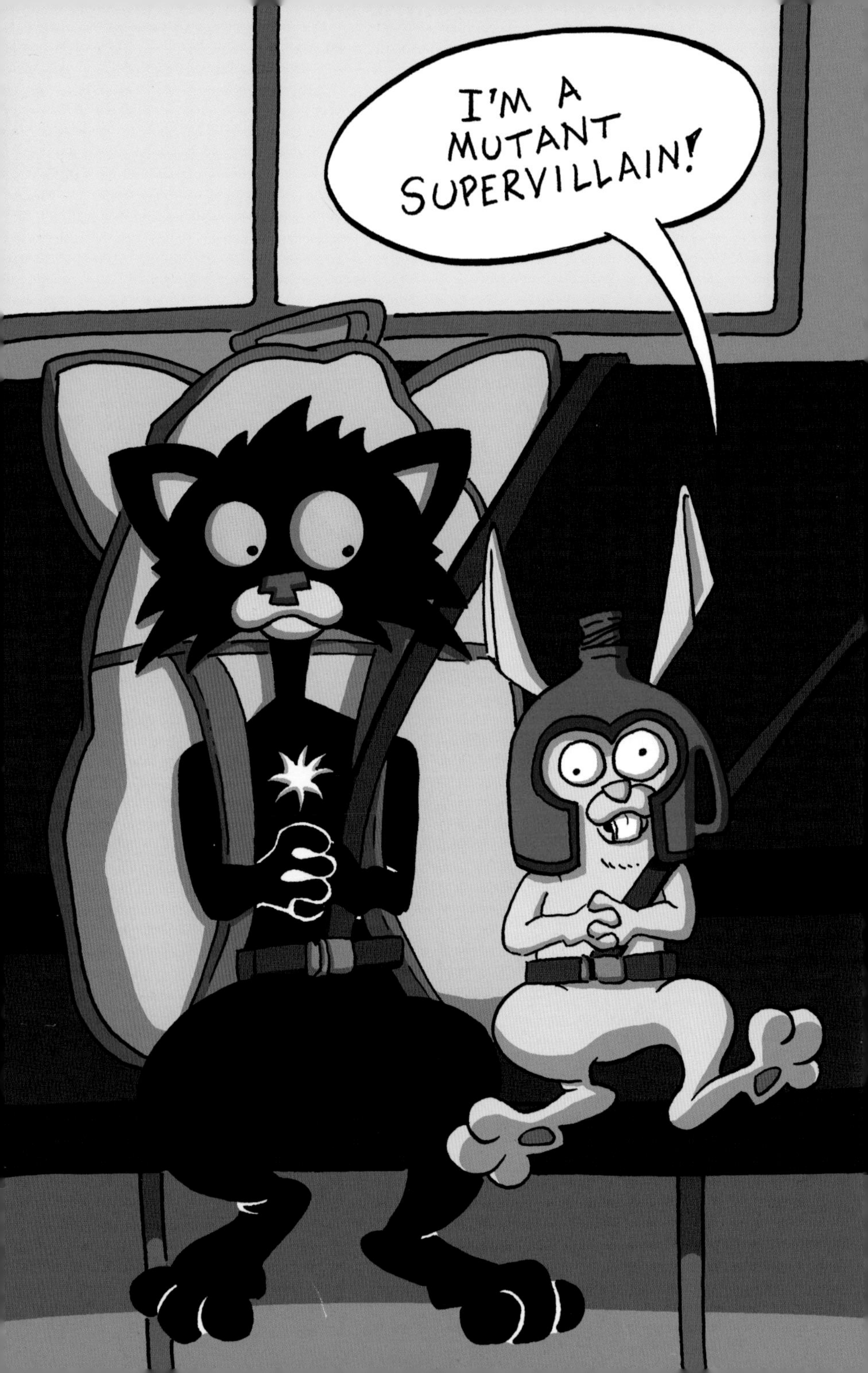
I'M A MUTANT SUPERVILLAIN!

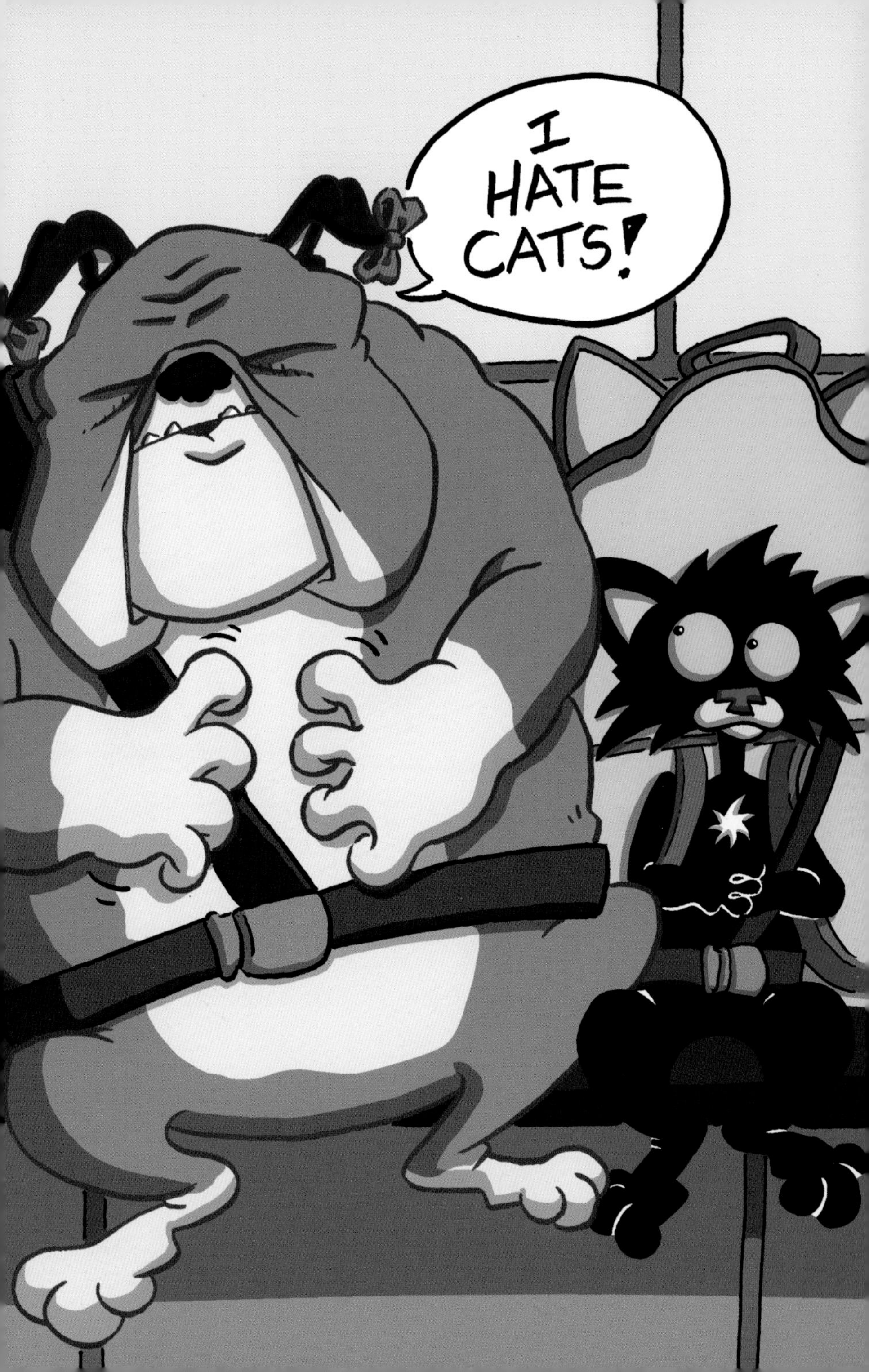
I HATE CATS!

Bye, Kitty! Bye, Puppy! I'll see you at the end of the day!

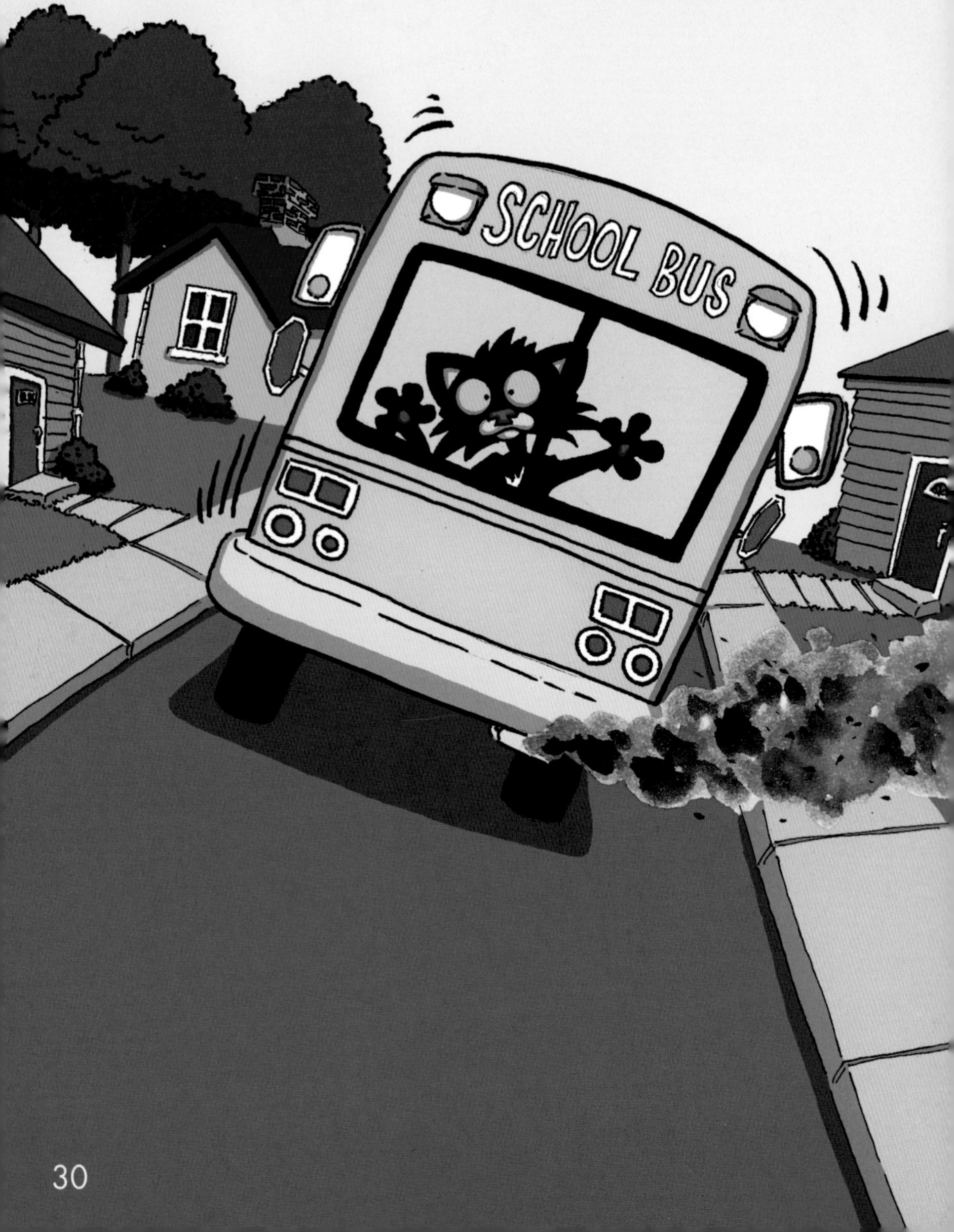
SCHOOL BUS

• CHAPTER THREE •

WELCOME

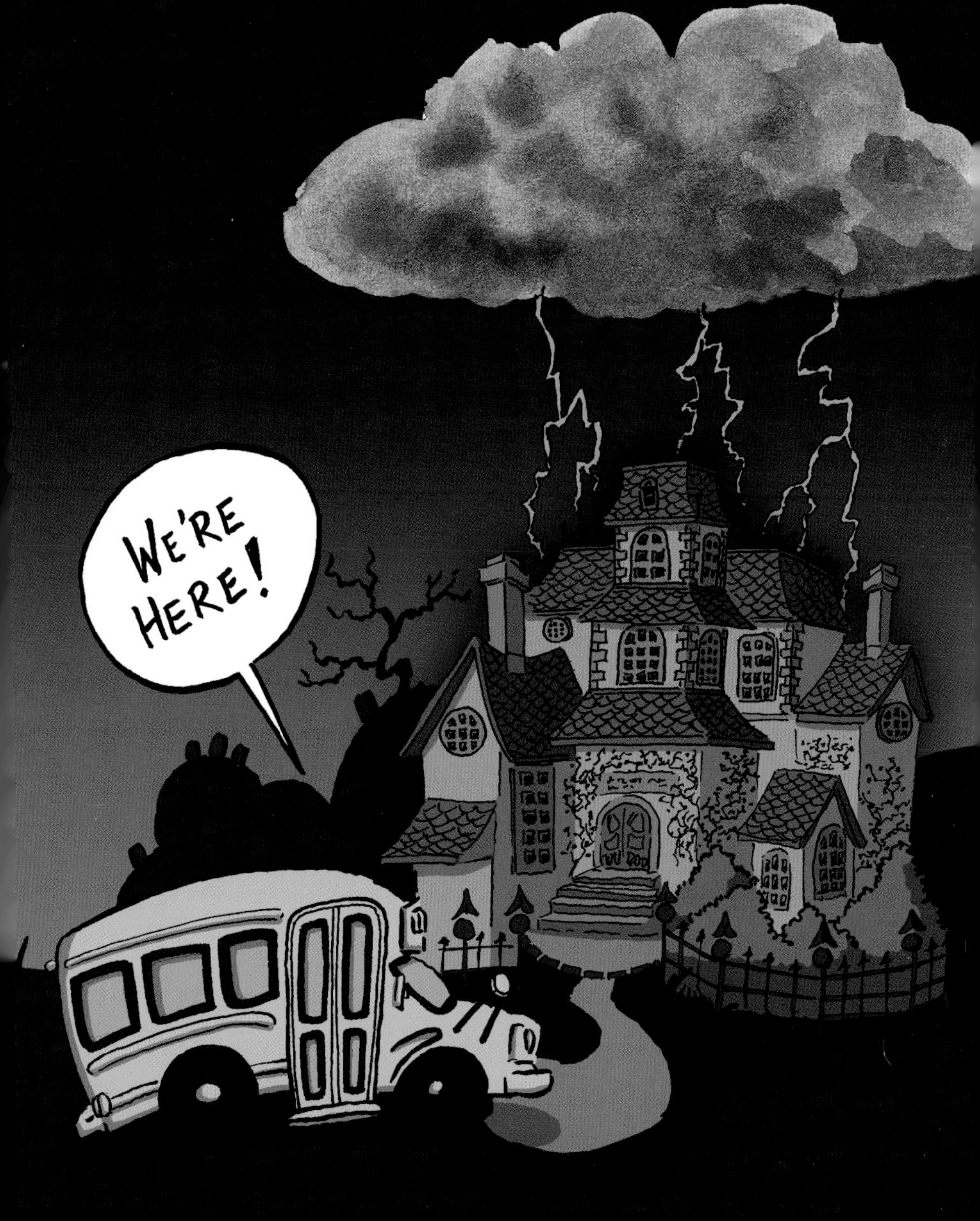
WE'RE HERE!

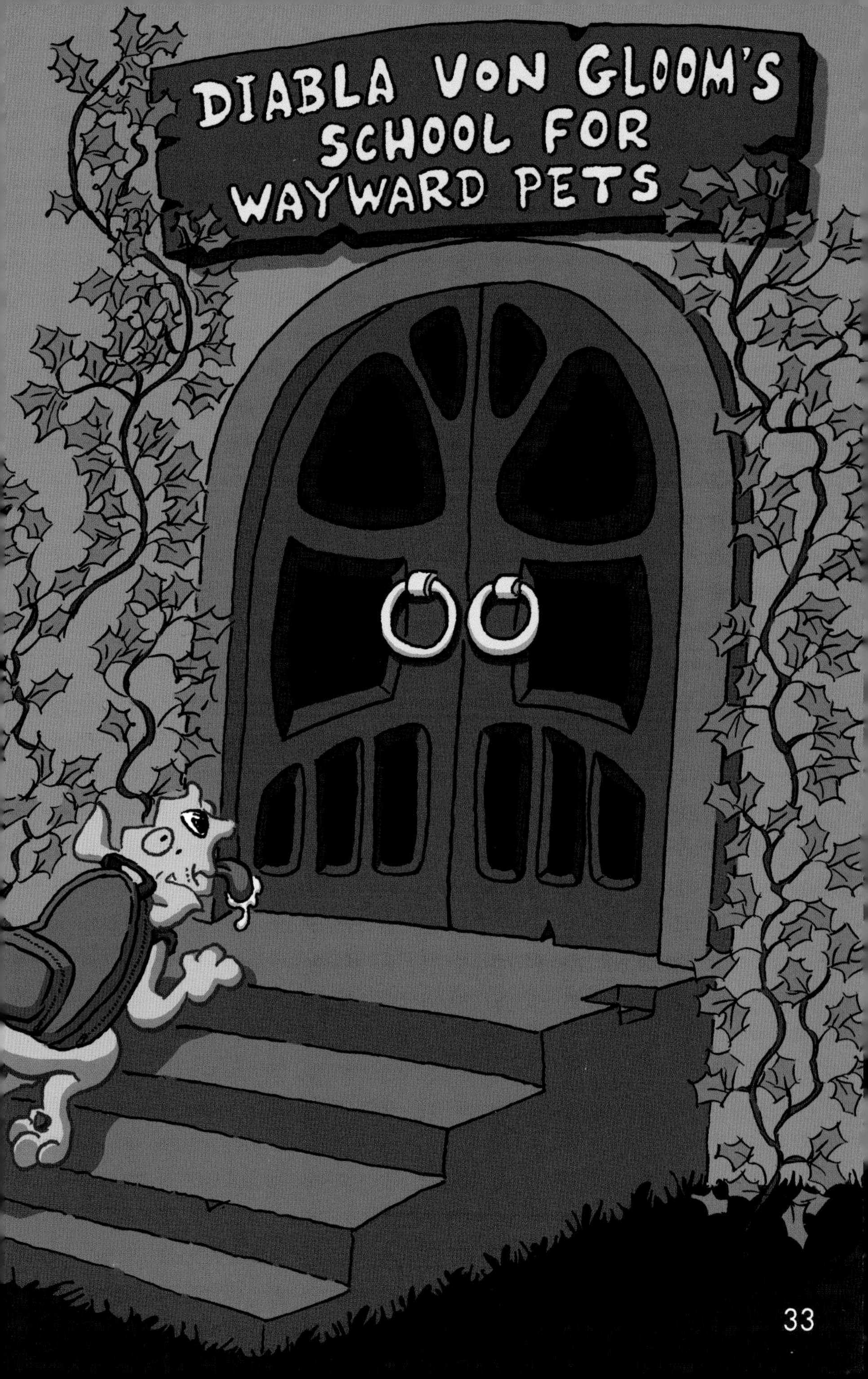
DIABLA VON GLOOM'S
SCHOOL FOR
WAYWARD PETS

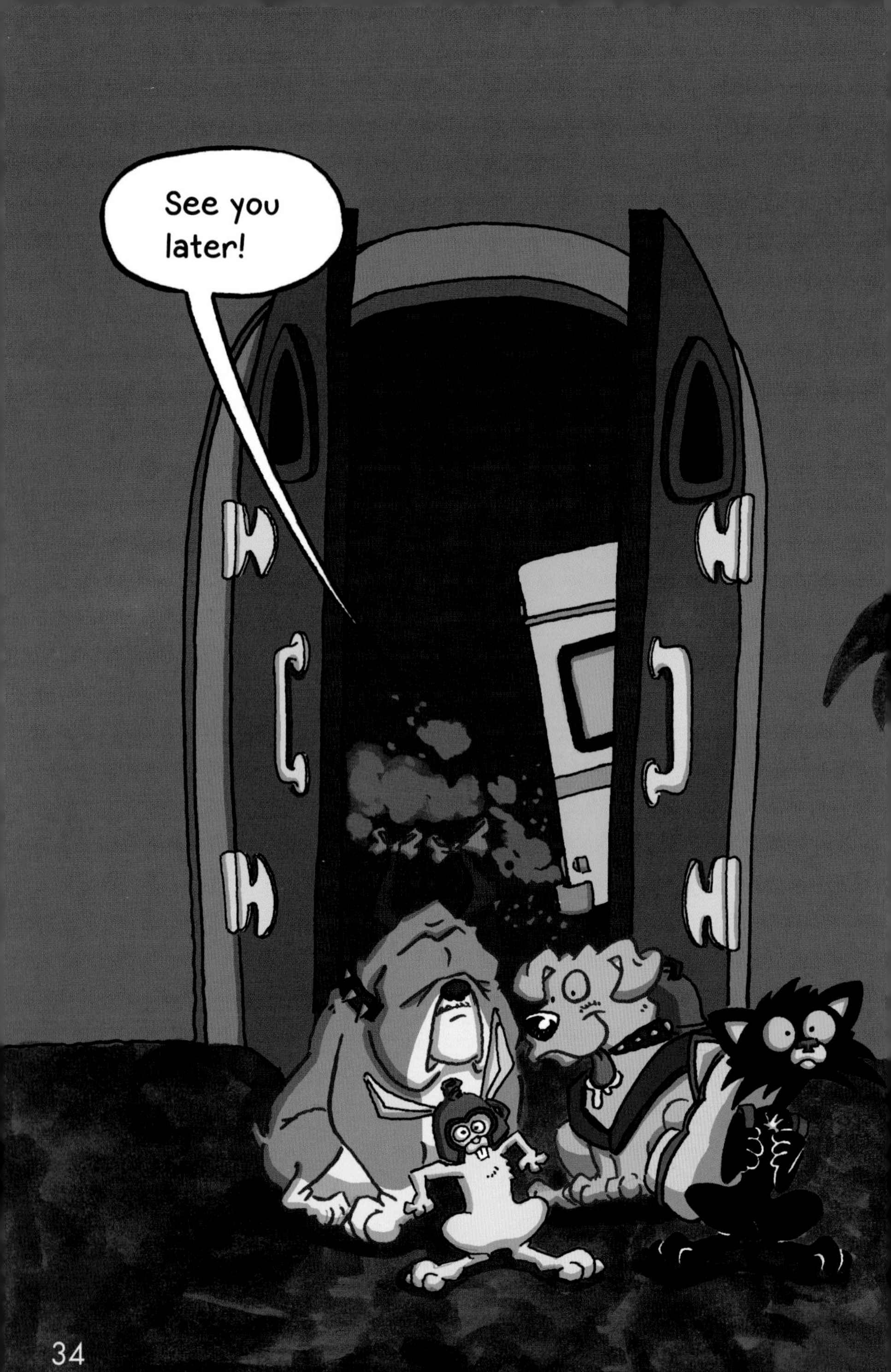
See you later!

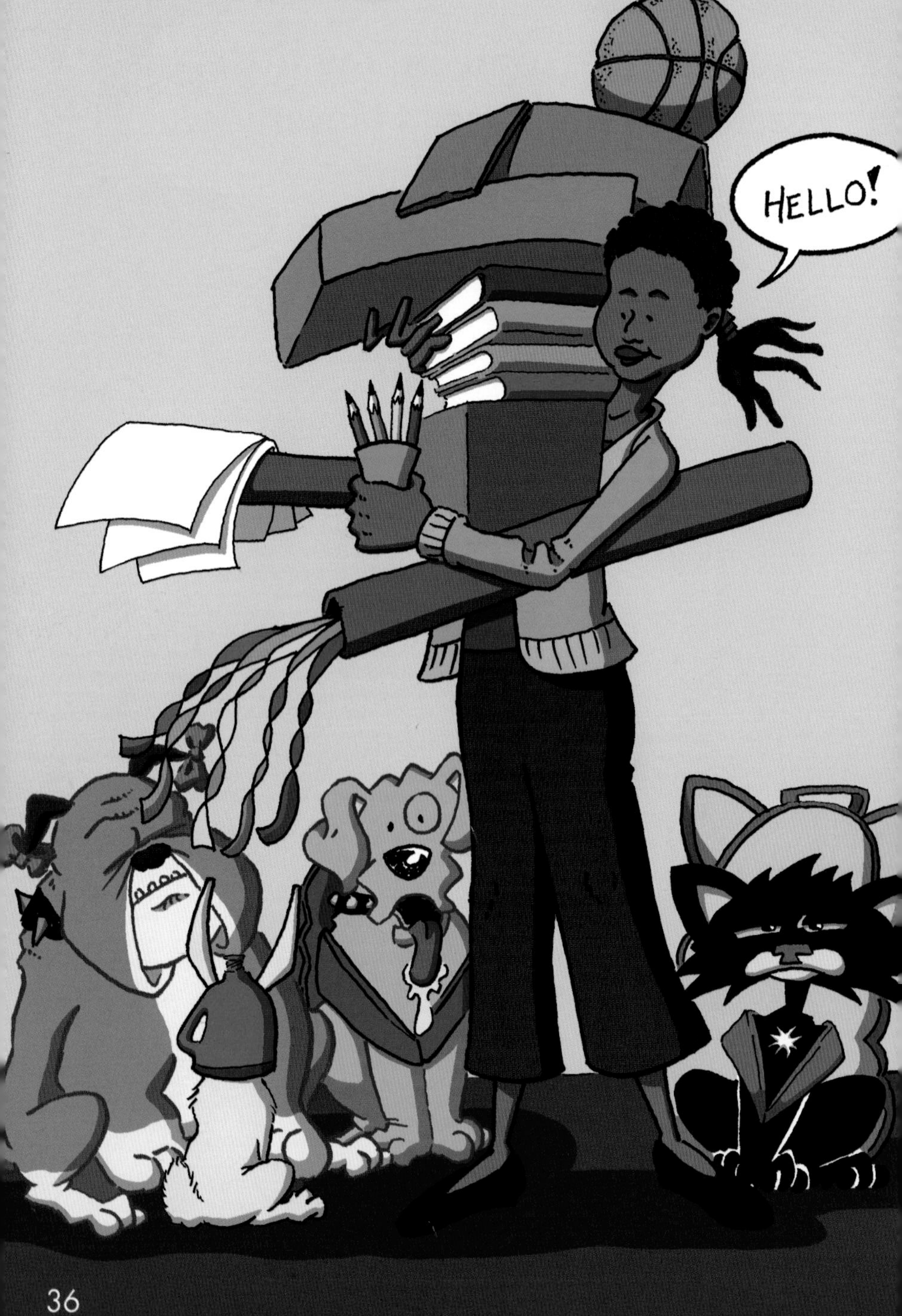
HELLO!

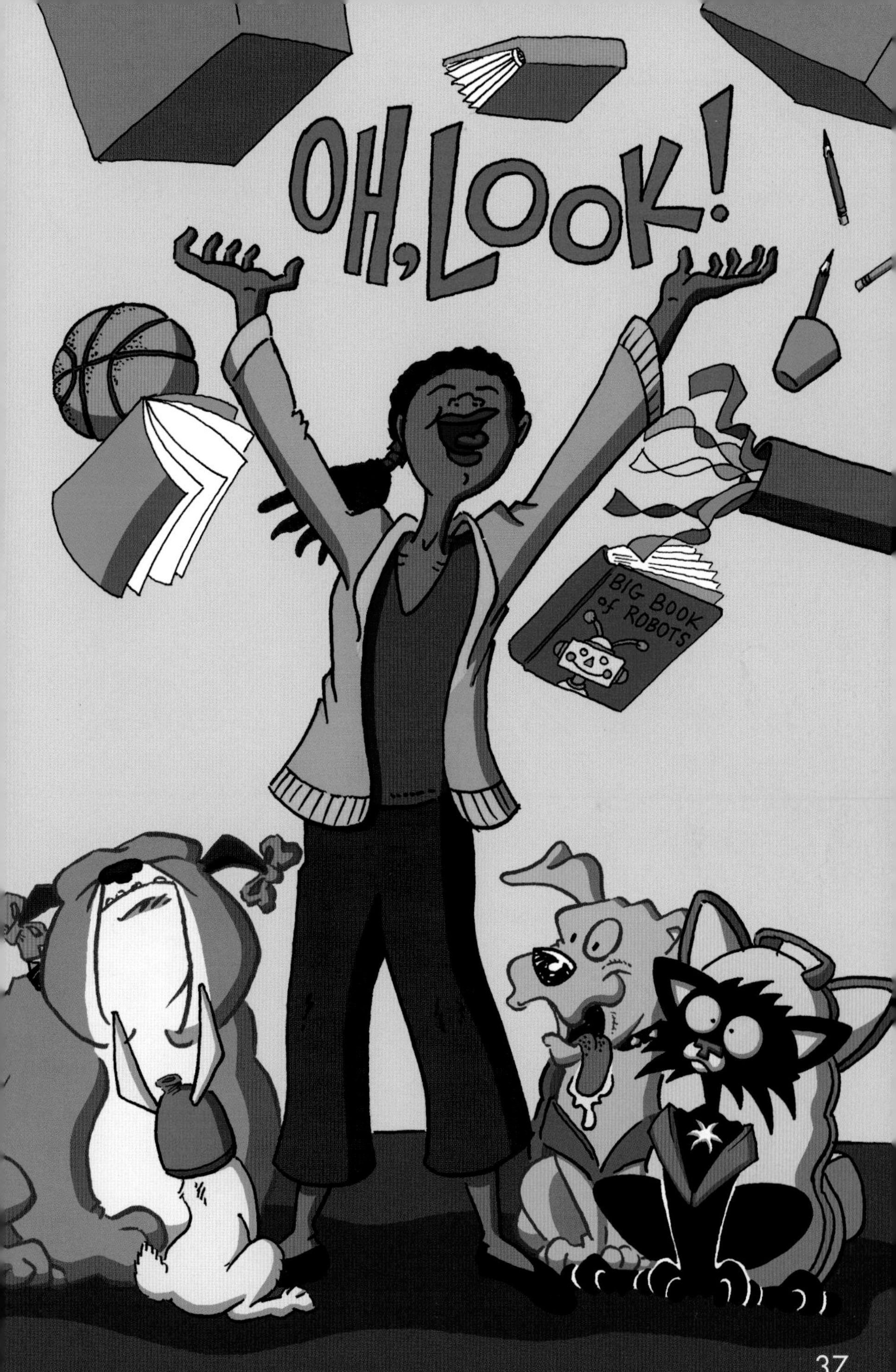
OH, LOOK!
BIG BOOK of ROBOTS

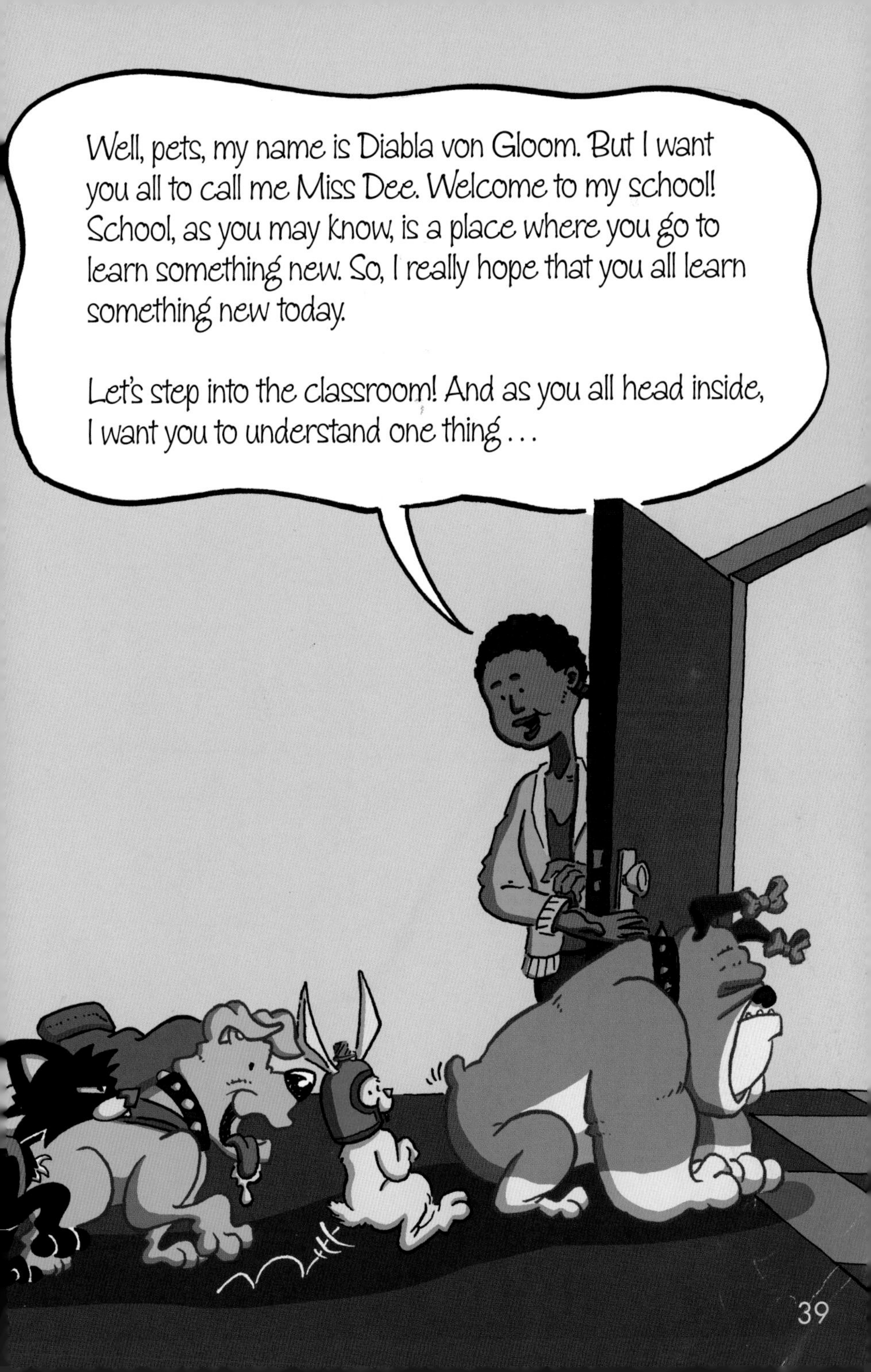
Well, pets, my name is Diabla von Gloom. But I want you all to call me Miss Dee. Welcome to my school! School, as you may know, is a place where you go to learn something new. So, I really hope that you all learn something new today.
Let's step into the classroom! And as you all head inside, I want you to understand one thing . . .

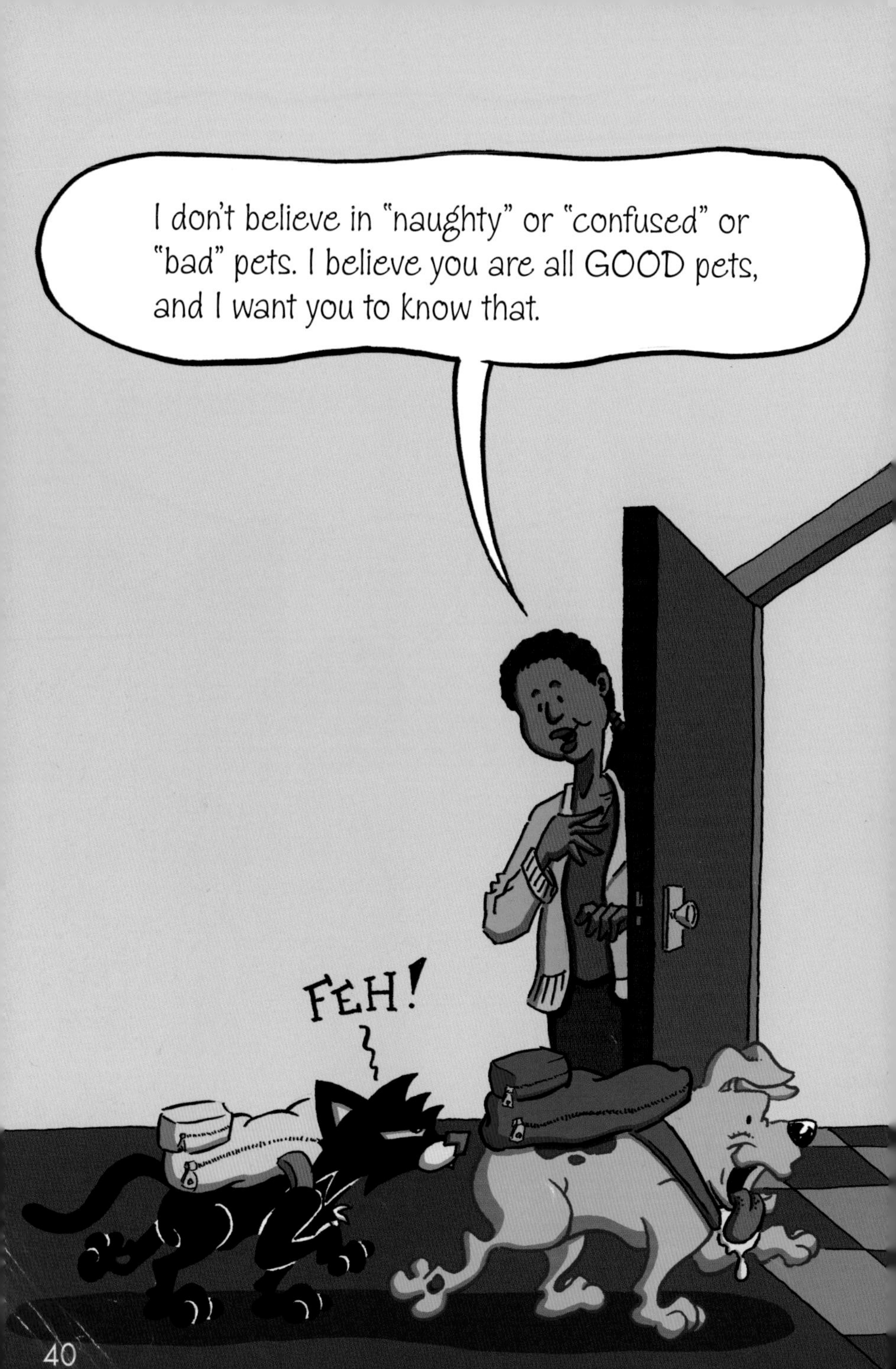
I don't believe in "naughty" or "confused" or "bad" pets. I believe you are all GOOD pets, and I want you to know that.
FEH!

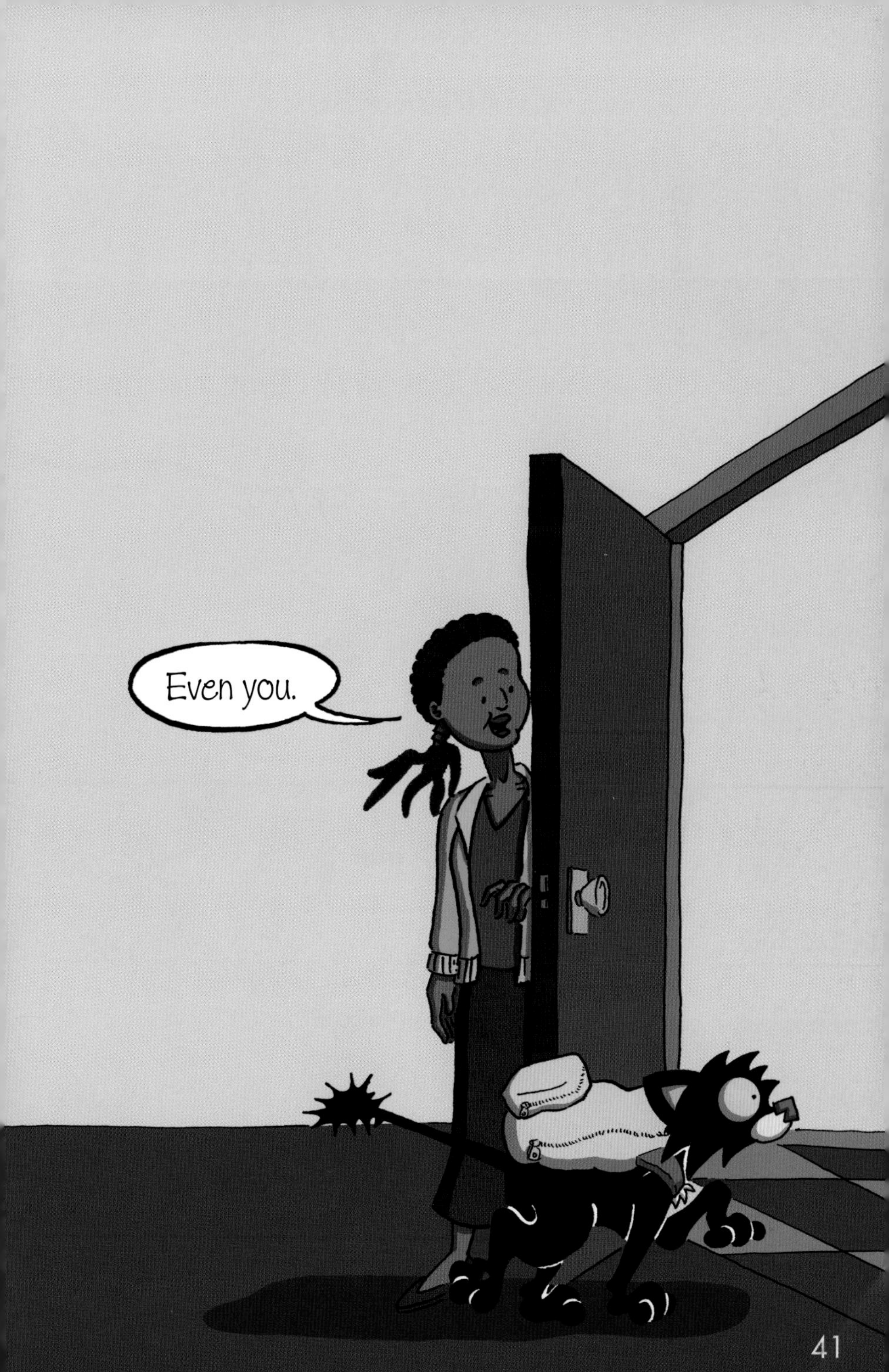
Even you.

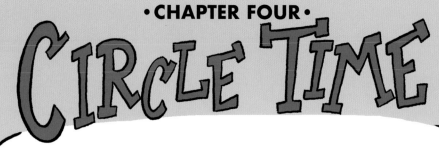

CHAPTER FOUR

Circle Time

Circle time is how I get to know all of you, and for all of you to get to know each other.

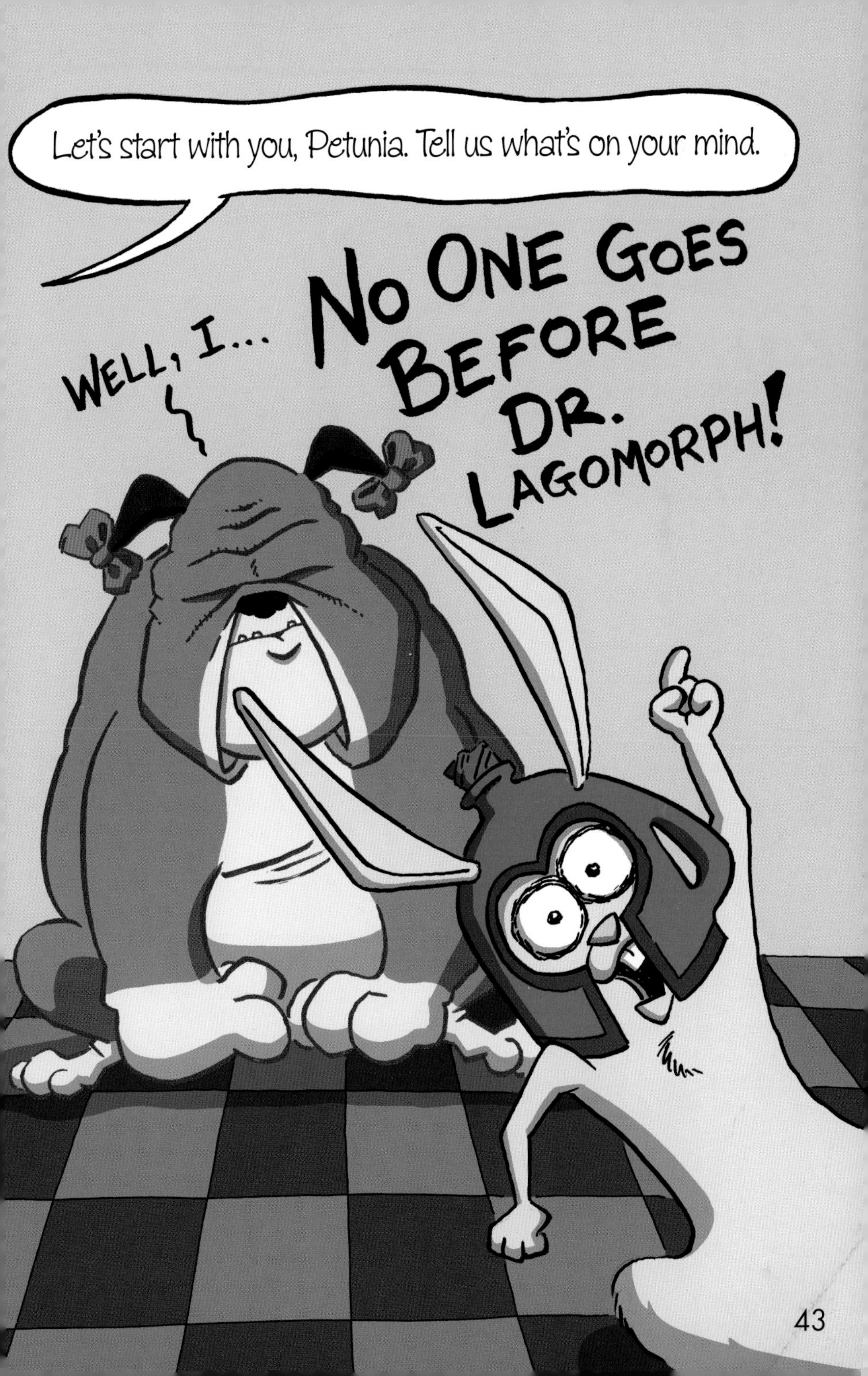
Let's start with you, Petunia. Tell us what's on your mind.
WELL, I...
NO ONE GOES BEFORE DR. LAGOMORPH!

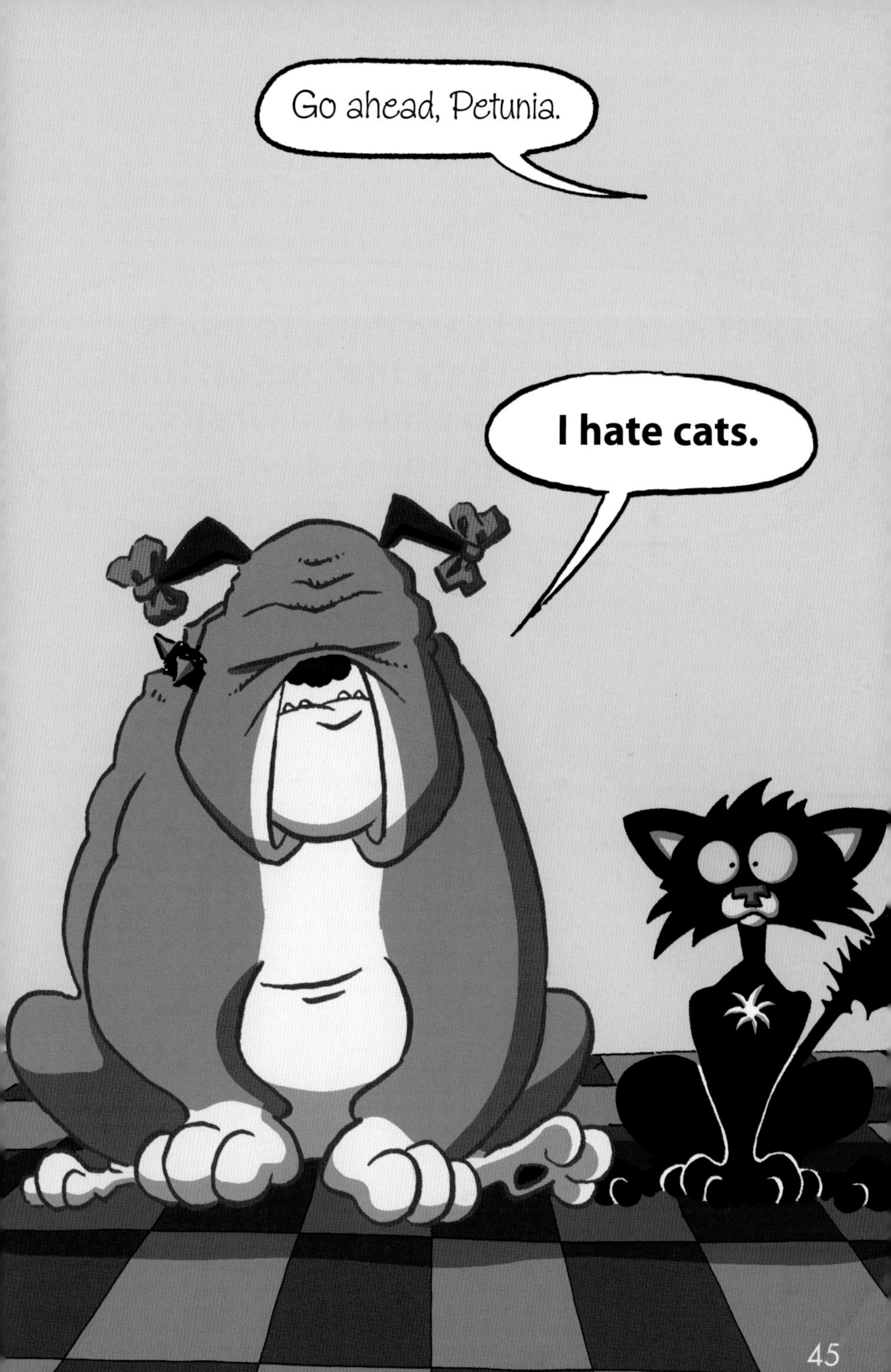
Go ahead, Petunia.
I hate cats.

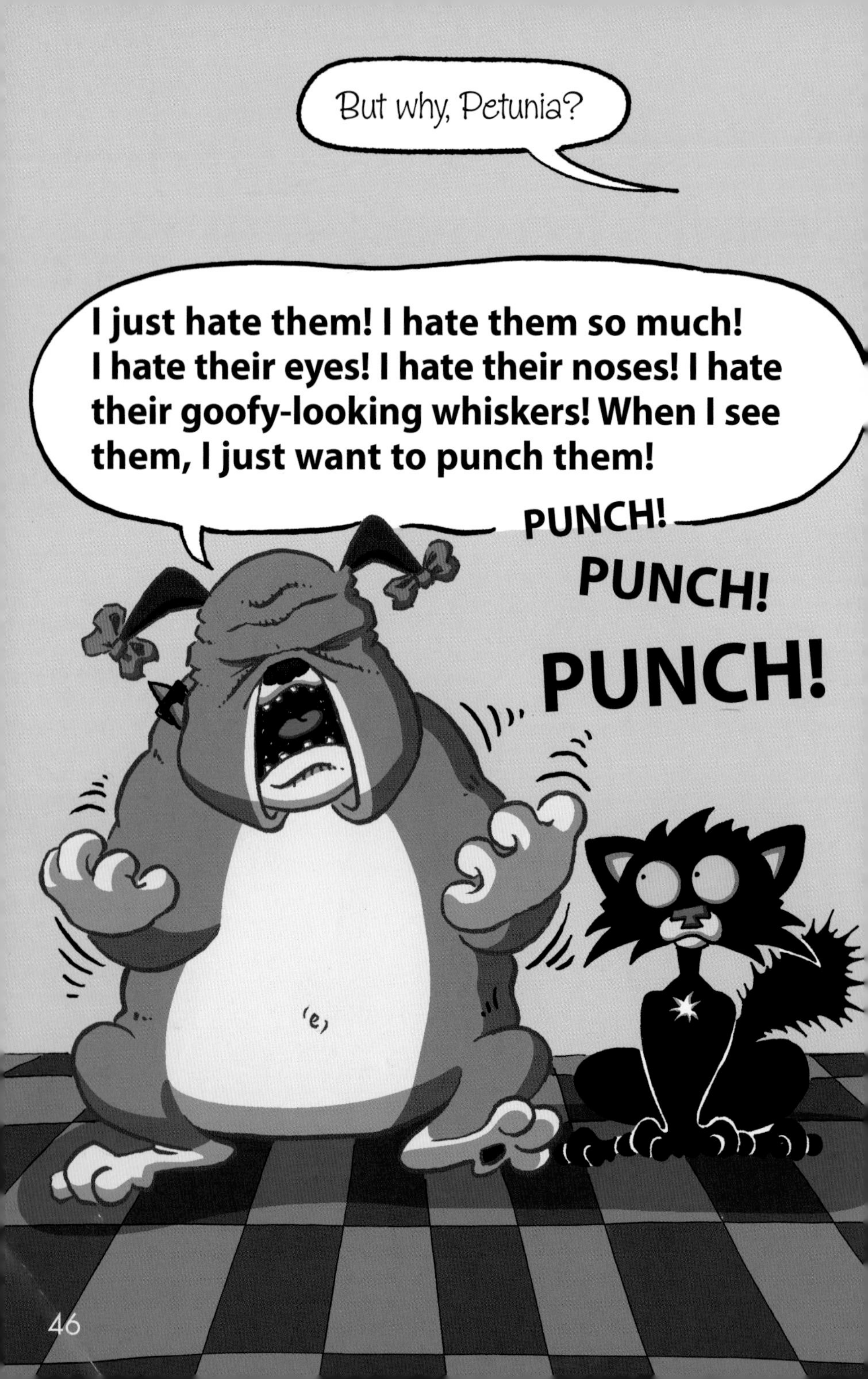
But why, Petunia?
I just hate them! I hate them so much! I hate their eyes! I hate their noses! I hate their goofy-looking whiskers! When I see them, I just want to punch them!
PUNCH!
PUNCH!
PUNCH!

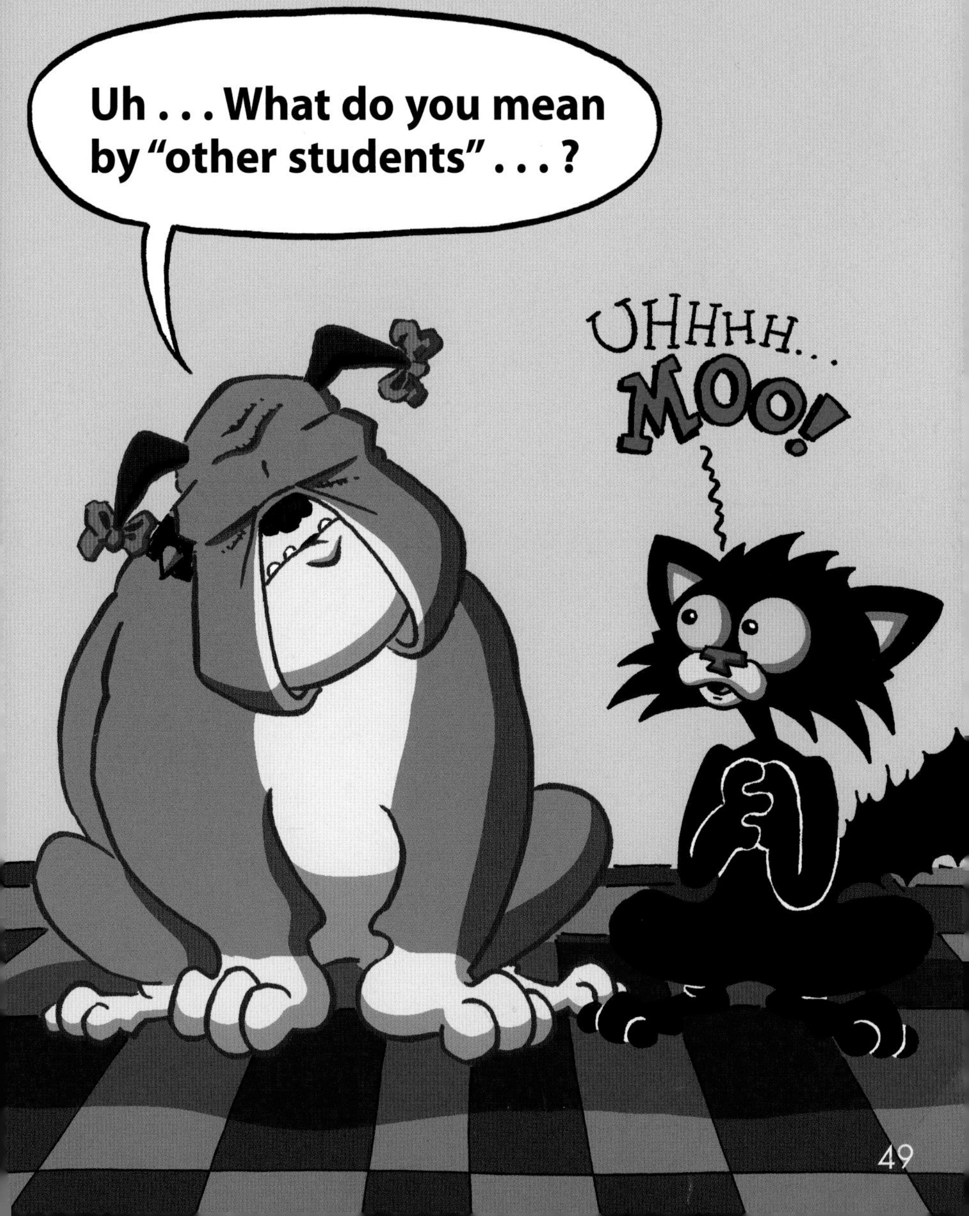
Uh . . . What do you mean by "other students" . . . ?
UHHHH...
MOO!

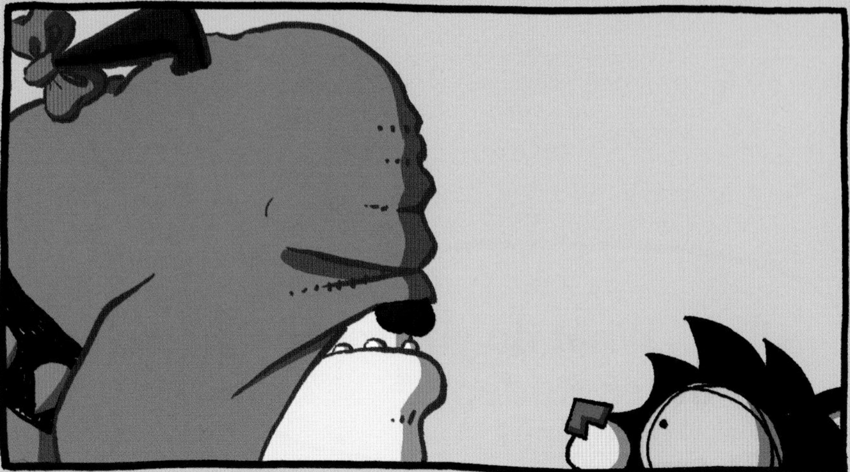

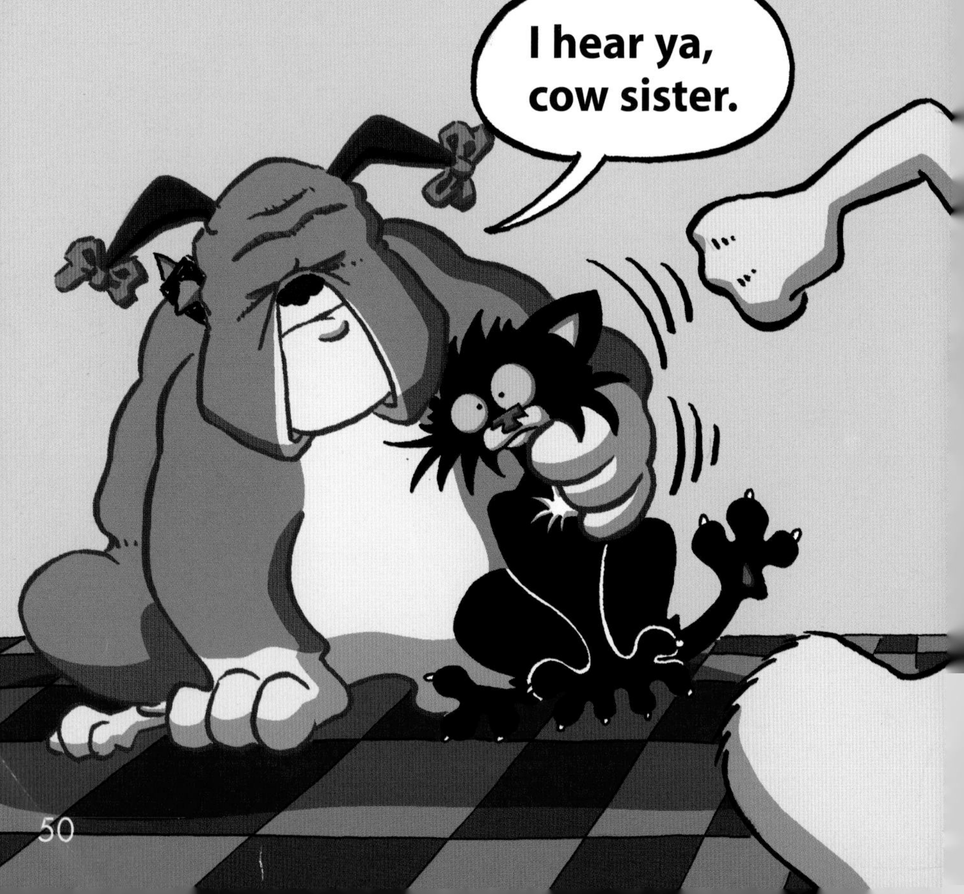
I hear ya,
cow sister.

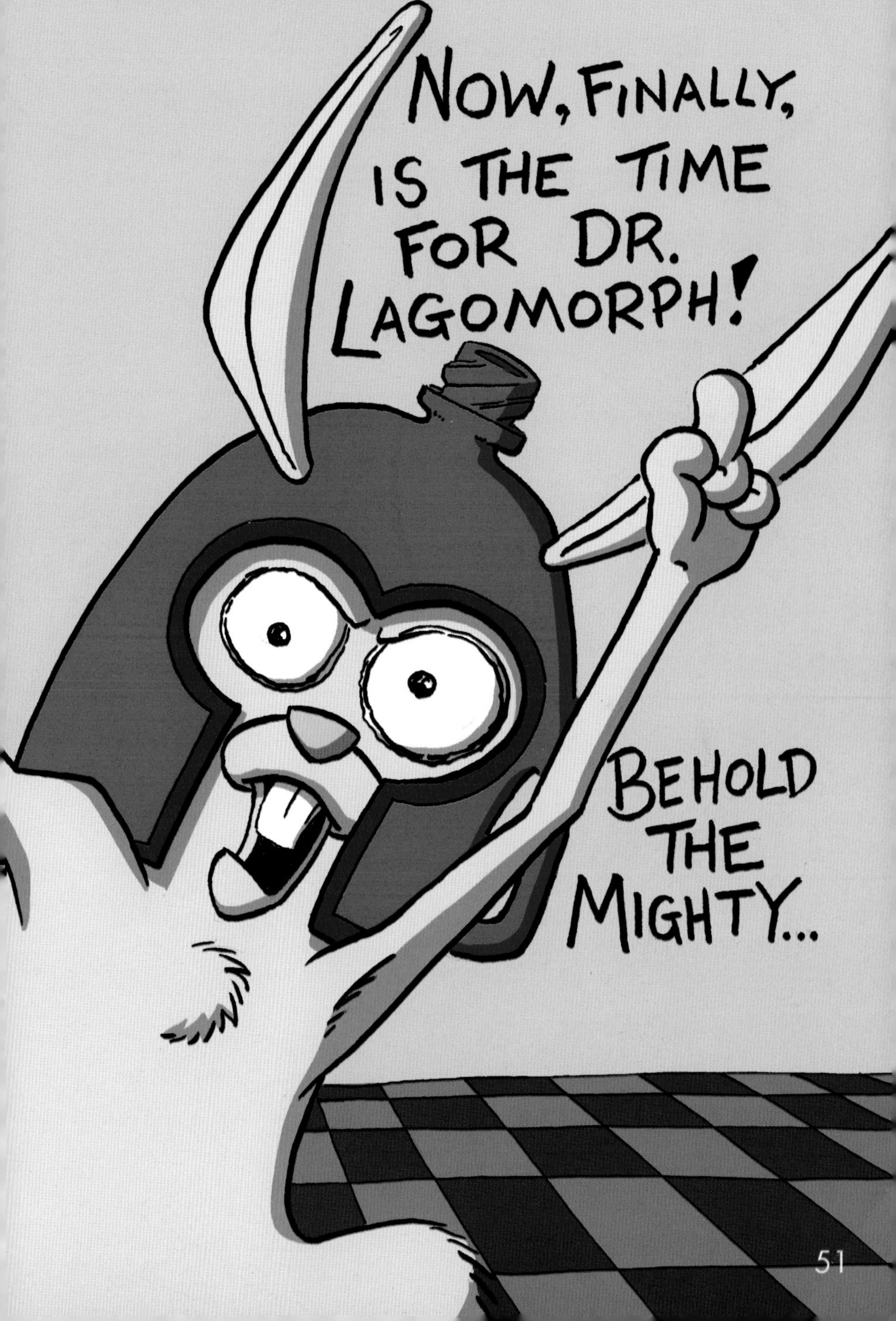
NOW, FINALLY, IS THE TIME FOR DR. LAGOMORPH!
BEHOLD THE MIGHTY...

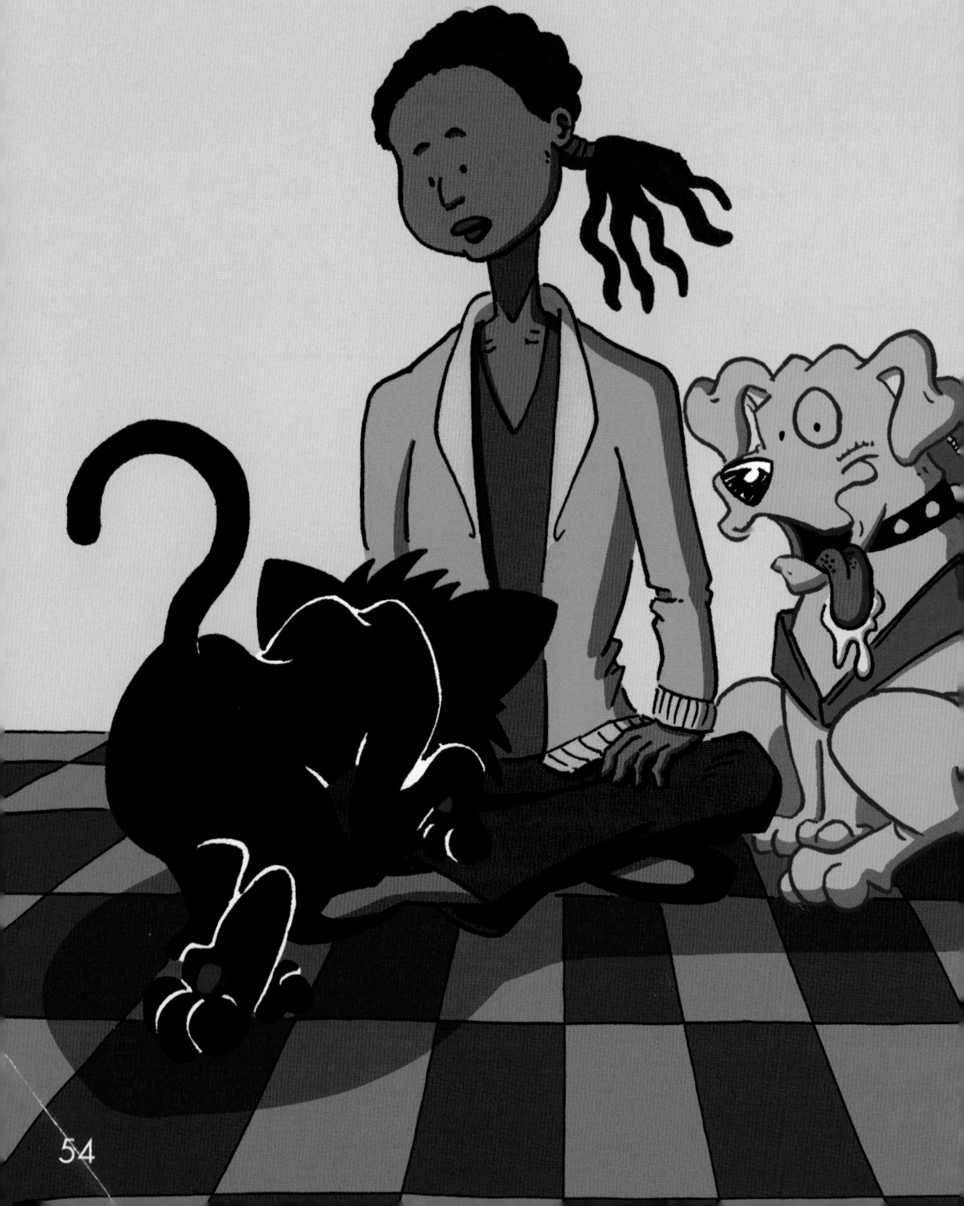

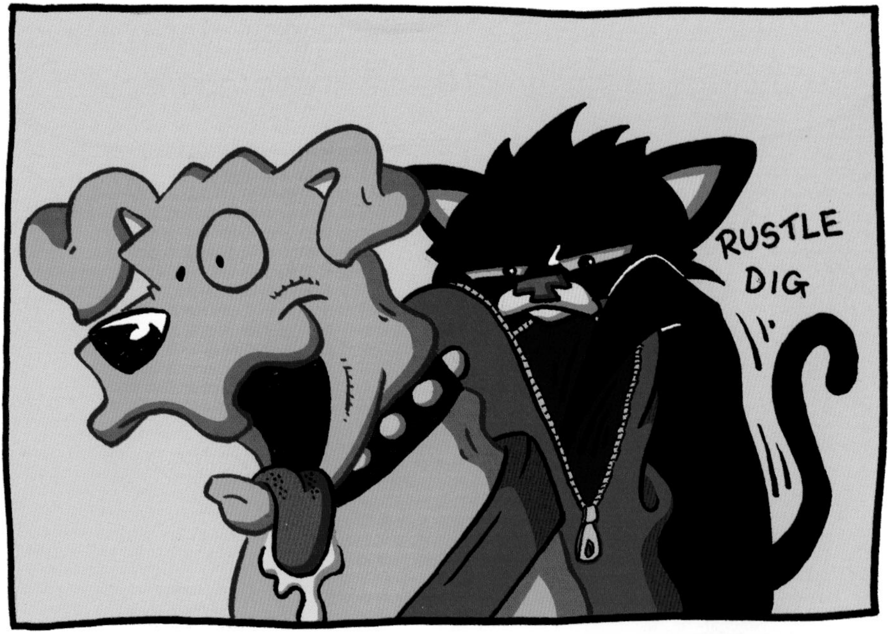
RUSTLE
DIG

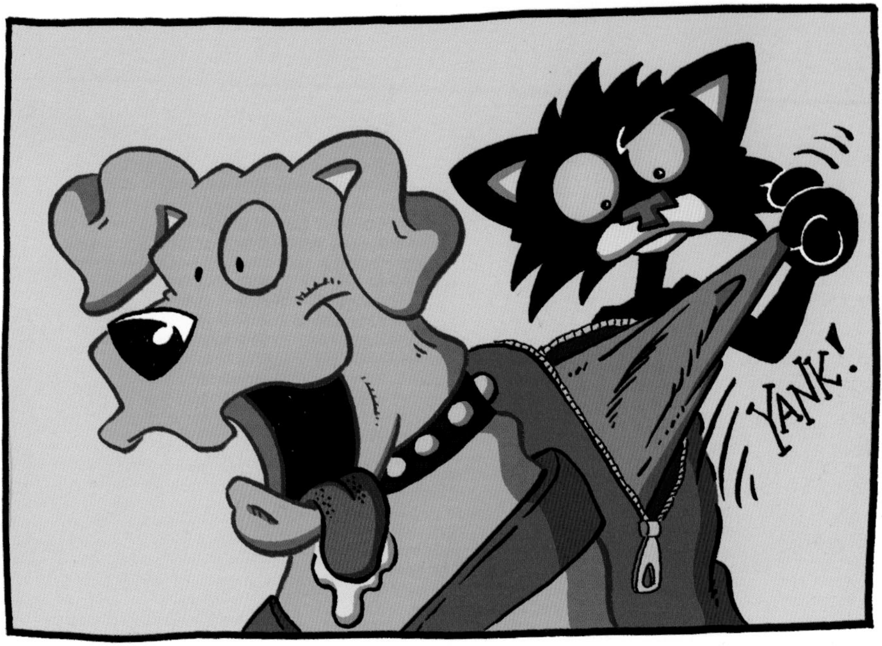
YANK!

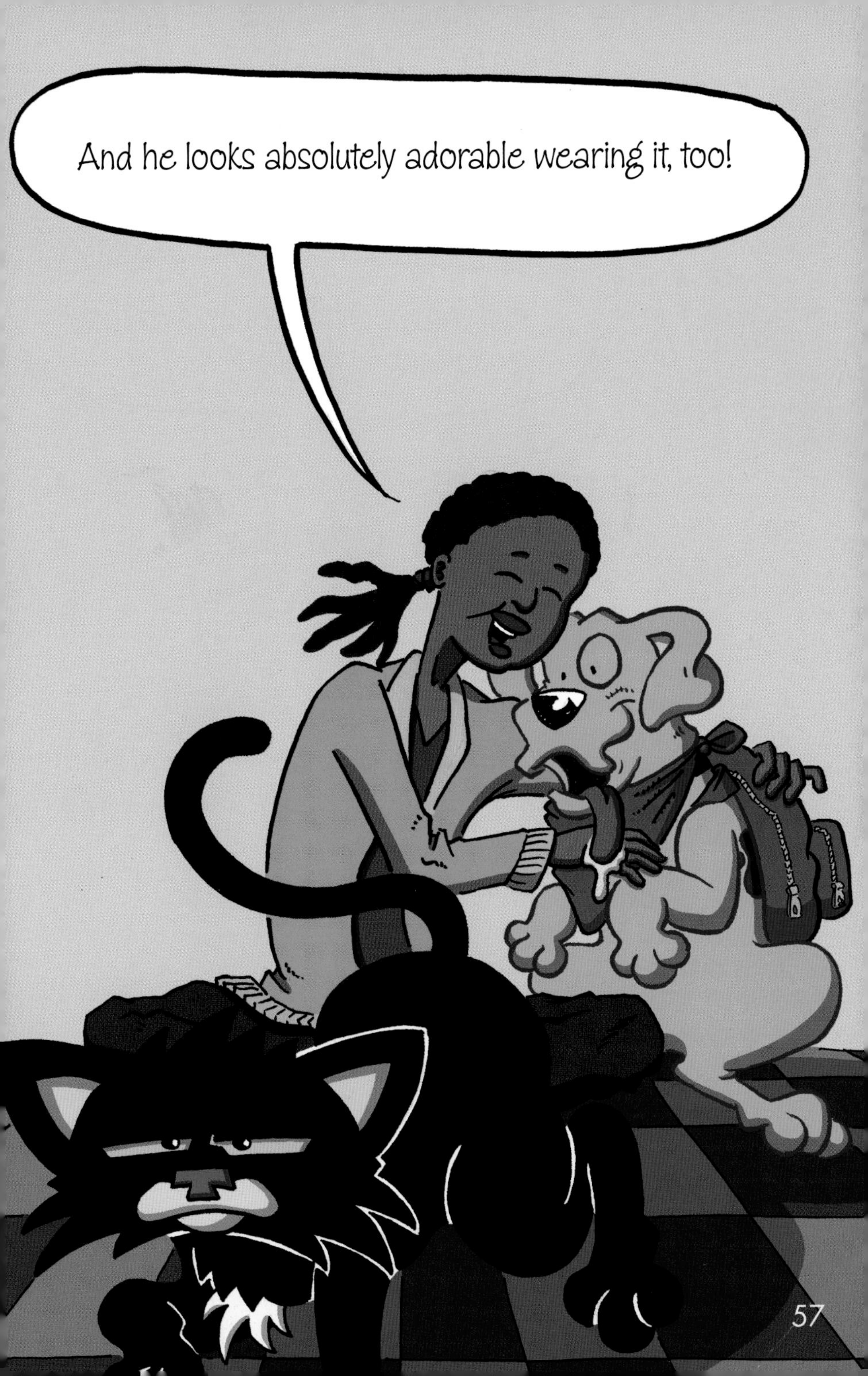
And he looks absolutely adorable wearing it, too!

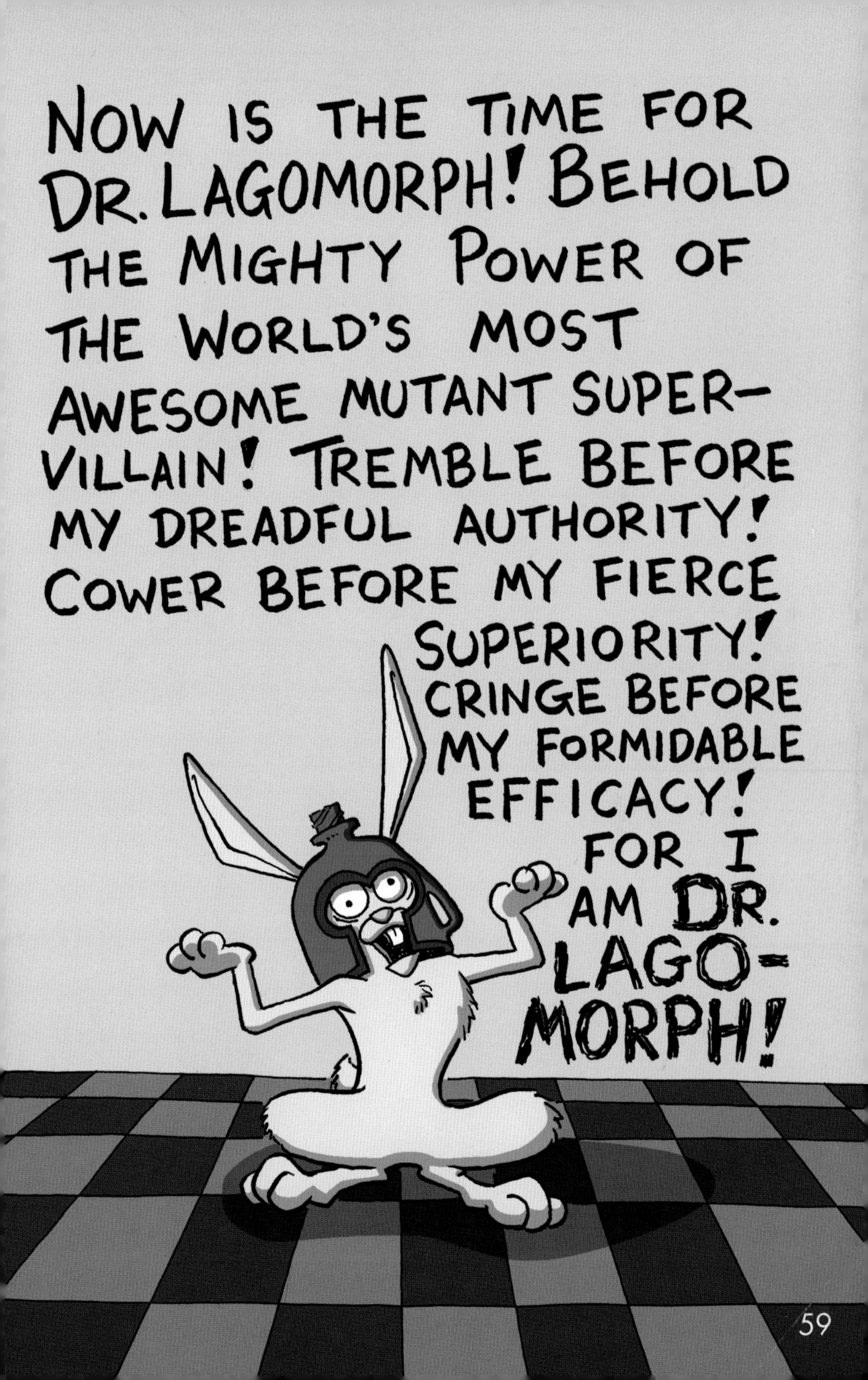
NOW IS THE TIME FOR DR. LAGOMORPH! BEHOLD THE MIGHTY POWER OF THE WORLD'S MOST AWESOME MUTANT SUPER-VILLAIN! TREMBLE BEFORE MY DREADFUL AUTHORITY! COWER BEFORE MY FIERCE SUPERIORITY! CRINGE BEFORE MY FORMIDABLE EFFICACY! FOR I AM DR. LAGO-MORPH!

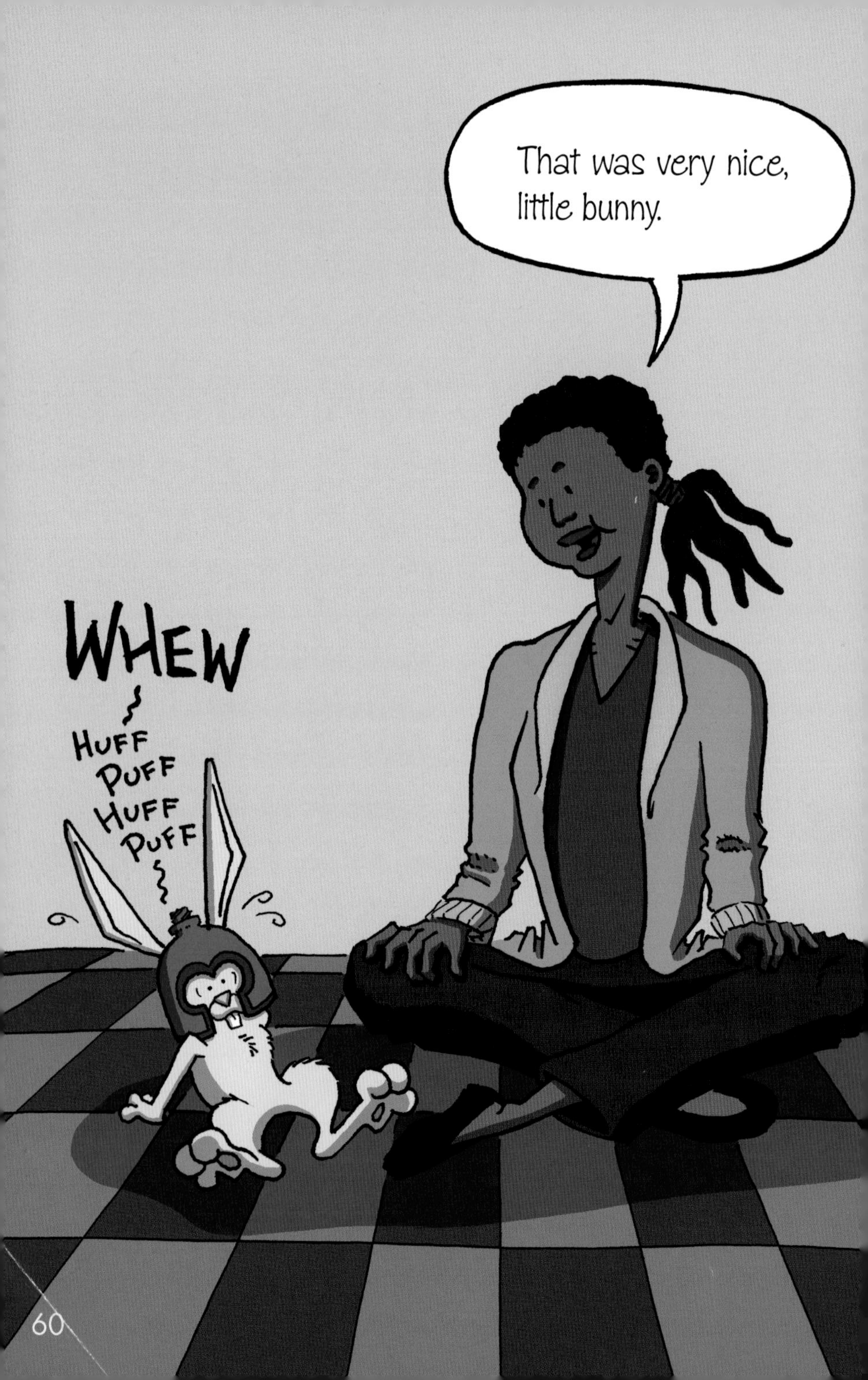
That was very nice, little bunny.
WHEW
HUFF
PUFF
HUFF
PUFF

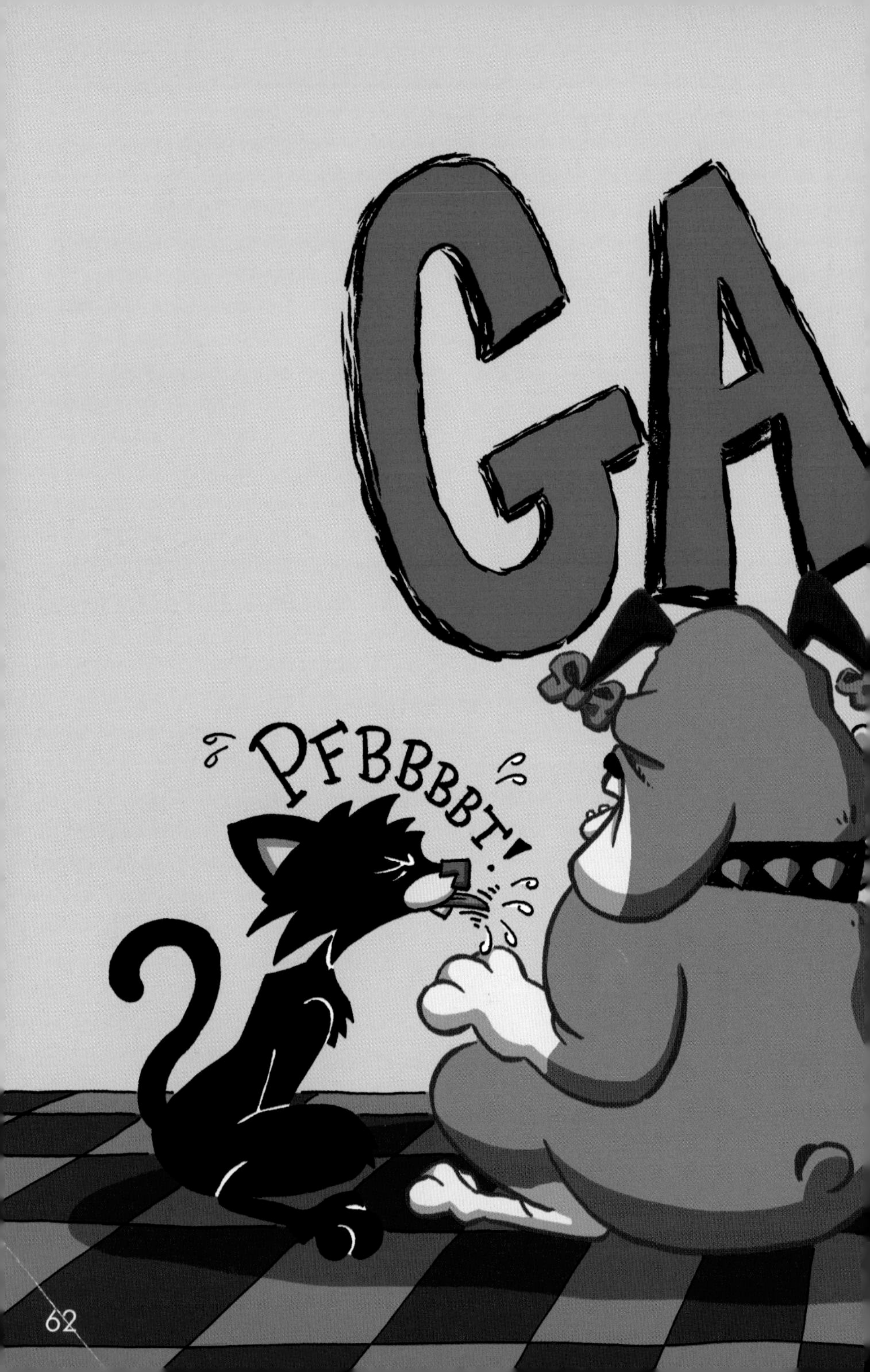
GA
PFBBBBT!

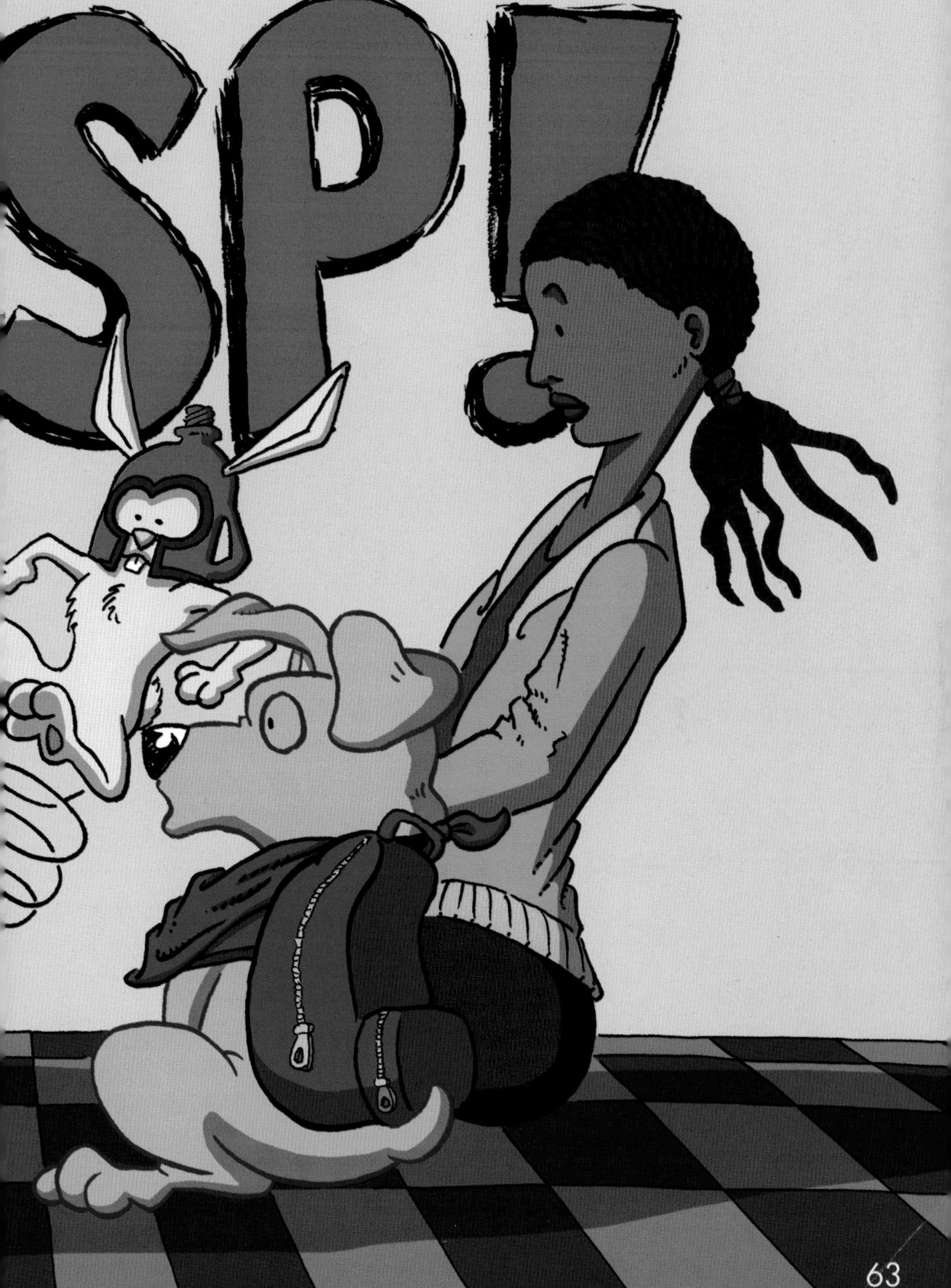
SP!

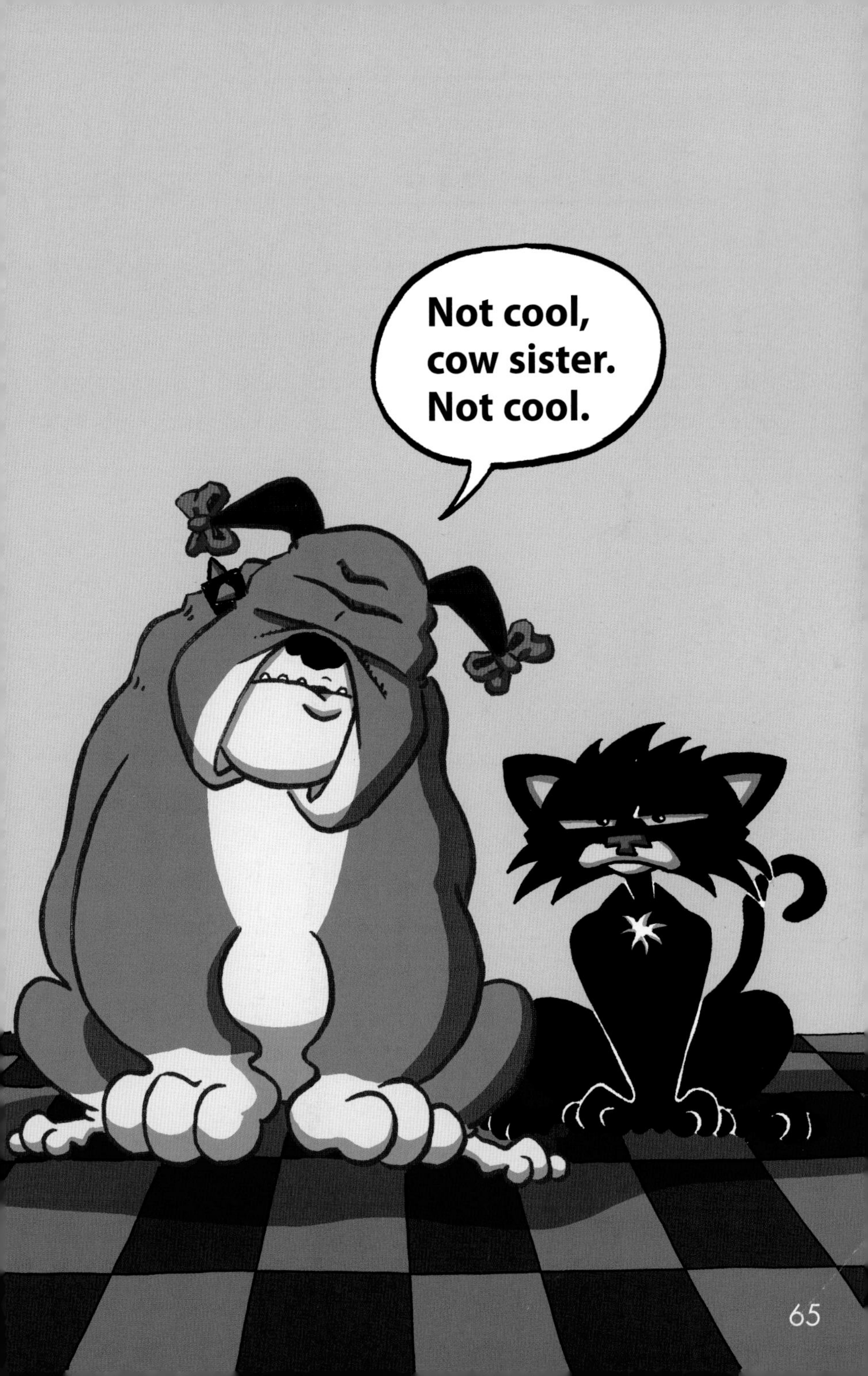
Not cool, cow sister. Not cool.

UNCLE MURRAY'S FUN FACTS

WHY DO DOGS AND CATS HATE EACH OTHER?

Stop blamin dogs! This all the faul of goofy cats!

The problem between dogs and cats isn't so much that they hate each other . . . they just don't understand each other. Let's think about how dogs and cats are different from each other.

NOSE—SNIFFS EVERYTHING

TONGUE—LICKS YOU BECAUSE HE LIKES YOU

TAIL—WAGS WHEN HAPPY.

Dogs are very social. They live in packs and usually enjoy the company of other dogs. Dogs like to play by wrestling and biting. When a dog first meets you, he likes to sniff you (especially in places where you may not like to be sniffed). When a dog likes you, he expresses it by licking you. When a dog is happy, he wags his tail.

Cats, on the other hand, are not social animals. They lead independent lives and usually do not seek the company of other cats. Except for when they're young, cats do not play with each other and especially not by wrestling or biting. Cats don't sniff things nearly as much as dogs. Cats generally only lick themselves, and then only to clean themselves. And cats only shake their tails when they're feeling nervous or angry.

TAIL— SHAKES WHEN NERVOUS

NOSE—USUALLY ONLY SNIFFS TO SENSE DANGER OR SAFETY

TONGUE — ONLY LICKS HERSELF

Now imagine what happens when a strange dog and cat meet for the first time. The dog runs up to the cat with his tail wagging, expecting to sniff her, lick her, and play with her. But the cat, meanwhile, sees the dog's running as an attack. She sees the wagging tail as a sign of anger. And the last thing the cat wants is to be sniffed (especially in a place where she doesn't want to be sniffed), licked, and played with. So the cat either runs away or attacks, neither of which the dog expected.

Okay, so maybe the dogs are just kinda sorta partly to blame.

So now the dog has a perception that cats just *aren't* friendly. This isn't going to encourage the dog to be friendly with any cats in the future. And so begins a cycle of misunderstanding that can sometimes lead to a real mess.

• CHAPTER FIVE •

Arts + Crafts

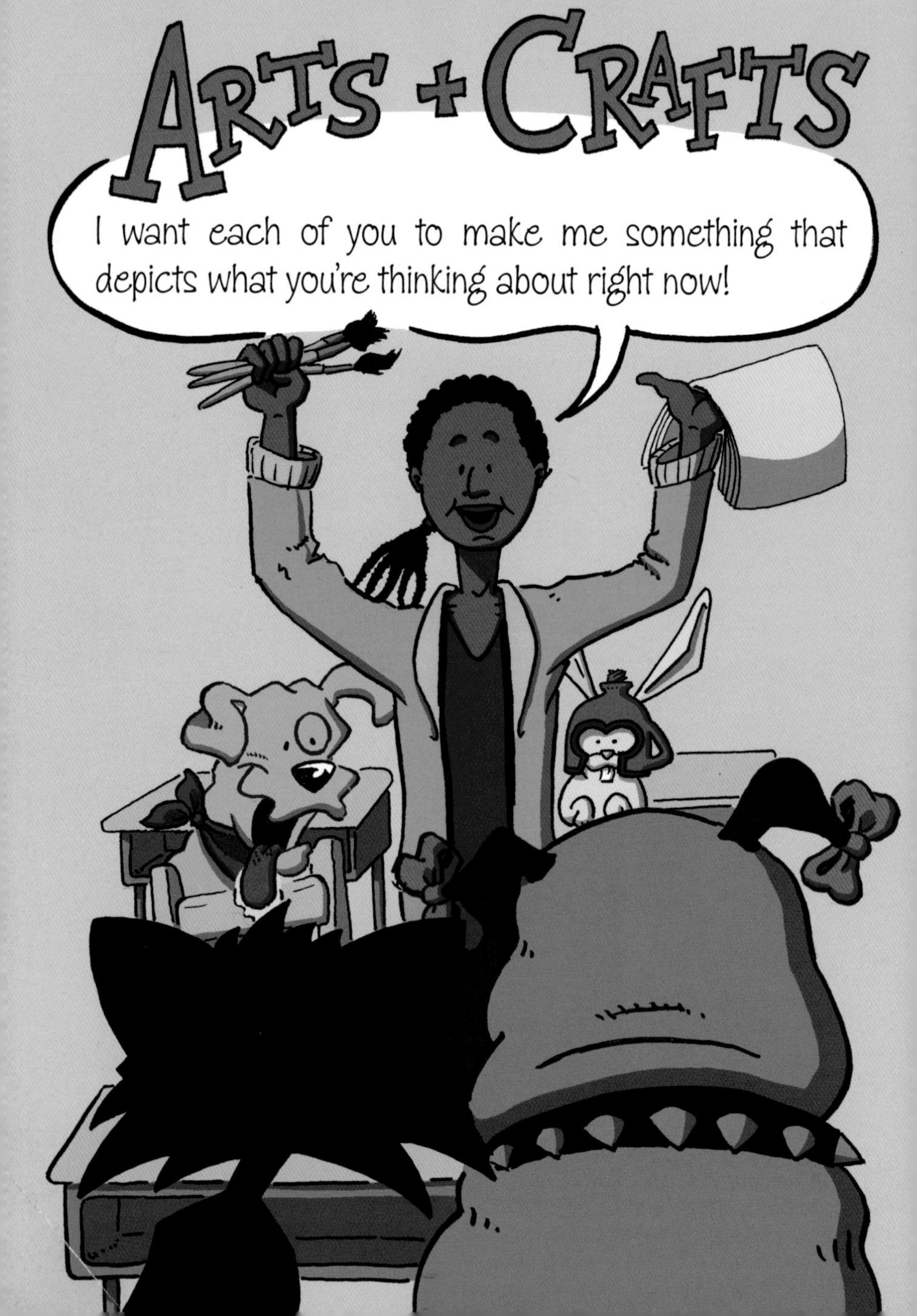
I want each of you to make me something that depicts what you're thinking about right now!

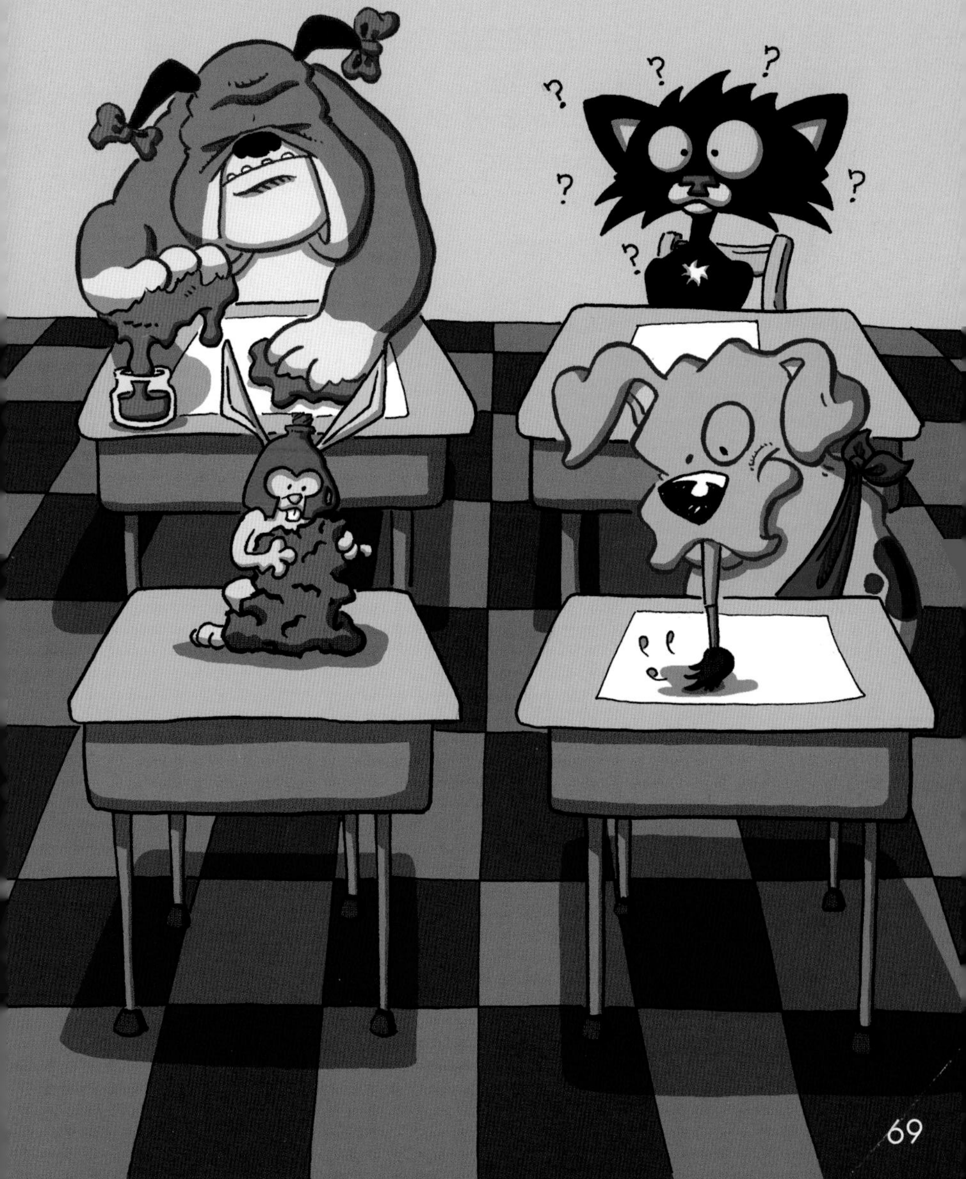
???????

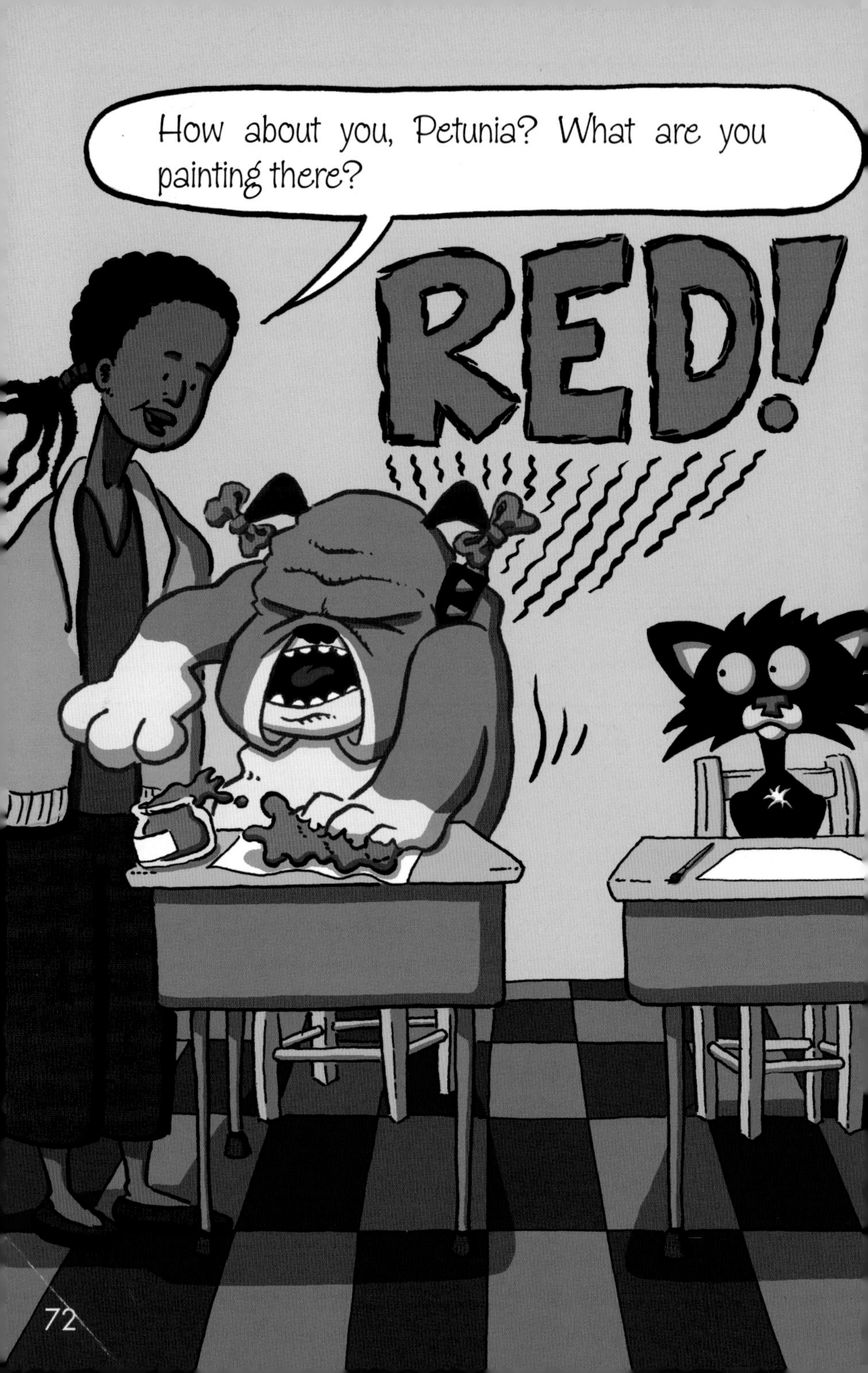
How about you, Petunia? What are you painting there?
RED!

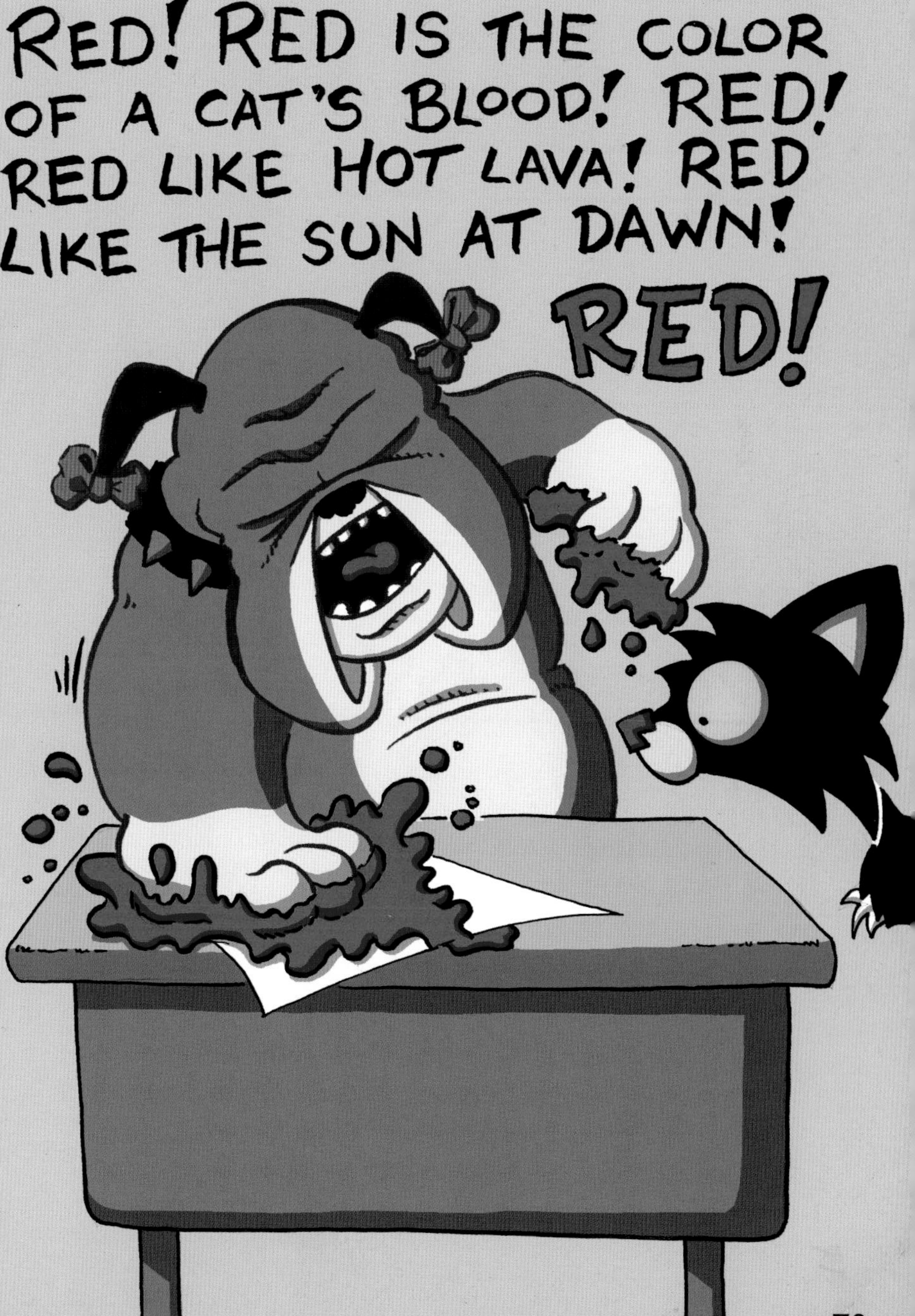
RED! RED IS THE COLOR OF A CAT'S BLOOD! RED! RED LIKE HOT LAVA! RED LIKE THE SUN AT DAWN!
RED!

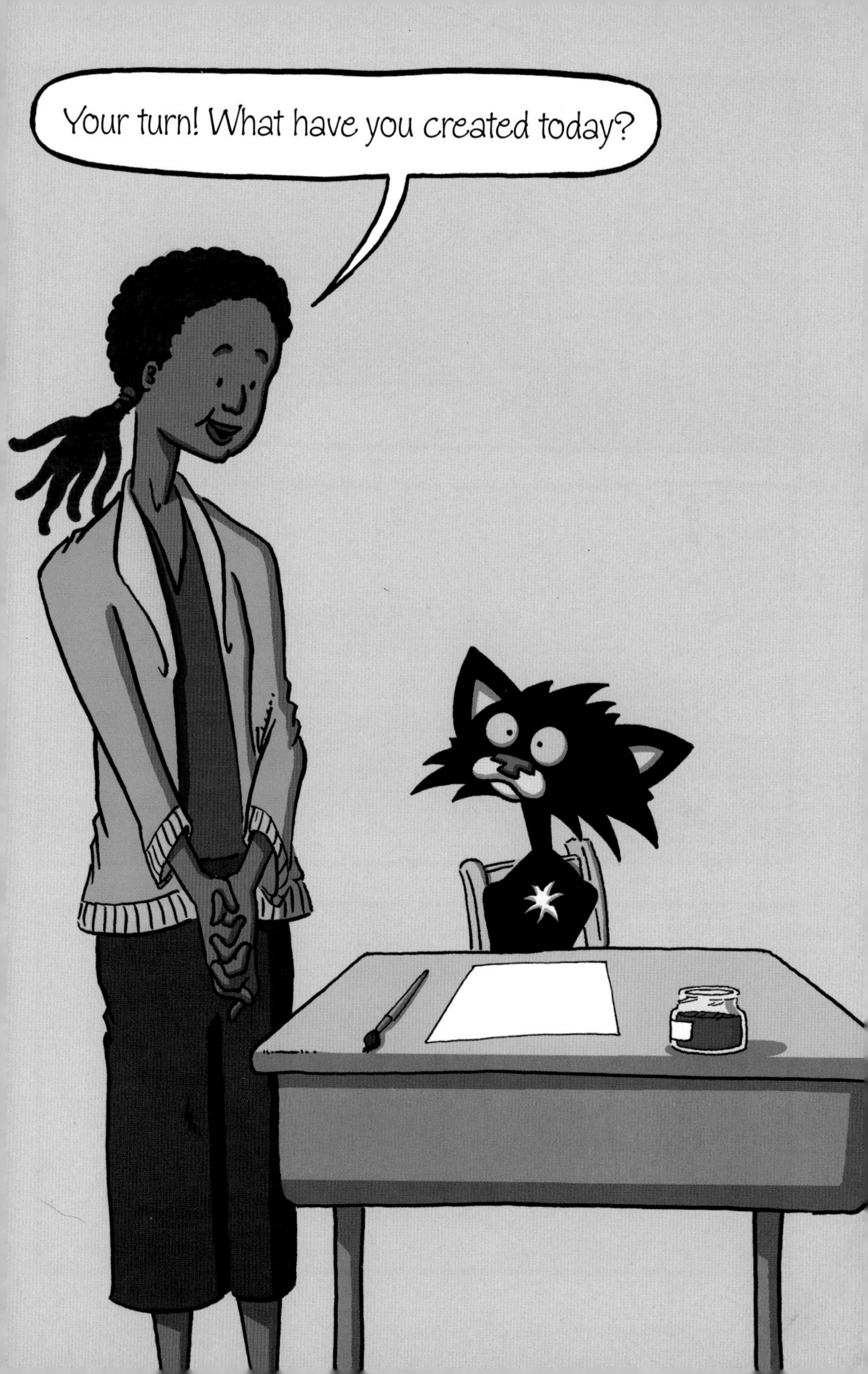
Your turn! What have you created today?

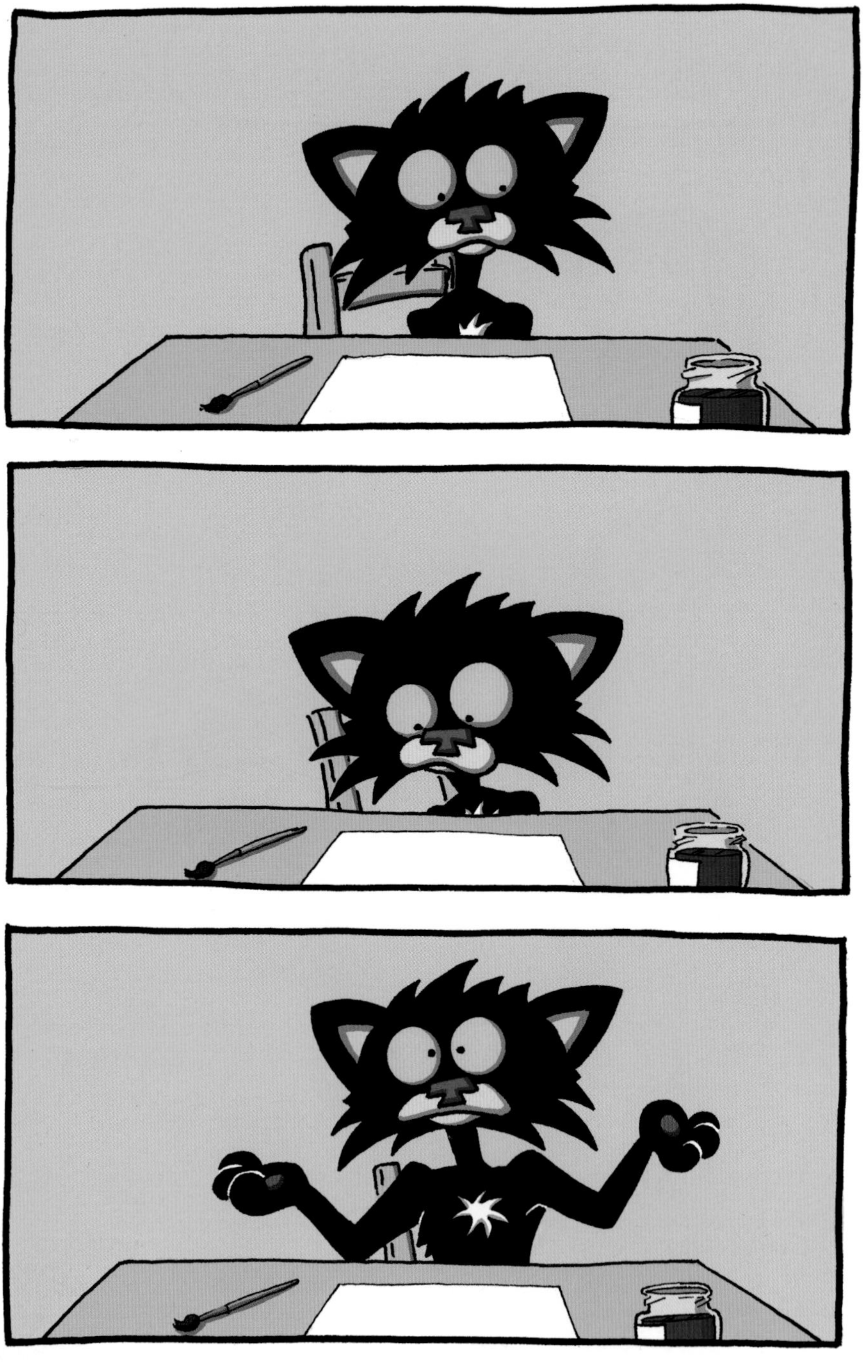

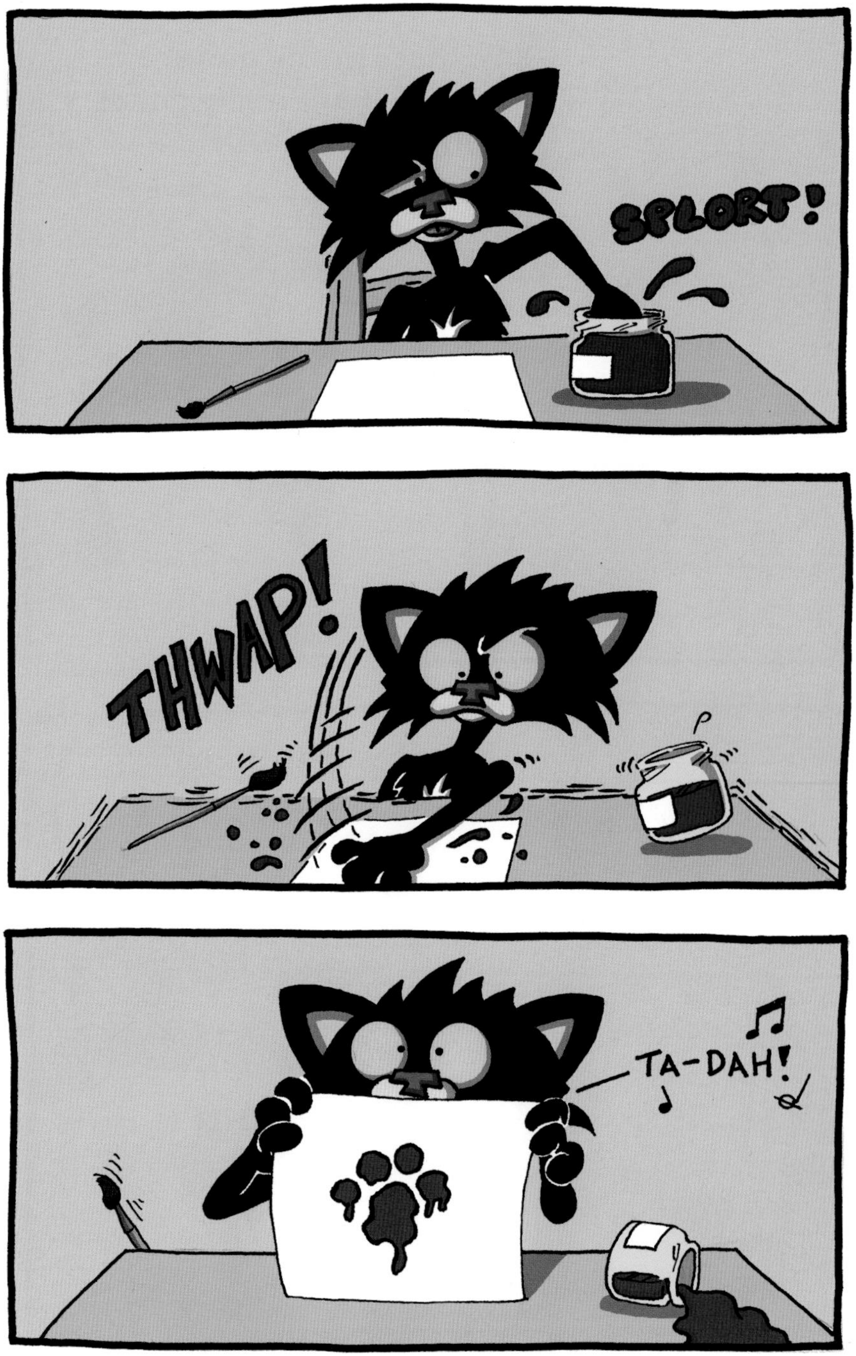
SPLORT!
THWAP!
TA-DAH!

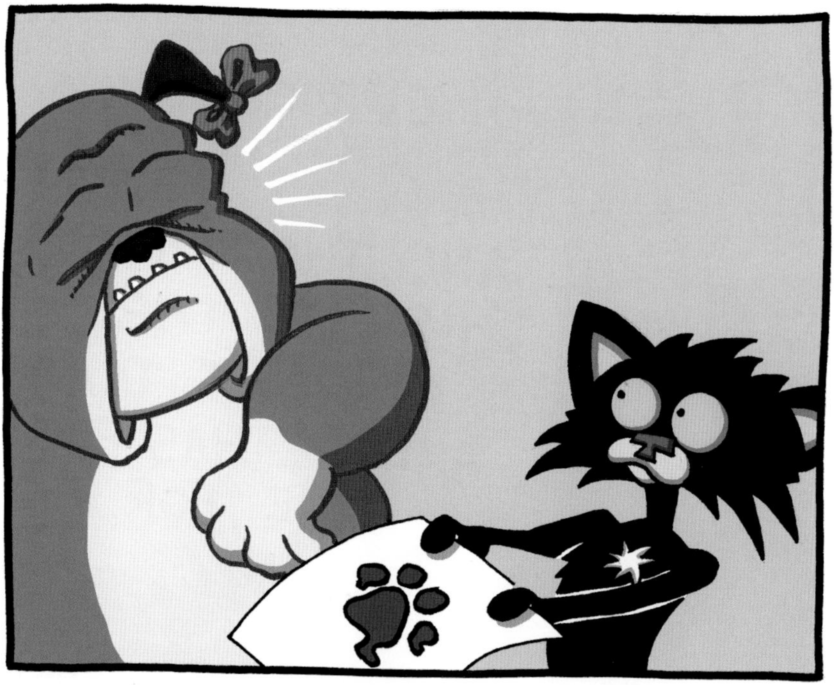

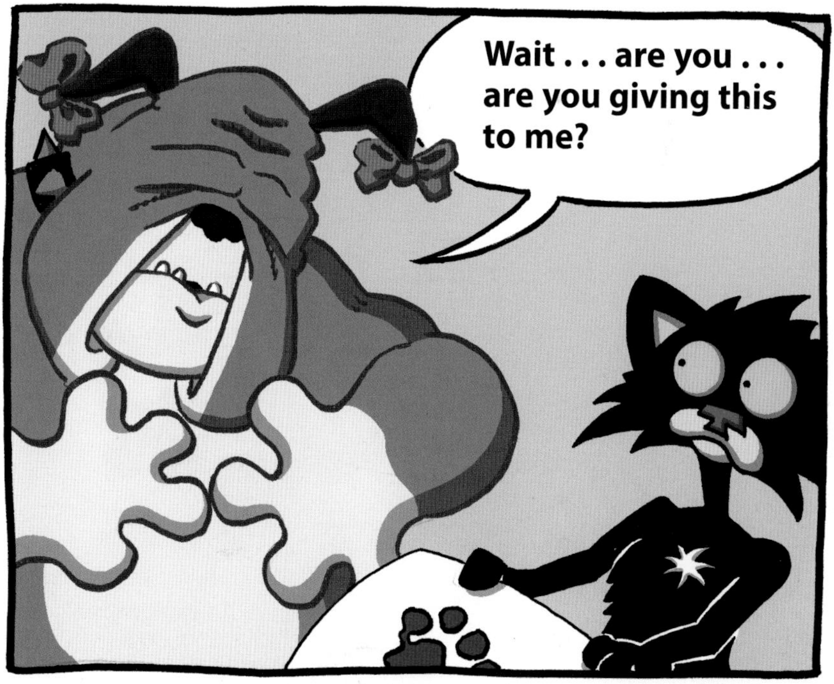
Wait . . . are you . . . are you giving this to me?

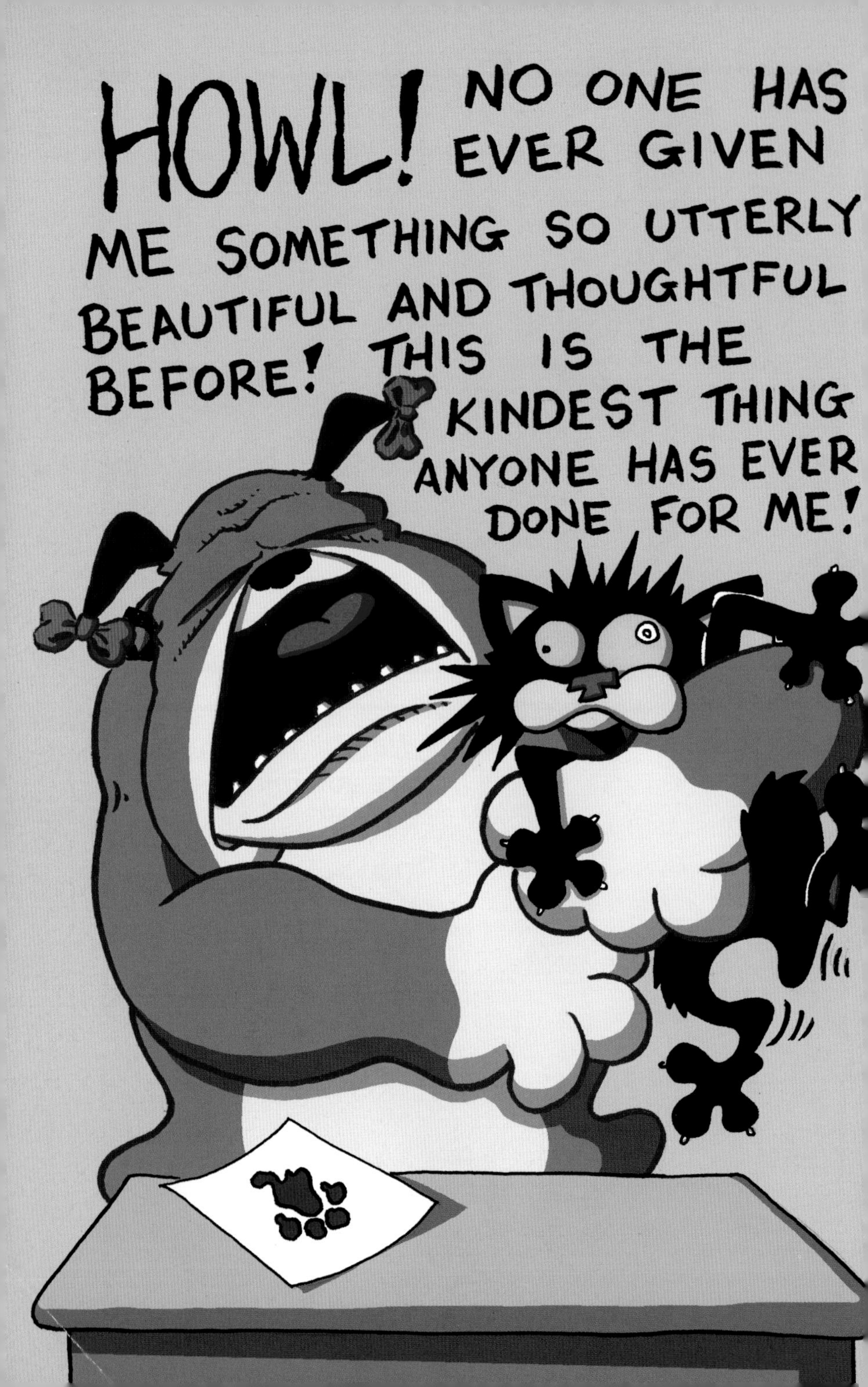
HOWL! NO ONE HAS EVER GIVEN ME SOMETHING SO UTTERLY BEAUTIFUL AND THOUGHTFUL BEFORE! THIS IS THE KINDEST THING ANYONE HAS EVER DONE FOR ME!

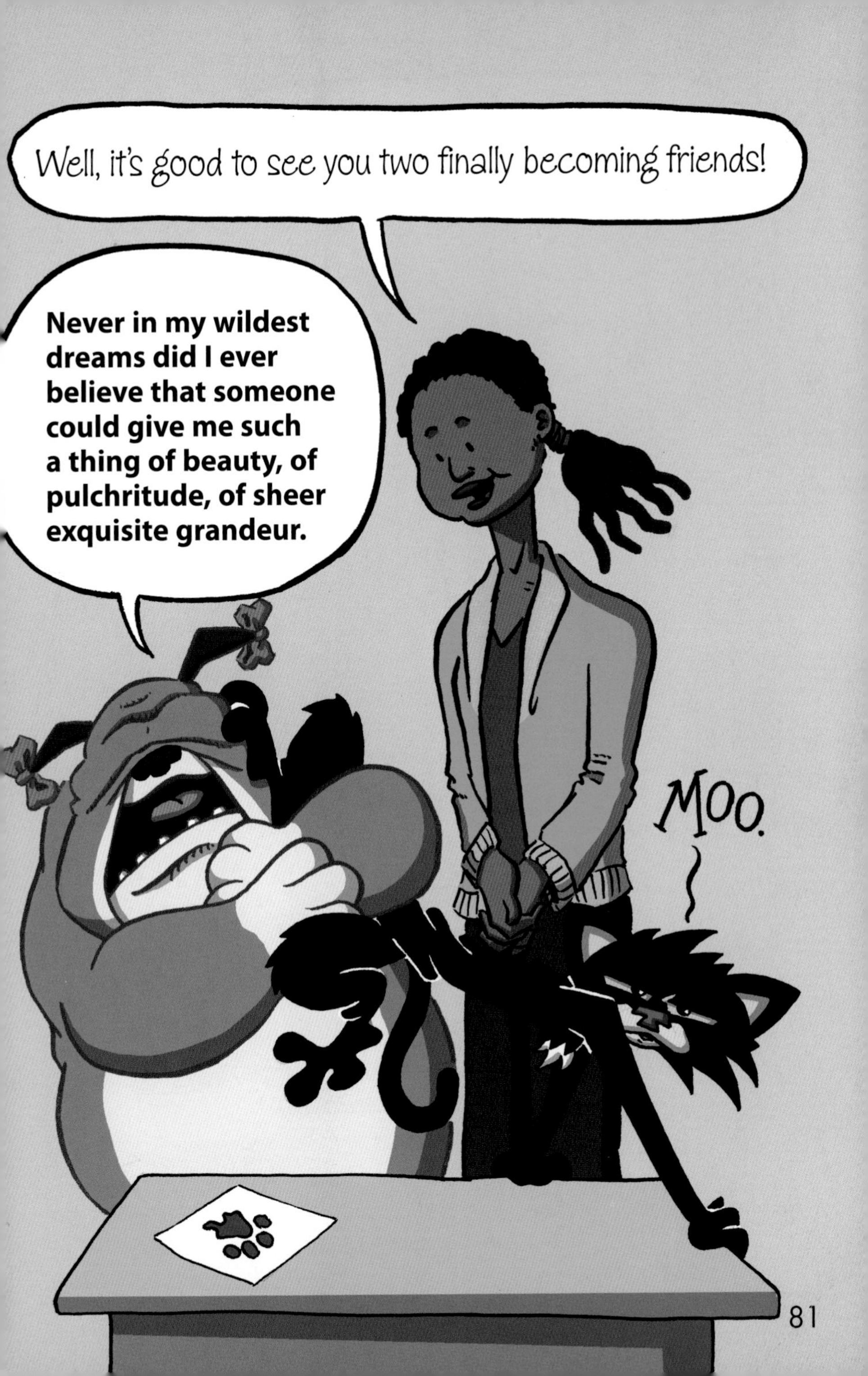
Well, it's good to see you two finally becoming friends!
Never in my wildest dreams did I ever believe that someone could give me such a thing of beauty, of pulchritude, of sheer exquisite grandeur.
MOO.

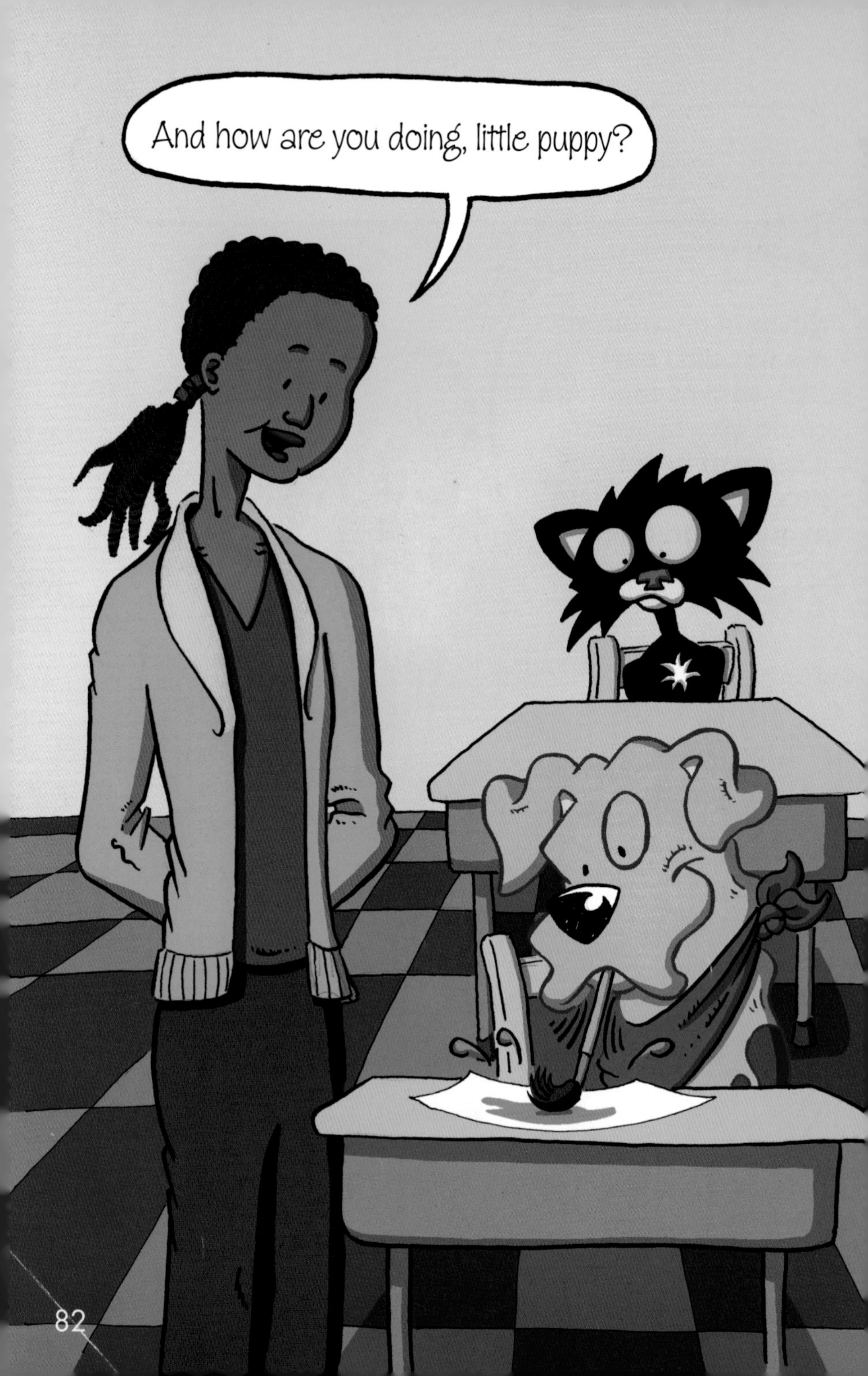
And how are you doing, little puppy?

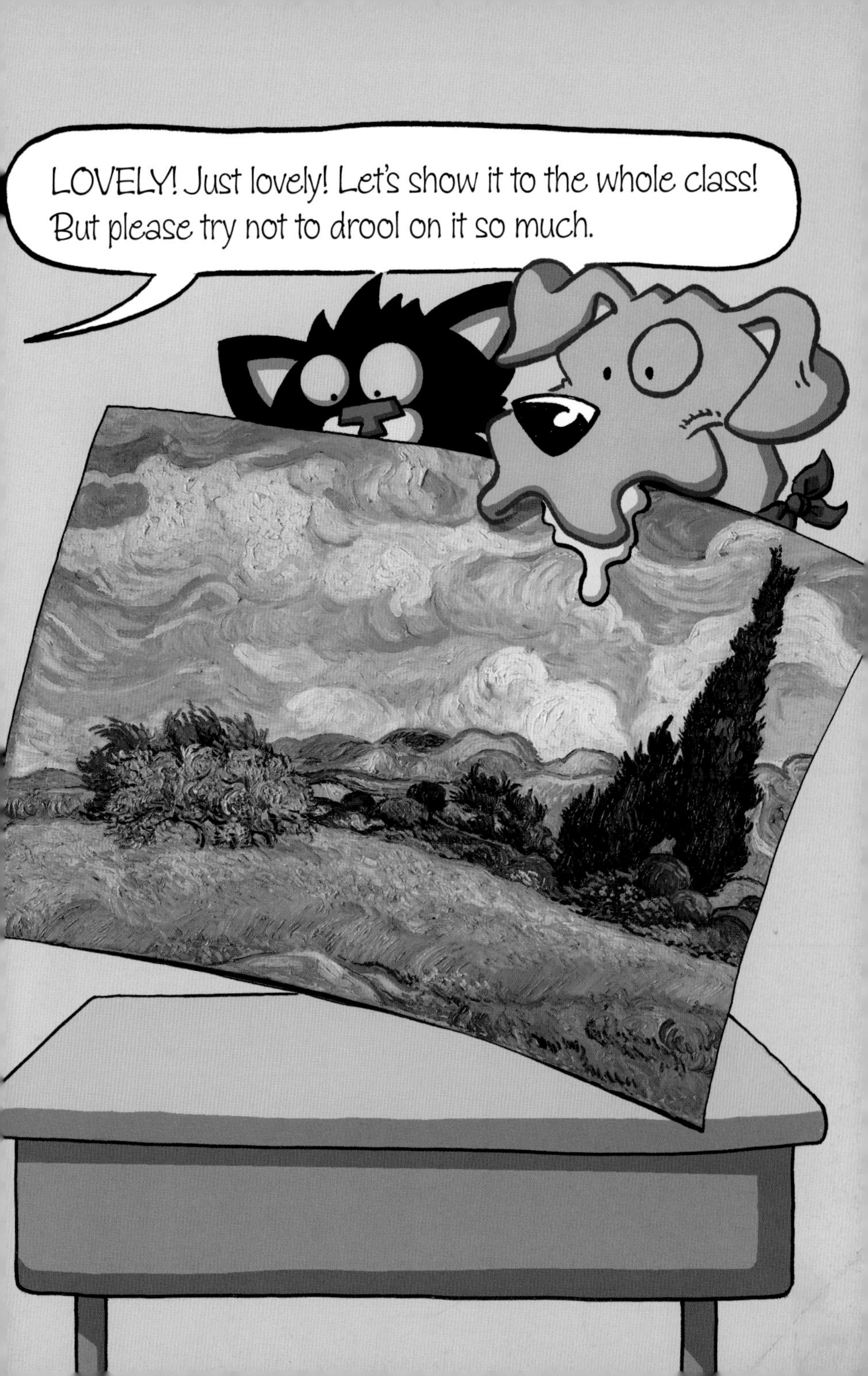
LOVELY! Just lovely! Let's show it to the whole class! But please try not to drool on it so much.

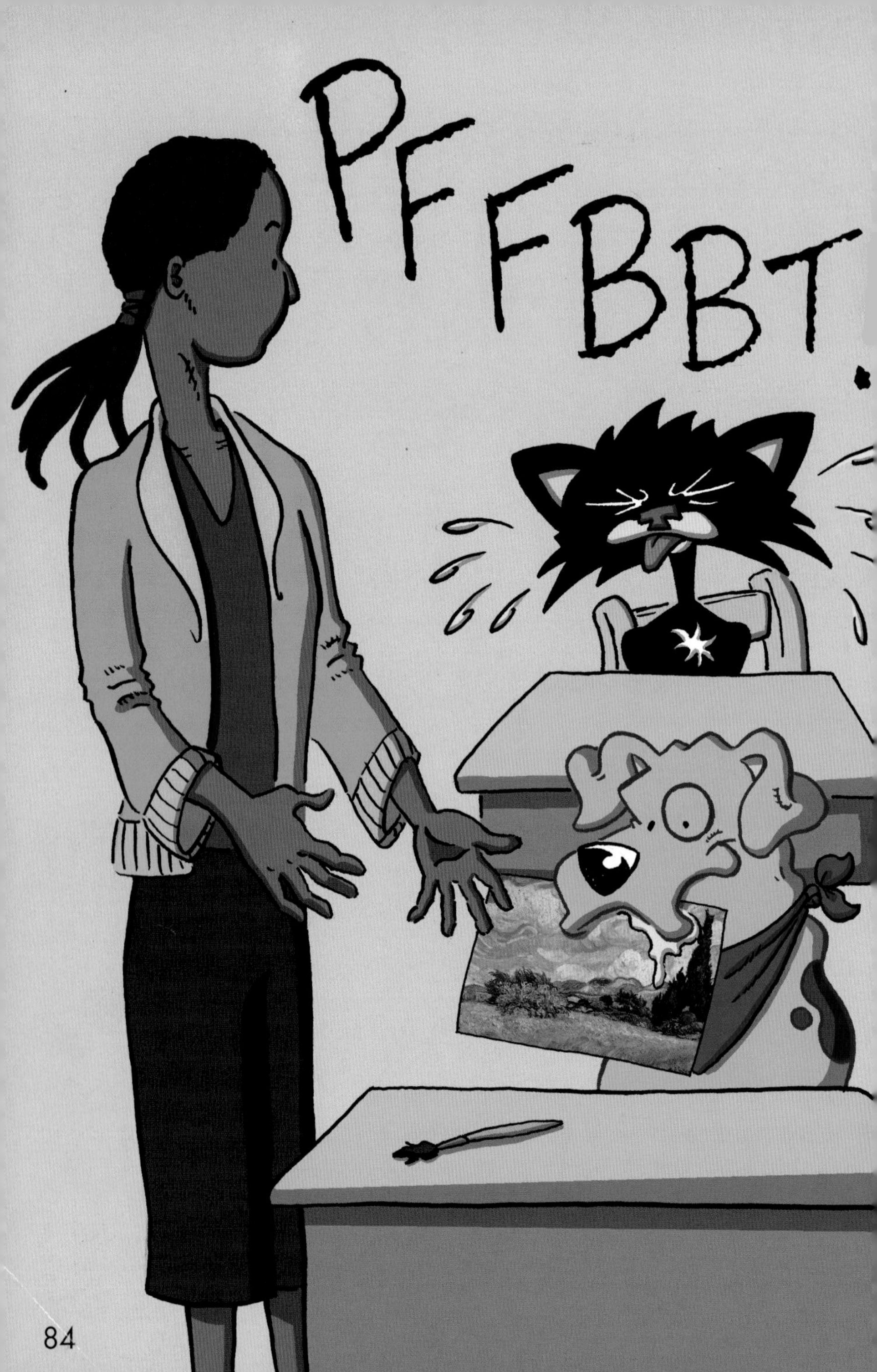
PFFBBT!

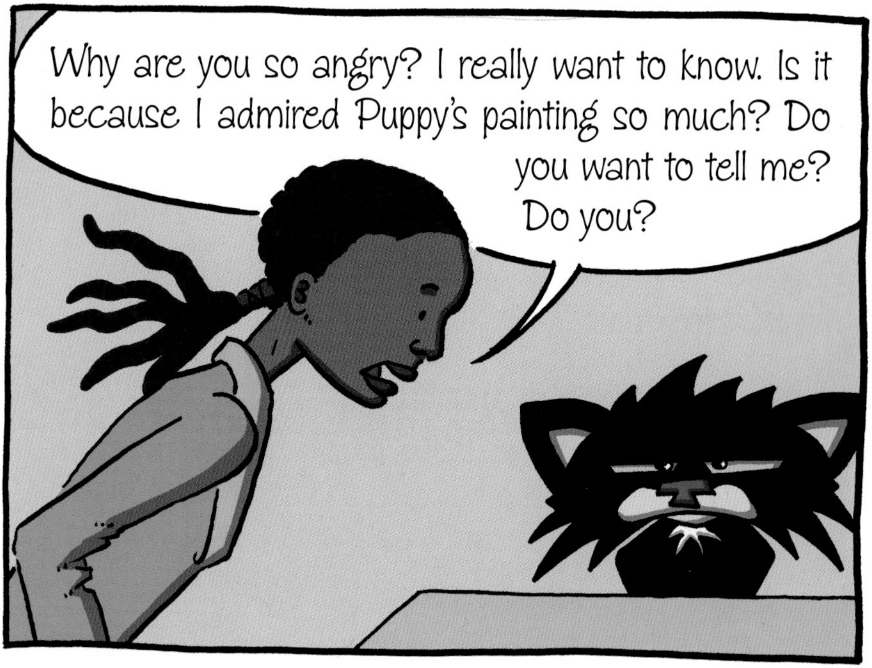
Why are you so angry? I really want to know. Is it because I admired Puppy's painting so much? Do you want to tell me? Do you?

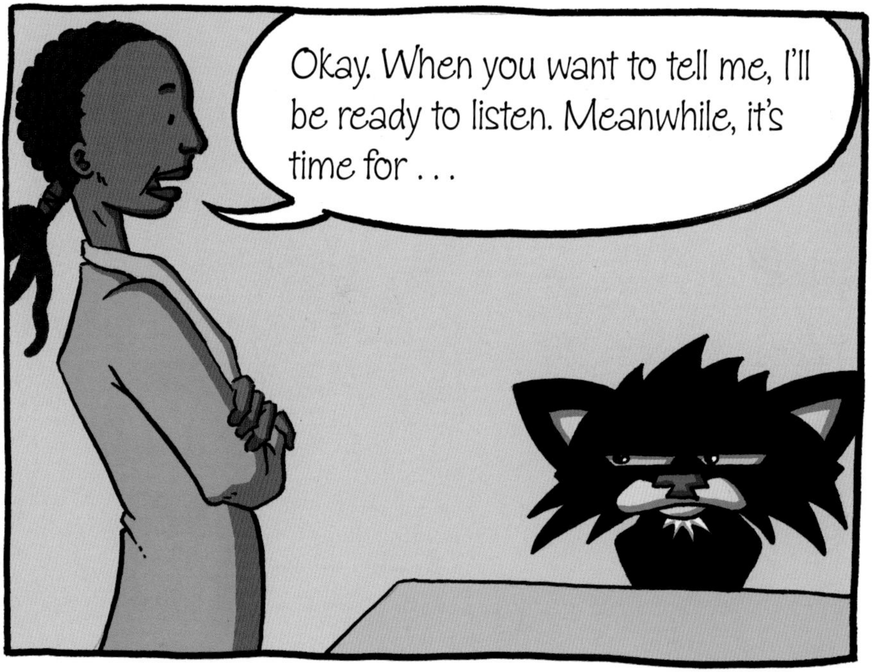
Okay. When you want to tell me, I'll be ready to listen. Meanwhile, it's time for . . .

•CHAPTER SIX•

SHOW + TELL

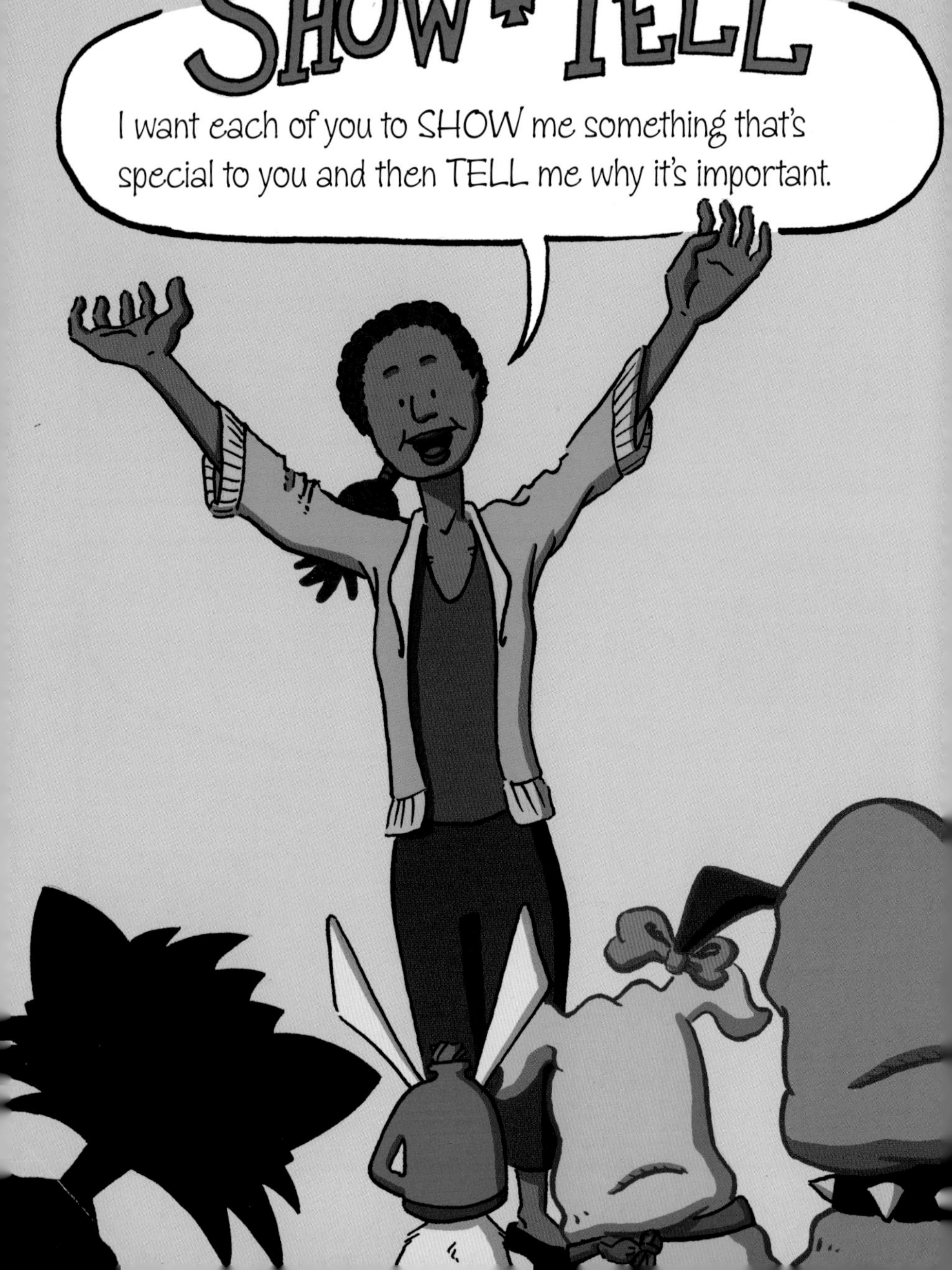
I want each of you to SHOW me something that's special to you and then TELL me why it's important.

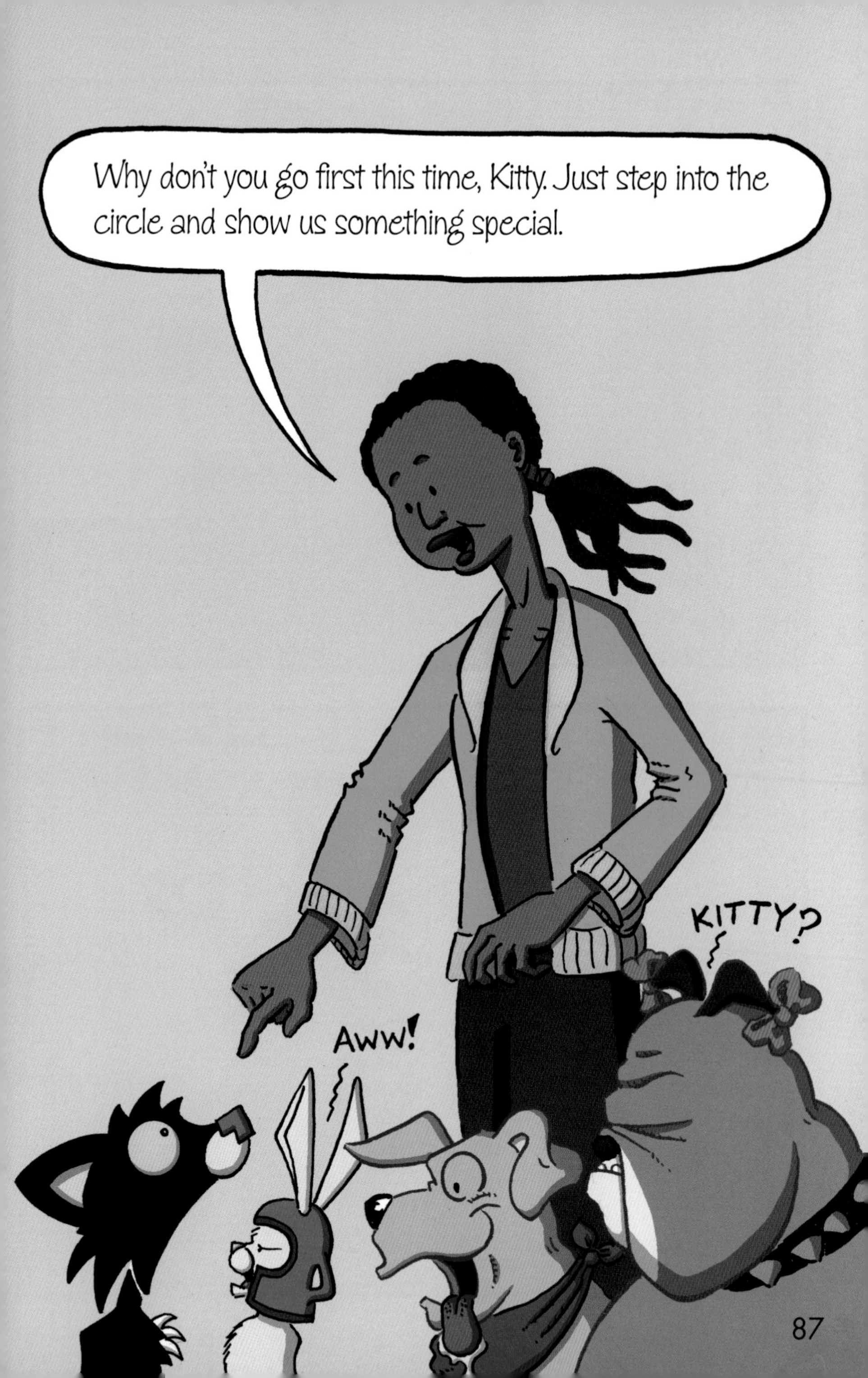
Why don't you go first this time, Kitty. Just step into the circle and show us something special.
KITTY?
AWW!

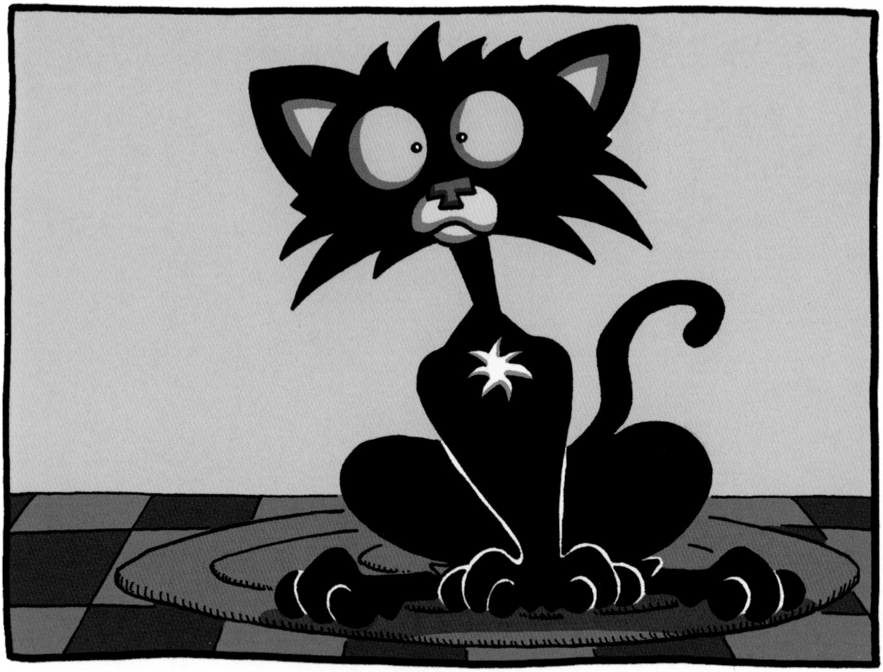

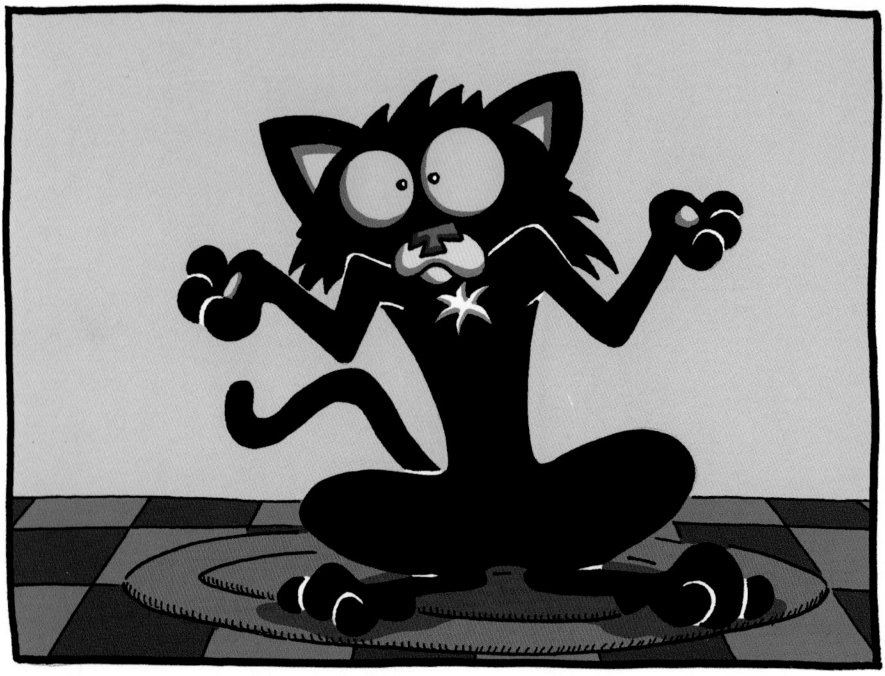

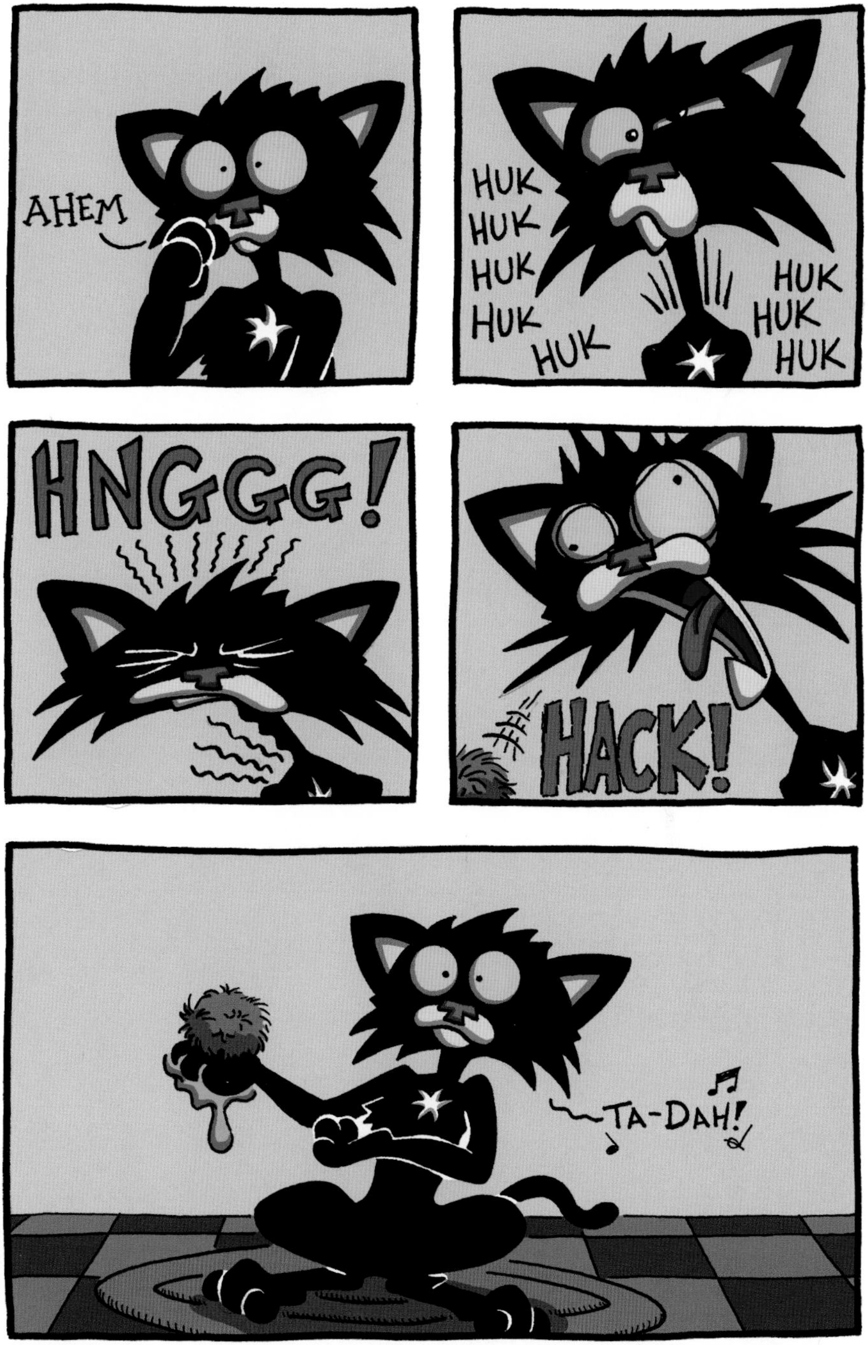
AHEM
HUK
HUK
HUK
HUK
HUK
HUK
HUK
HUK
HNGGG!
HACK!
TA-DAH!

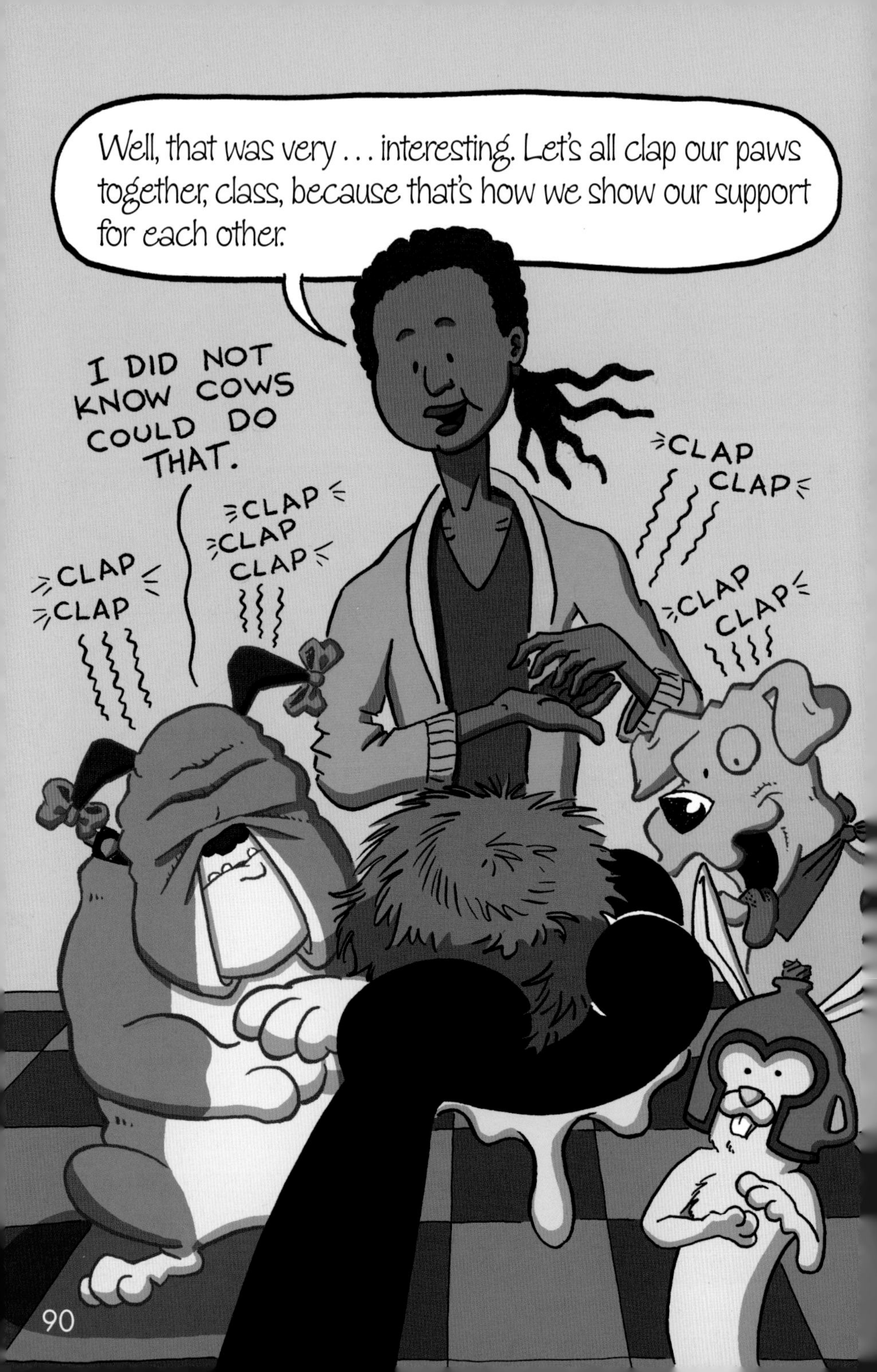

Well, that was very . . . interesting. Let's all clap our paws together, class, because that's how we show our support for each other.
I DID NOT KNOW COWS COULD DO THAT.
CLAP CLAP
CLAP CLAP CLAP
CLAP CLAP
CLAP CLAP

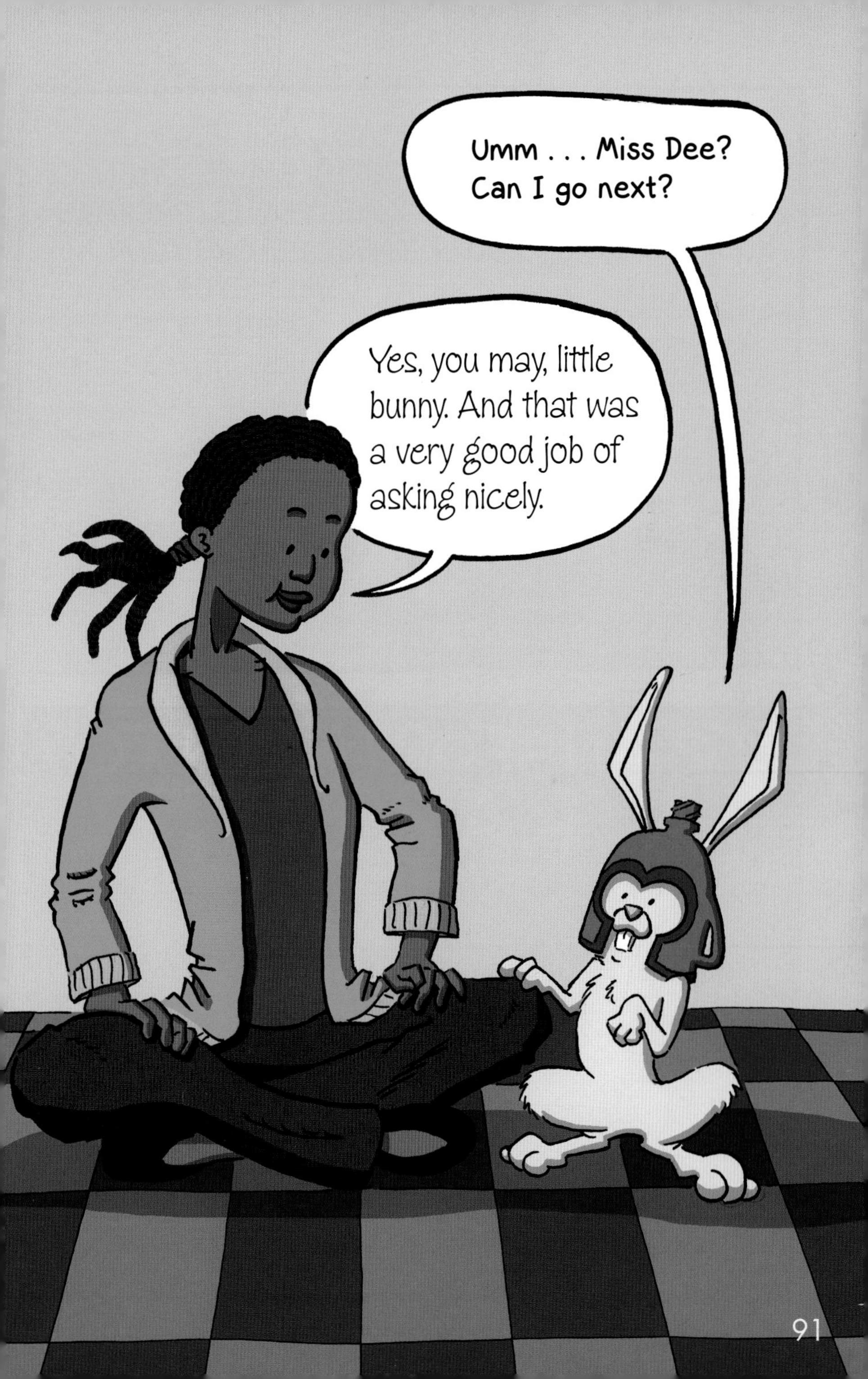
Umm . . . Miss Dee? Can I go next?
Yes, you may, little bunny. And that was a very good job of asking nicely.

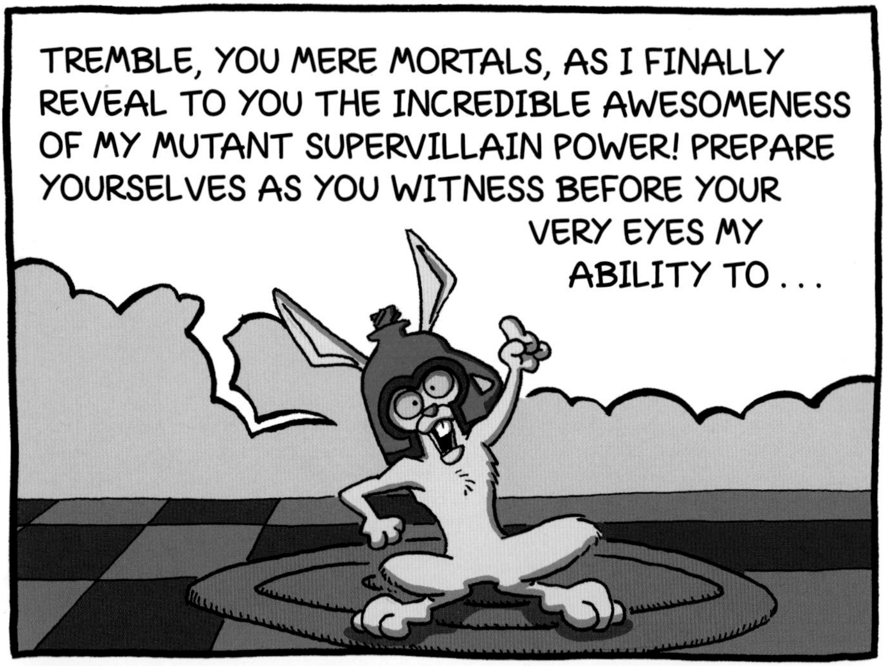
TREMBLE, YOU MERE MORTALS, AS I FINALLY REVEAL TO YOU THE INCREDIBLE AWESOMENESS OF MY MUTANT SUPERVILLAIN POWER! PREPARE YOURSELVES AS YOU WITNESS BEFORE YOUR VERY EYES MY ABILITY TO . . .

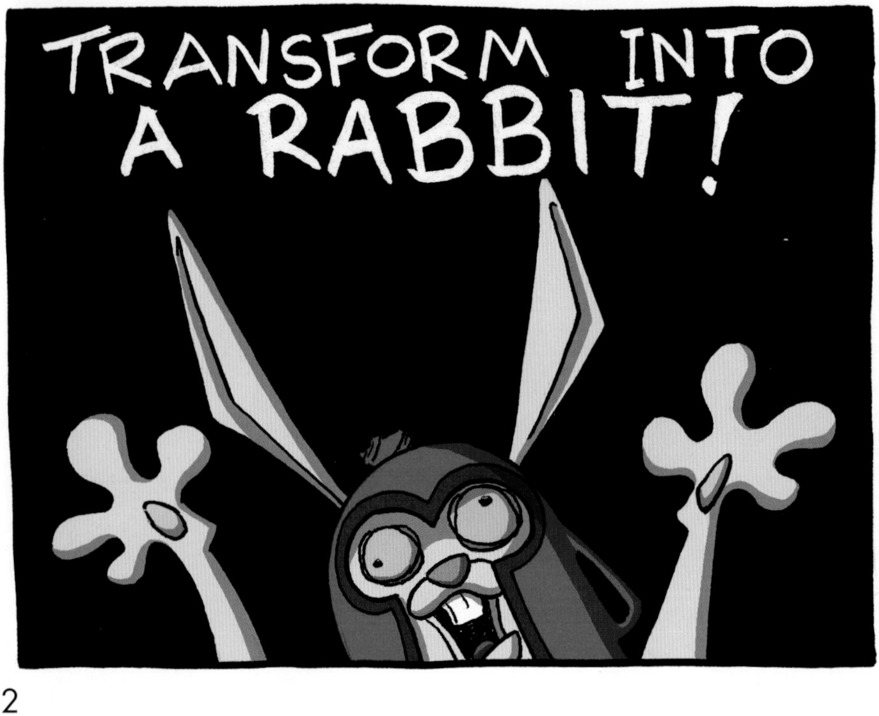
TRANSFORM INTO A RABBIT!

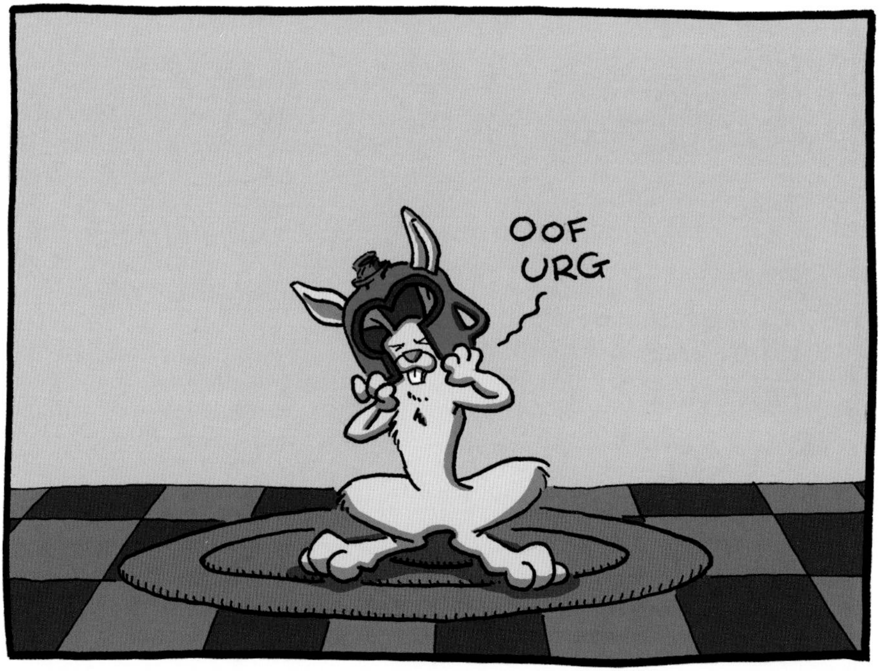
OOF
URG

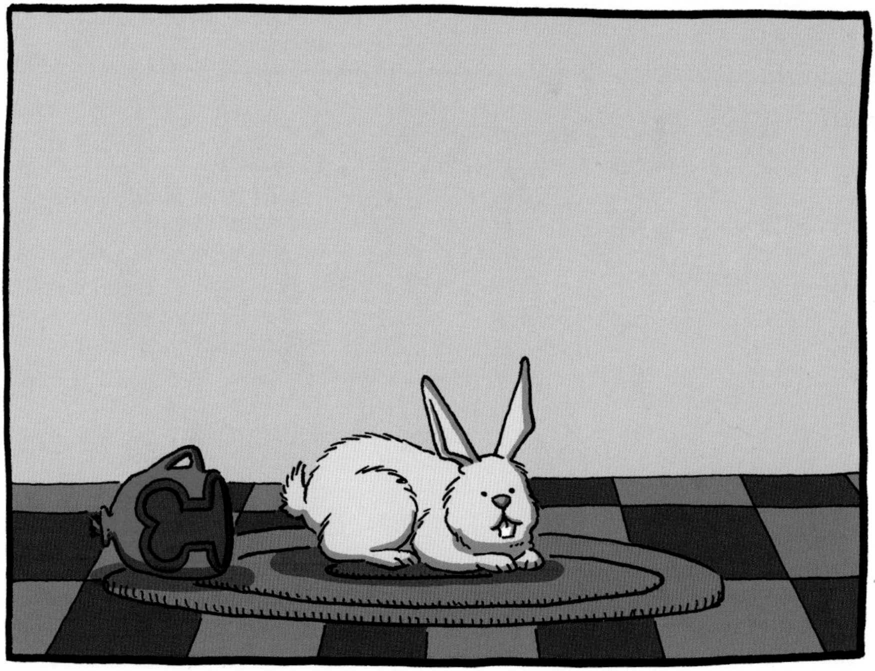

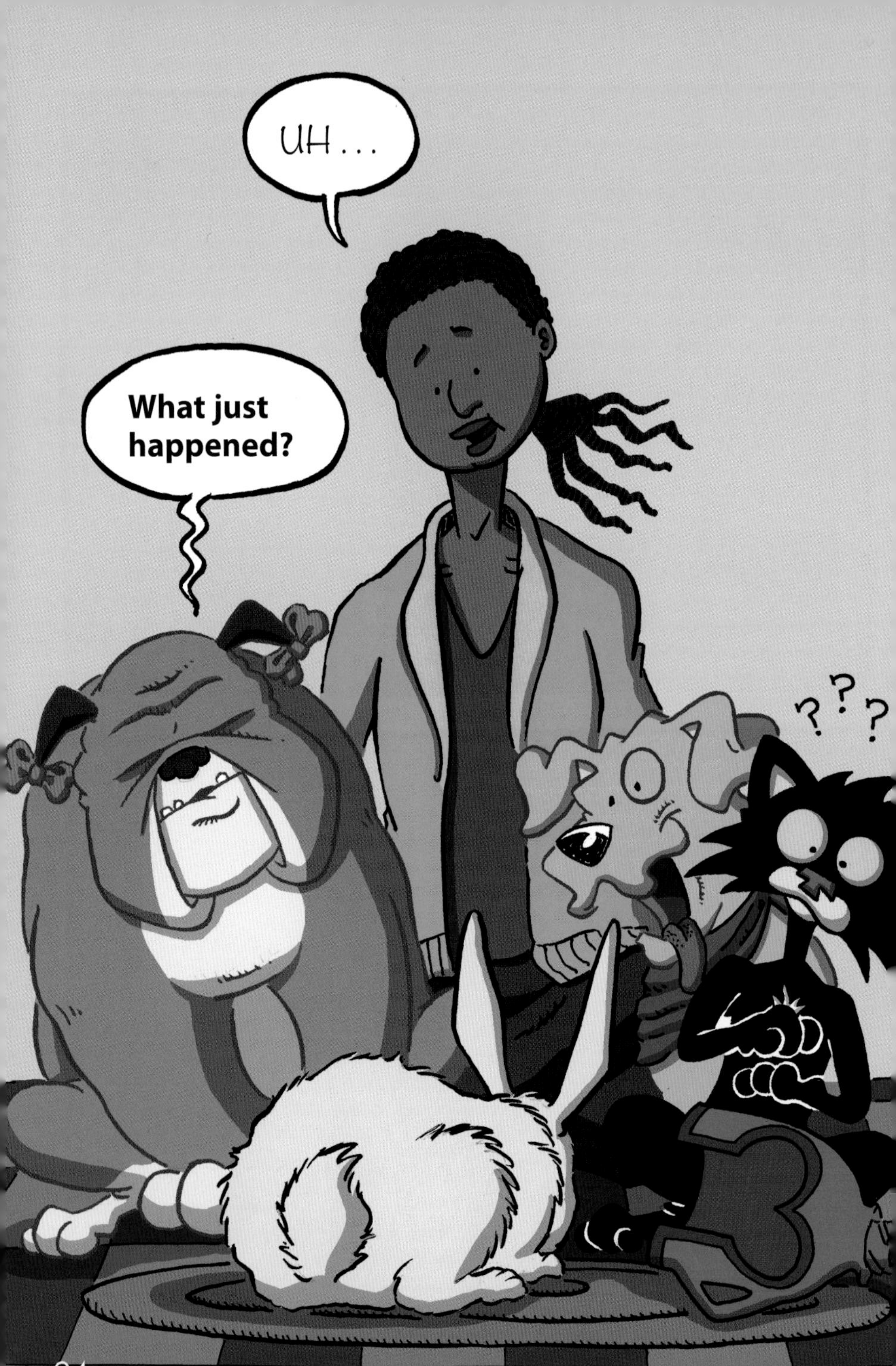
UH...
What just happened?
???

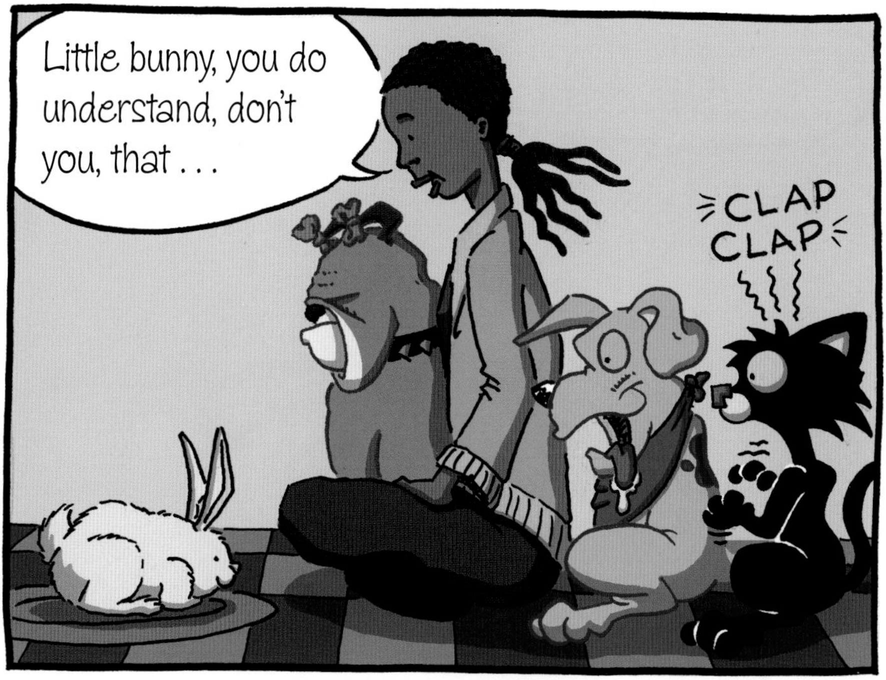
Little bunny, you do understand, don't you, that . . .
CLAP
CLAP

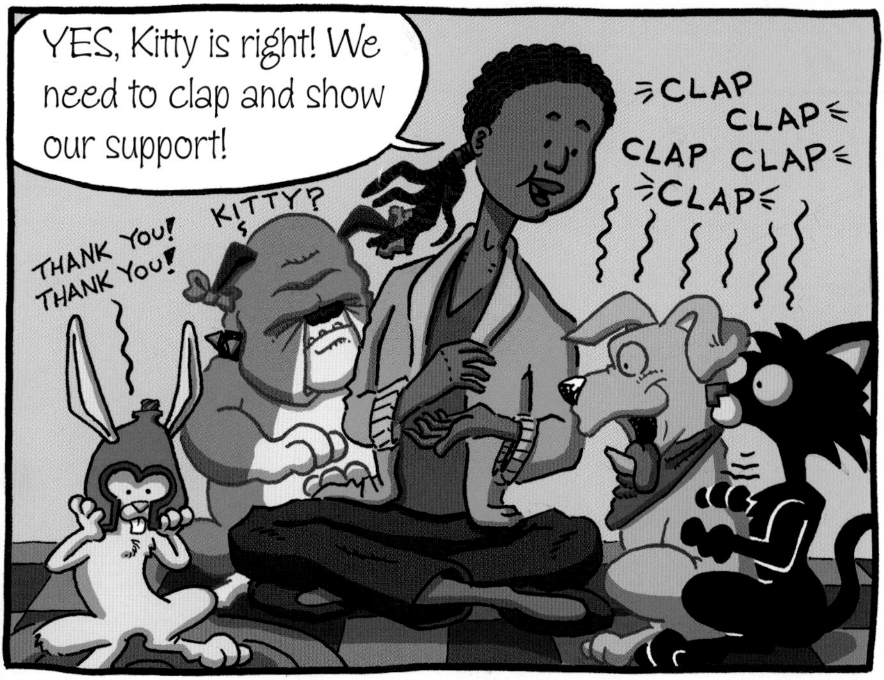
YES, Kitty is right! We need to clap and show our support!
KITTY?
THANK YOU! THANK YOU!
CLAP
CLAP
CLAP CLAP
CLAP

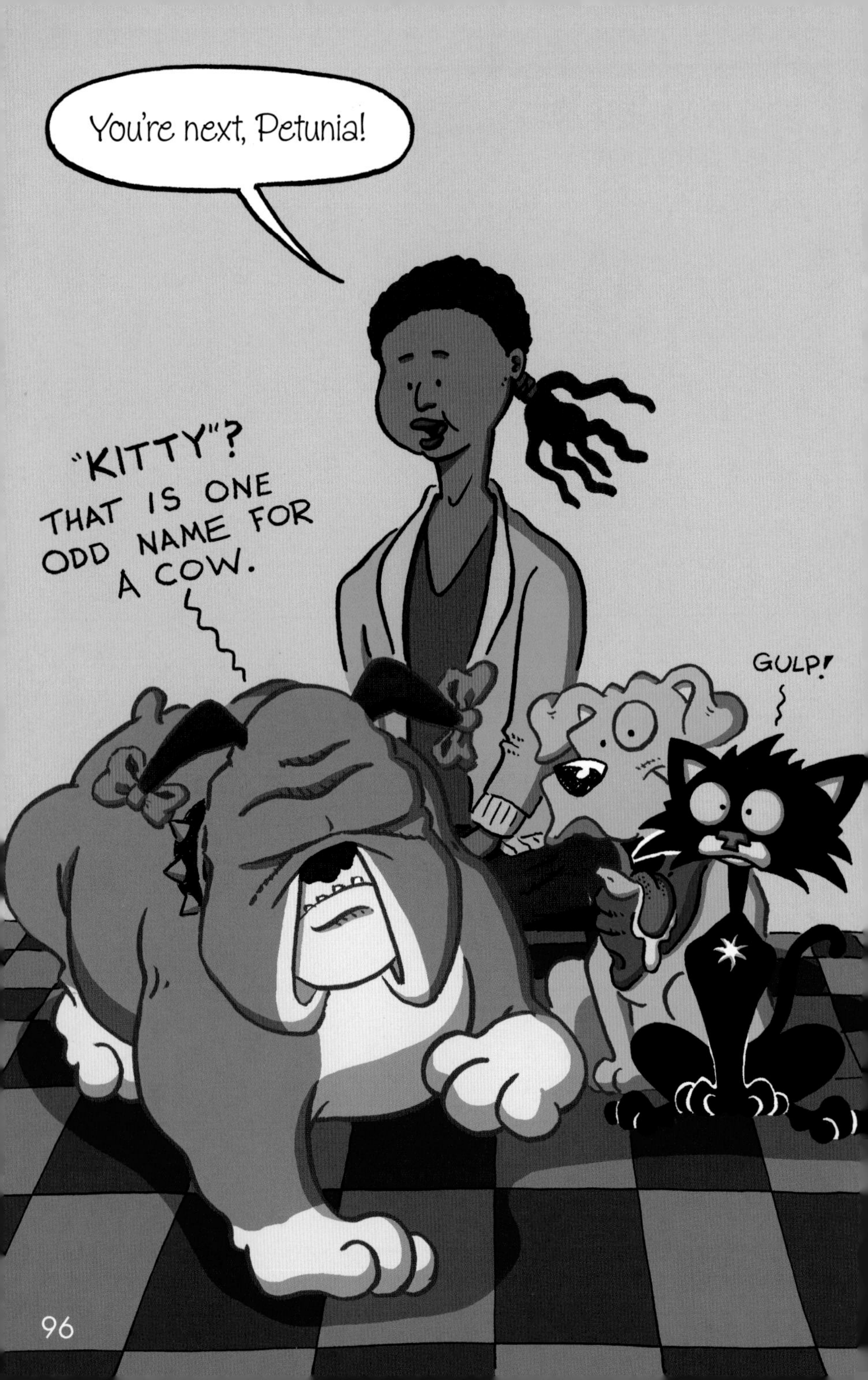

You're next, Petunia!
"KITTY"? THAT IS ONE ODD NAME FOR A COW.
GULP!

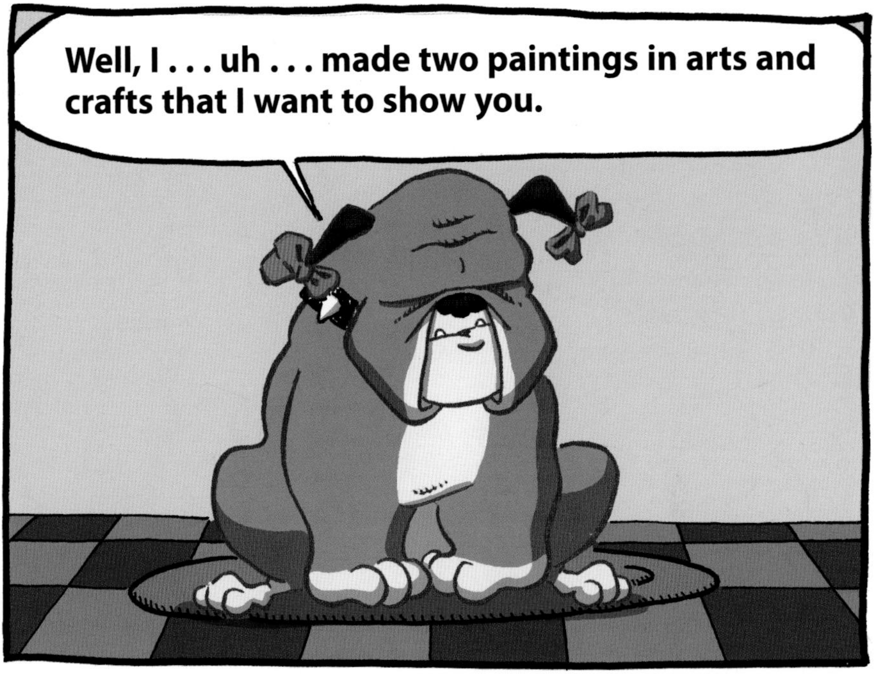
Well, I . . . uh . . . made two paintings in arts and crafts that I want to show you.

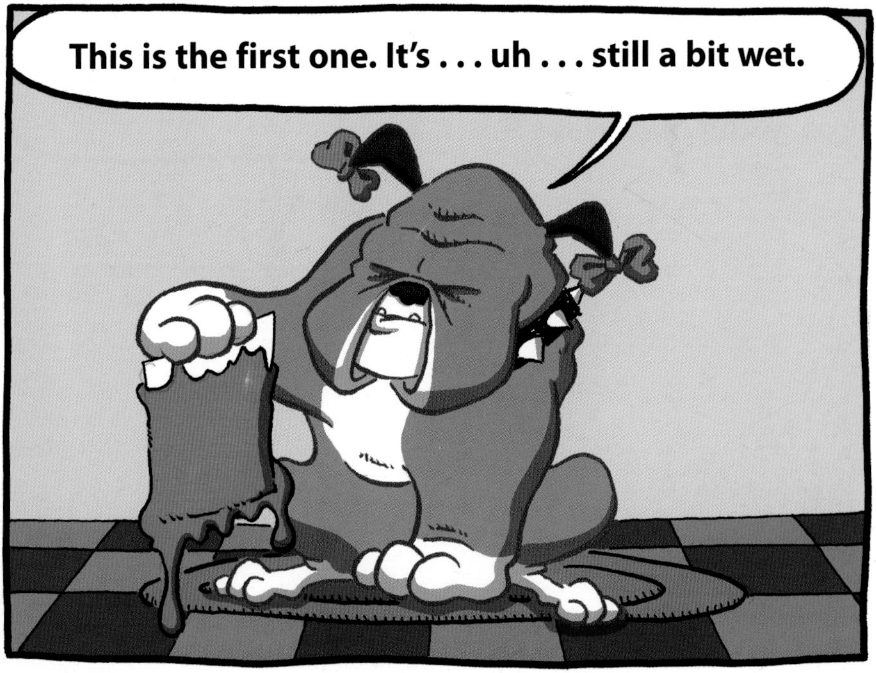
This is the first one. It's . . . uh . . . still a bit wet.

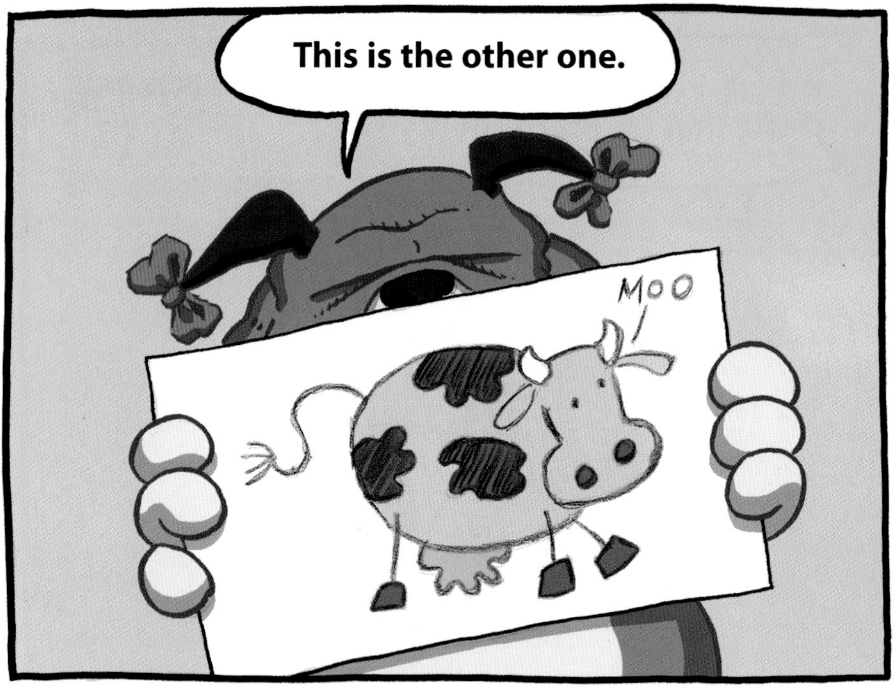
This is the other one.
MOO

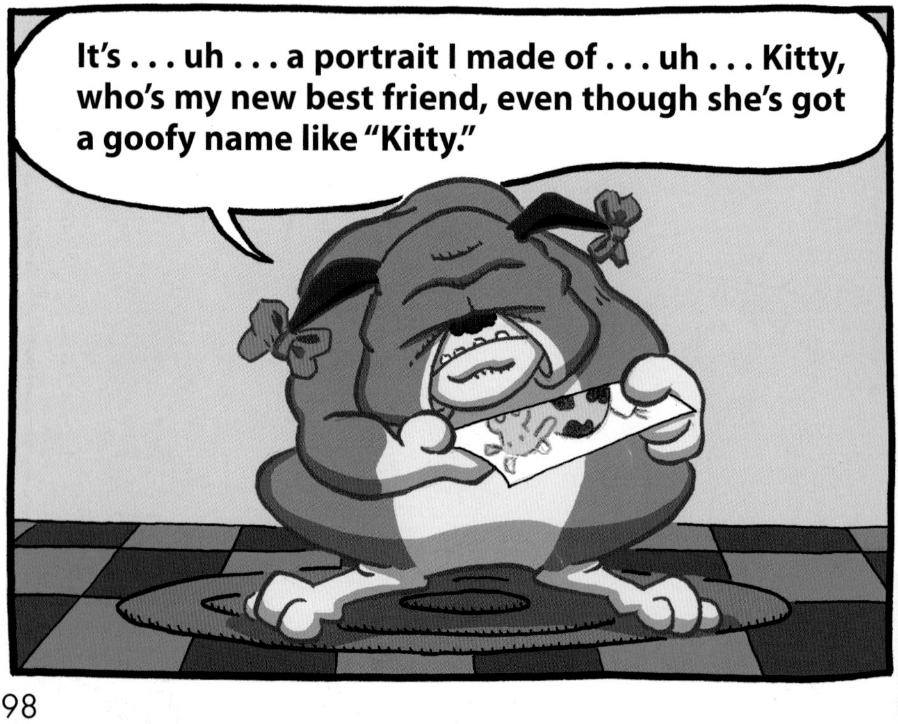
It's . . . uh . . . a portrait I made of . . . uh . . . Kitty, who's my new best friend, even though she's got a goofy name like "Kitty."

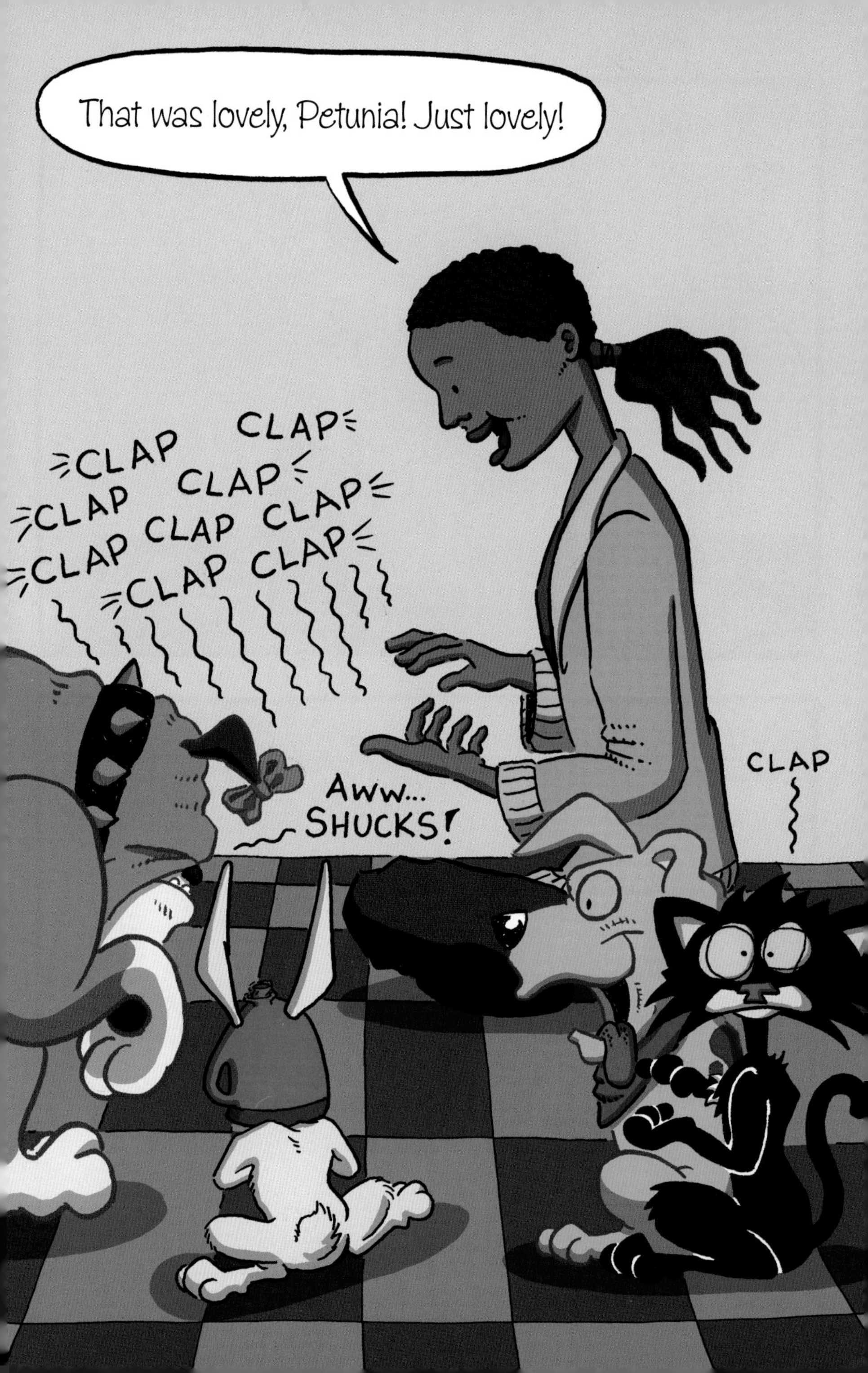
That was lovely, Petunia! Just lovely!
CLAP CLAP CLAP CLAP CLAP CLAP CLAP CLAP CLAP CLAP
AWW... SHUCKS!
CLAP

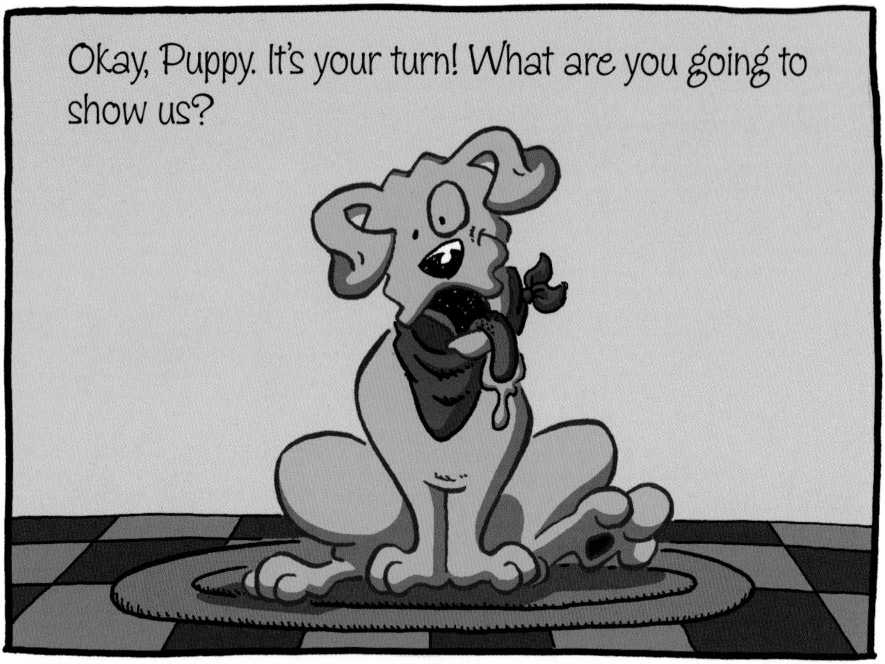
Okay, Puppy. It's your turn! What are you going to show us?

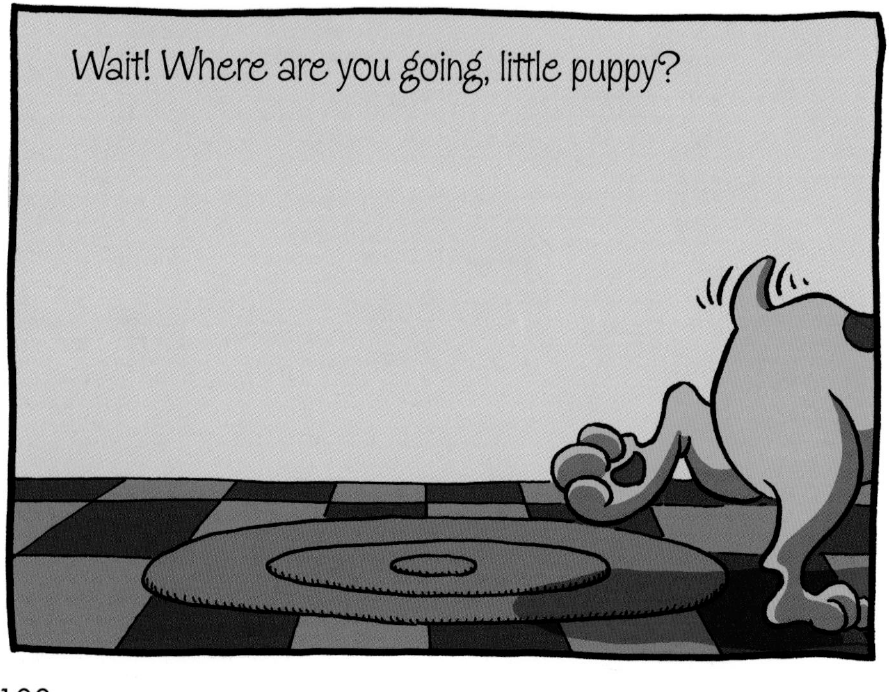
Wait! Where are you going, little puppy?

Partita in A minor

for solo flute

J. S. Bach
BWV 1013

Allemande

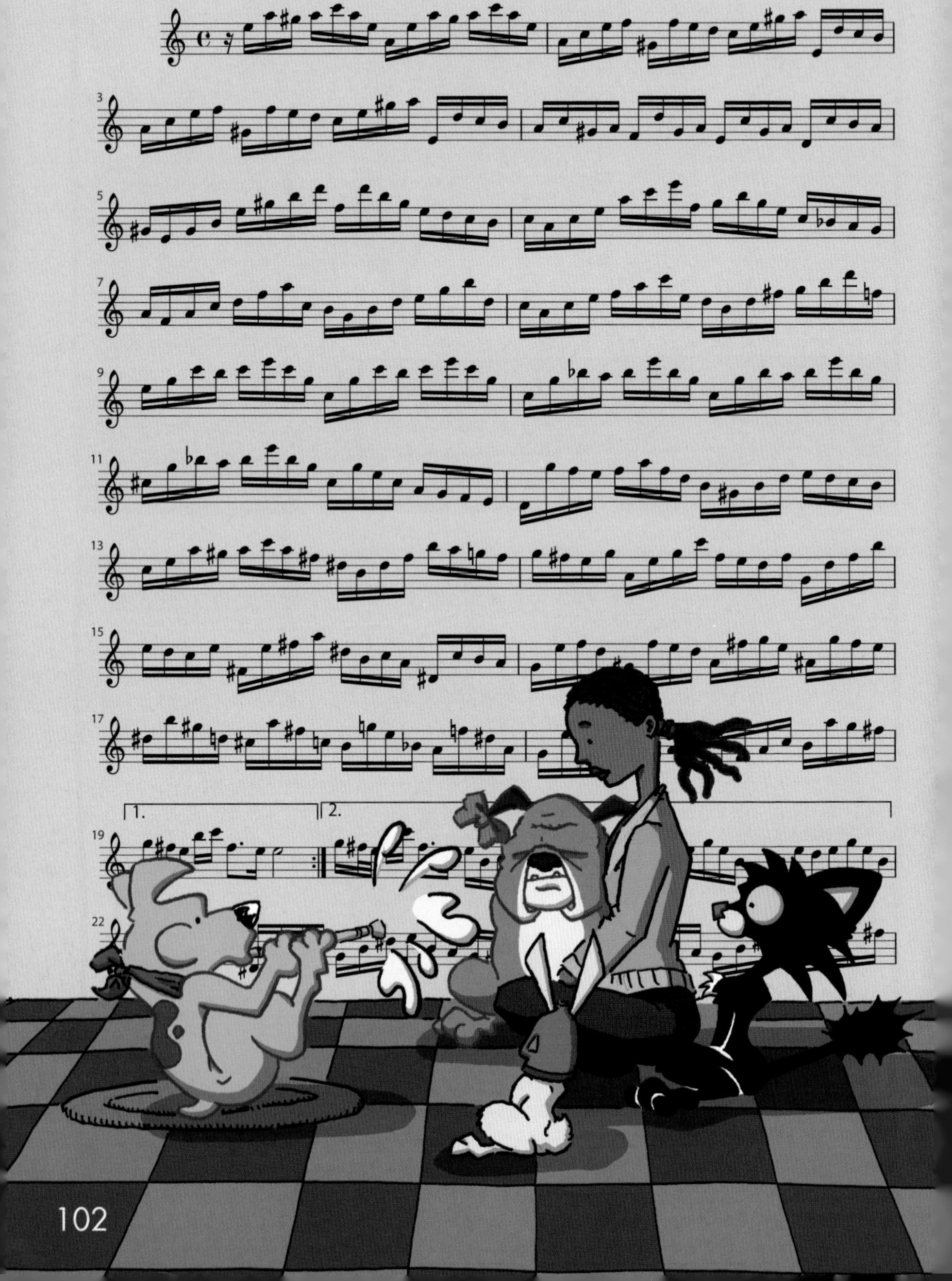
1.
2.

That was very nice, Puppy. But I think we still have to work on this drooling issue of yours.
CLAP
CLAP CLAP
CLAP
BLEH!

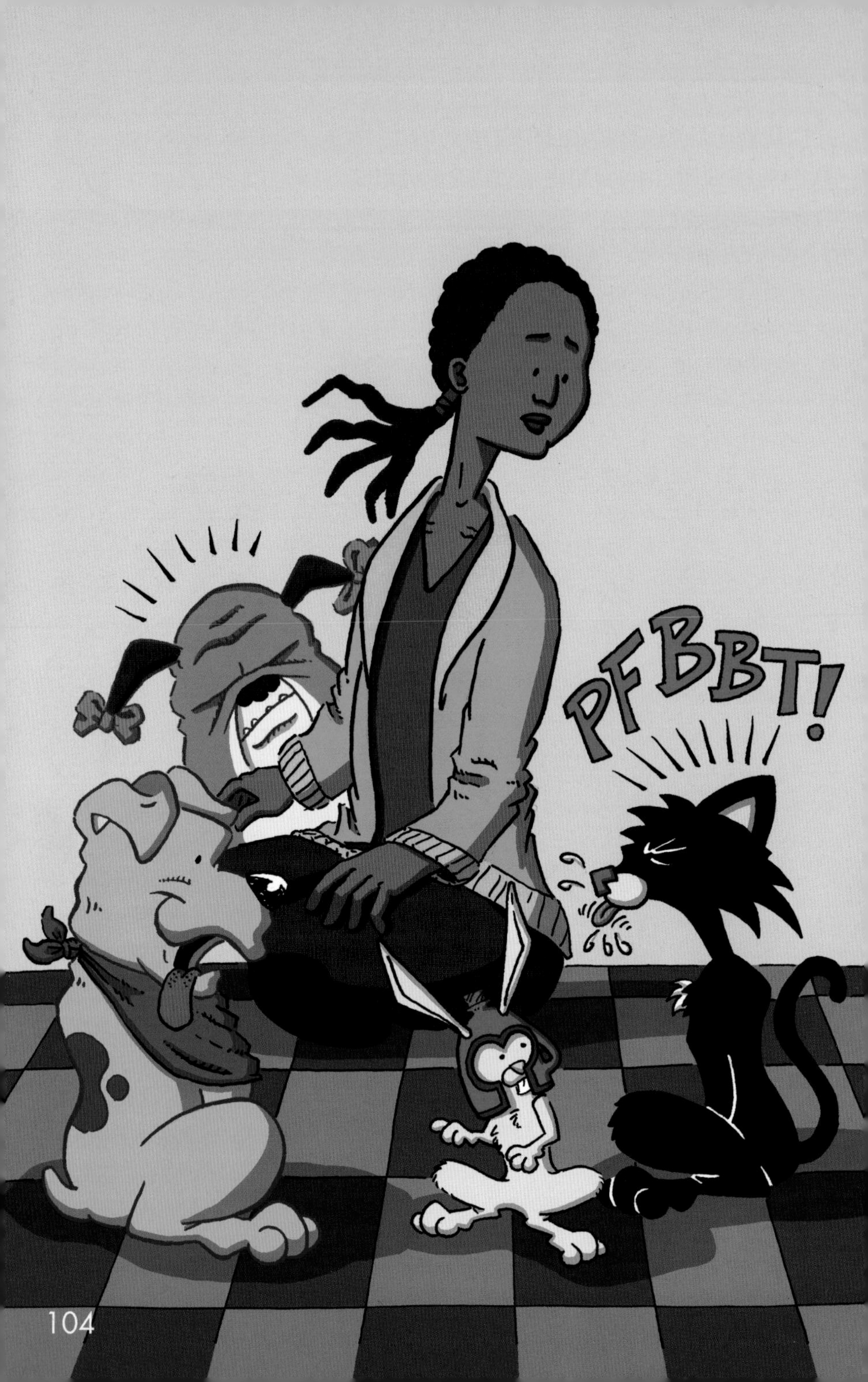
PFBBT!

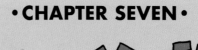

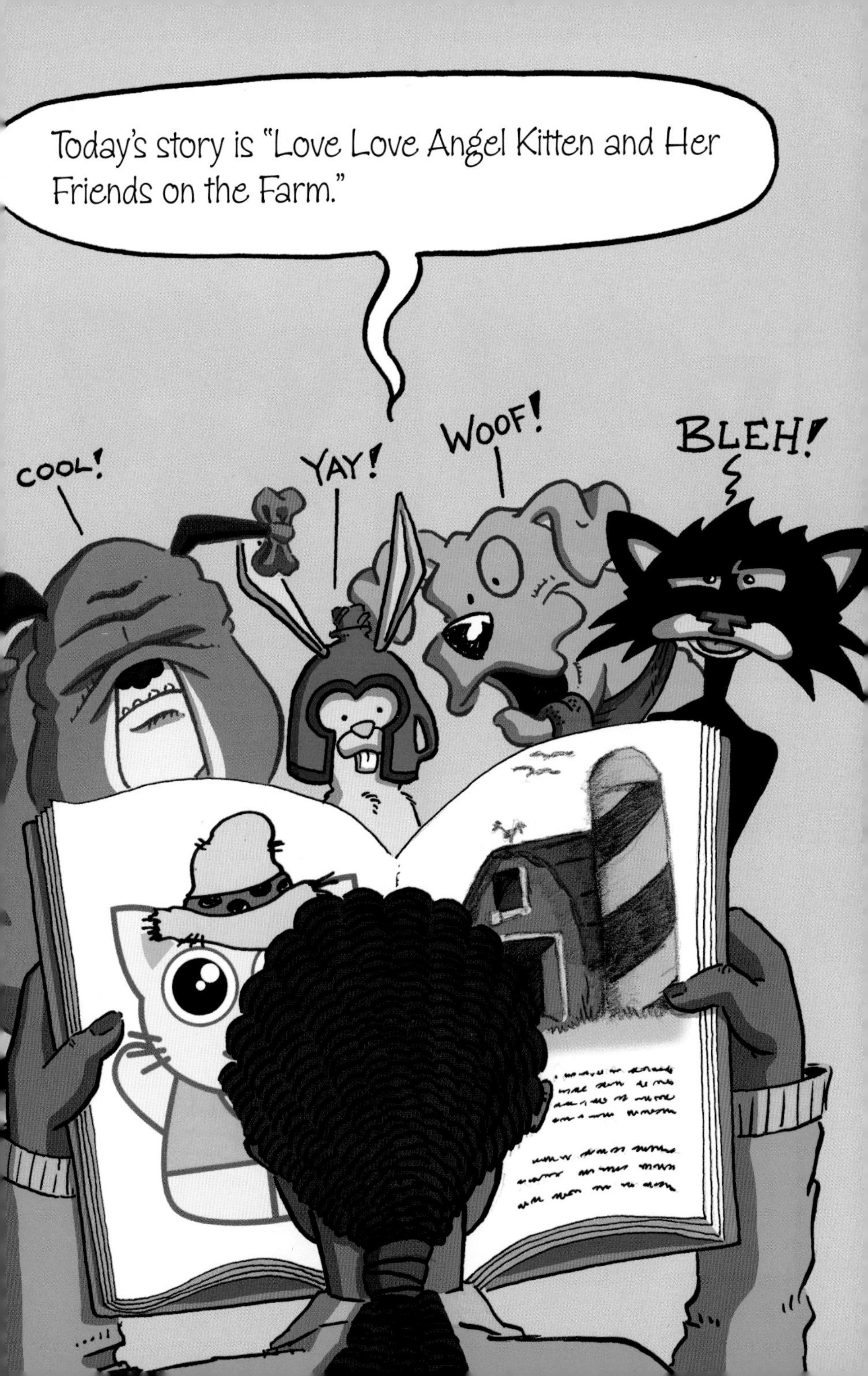
Today's story is "Love Love Angel Kitten and Her Friends on the Farm."
COOL!
YAY!
WOOF!
BLEH!

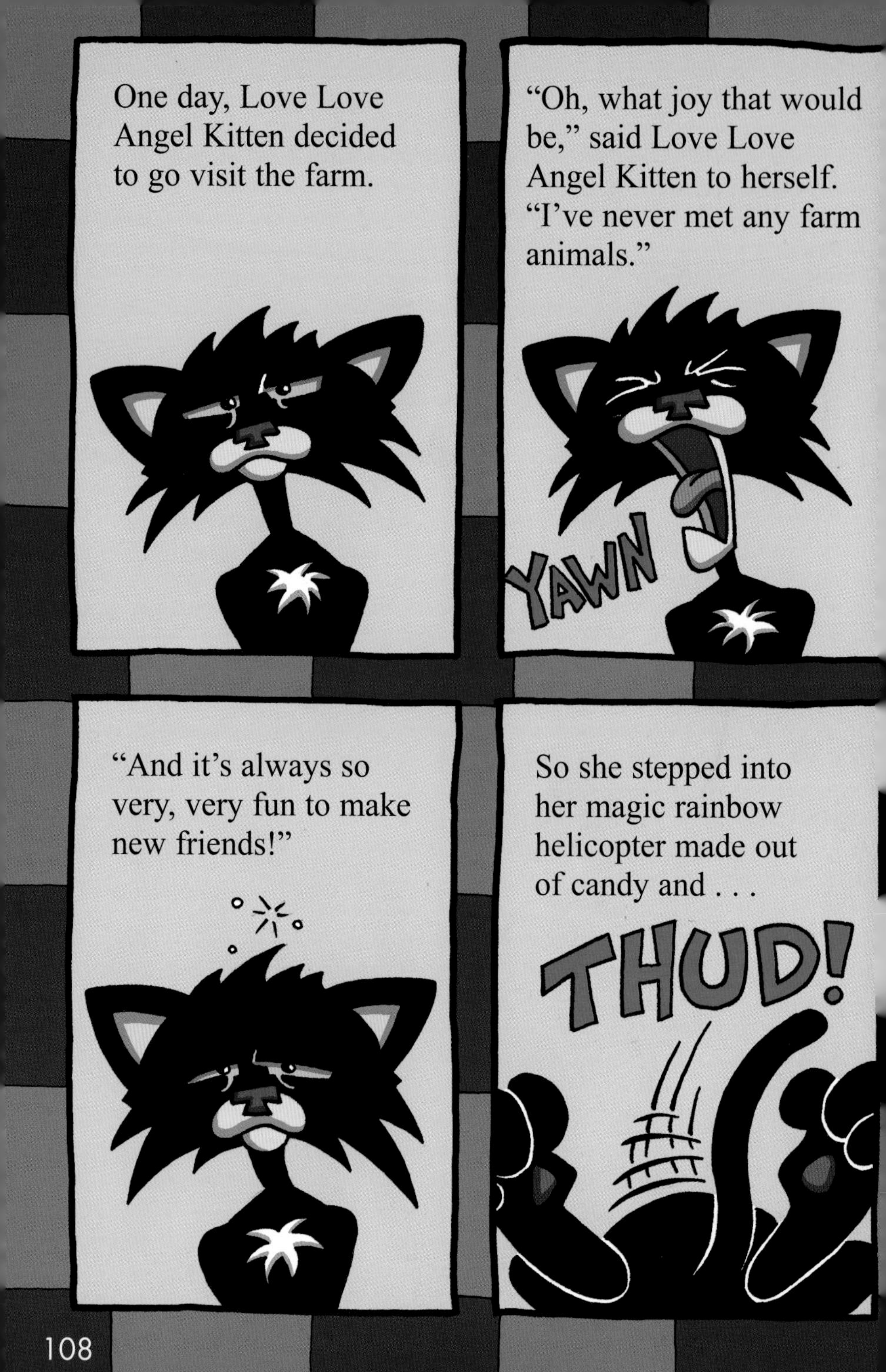
One day, Love Love Angel Kitten decided to go visit the farm.
"Oh, what joy that would be," said Love Love Angel Kitten to herself. "I've never met any farm animals."
YAWN
"And it's always so very, very fun to make new friends!"
So she stepped into her magic rainbow helicopter made out of candy and . . .
THUD!

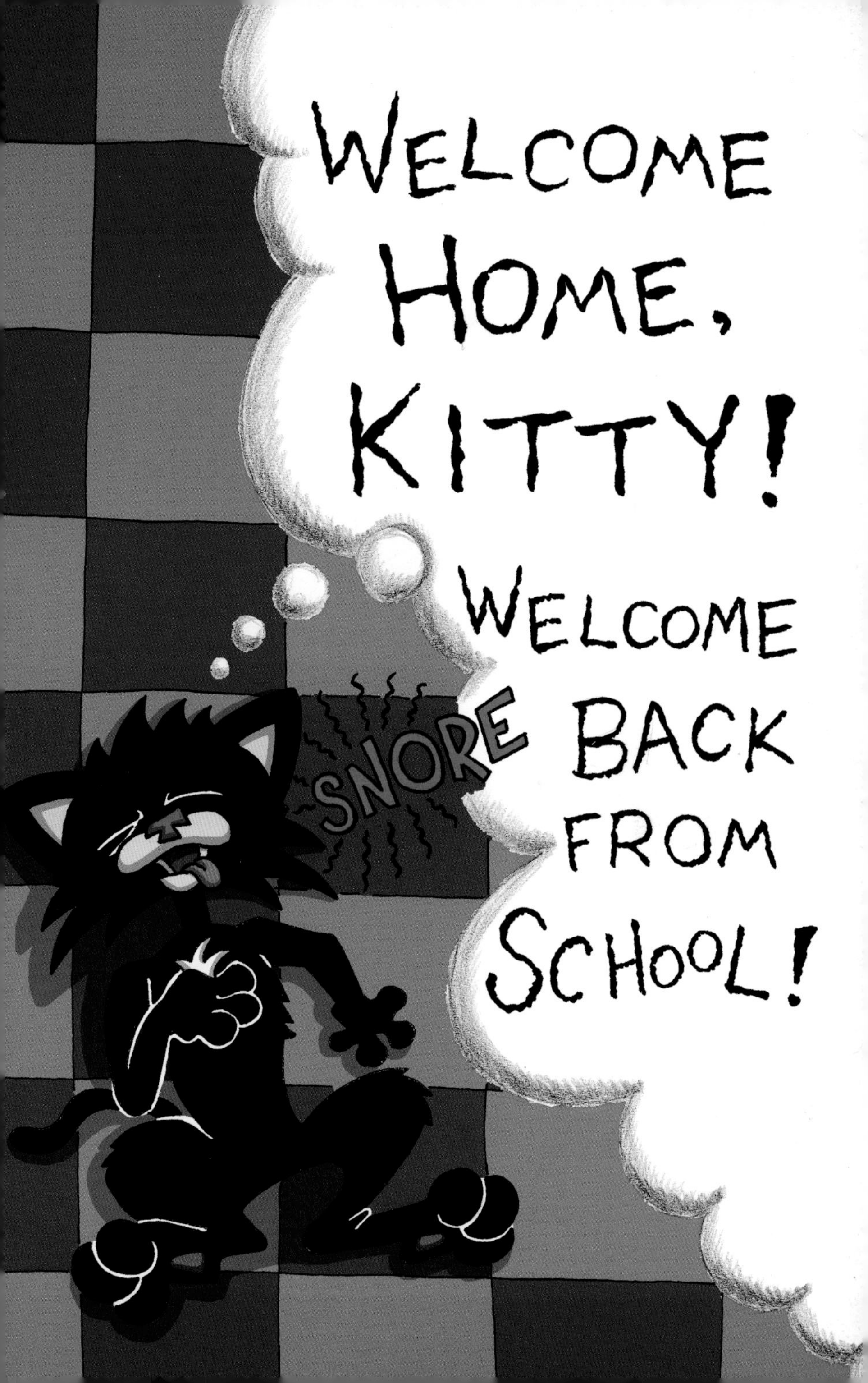
WELCOME HOME, KITTY!
WELCOME BACK FROM SCHOOL!
SNORE

But you're not just plain ol' Kitty anymore, are you? No, now you're . . .

LOVE LOVE ANGEL KITTY!

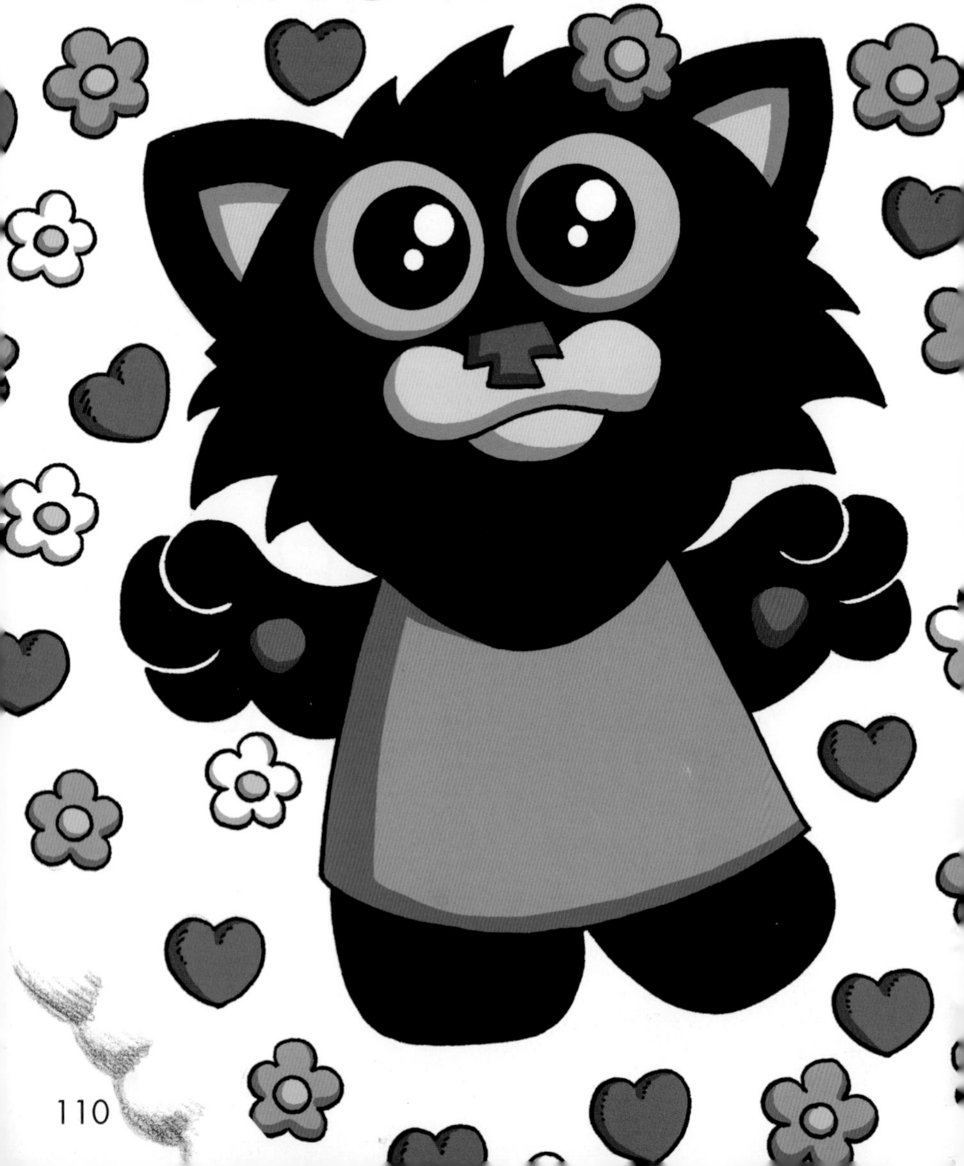

HEY, EVERYBODY! Look at Love Love Angel Kitty!

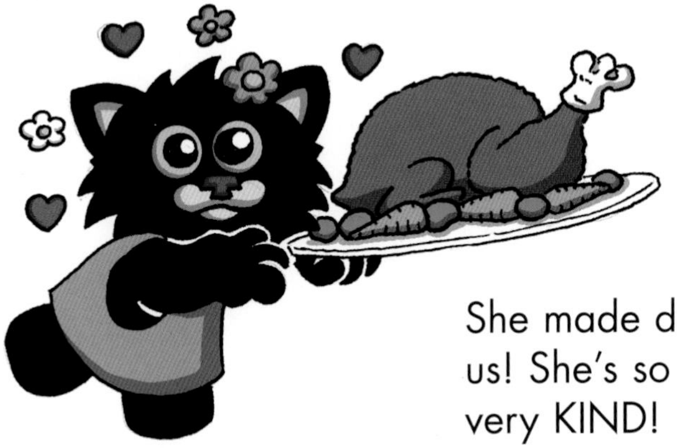

She made dinner for us! She's so very, very KIND!

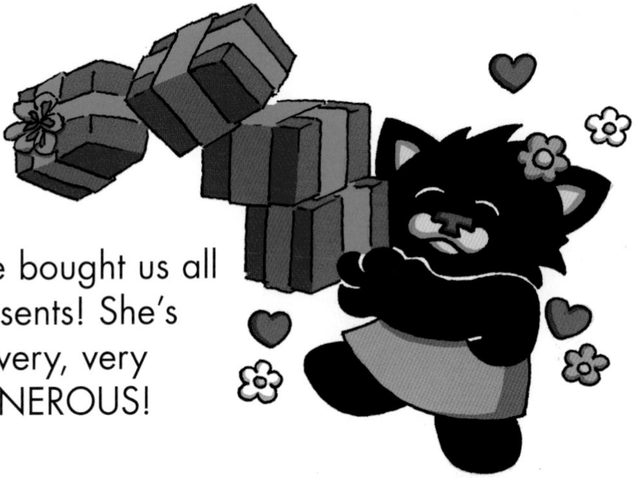

She bought us all presents! She's so very, very GENEROUS!

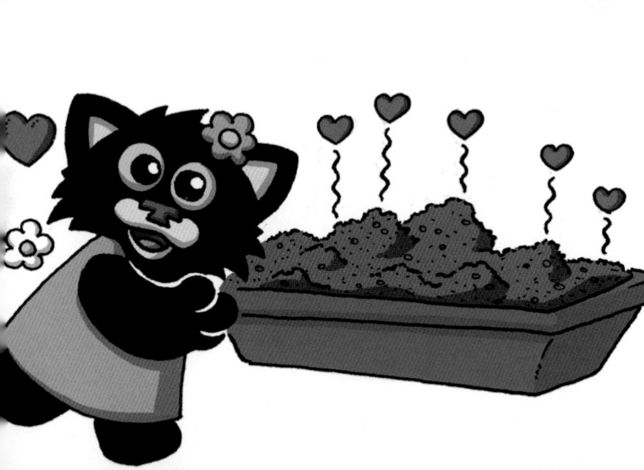

She cleaned her own litter box! She's so very, very HELPFUL!

Love Love Angel Kitty is such a very, very, good, good, GOOD Kitty! Look at how much she loves Baby!

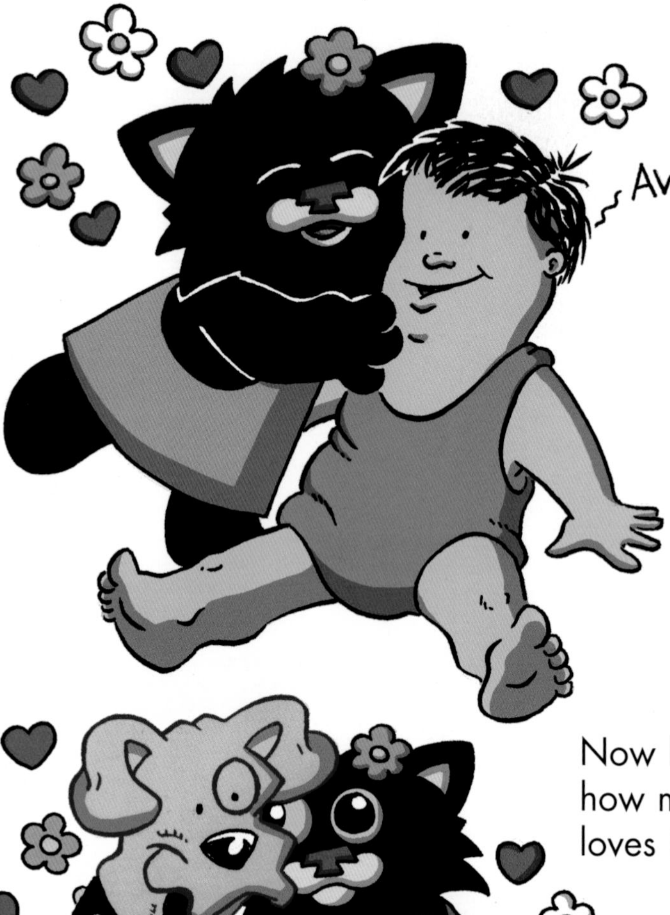
AWWW!

Now look at how much she loves Puppy!

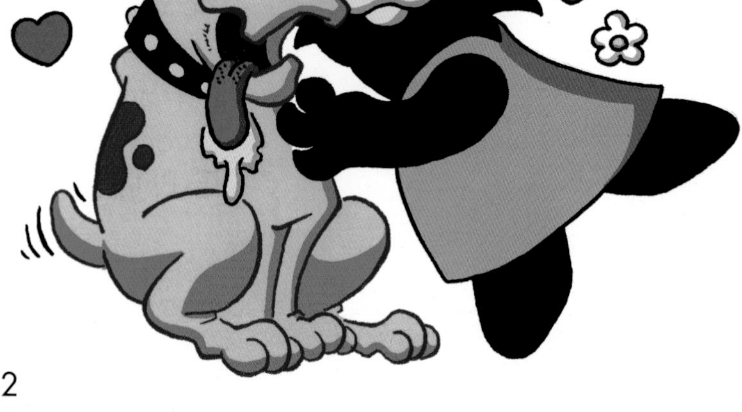

Finally, there is peace in our home. Where once there were screaming temper tantrums, now there are only kisses. Where once there were fights and shrieks and howls, now there are only hugs. Where once there was only mayhem, now there is only love. Sweet, wonderful LOVE.

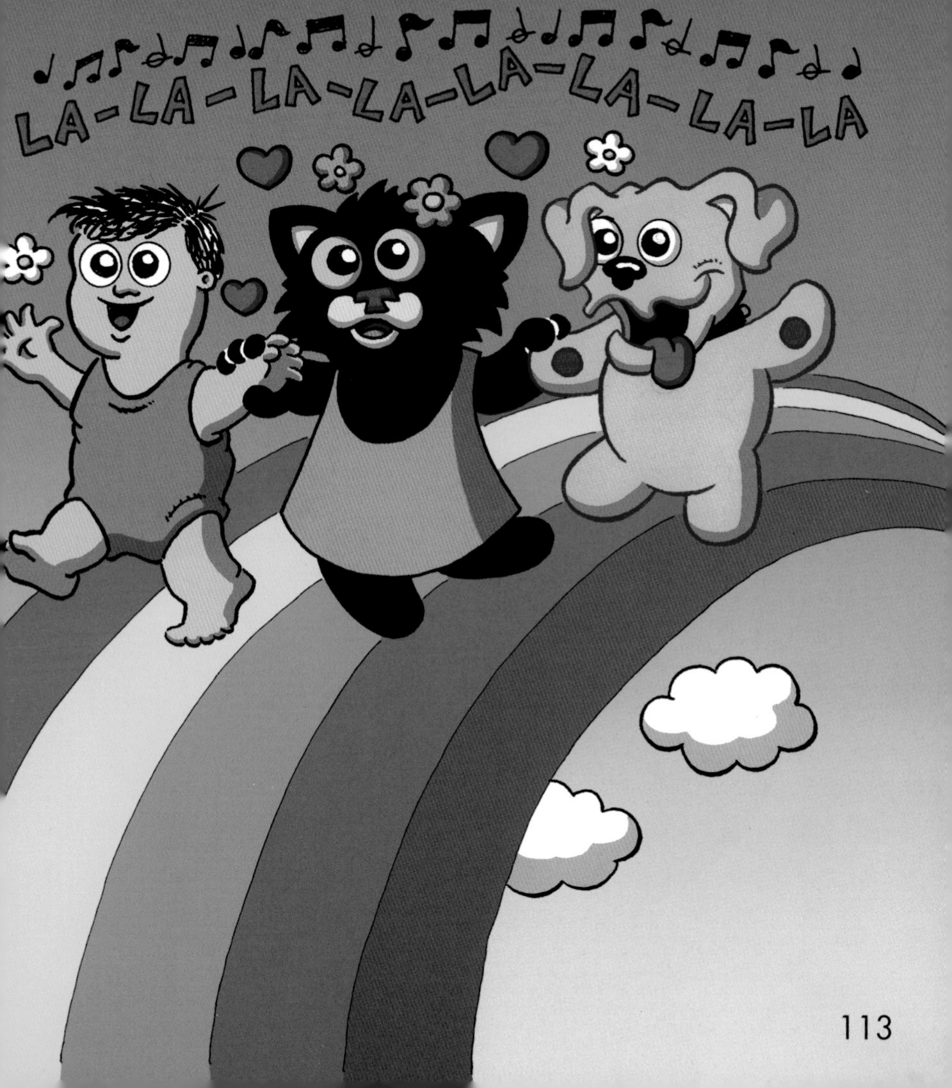
LA-LA-LA-LA-LA-LA-LA-LA

And it's all thanks to

SCHOOL
SCHOOL
SCHOOL
SCHOOL
SCHOOL
SCHOOL

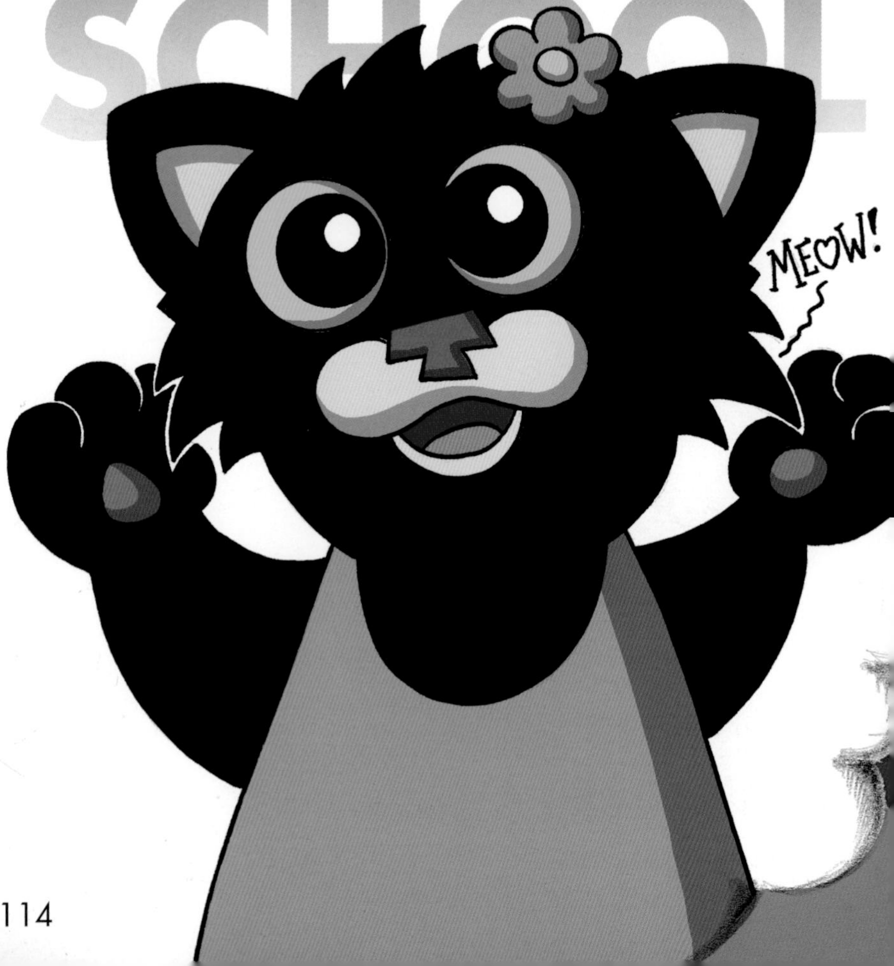
MEOW!

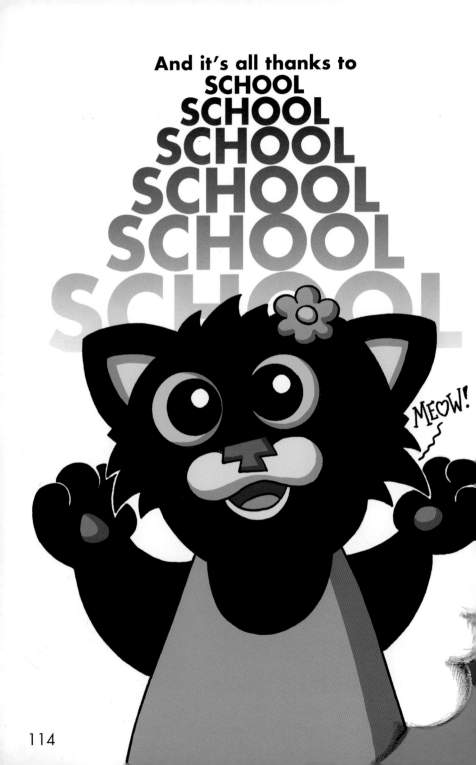

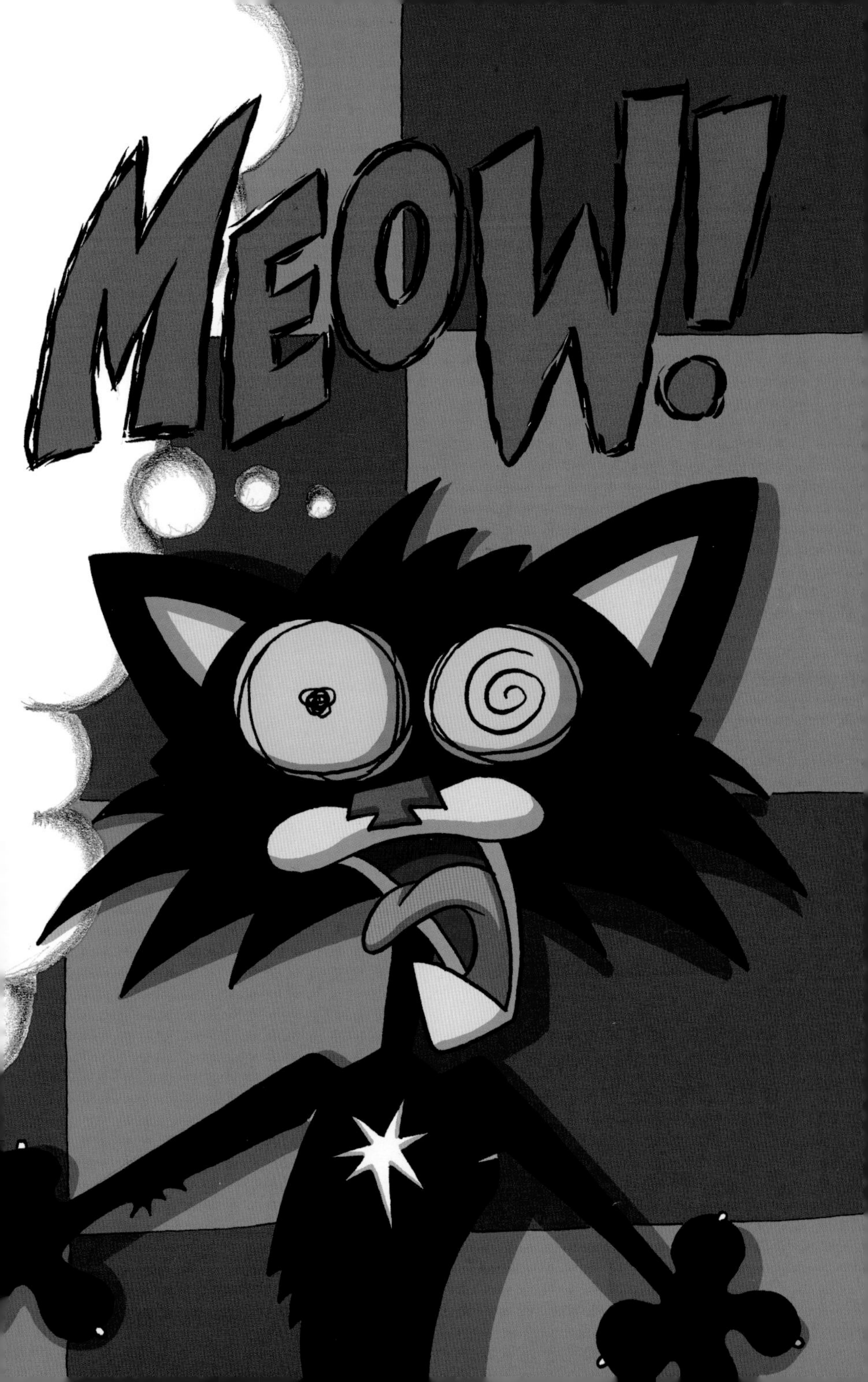
MEOW!

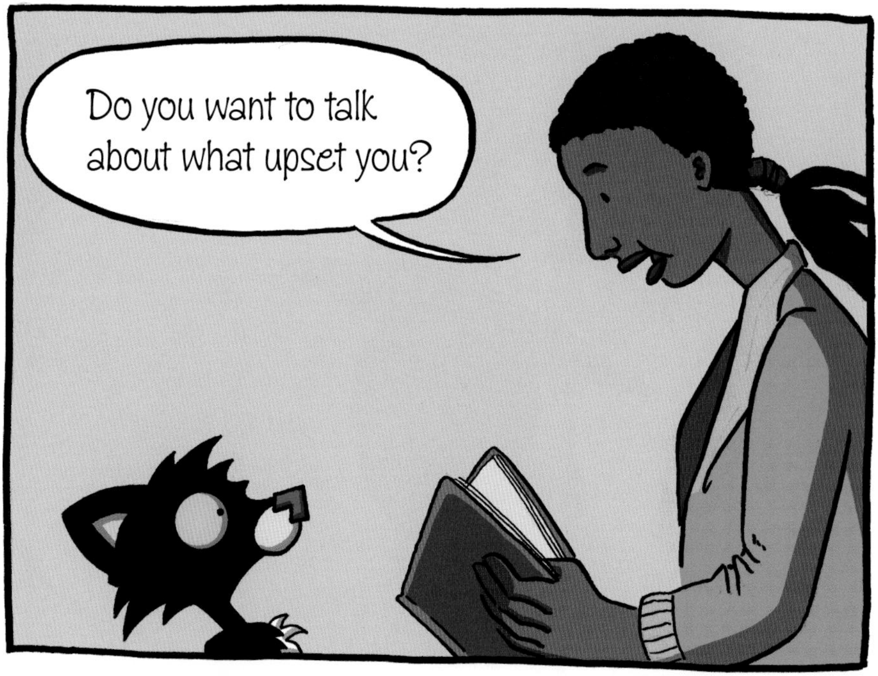
Do you want to talk about what upset you?

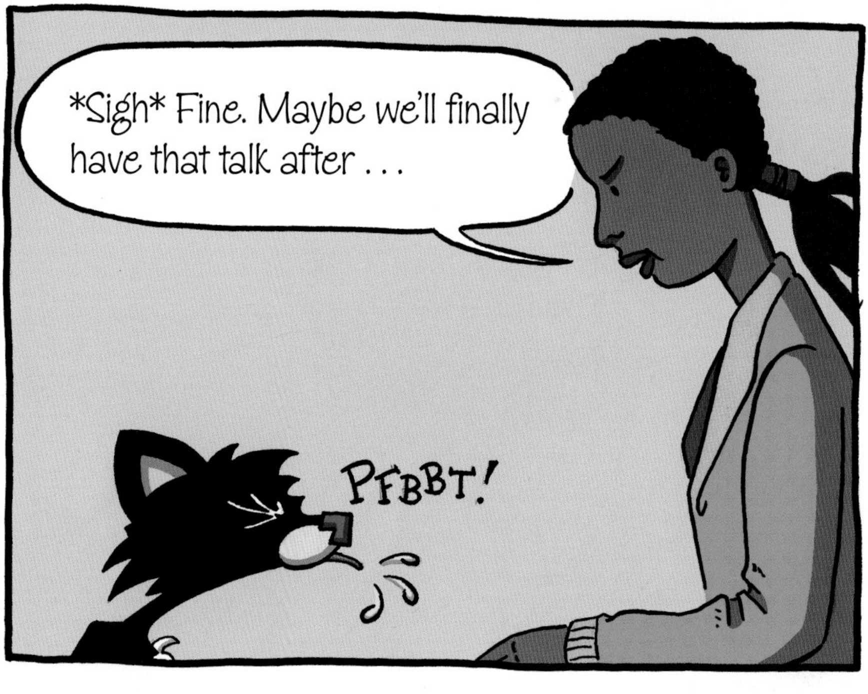
Sigh Fine. Maybe we'll finally have that talk after . . .
PFBBT!

•CHAPTER EIGHT•

GRADUATION

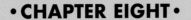

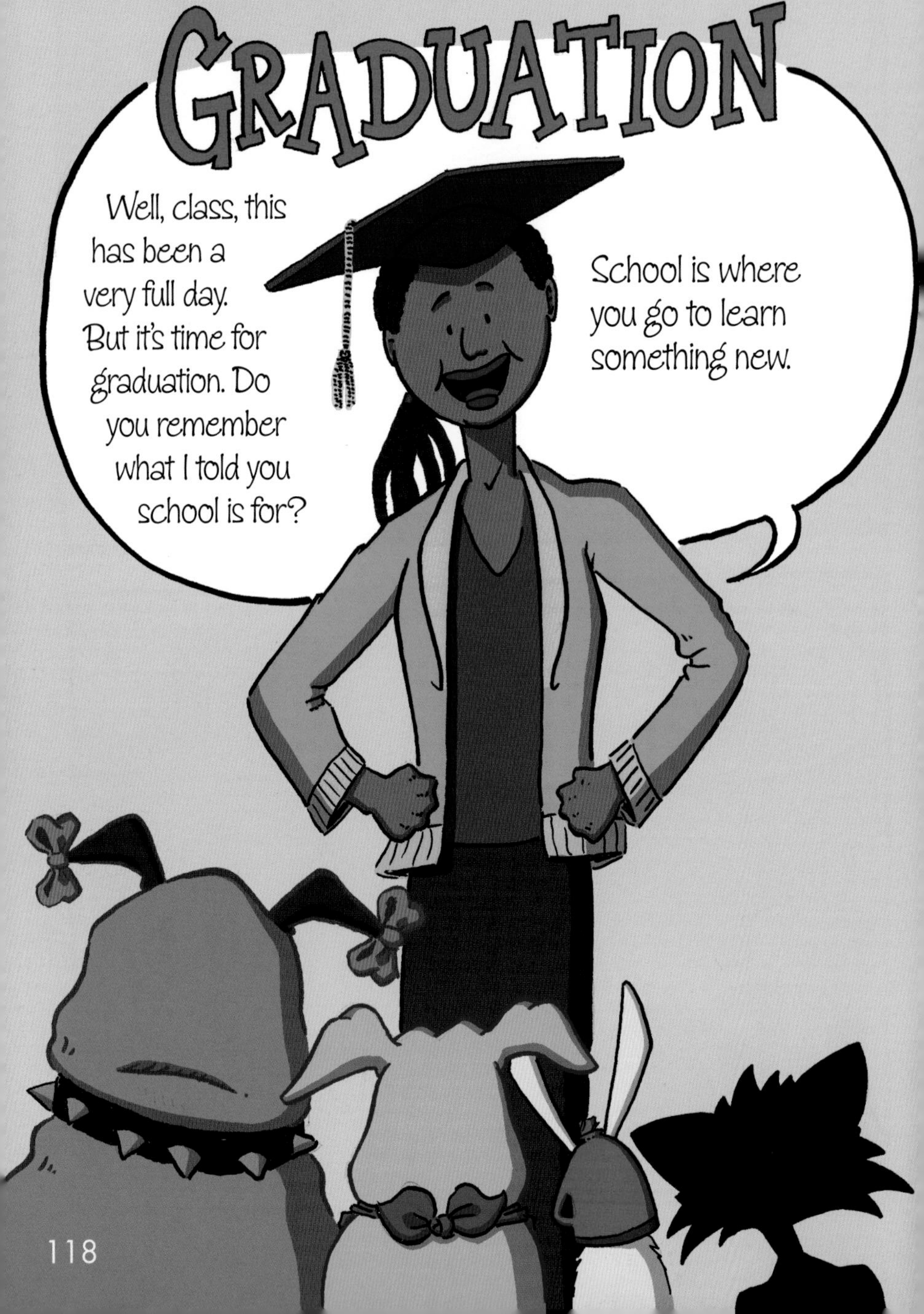
Well, class, this has been a very full day. But it's time for graduation. Do you remember what I told you school is for?
School is where you go to learn something new.

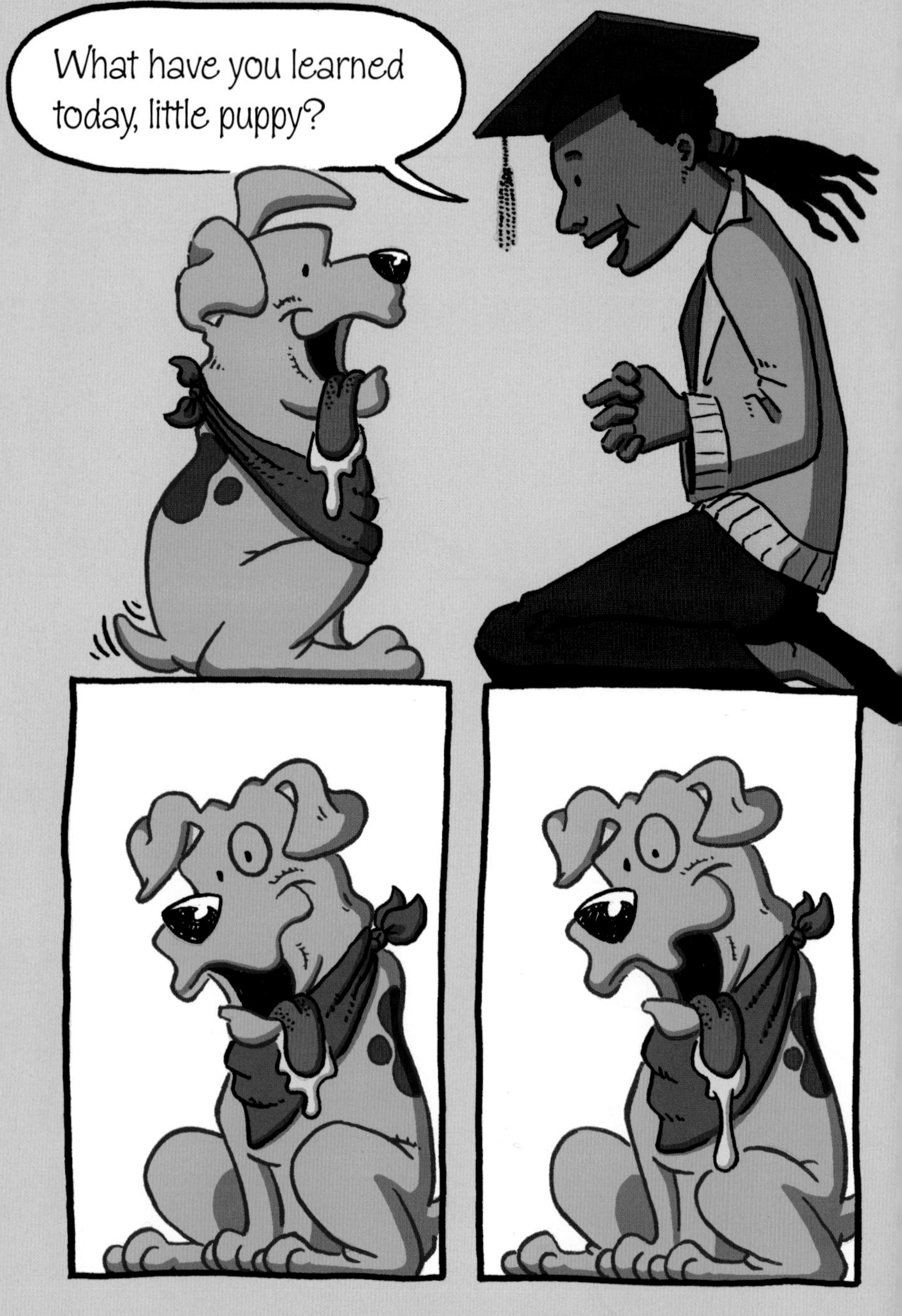
What have you learned today, little puppy?

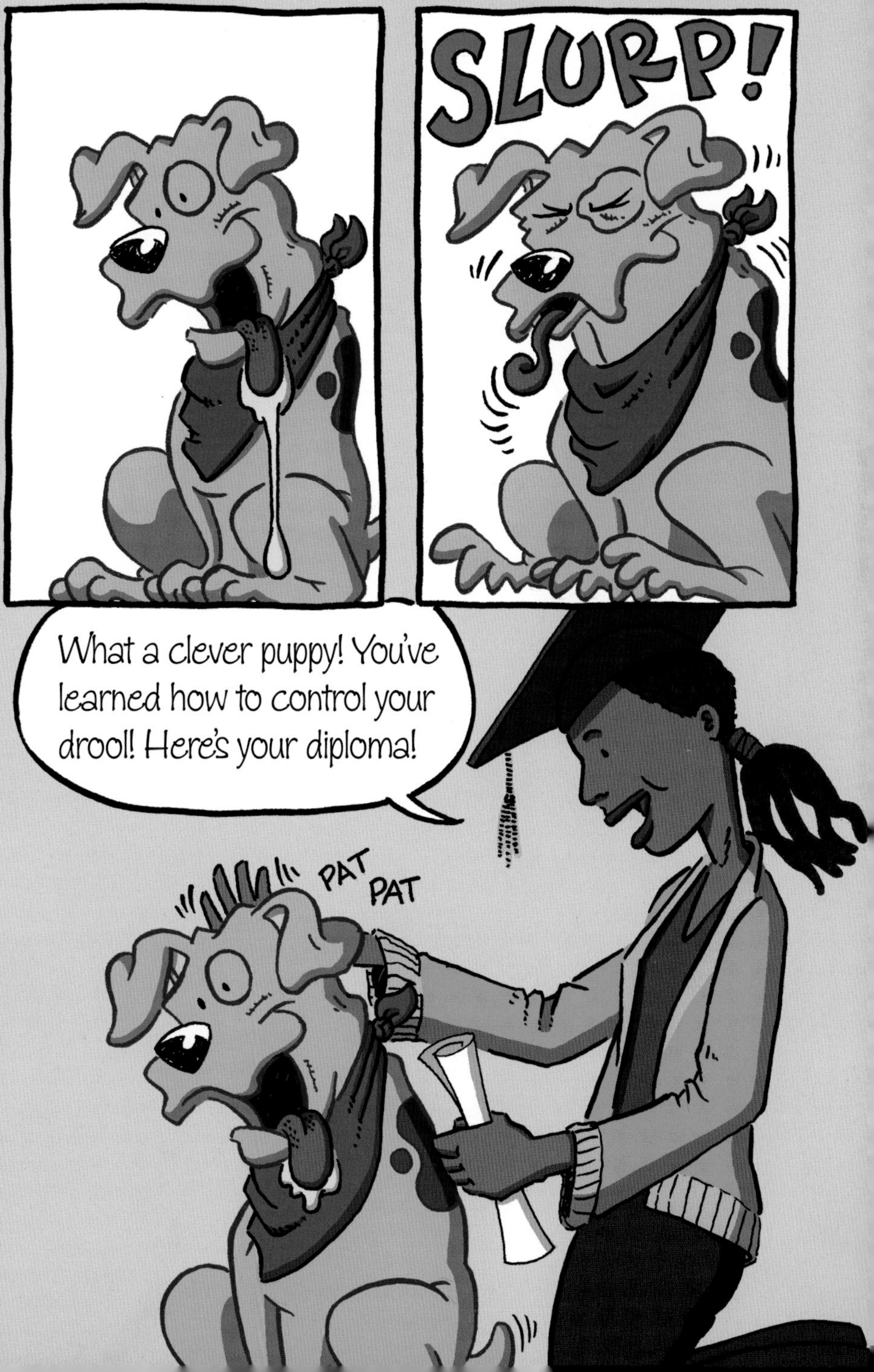
SLURP!
What a clever puppy! You've learned how to control your drool! Here's your diploma!
PAT PAT

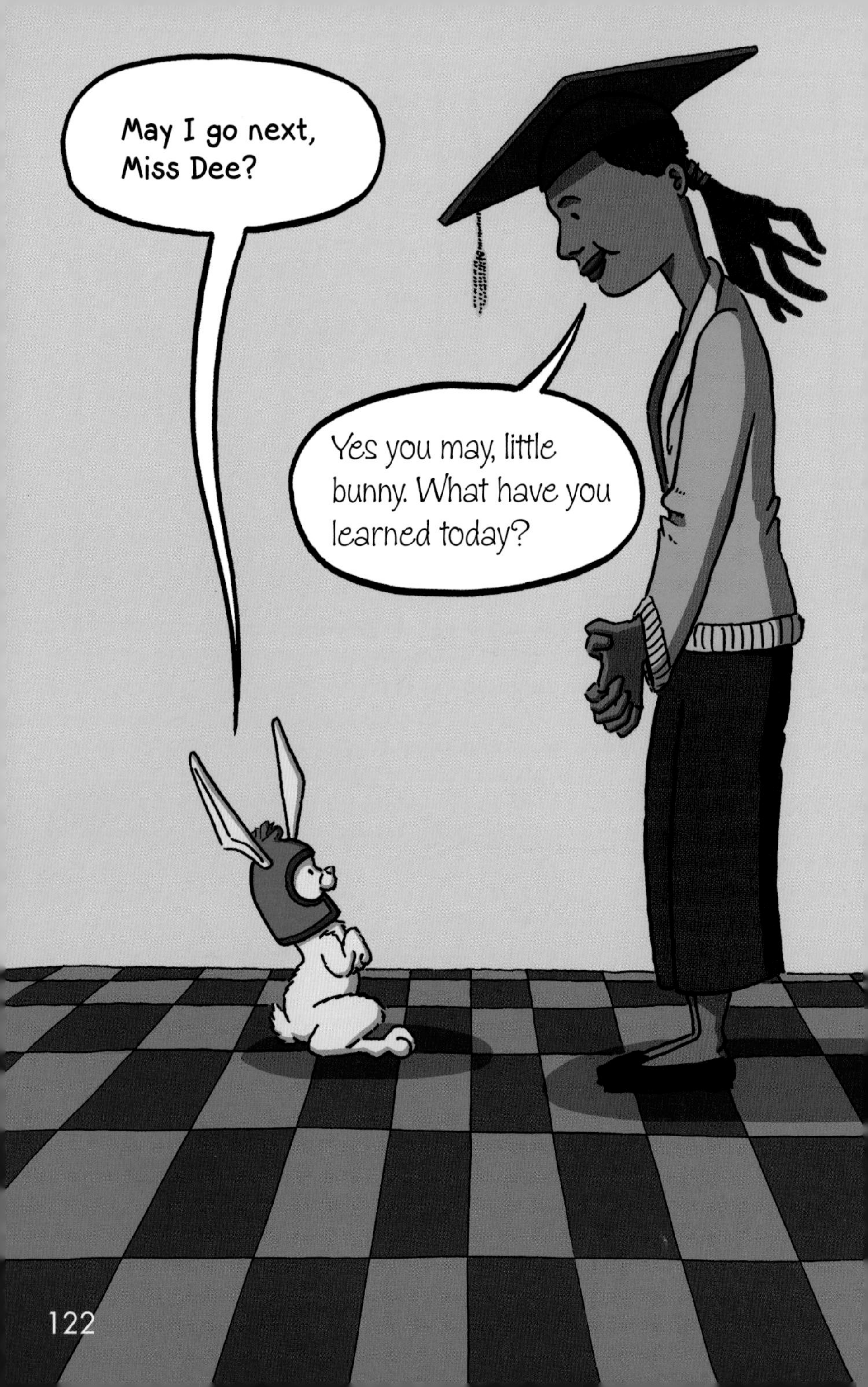
May I go next, Miss Dee?
Yes you may, little bunny. What have you learned today?

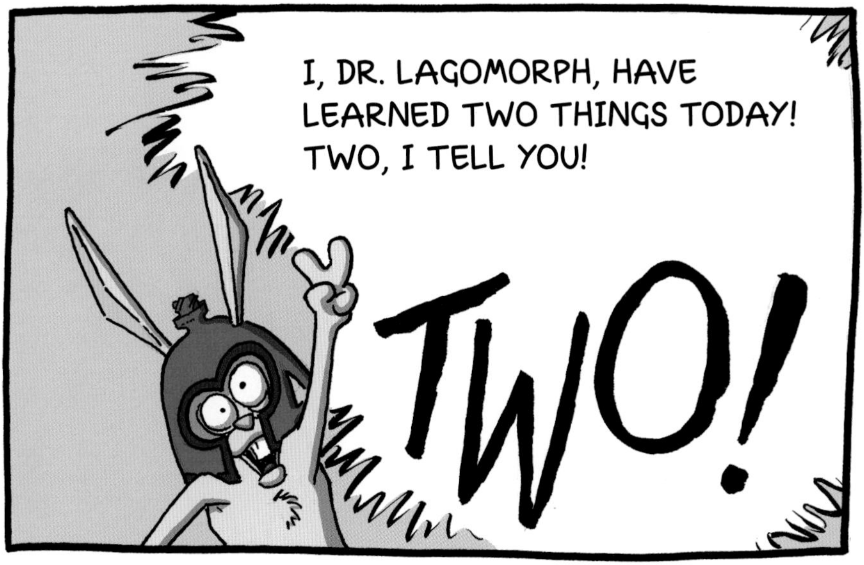
I, DR. LAGOMORPH, HAVE LEARNED TWO THINGS TODAY! TWO, I TELL YOU!
TWO!

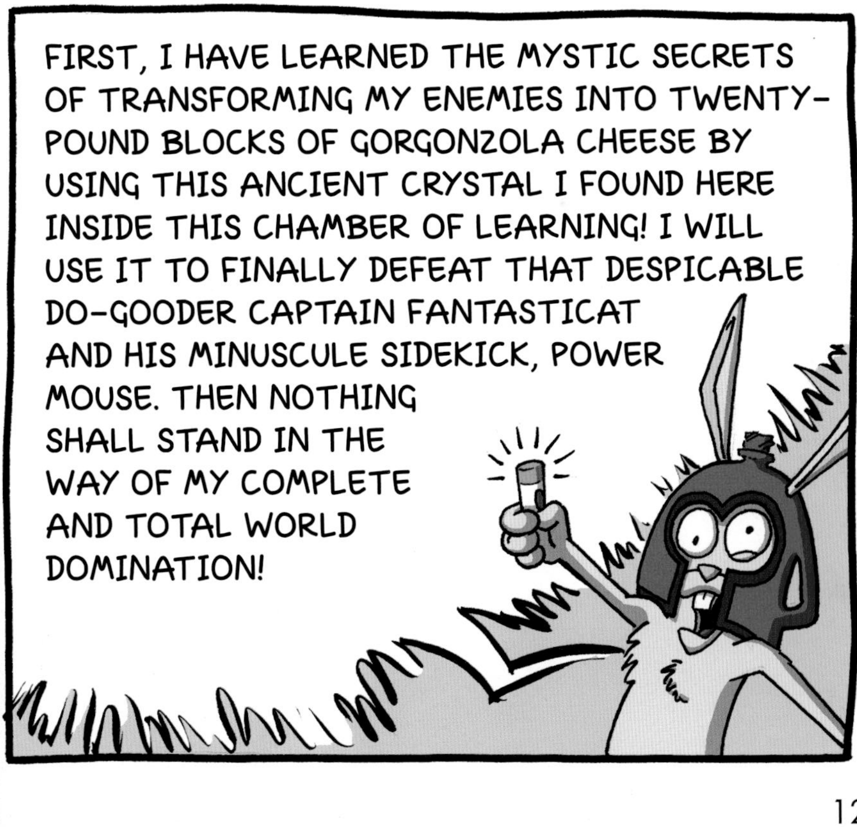
FIRST, I HAVE LEARNED THE MYSTIC SECRETS OF TRANSFORMING MY ENEMIES INTO TWENTY-POUND BLOCKS OF GORGONZOLA CHEESE BY USING THIS ANCIENT CRYSTAL I FOUND HERE INSIDE THIS CHAMBER OF LEARNING! I WILL USE IT TO FINALLY DEFEAT THAT DESPICABLE DO-GOODER CAPTAIN FANTASTICAT AND HIS MINUSCULE SIDEKICK, POWER MOUSE. THEN NOTHING SHALL STAND IN THE WAY OF MY COMPLETE AND TOTAL WORLD DOMINATION!

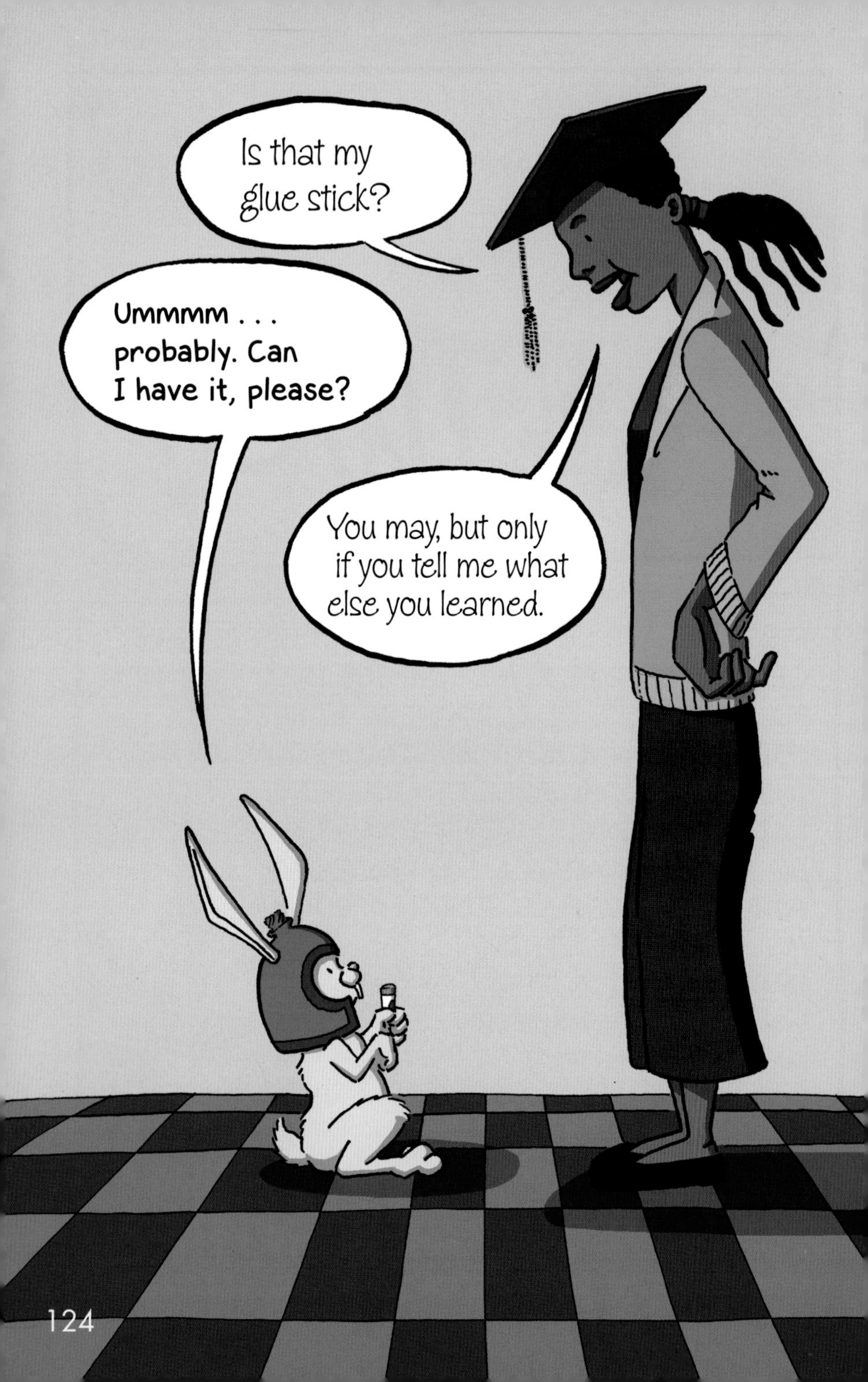
Is that my glue stick?
Ummmm . . . probably. Can I have it, please?
You may, but only if you tell me what else you learned.

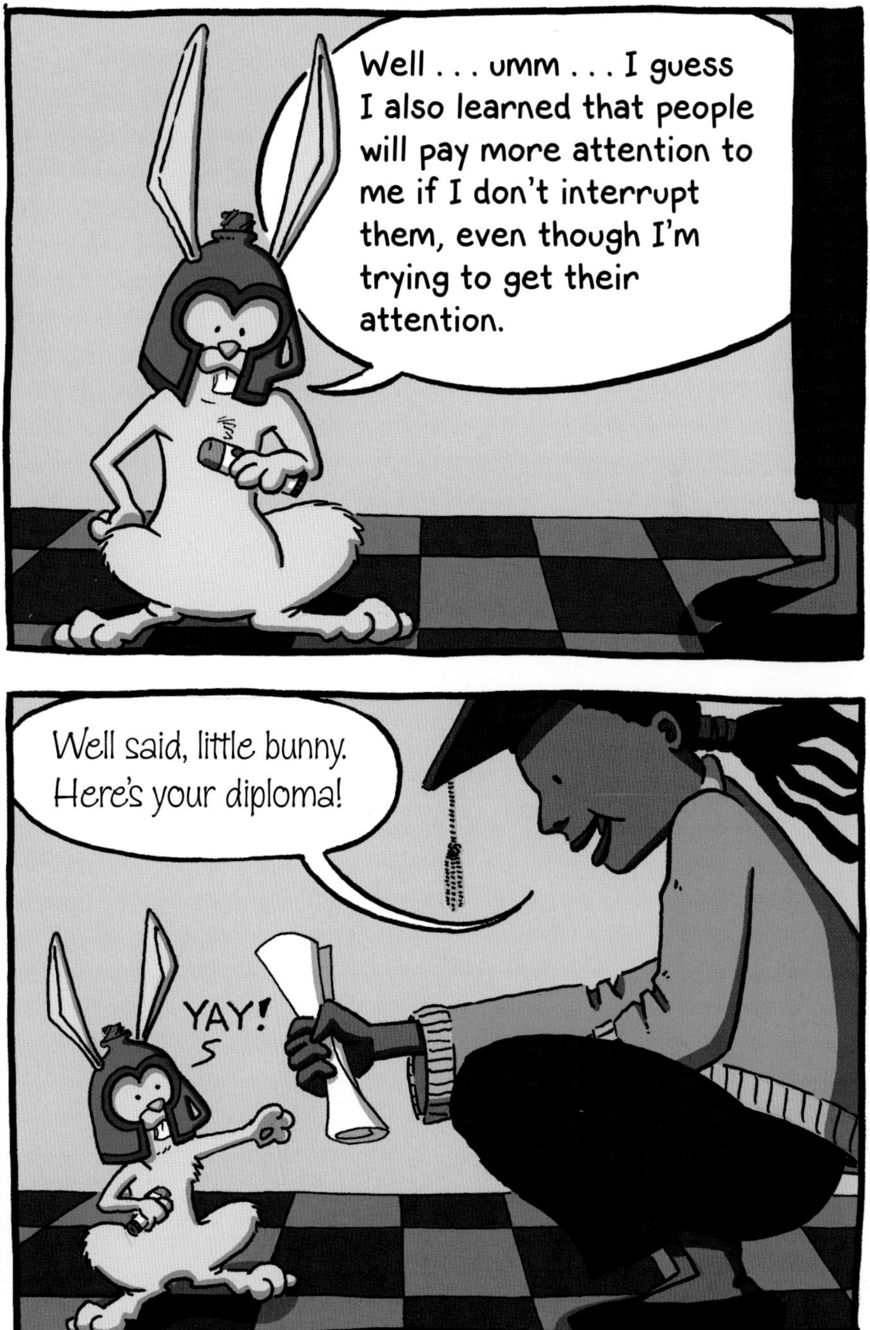
Well . . . umm . . . I guess I also learned that people will pay more attention to me if I don't interrupt them, even though I'm trying to get their attention.
Well said, little bunny. Here's your diploma!
YAY!

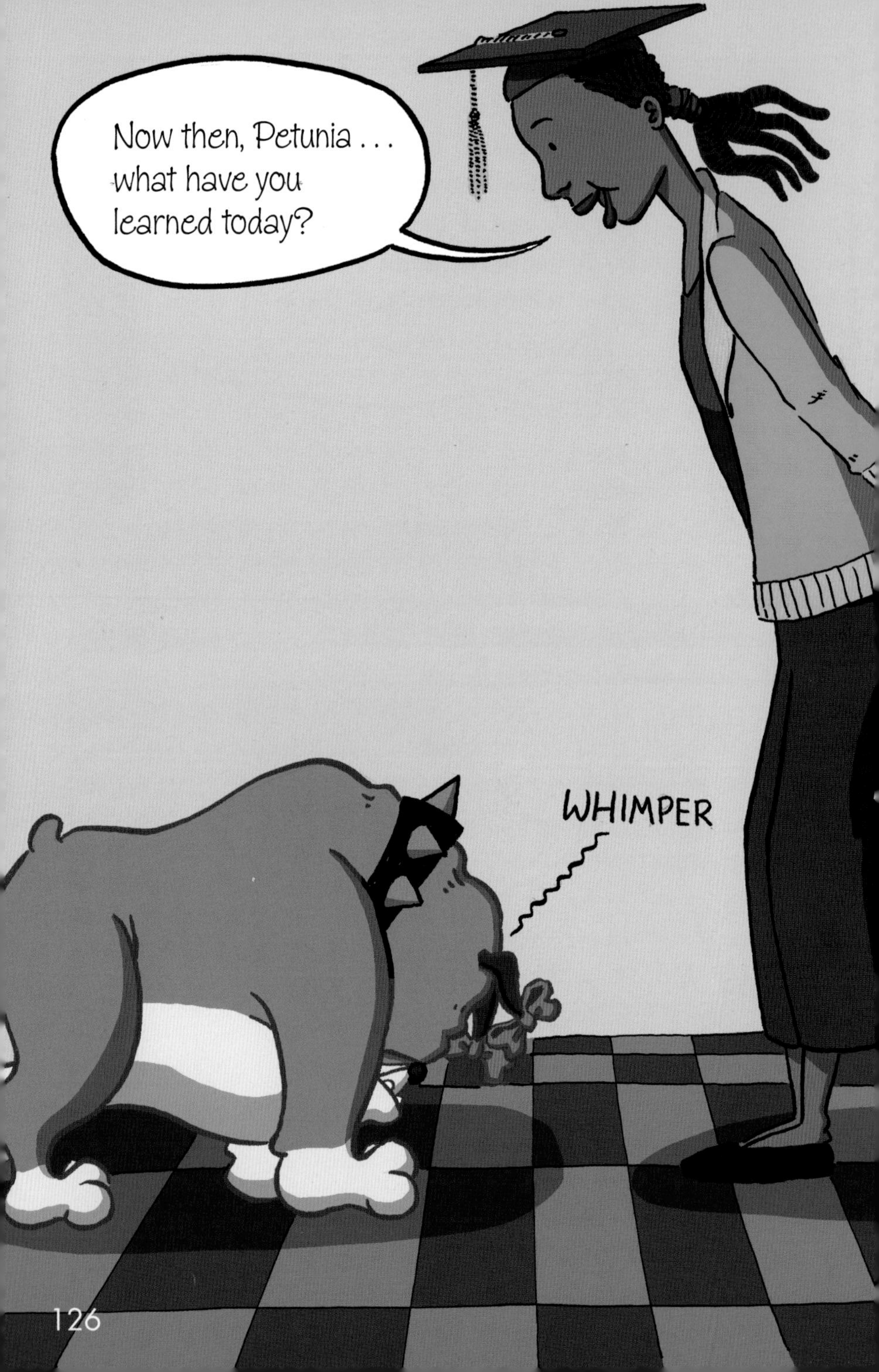
Now then, Petunia . . . what have you learned today?
WHIMPER

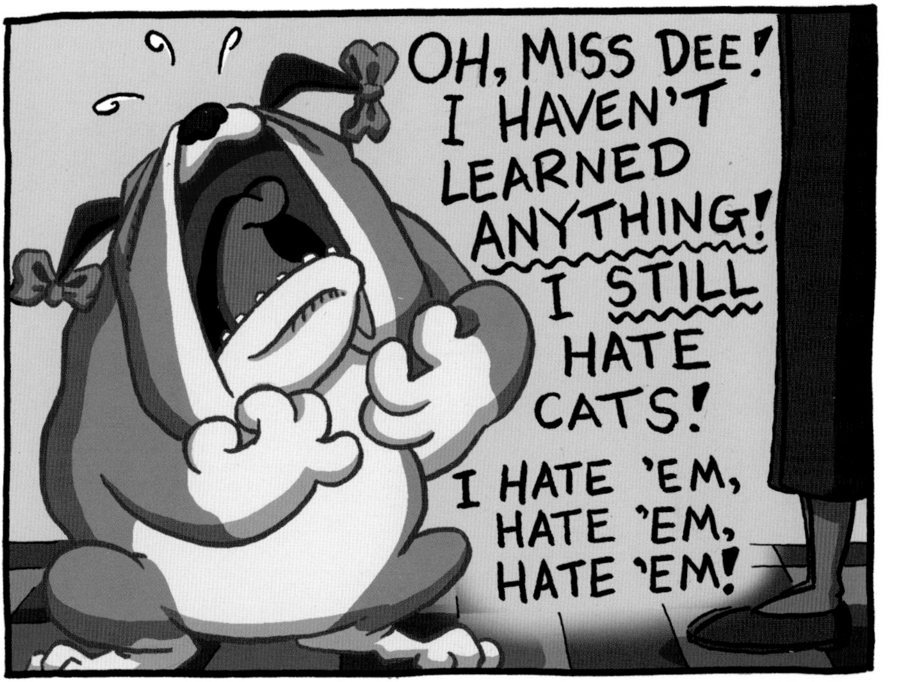
OH, MISS DEE! I HAVEN'T LEARNED ANYTHING! I STILL HATE CATS!
I HATE 'EM, HATE 'EM, HATE 'EM!

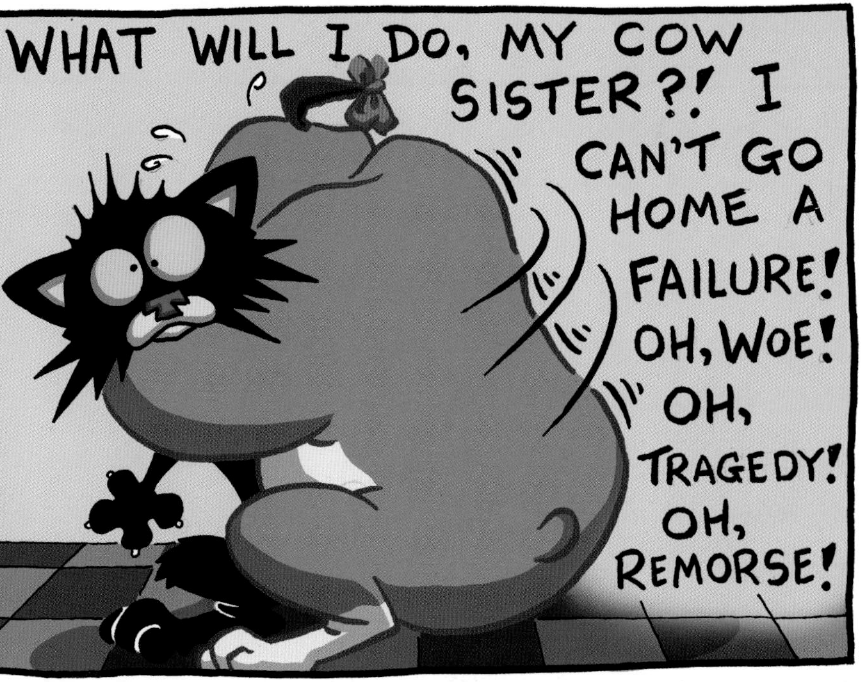
WHAT WILL I DO, MY COW SISTER?! I CAN'T GO HOME A FAILURE! OH, WOE! OH, TRAGEDY! OH, REMORSE!

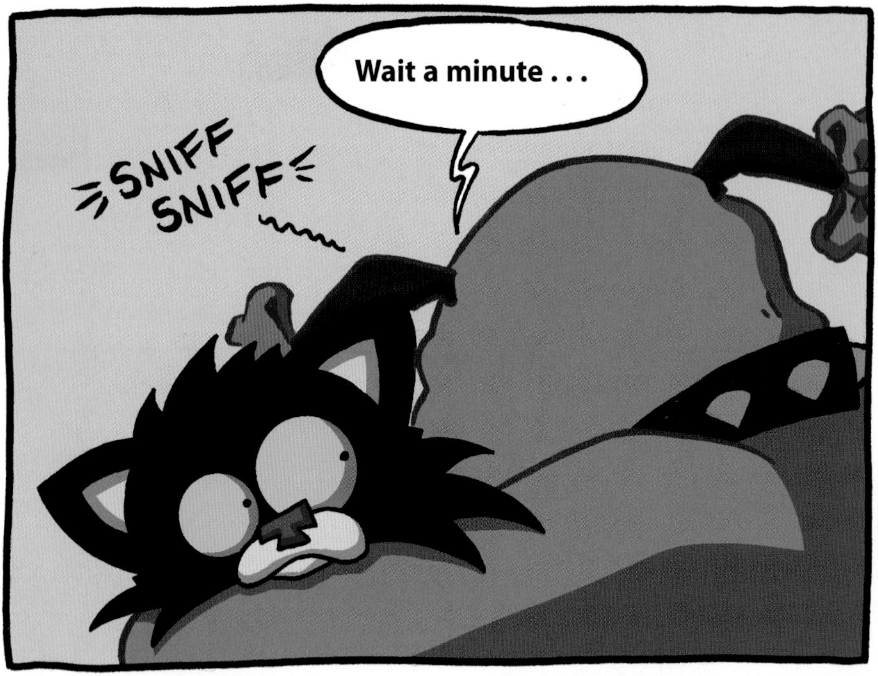
Wait a minute . . .
SNIFF
SNIFF

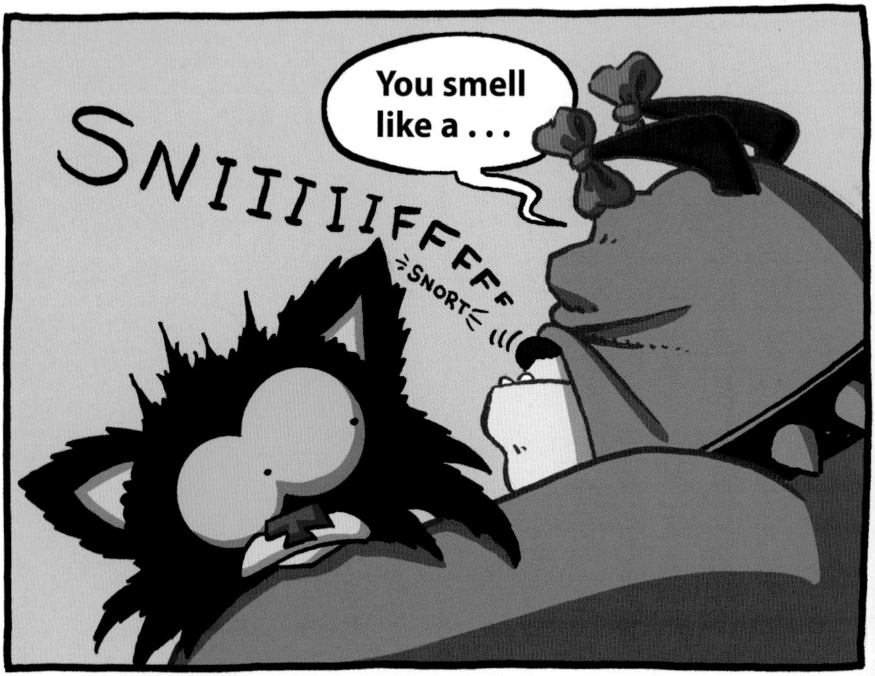
You smell like a . . .
SNIIIIIIFFFFF
SNORT

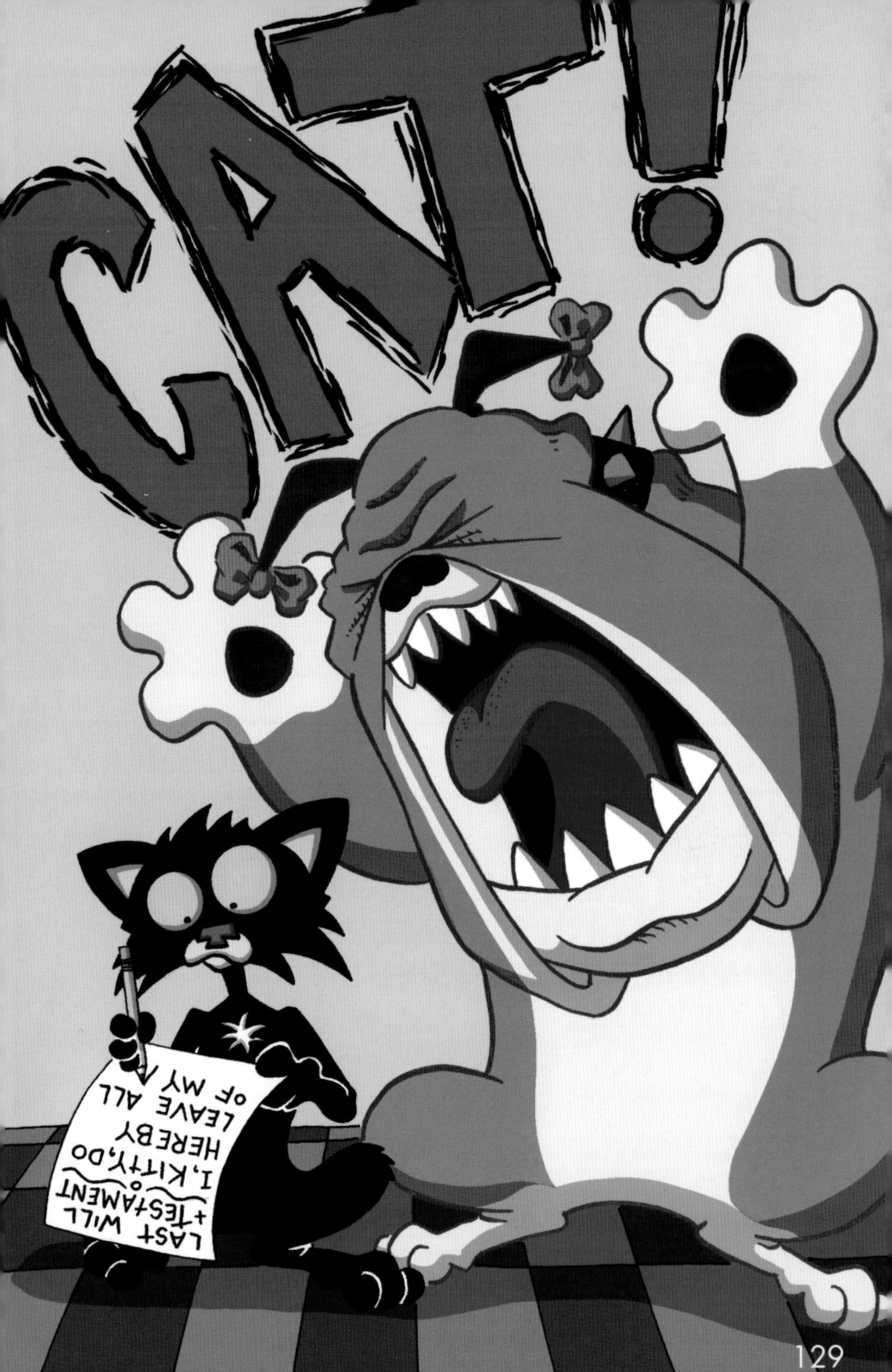
CAT!
LAST WILL
+ TESTAMENT
I, KITTY, DO
HEREBY
LEAVE ALL
OF MY

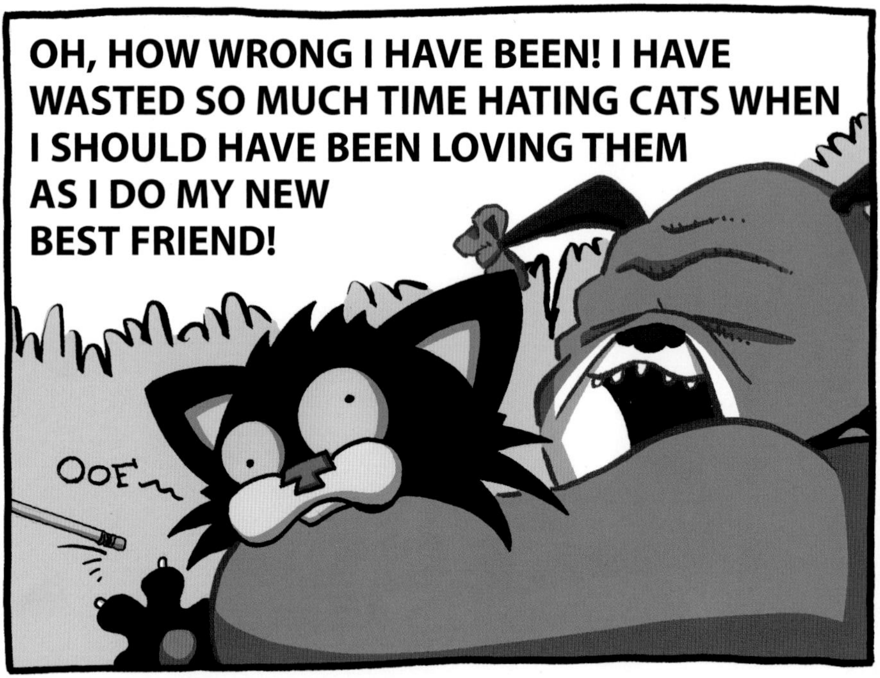
OH, HOW WRONG I HAVE BEEN! I HAVE WASTED SO MUCH TIME HATING CATS WHEN I SHOULD HAVE BEEN LOVING THEM AS I DO MY NEW BEST FRIEND!
OOF

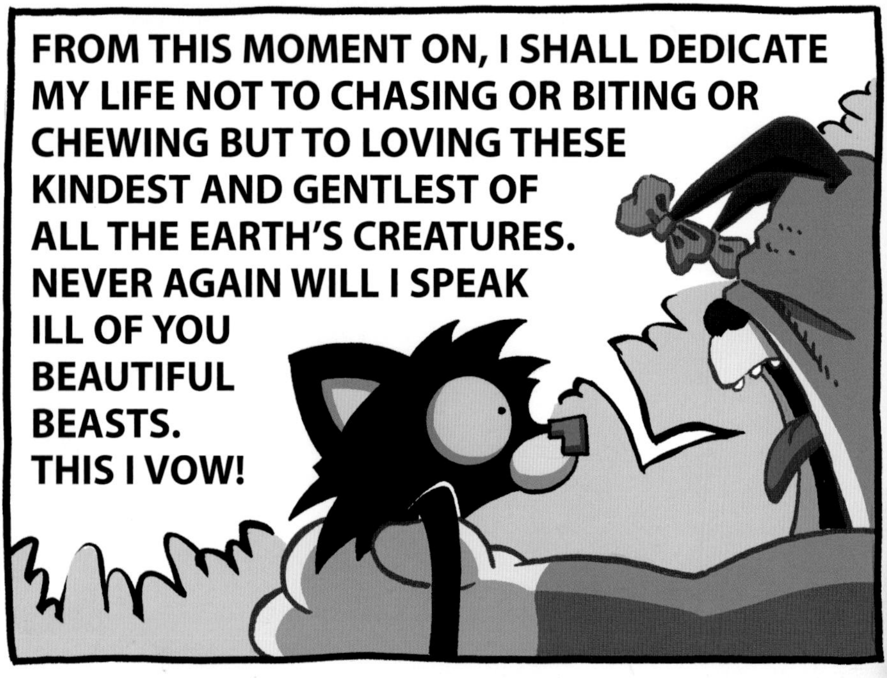
FROM THIS MOMENT ON, I SHALL DEDICATE MY LIFE NOT TO CHASING OR BITING OR CHEWING BUT TO LOVING THESE KINDEST AND GENTLEST OF ALL THE EARTH'S CREATURES. NEVER AGAIN WILL I SPEAK ILL OF YOU BEAUTIFUL BEASTS. THIS I VOW!

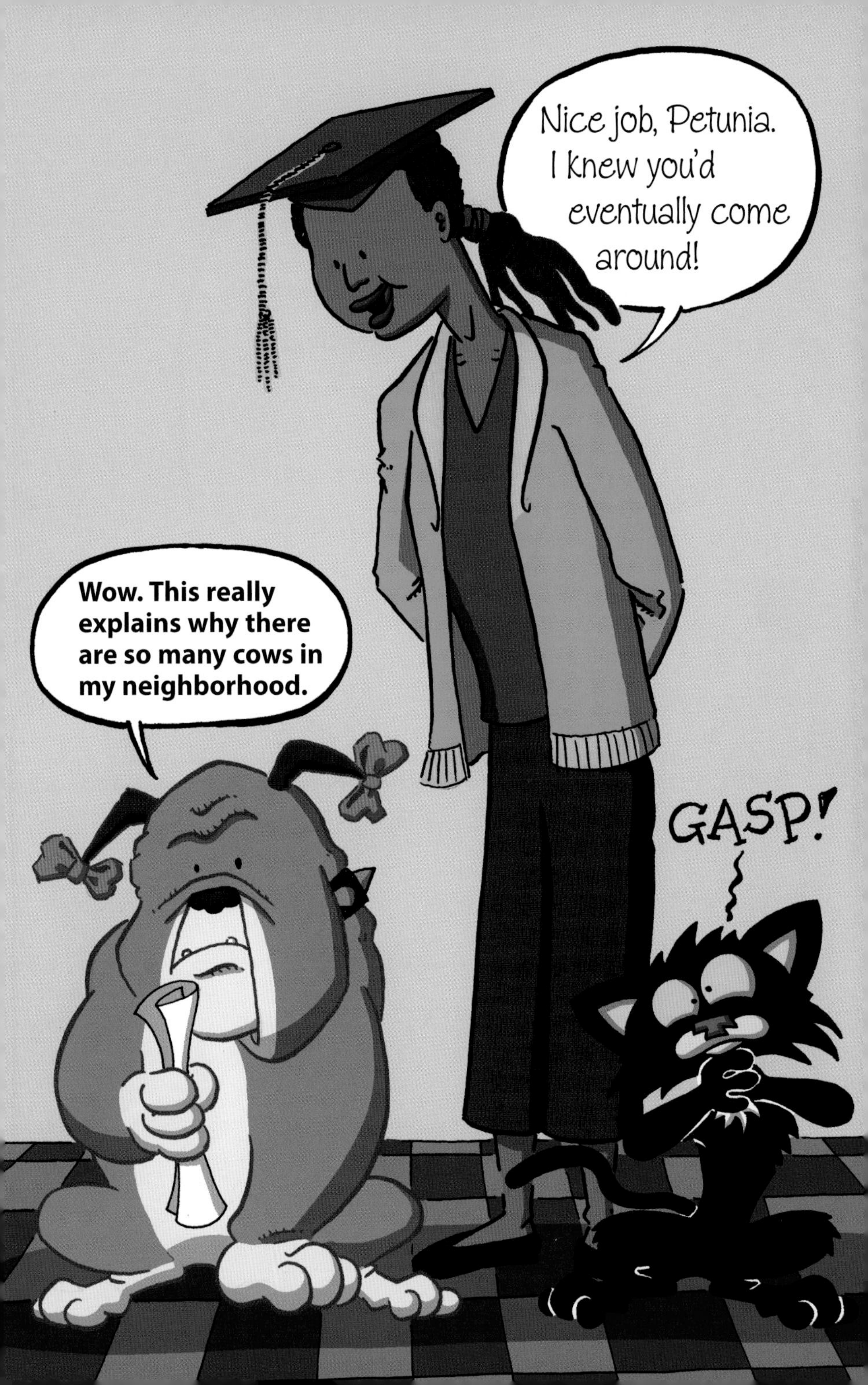
Nice job, Petunia. I knew you'd eventually come around!
Wow. This really explains why there are so many cows in my neighborhood.
GASP!

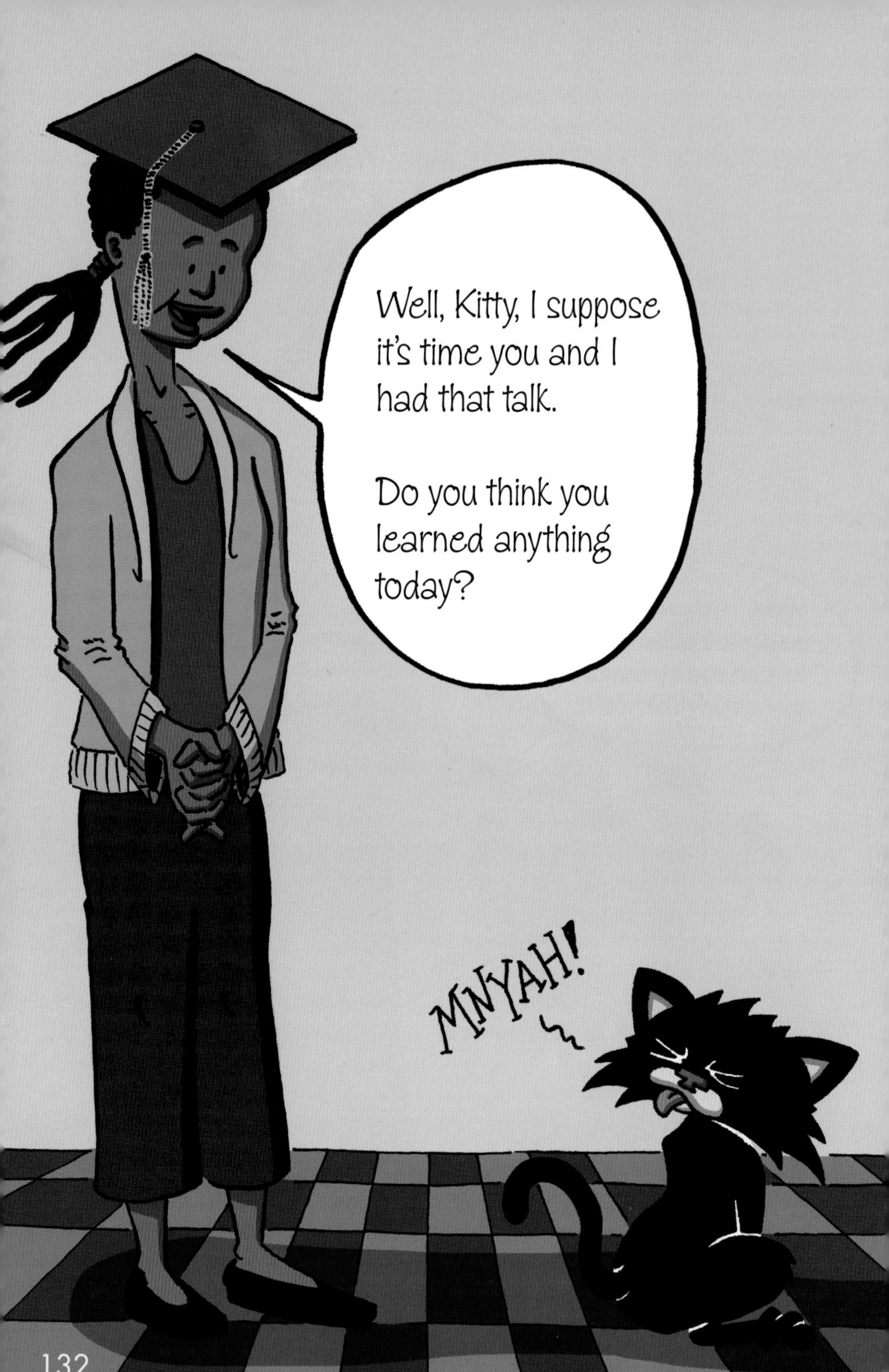
Well, Kitty, I suppose it's time you and I had that talk.
Do you think you learned anything today?
MNYAH!

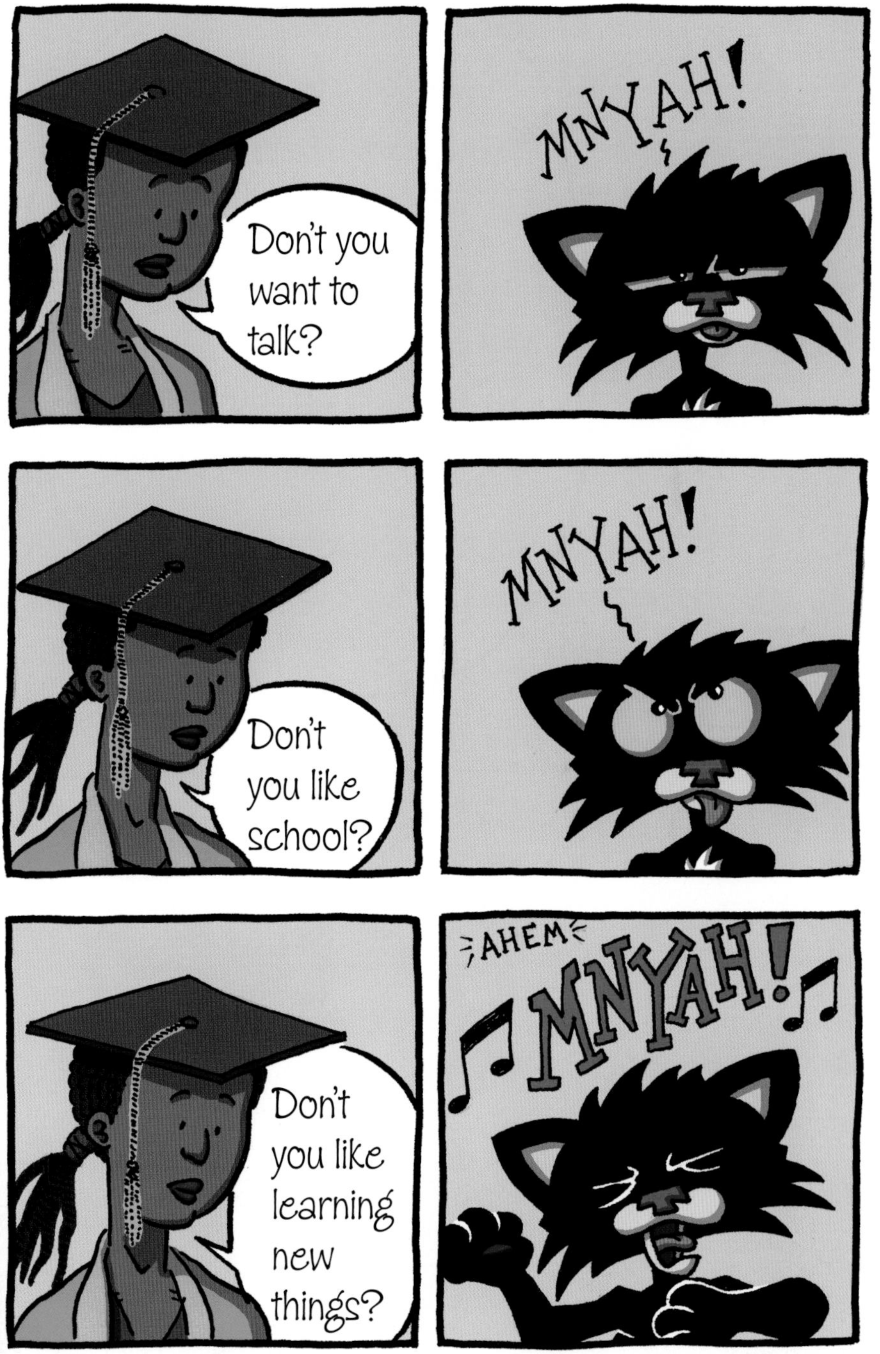
Don't you want to talk?
MNYAH!
Don't you like school?
MNYAH!
Don't you like learning new things?
AHEM
MNYAH!

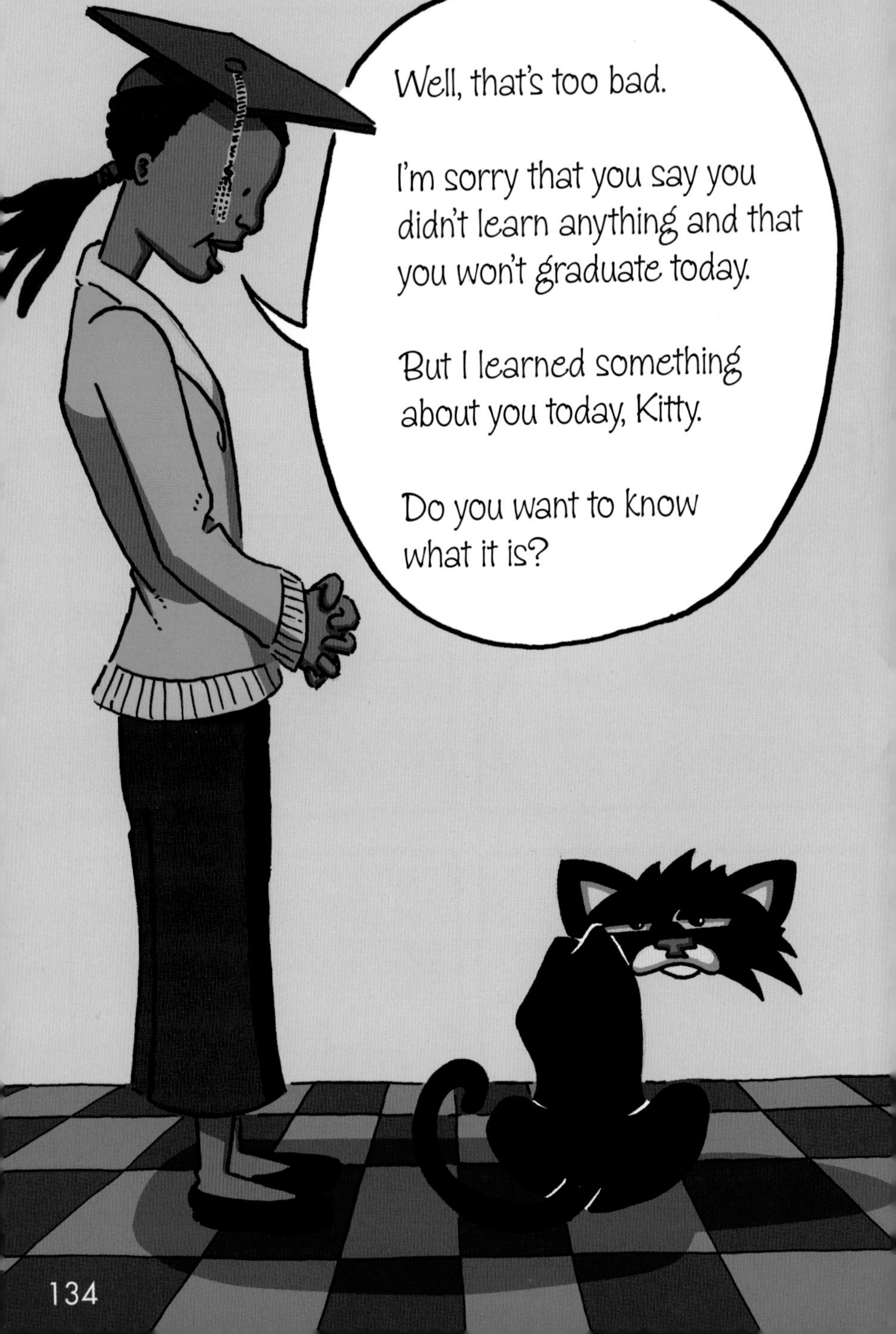
Well, that's too bad.
I'm sorry that you say you didn't learn anything and that you won't graduate today.
But I learned something about you today, Kitty.
Do you want to know what it is?

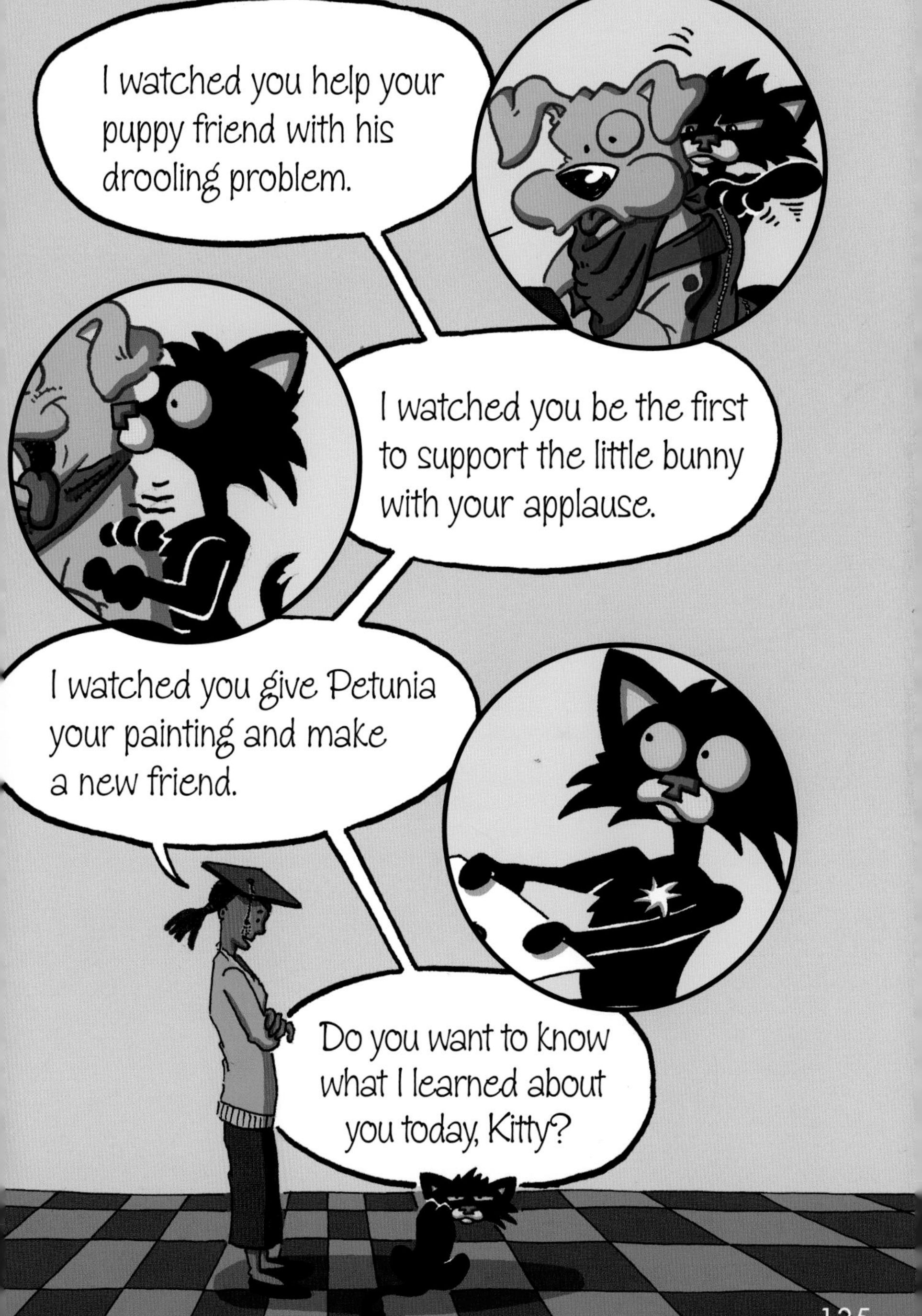
I watched you help your puppy friend with his drooling problem.
I watched you be the first to support the little bunny with your applause.
I watched you give Petunia your painting and make a new friend.
Do you want to know what I learned about you today, Kitty?

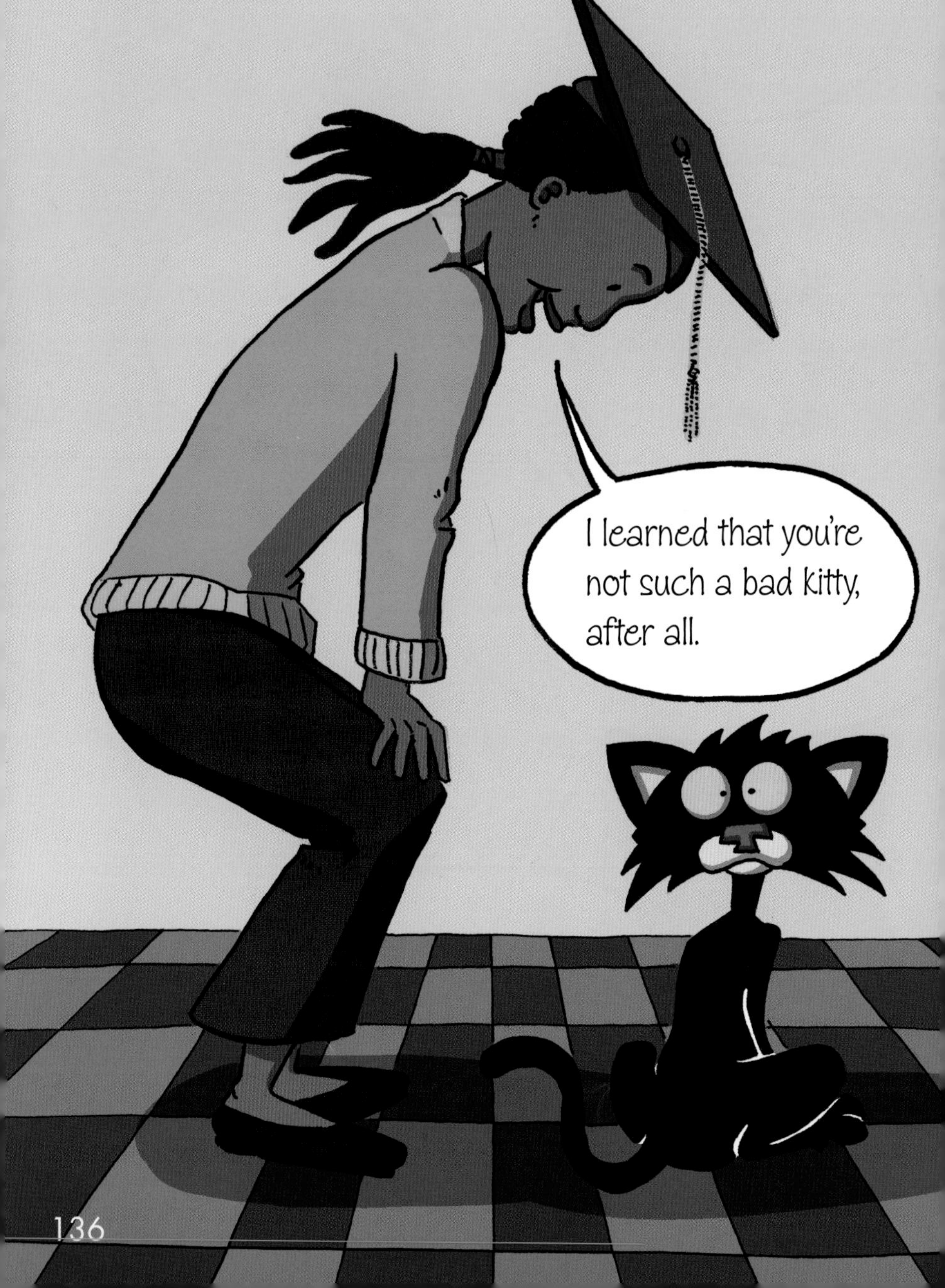
I learned that you're not such a bad kitty, after all.

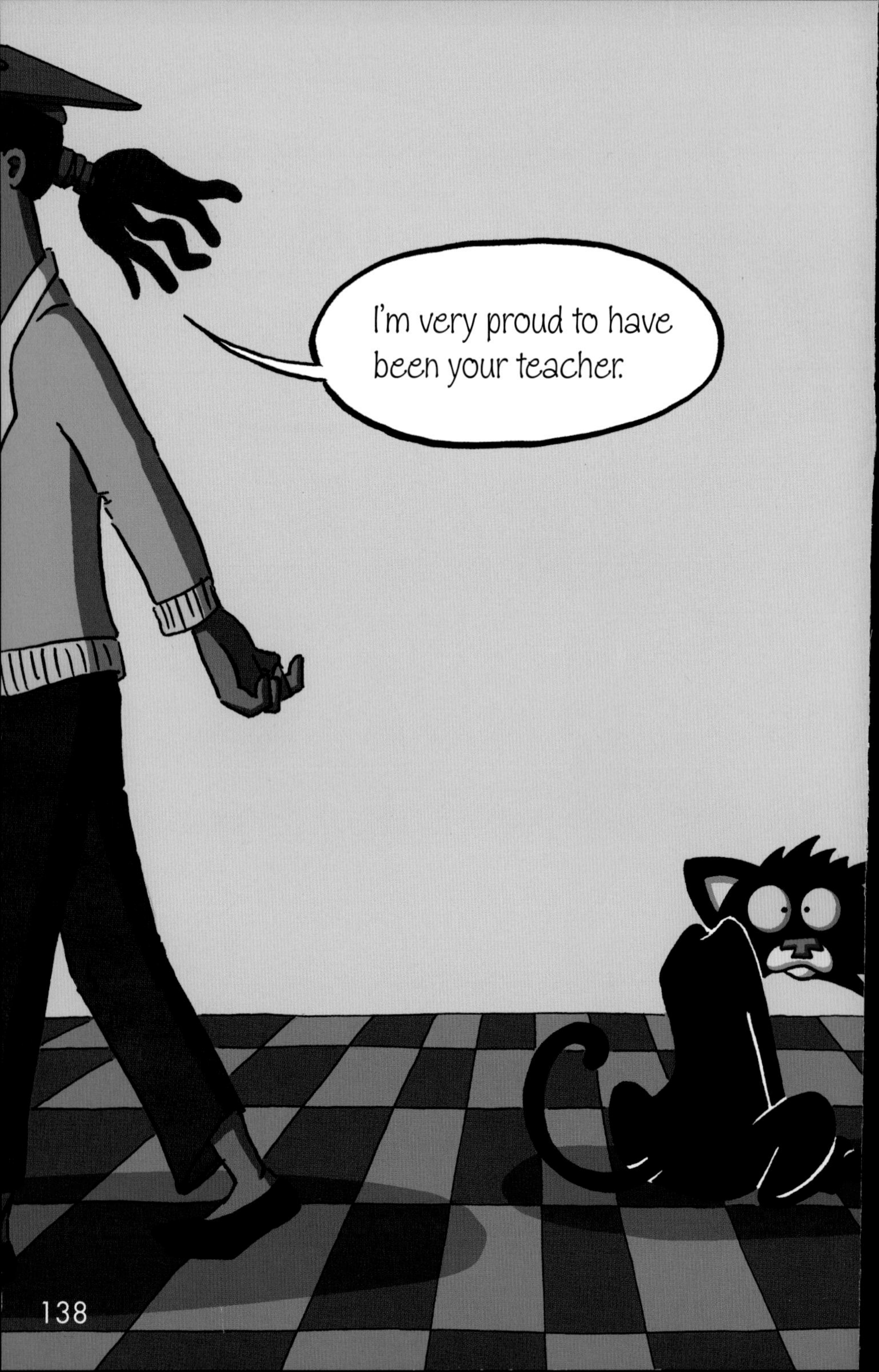
I'm very proud to have been your teacher.

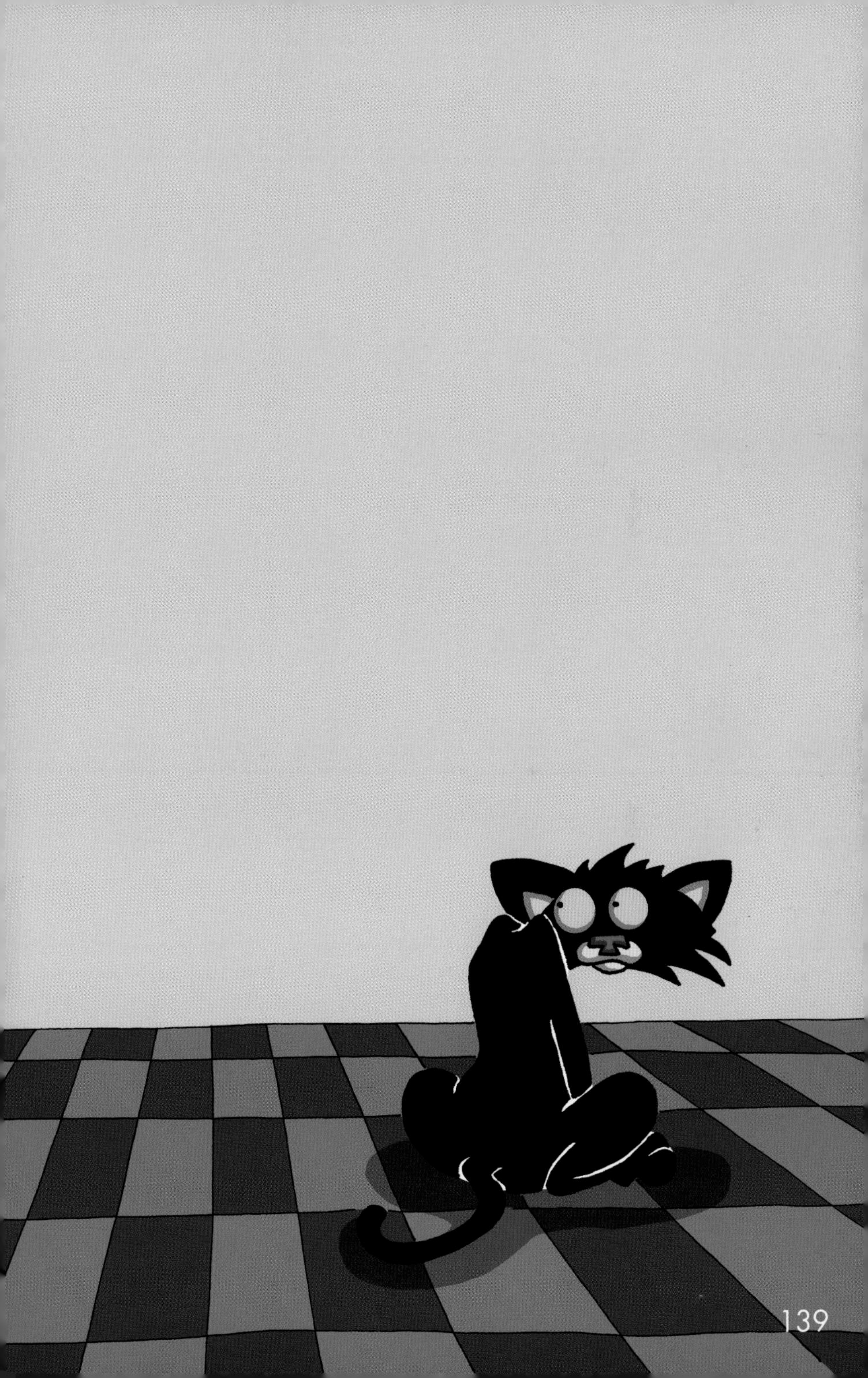

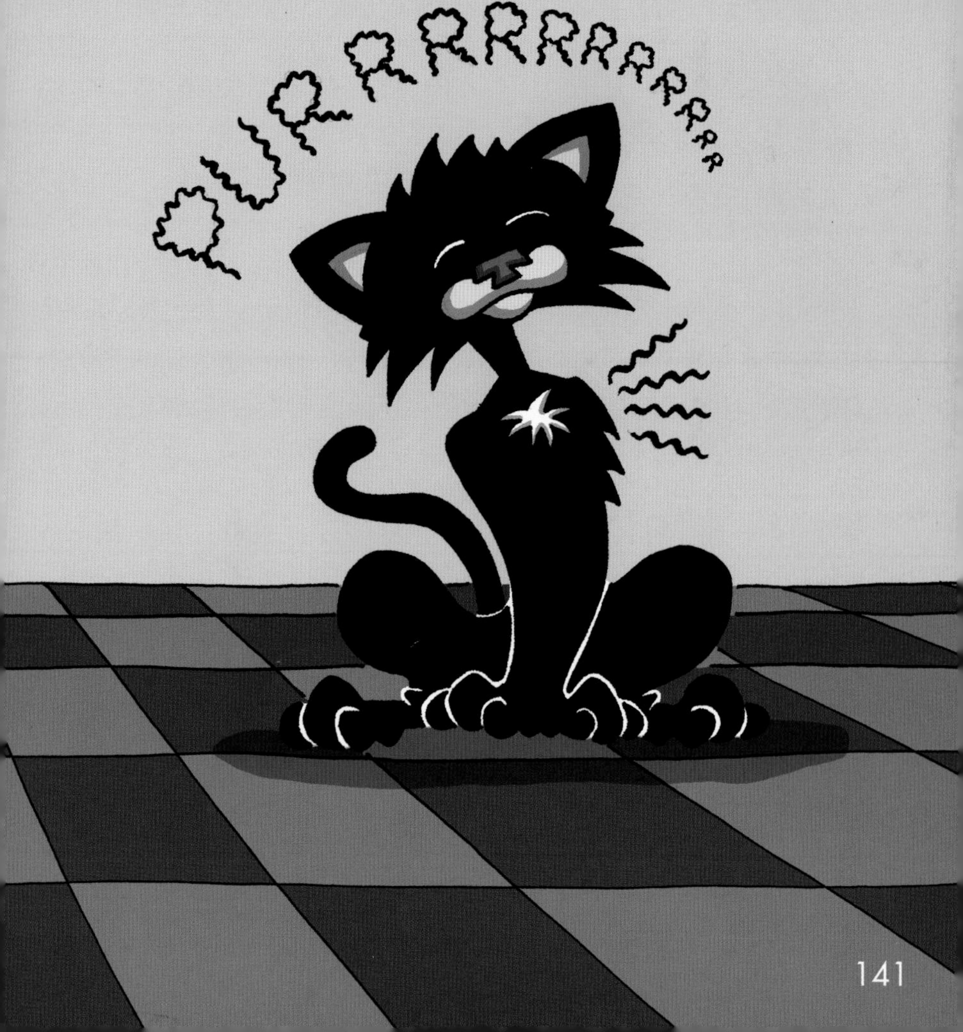
PURRRRRRRRRRRRR

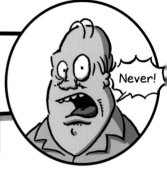

Never!

UNCLE MURRAY'S FUN FACTS

CAN DOGS AND CATS EVER BECOME FRIENDS?

Dogs and cats can and will become friends, but they can't do this by themselves. They'll need your help. The key is PATIENCE. Helping your pets to get along could take a long time and will require a lot of your attention.

MEOW?

First, take a few precautions. Trim the claws on your cat. Put the dog on a leash. Make sure the cat has a place to hide or escape to if things get out of hand. And keep some treats on hand . . . you'll see why in a moment.

If you're bringing a cat into the home, keep her in her carrier and let the dog sniff the cat through the air holes. If the dog is calm, give him some treats as a reward. If he barks or is excitable, pull on the leash and tell him "NO" until he calms down.

ARF?

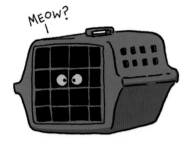

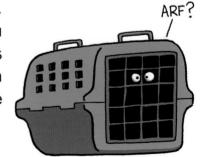

If you're bringing a dog into the home, also keep the dog in a cage if you can, at first. Bring the cat into the room by carrying her and petting her to let her know it's okay. If your cat gets wiggly or runs, don't punish her for being understandably anxious. Just pet her and console her.

Another tactic you might try is to keep both animals inside their respective carriers and place them

both in the same room with their doors facing each other. You should stay in the room, too, if only to give them both treats when they are calm. If either of your pets continues to be anxious about the

situation, you should be prepared to keep them separate from each other the best you can and repeat this process each day for as long as it takes.

In time, you should be able to train each pet to think of the other as another member of the family . . . an annoying member, perhaps, but part of the family nonetheless.

• EPILOGUE •

Well, Kitty, I'm pretty disappointed with you that you didn't graduate. I can't help but think that maybe you just didn't try hard enough.

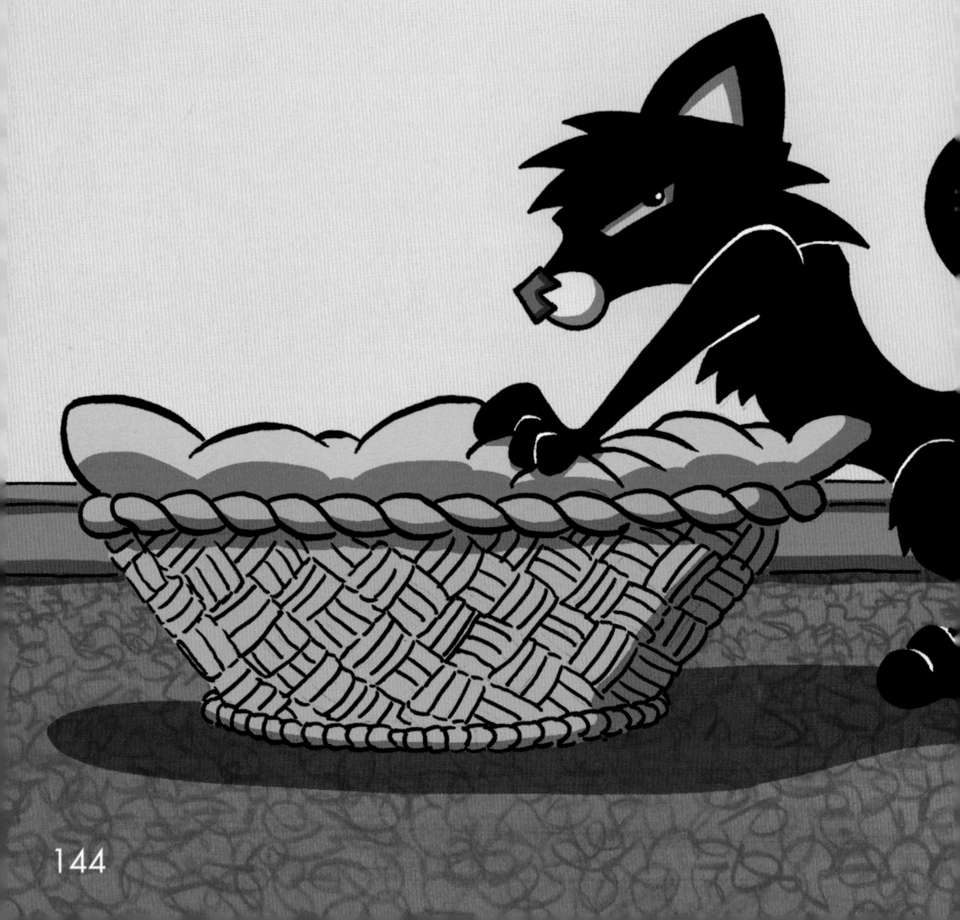

SIGH And I guess this means that you're the same old, cranky, ornery, disagreeable Kitty you've always been.

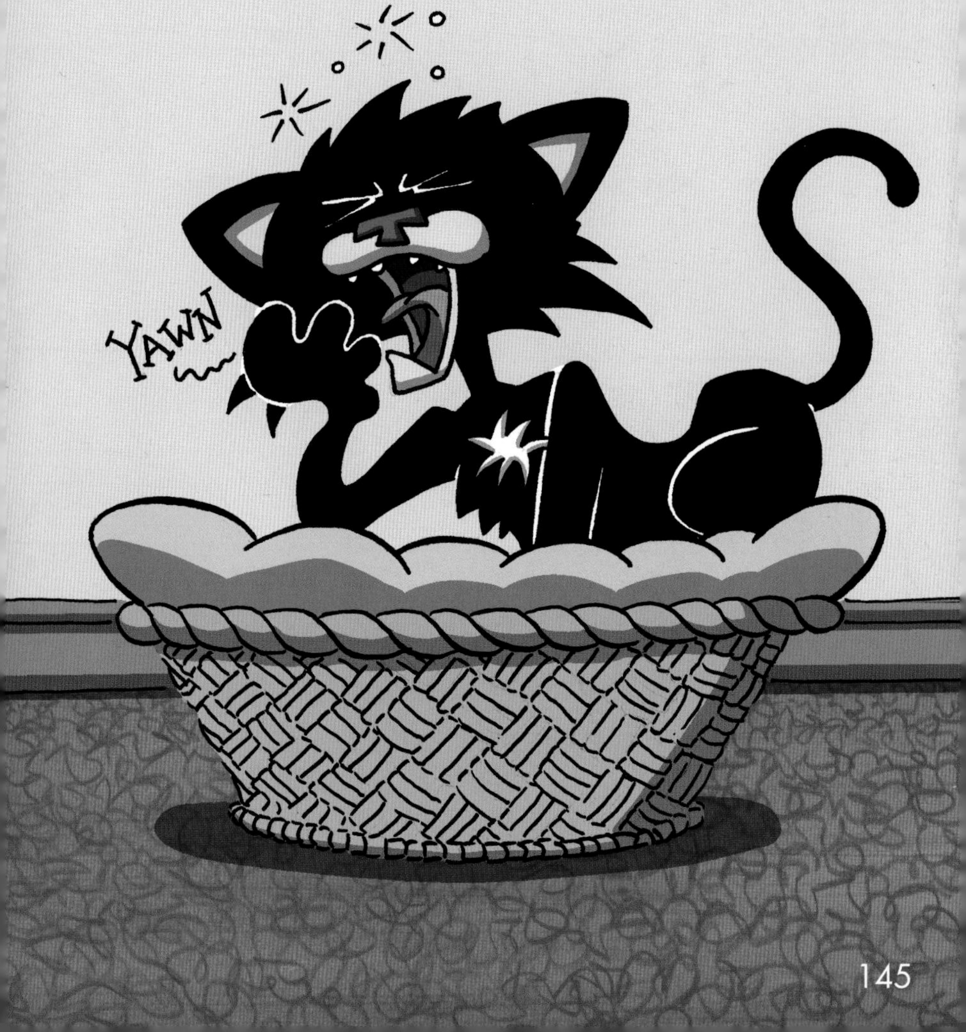
YAWN

Your teacher, Miss Dee, kept telling me how much she likes you and how much she hopes that you'll be able to go back to school for another chance. She seemed to really like you, Kitty. But I don't know. I just don't see any reason to send you back to that school . . .

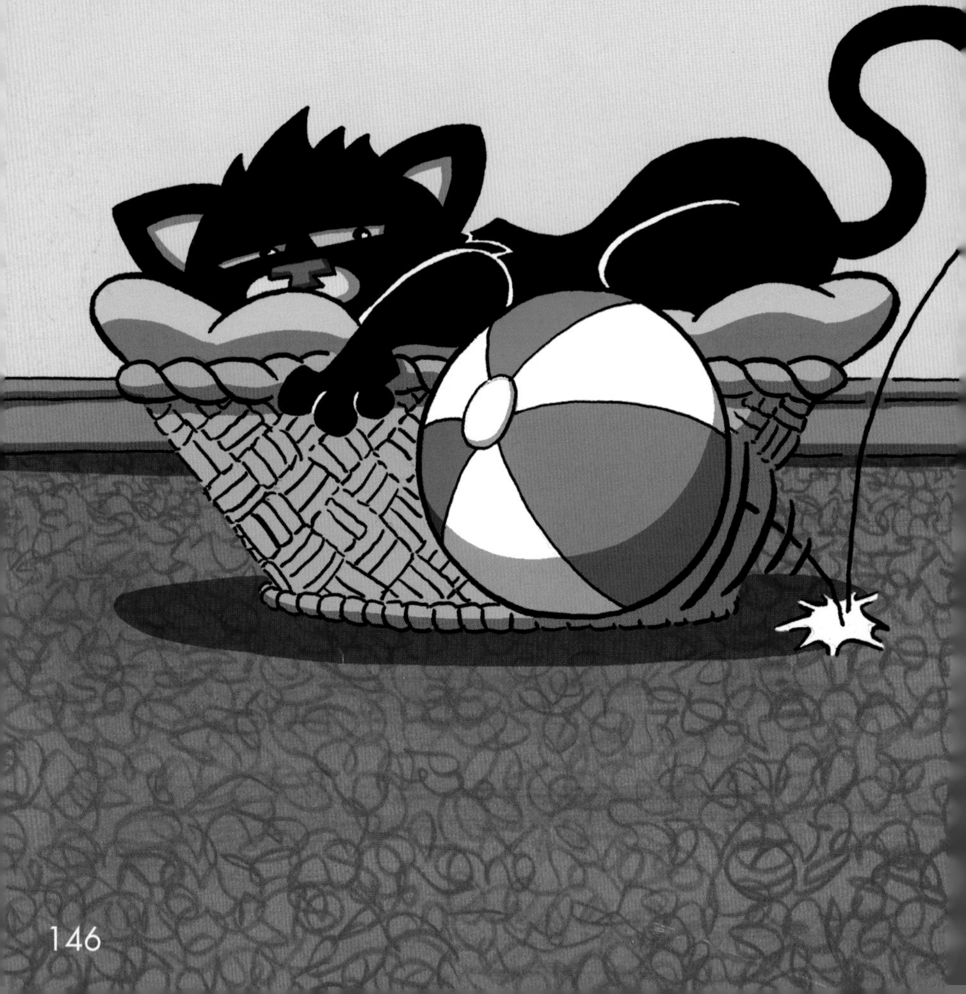

unless we really, really, REALLY have to.

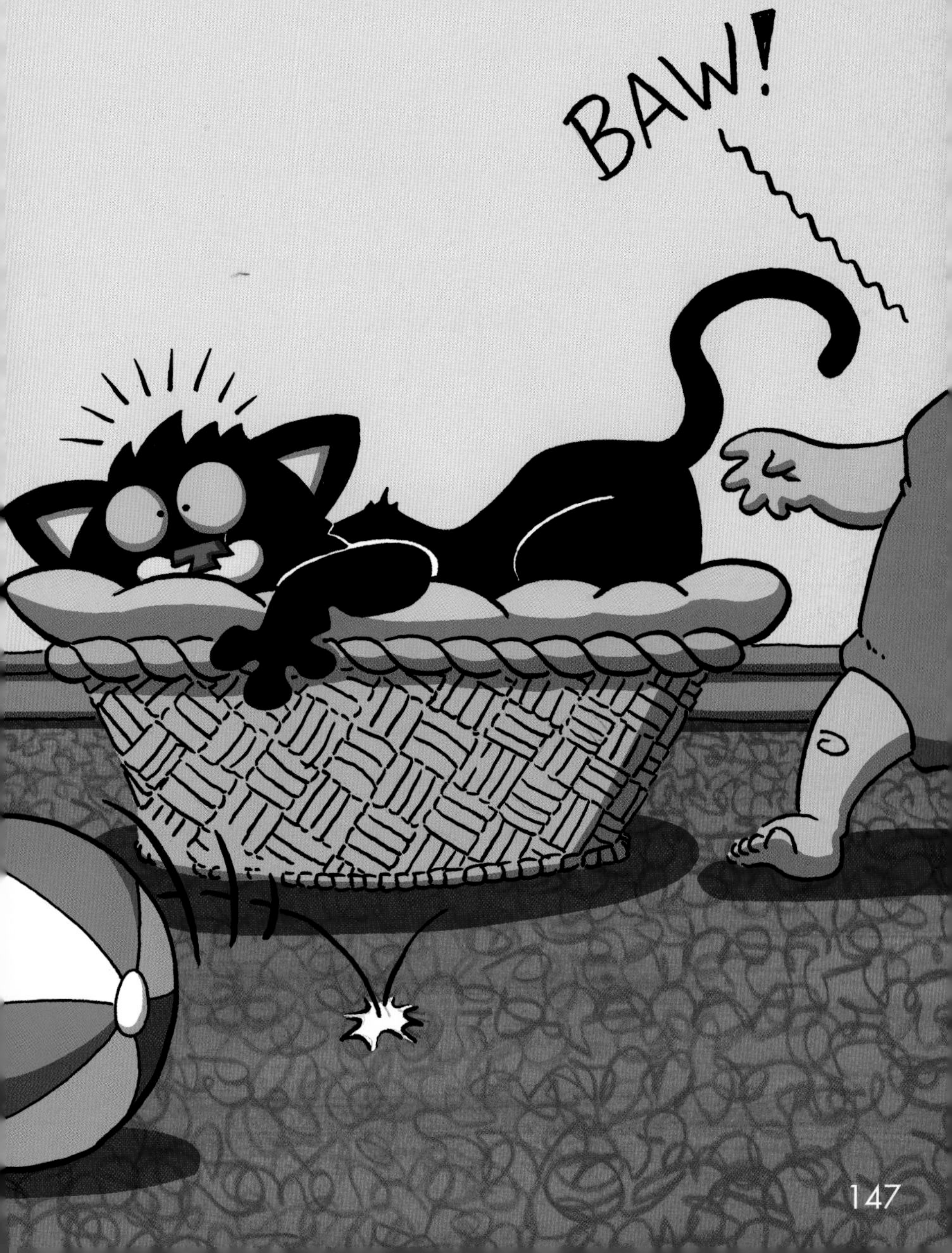
BAW!

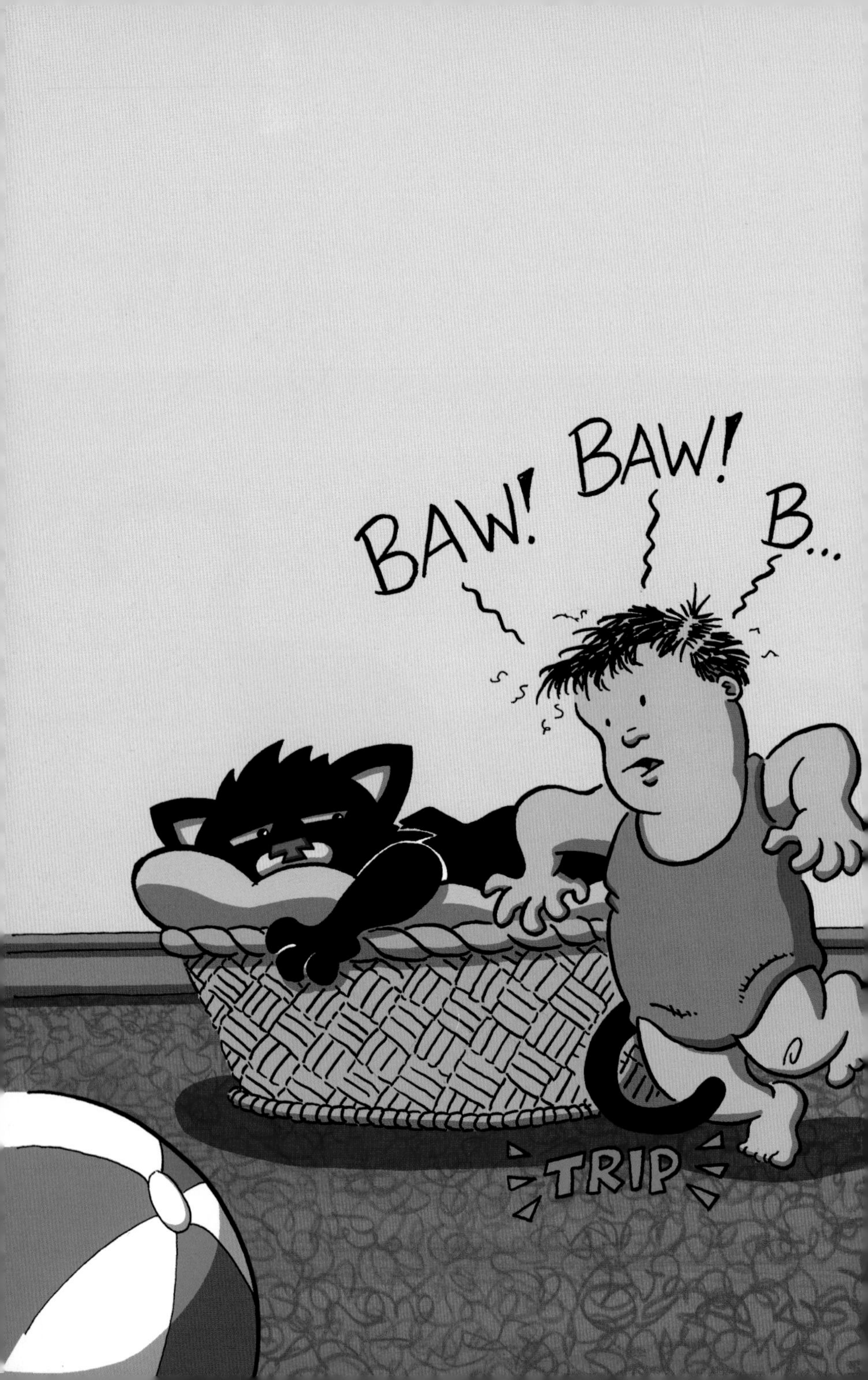
BAW! BAW! B...
TRIP

KITTY!

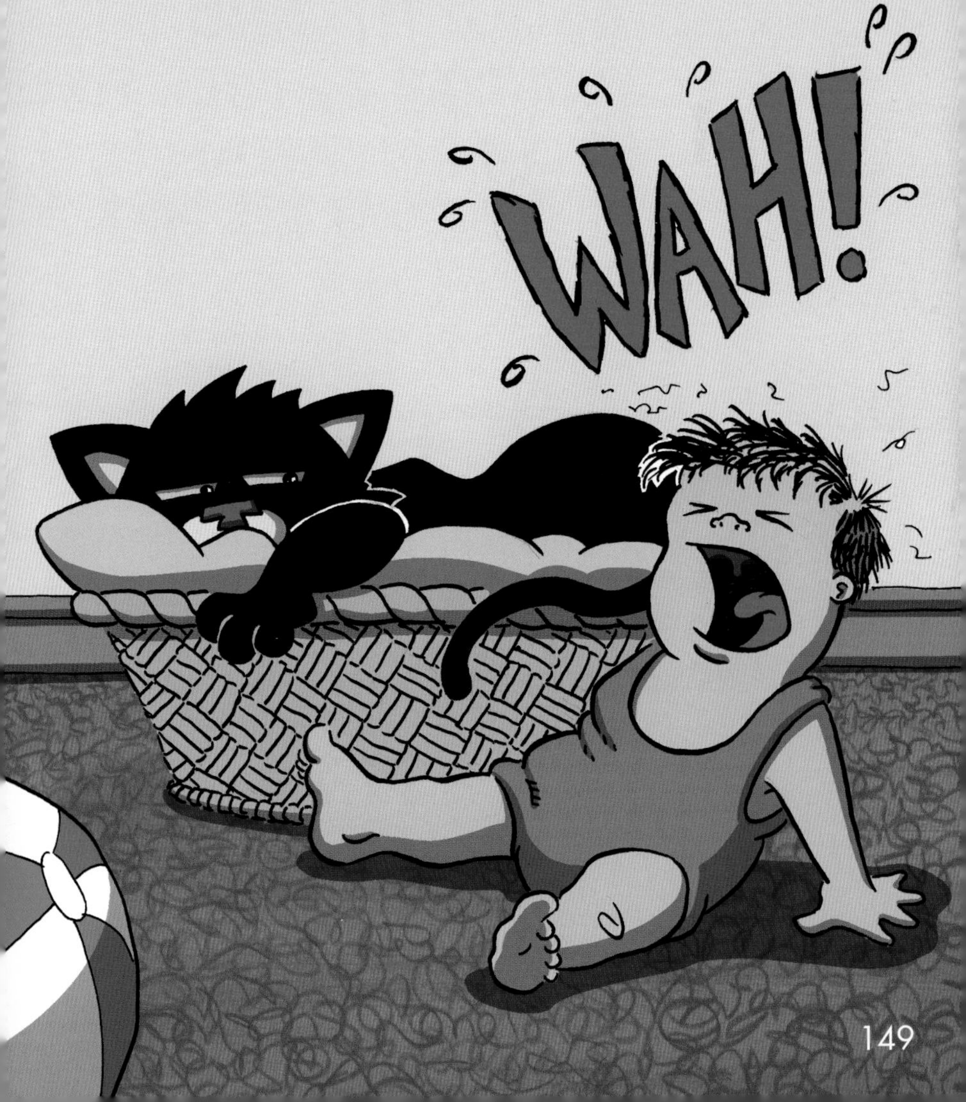
WAH!

THAT DOES IT! THAT'S THE LAST STRAW! I'M SENDING YOU BACK TO THAT SCHOOL AND I DON'T WANT TO HEAR ONE SINGLE COMPLAINT OUT OF YOU ABOUT IT! AND THIS TIME YOU BETTER BE NICE TO THAT TEACHER! I MEAN IT, KITTY. SHE SEEMS TO LIKE YOU, BUT I DON'T KNOW WHY! FIRST THIING IN THE ... **I'M CA**...

PURRR

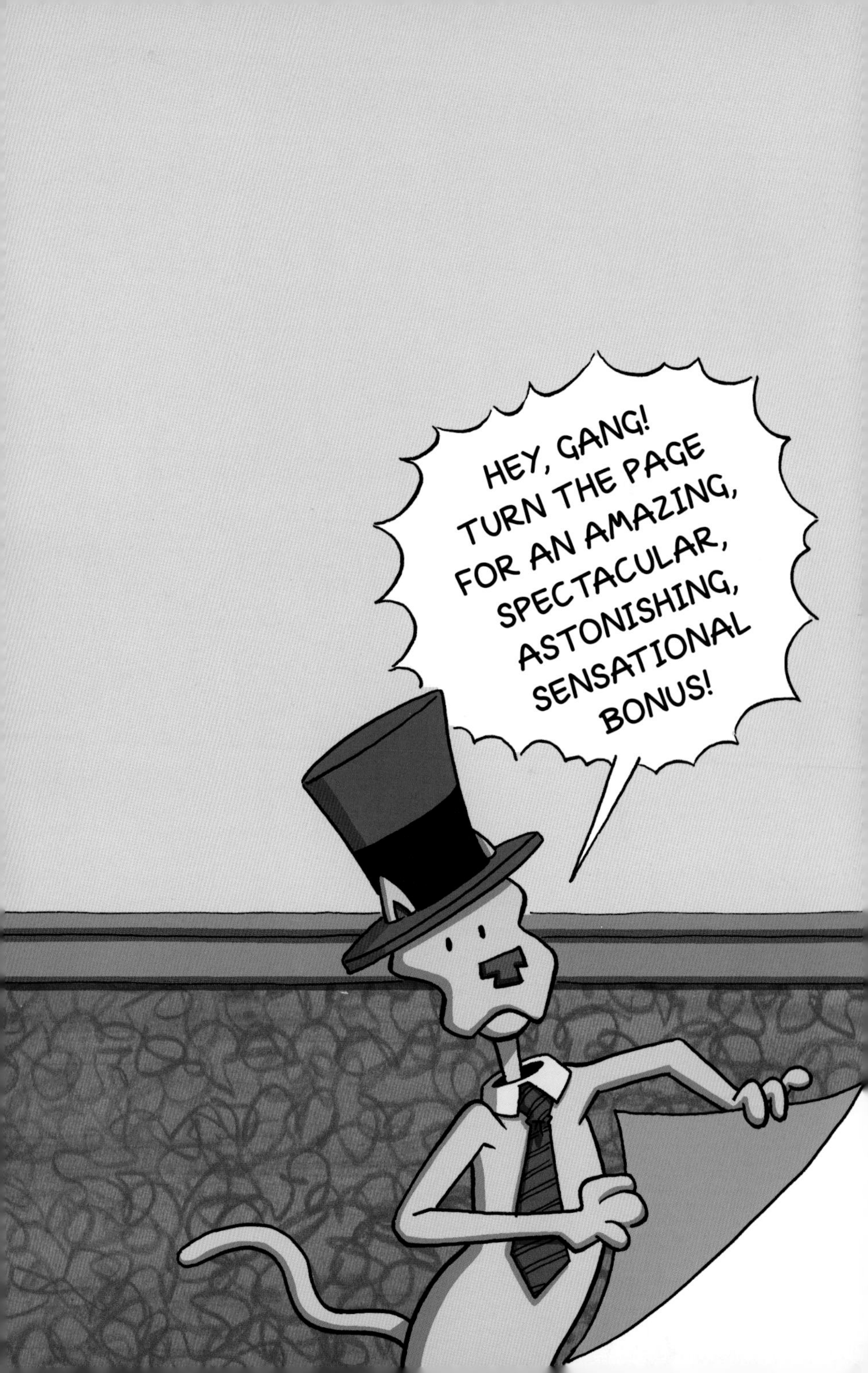
HEY, GANG! TURN THE PAGE FOR AN AMAZING, SPECTACULAR, ASTONISHING, SENSATIONAL BONUS!

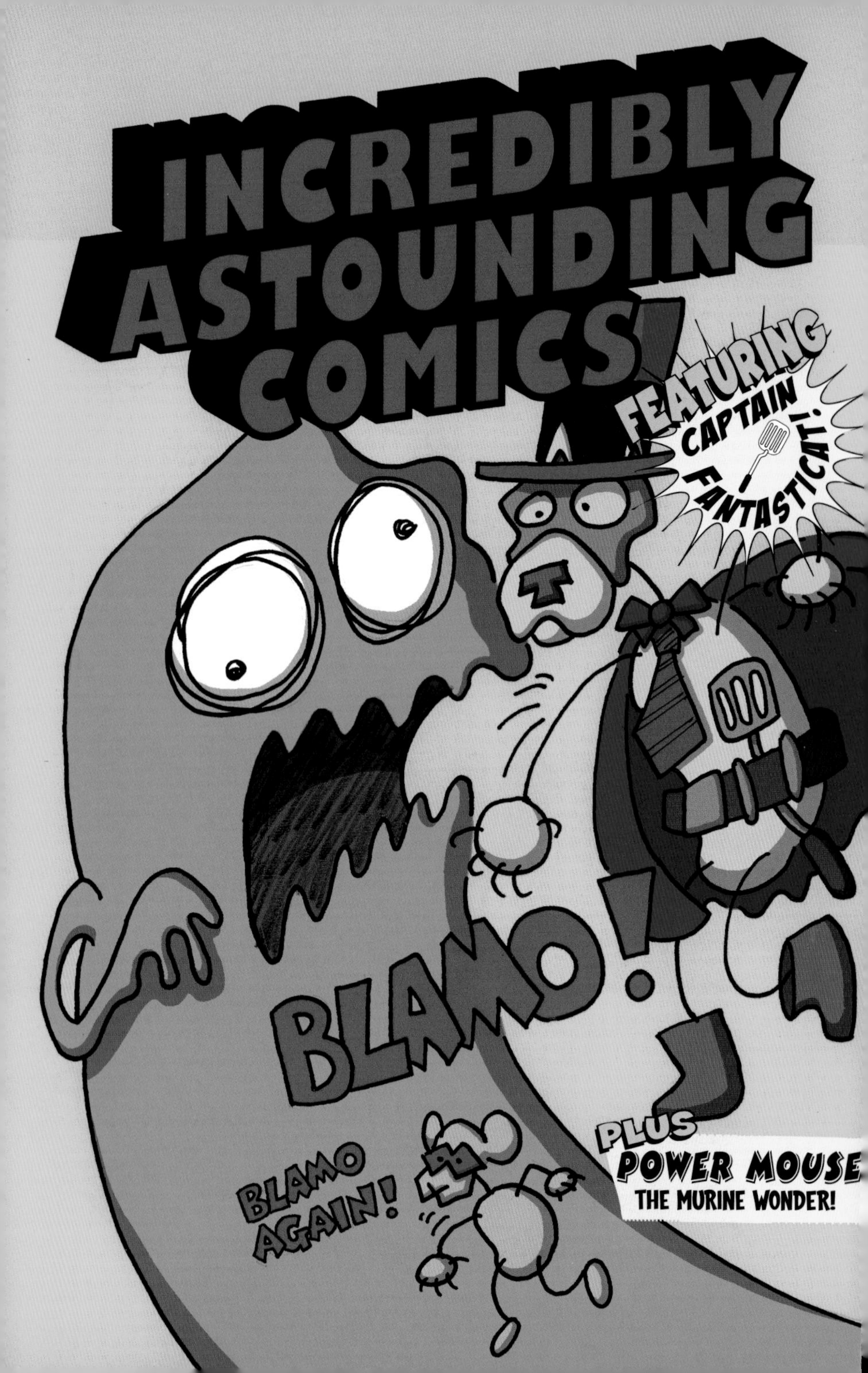
INCREDIBLY ASTOUNDING COMICS!
FEATURING CAPTAIN FANTASTICAT!
BLAMO!
BLAMO AGAIN!
PLUS
POWER MOUSE
THE MURINE WONDER!

IN THEIR SUBTERRANEAN LAIR, CAPTAIN FANTASTICAT AND POWER MOUSE AWAIT THEIR NEXT ADVENTURE.

BORED!

ME, TOO!

SUDDENLY, THE FANTAS-TIPHONE RINGS!

RING!

(PHONE)

HELLO?

IF IT'S MY MOM, TELL HER I'M AT THE LIBRARY!

CAPTAIN FANTASTICAT! SOMEONE IS ROBBING THE NATIONAL BANK... THE ONE WITH ALL THE MONEY!

(POLICE CHIEF)

TO THE FANTAS-TICAR!

WAS IT MY MOM?

ROAR!

ZOOOOOOM!

NO, IT WASN'T YOUR MOM.

1

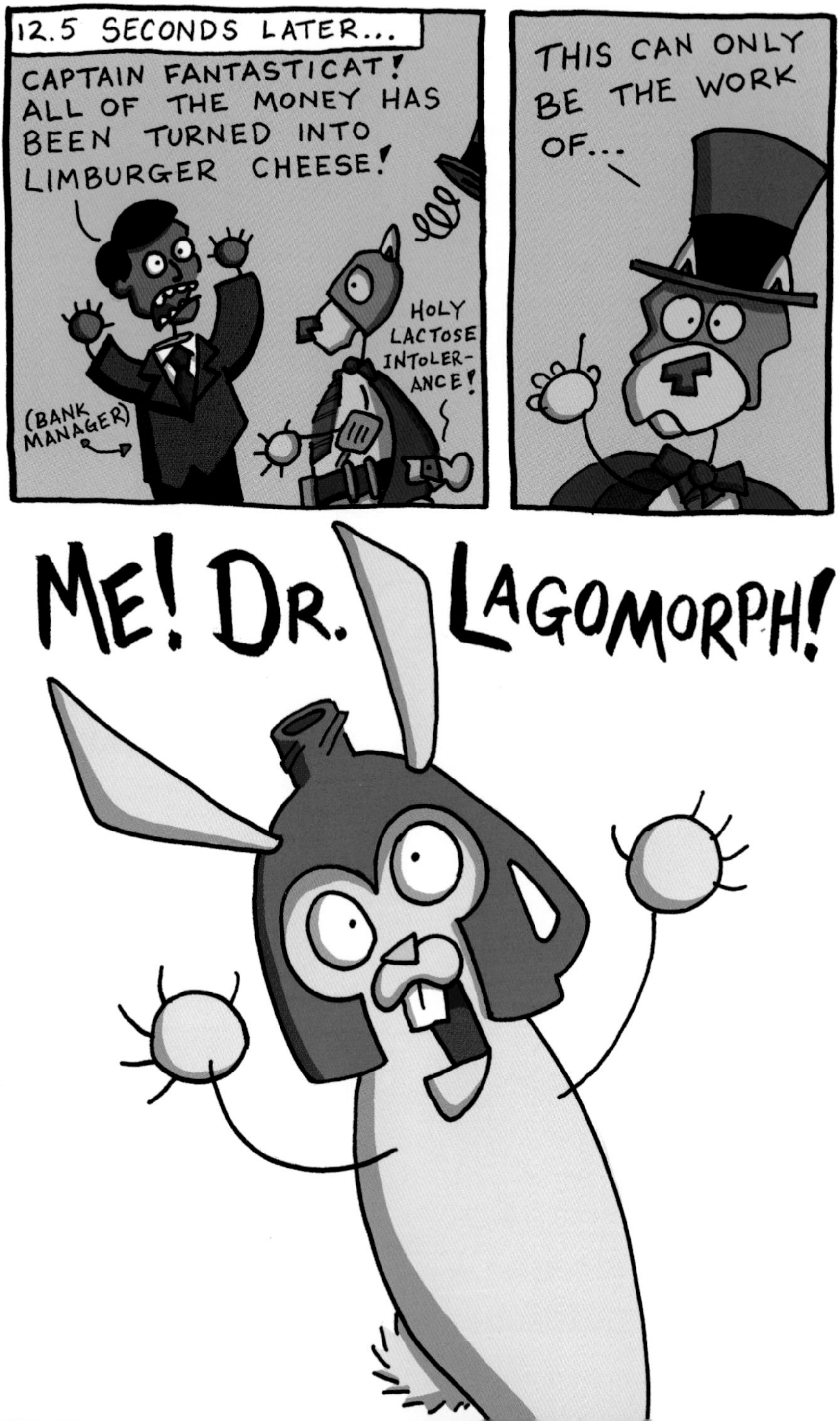
12.5 SECONDS LATER...
CAPTAIN FANTASTICAT! ALL OF THE MONEY HAS BEEN TURNED INTO LIMBURGER CHEESE!
(BANK MANAGER)
HOLY LACTOSE INTOLER-ANCE!
THIS CAN ONLY BE THE WORK OF...
ME! DR. LAGOMORPH!

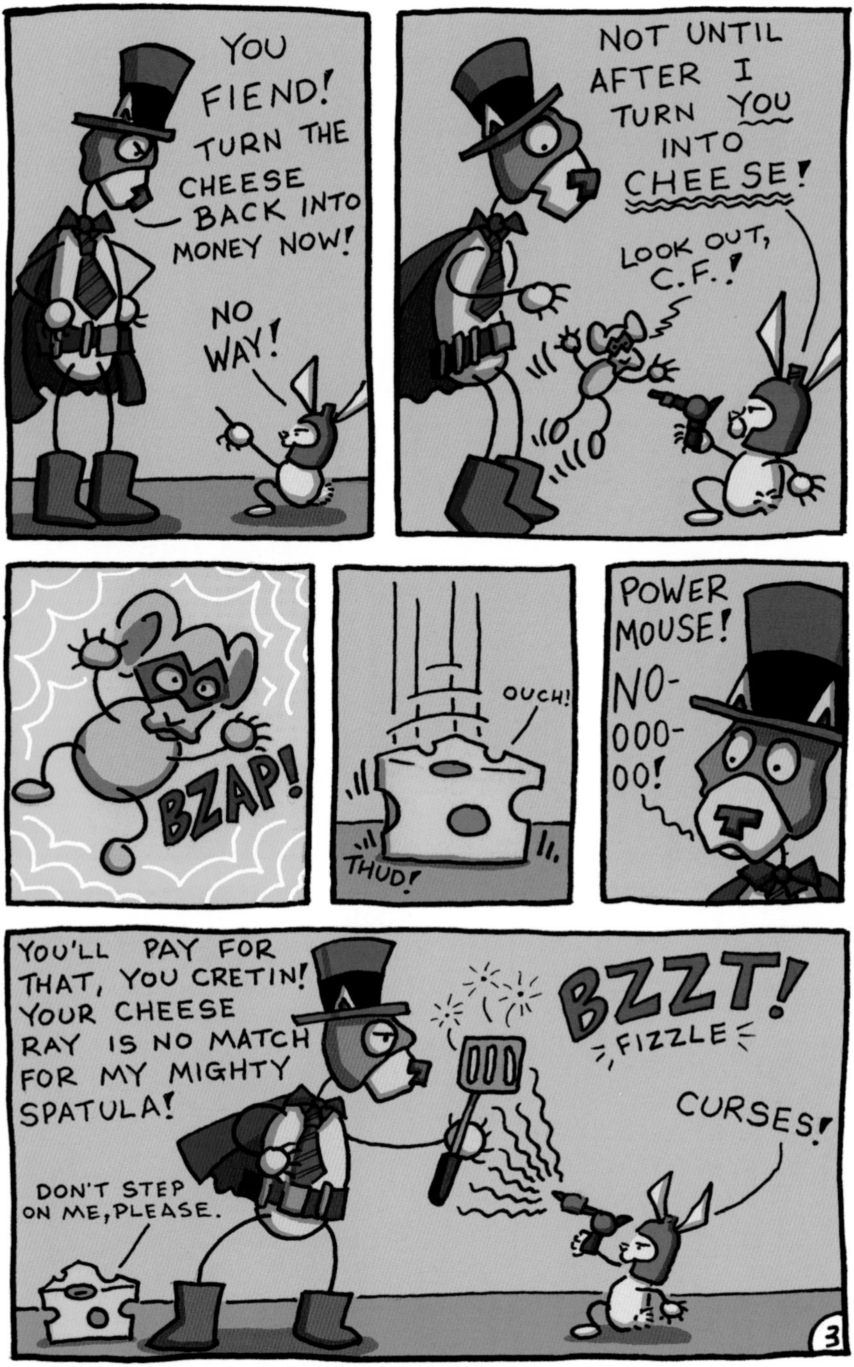

YOU FIEND! TURN THE CHEESE BACK INTO MONEY NOW!
NO WAY!
NOT UNTIL AFTER I TURN YOU INTO CHEESE!
LOOK OUT, C.F.!
BZAP!
OUCH!
THUD!
POWER MOUSE! NO-OOO-OO!
YOU'LL PAY FOR THAT, YOU CRETIN! YOUR CHEESE RAY IS NO MATCH FOR MY MIGHTY SPATULA!
BZZT!
FIZZLE
CURSES!
DON'T STEP ON ME, PLEASE.
3

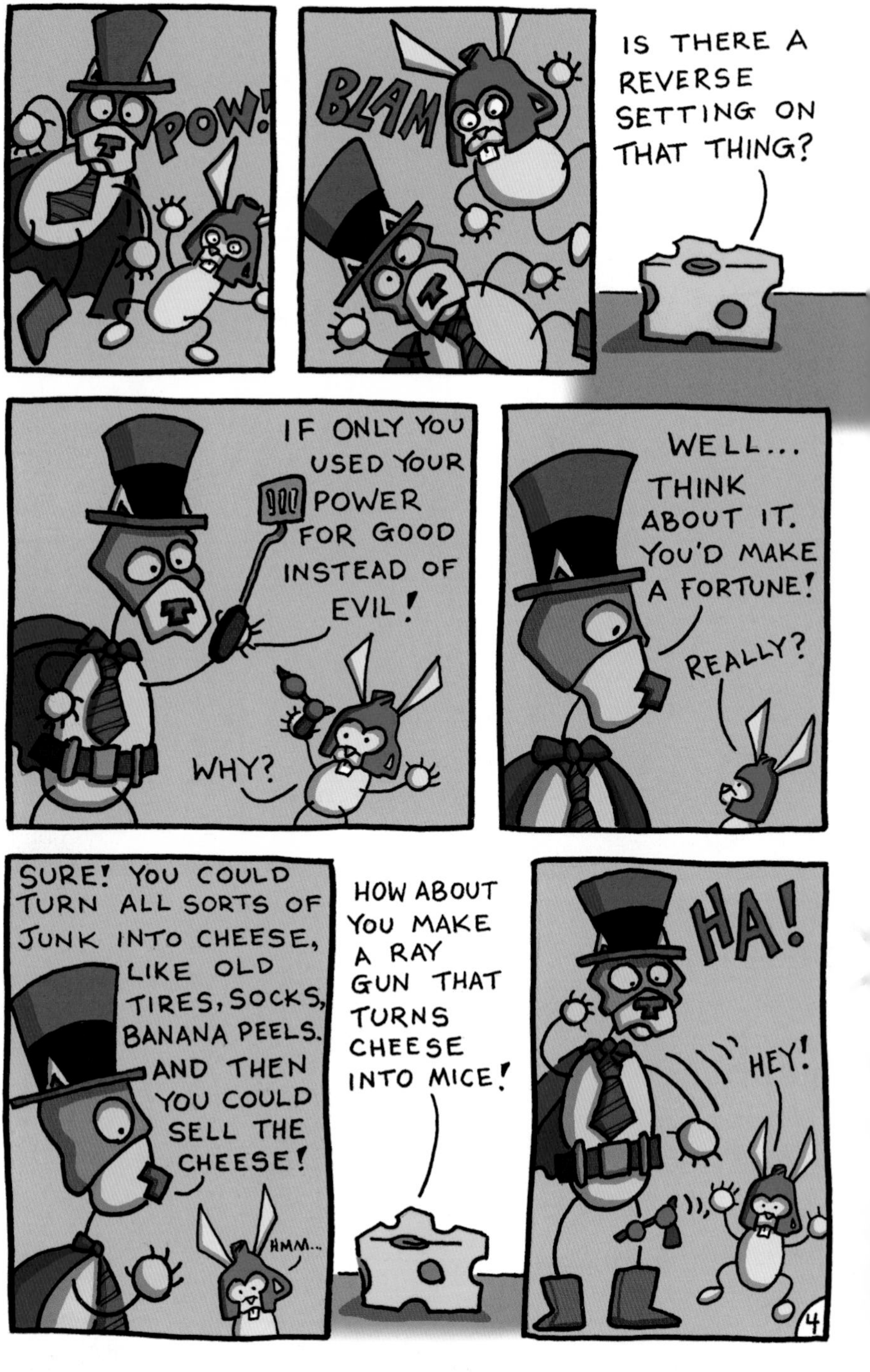
POW!
BLAM
IS THERE A REVERSE SETTING ON THAT THING?
IF ONLY YOU USED YOUR POWER FOR GOOD INSTEAD OF EVIL!
WHY?
WELL... THINK ABOUT IT. YOU'D MAKE A FORTUNE!
REALLY?
SURE! YOU COULD TURN ALL SORTS OF JUNK INTO CHEESE, LIKE OLD TIRES, SOCKS, BANANA PEELS. AND THEN YOU COULD SELL THE CHEESE!
HMM...
HOW ABOUT YOU MAKE A RAY GUN THAT TURNS CHEESE INTO MICE!
HA!
HEY!
4

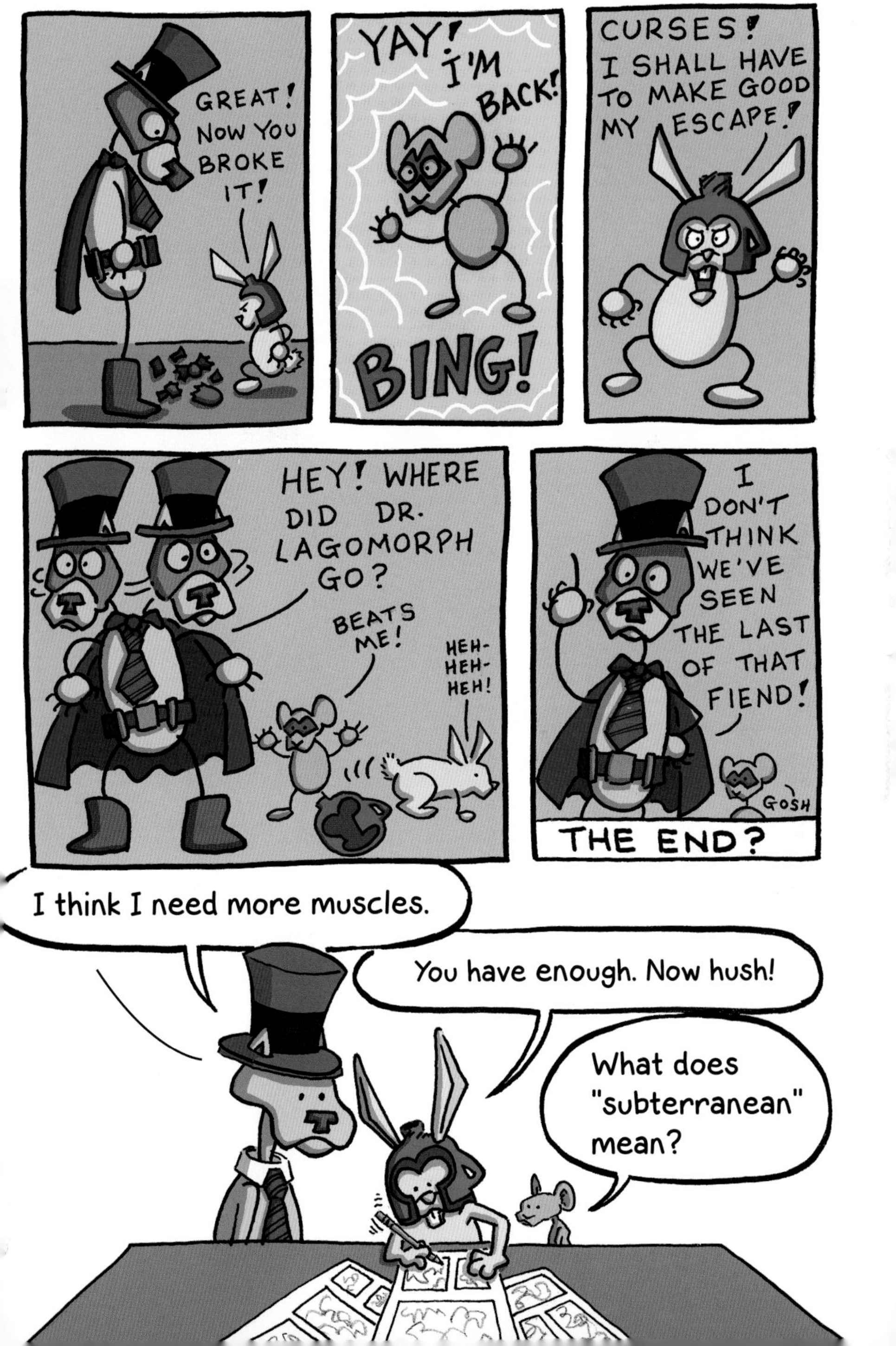
GREAT! NOW YOU BROKE IT!
YAY! I'M BACK!
BING!
CURSES! I SHALL HAVE TO MAKE GOOD MY ESCAPE!
HEY! WHERE DID DR. LAGOMORPH GO?
BEATS ME!
HEH-HEH-HEH!
I DON'T THINK WE'VE SEEN THE LAST OF THAT FIEND!
GOSH
THE END?
I think I need more muscles.
You have enough. Now hush!
What does "subterranean" mean?

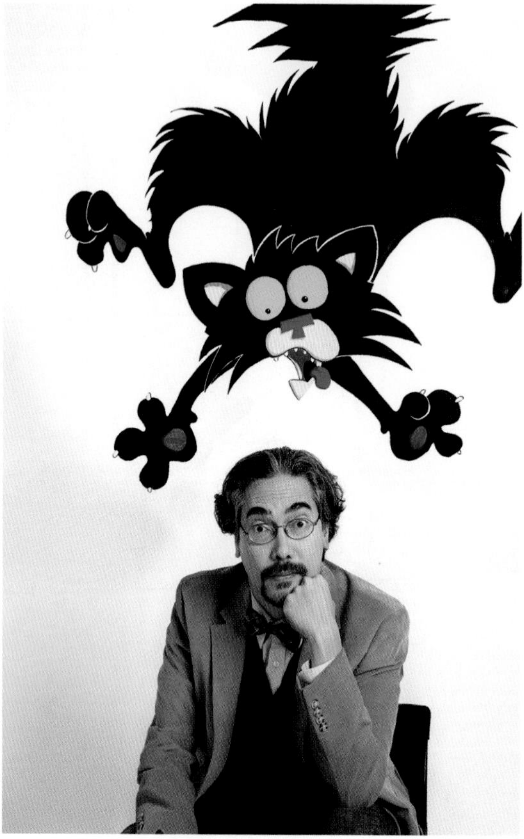

Author photo by Marty Umans

NICK BRUEL is the author and illustrator of the phenomenally successful *New York Times*–bestselling Bad Kitty series, including the 2012 and 2013 CBC Children's Choice Book Award winners *Bad Kitty Meets the Baby* and *Bad Kitty for President.* Nick has also written and illustrated popular picture books including *Who Is Melvin Bubble?*, *Bob and Otto*, and his most recent, *A Wonderful Year*. He lives with his wife and daughter in Westchester, New York.

nickbruelbooks.com

Check out Bad Kitty in FULL COLOR! Available meow:

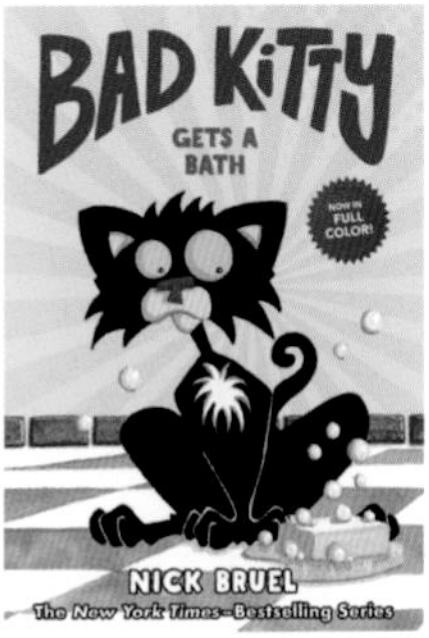
BAD KITTY
GETS A BATH
NOW IN FULL COLOR!
NICK BRUEL
The New York Times–Bestselling Series

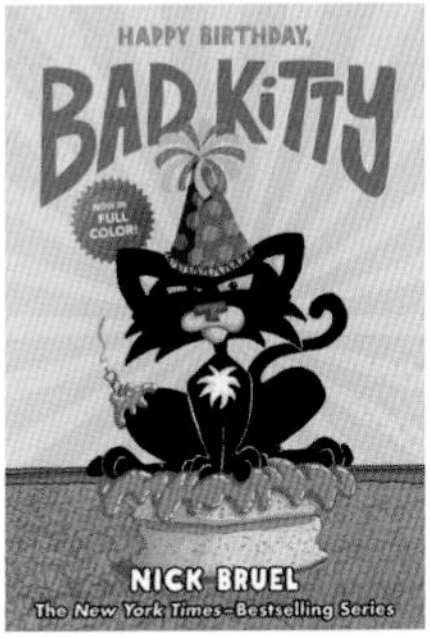
HAPPY BIRTHDAY,
BAD KITTY
NOW IN FULL COLOR!
NICK BRUEL
The New York Times–Bestselling Series

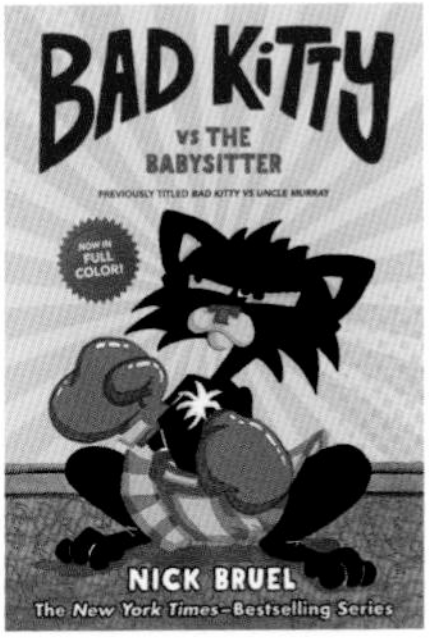
BAD KITTY
VS THE BABYSITTER
PREVIOUSLY TITLED BAD KITTY VS UNCLE MURRAY
NOW IN FULL COLOR!
NICK BRUEL
The New York Times–Bestselling Series

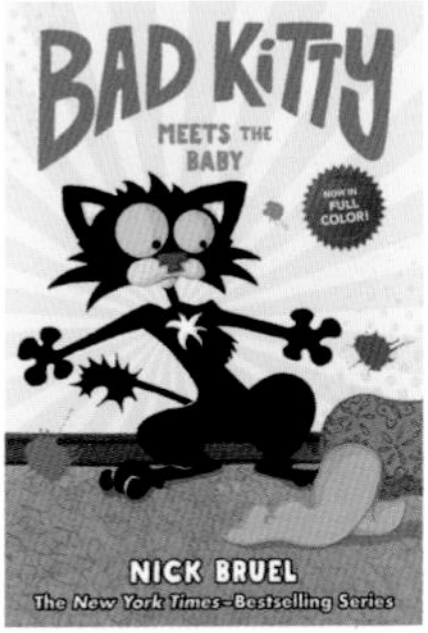
BAD KITTY
MEETS THE BABY
NOW IN FULL COLOR!
NICK BRUEL
The New York Times–Bestselling Series

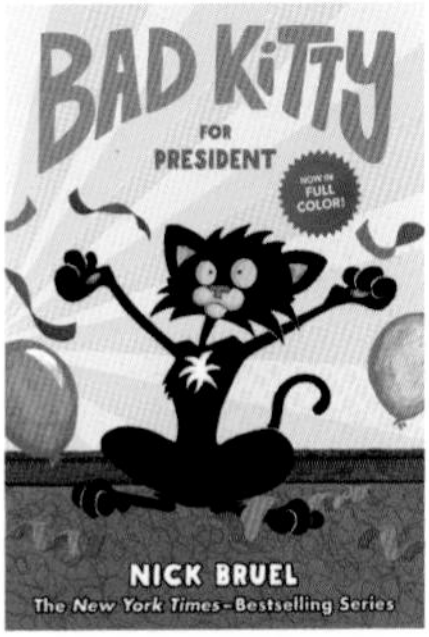
BAD KITTY
FOR PRESIDENT
NOW IN FULL COLOR!
NICK BRUEL
The New York Times–Bestselling Series

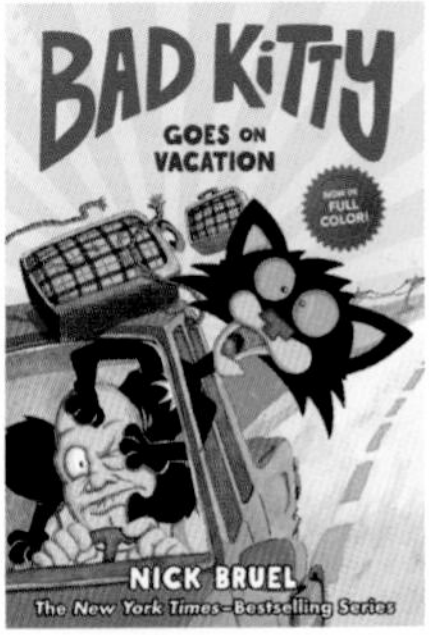
BAD KITTY
GOES ON VACATION
NOW IN FULL COLOR!
NICK BRUEL
The New York Times–Bestselling Series

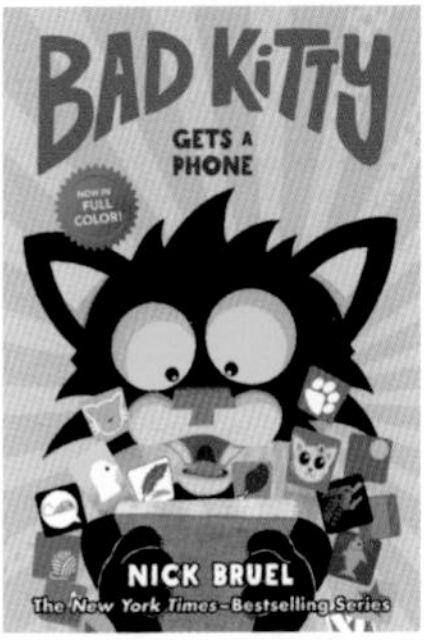
BAD KITTY
GETS A PHONE
NOW IN FULL COLOR!
NICK BRUEL
The New York Times–Bestselling Series

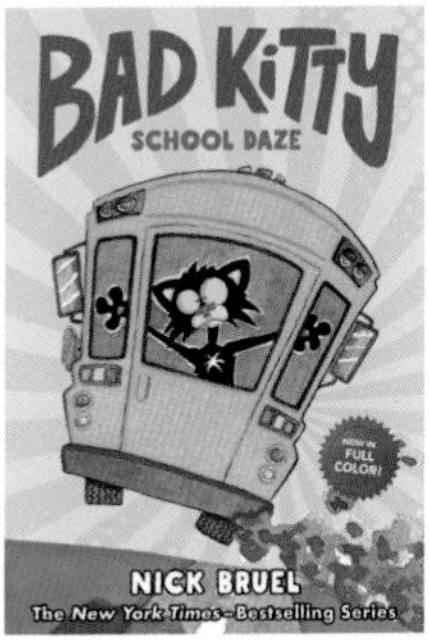
BAD KITTY
SCHOOL DAZE
NOW IN FULL COLOR!
NICK BRUEL
The New York Times–Bestselling Series

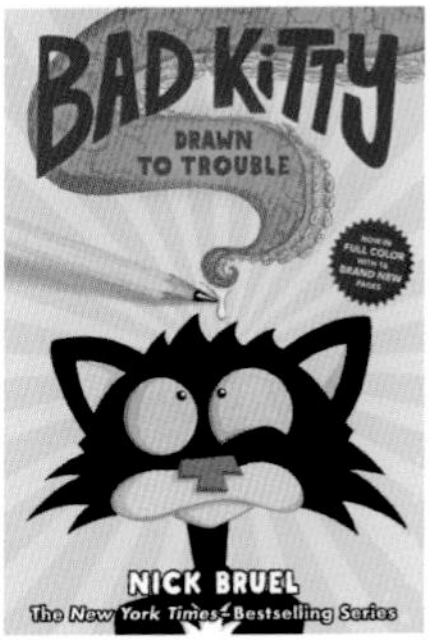
BAD KITTY
DRAWN TO TROUBLE
NICK BRUEL
The New York Times–Bestselling Series

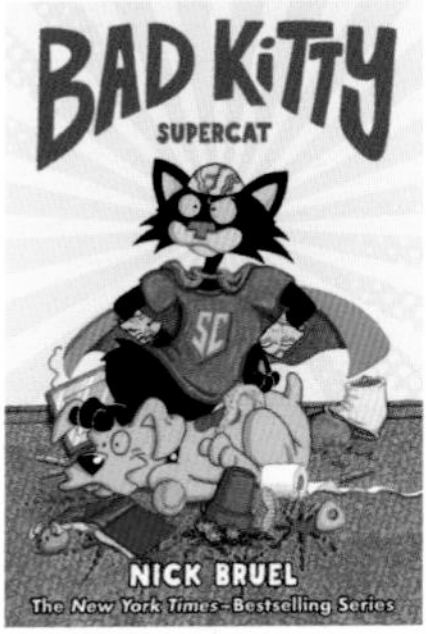
BAD KITTY
SUPERCAT
NICK BRUEL
The New York Times–Bestselling Series